Michelle Jackson

One Kiss in
Havana

POOLBEG

Published 2011
by Poolbeg Press Ltd
123 Grange Hill, Baldoyle
Dublin 13, Ireland
E-mail: poolbeg@poolbeg.com
www.poolbeg.com

© Michelle Jackson 2010

Copyright for typesetting, layout, design
© Poolbeg Press Ltd

The moral right of the author has been asserted.

1

A catalogue record for this book is available from the British Library.

ISBN 978-1-84223-484-6

Typeset by Patricia Hope in Sabon 11.5/15.5
Printed by CPI Cox & Wyman, UK

www.poolbeg.com

Note on the Author

Michelle Jackson is the bestselling author of *Two Days in Biarritz* and *Three Nights in New York*. In the 1980s Michelle attended the National College of Art and Design where she nurtured her love of the visual arts, majoring in printed textiles for fashion. She kicked off her career as a sock designer in the 1980s and spent many years teaching art at secondary school level. Writing novels gives her the chance to blend her love of travel with telling stories. Her recent visit to Las Vegas will be the inspiration for her fourth novel with Poolbeg, which will be coming up next year.

Michelle lives in Howth, Co Dublin with her husband and two children.

If you would like Michelle to visit your book club or talk to community groups etc, she is contactable through her website www.michellejackson.ie.

Also by Michelle Jackson

Two Days in Biarritz

Three Nights in New York

Published by Poolbeg

Acknowledgements

As always this is the hardest bit of writing a book. There are so many people that I have to thank that it would take up far too many pages if I were to fit everyone in – so I will say a massive big thank you to my friends and, if I have missed you in these few paragraphs, I am still deeply indebted and haven't forgotten anyone who has helped me on the journey to this, my third book.

To the person who has helped me more than anyone could ever know – thank you, Gaye Shortland my FGE (we know what that stands for!). To Paula and Sarah, Kieran, David and everyone in Poolbeg, you have been wonderful to work with and I am looking forward to the next three novels!

Many thanks to my readers Clodagh Hoey and Suzanne Barry who have been there since my first scribbles. Also to my new readers who have with such patience and diligence gone through this with a fine-tooth comb – Maressa O'Brien-Raleigh, Tryphavana Cross, Suzie Murphy et al. You have no idea how important your role is in this book.

To Emma Heatherington and all of my Facebook friends, whose constant support and encouragement online helps immeasurably – I never feel alone when sitting at the laptop!

Thanks to Rachel Targett and Susan O'Conor for your inspiration and insight into sisters. To my Cuban friends, especially Dehannys, who told about their country and gave me great insights while I was researching this book.

Thanks to all the angels in my life – especially the living ones, Angela, Joy and Philip.

To Juliet Bressan who has been on this rollercoaster ride with me since we met and without whom I would be lost. For your patience, sense of humour, understanding and listening to my ranting, thank you.

To my parents Pauline and Jim Walsh, for sending me off to Cuba for my fortieth birthday – you spoil me and I am so lucky to have you both. I thank you for all the other gifts and talents that you have passed to me.

To Brian for holding my hand as we walked the streets of Havana and all the other adventures we have been on as husband and wife.

Finally to Nicole and Mark for being so wonderful and beautiful and inspiring – I am a very lucky mummy.

Dedicated in Ernest to –
Hemingway and Che Guevara.
Two inspiring men who were touched by Cuba!

Prologue

The sun also riseth and the sun goeth down
Ecclesiastes 1

SEPTEMBER 3RD

Emma woke as the first beam of daylight slipped through the break in the bedroom curtains. She rubbed her eyelids and lifted her head with its raven-black hair off the pillow – careful not to wake her husband. She was trying to relieve writer's block and getting up extra early was her latest attempt at establishing a new routine. Emma was by nature a night-owl and found six o'clock a difficult start. She went down to her study, turned on her laptop and waited as the icons appeared one by one. She had waited her whole life to write her first novel – now she was beginning to wonder if that was all she had to contribute to the world of words. Her husband Paul was so patient, giving her all the support and space that she needed to get the second one finished. She continued working as a journalist on a part-time basis, taking only jobs in magazines and periodicals that interested her, and had plenty of time to work on her novel as she pleased. She realised that she was in a position of freedom that most writers only dream of.

She organized her documents folder and went online to check for emails. Then she put down a few words and, before she realised it, it was seven thirty and time to wake the men of the house.

1

Finn was snoring gently but she crept into his bedroom to check that he was sound asleep. She watched his chest rise and fall and smiled with the satisfaction that only a mother can feel when watching her child sleep. He wouldn't be a child for much longer – he was already in fourth class.

Confident that her son would lie on for another few minutes at least, she set about waking her husband. This morning she was feeling alert and sexy after tapping at the keyboard for nearly two hours. It would be a nice midweek treat!

She laid a hand on to his forehead which was surprisingly cold to the touch. Very gently she put her lips down to his cheek – it was then she noticed that something was terribly wrong.

Louise was cutting the crusts off the sandwiches and putting the neat little squares of bread and ham into plastic bags, wondering how she ever managed when she used to rush out every morning to her job as a music teacher as well as get her children up for school and crèche.

She was still wearing her pyjamas but had been the second member of the Scott household to get up. Donal was already on his way to work – he liked to get to work early so he could finish in the evening and be out of town before the rush-hour traffic. During the summer and early autumn he used that extra time to go out to the yacht club for a sail before the light disappeared.

Suddenly her house phone rang out, startling her – it seldom rang in the mornings. The usual callers at this hour were the mums she knew through the local school calling to arrange lifts and play dates and they would always ring her mobile. She lifted it to hear her sister's voice on the other end of the line.

"Louise!" Emma sobbed. "Help – it's Paul – he's not breathing!"

Sophie breezed past the receptionist with a friendly nod, a cup of Starbucks coffee in her hand. It was going to be a great day – most days were great for Sophie. As she sat at the desk in her small but smart design office she opened the drawer and removed her mirror to check how she looked after her brief walk to work. Her strawberry-blonde curls held their shape perfectly and her lips were glossy and shiny. She hit the mouse on her state-of-the-art Apple Mac and waited for her emails to appear on the screen. She quickly scanned through them, looking for something from *him*, then double-checked the list – not quite believing her eyes – he always sent her an email before he started work. Suddenly her mobile phone rang and she searched her bag frantically – eager to hear his voice.

But it wasn't him.

"Sophie, it's Louise."

Sophie knew by her older sister's tone that something was not as it should be and she took a deep breath.

"Yes?"

"It's Paul – I'm on my way to hospital now – he's had a heart attack."

Sophie felt the blood drain from her face and rush all the way down to her toes.

"Oh my God! How bad is it?"

"It's bad, Sophie."

"What? He's going to be all right – isn't he?"

"He's in an ambulance – they're trying to resuscitate him."

"What do you mean?"

"I think he's dead – I'll call you back when I know more."

Sophie wasn't able to reply. Her stomach clenched in spasm with the shock and she felt as if she was about to vomit. She closed her eyes to keep from fainting. It couldn't be – not her beloved Paul. He was her favourite brother-in-law. He was her rock. He was her lover.

Chapter 1

MARCH 20TH

Easter was falling early this year and Louise wanted to be prepared for it – in the same way that she had come to be for all festivals and holidays. When she was working she used to imagine how relaxed her life would be if she didn't have to go into school every day and jump to attention every time the bell rang to signal the end of a class. But staying at home hadn't proved to be the bed of roses she had expected. For one thing, since she gave up work Donal quizzed her regularly about how she spent her day and she wasn't always able to give a satisfactory answer. The truth was, she often found herself fussing over the trivial things that before she used to do on her way to and from work without thinking. She also seemed to create work for herself by choosing the more time-consuming option of doing a task. For instance, this morning she needn't have gone all the way into Dublin city to buy the Easter eggs.

The doors to the DART slid open and Louise took a seat immediately to her right. She settled the bags of chocolate eggs at her feet – not focusing on the man wearing the leather jacket sitting opposite.

He spoke first.

"Louise?"

She looked up, startled.

"It's Jack!" the young man said.

Louise's mouth dropped. It was him. His blond hair was now the colour of sand but his eyes were still that unmistakable translucent blue. She stared at his perfectly sculpted nose and the smooth line of his cheek – unable to reply.

Emma turned the key in the mailbox. Most of the letters seemed to be addressed to Paul – she never realised how much of the household mail came to him until he was gone and she was left to open them. The majority were bills or business-related – they weren't too hard to deal with but, when someone wrote a personal note who hadn't heard of his sudden death, she found it hard.

Nothing she had opened so far was to leave her so traumatised as the smooth white envelope in her hand.

She walked back into the hall and then the kitchen. Something told her that she would need a cuppa nearby before she opened the envelope. It was embossed on the front with the logo of Evans, the graphics house where Paul had worked.

Six months had passed so quickly. After his death she used to have six bad nights a week. Slowly as the months passed the bad nights were turning to good. But last night she woke at seven minutes past one and jumped out of bed to soothe the trembling. Wrapped in her dressing-gown, she went into Finn's room to check that he was breathing. It was something she had given up doing when he turned two but since finding his father dead on that bright September morning she didn't take anything for granted any more. If she lay in bed her mind would start to wander and she would torture herself for hours wondering why

Paul had decided to leave her and her son when he had so much to live for.

So she did what she usually did and rang her friend David in Sydney – he was the only other person apart from her brother-in-law that knew Paul had died under such dark circumstances. It was safe to tell someone who was so far away that they would never tell anyone else in her family.

When the call finished she turned to surfing the internet – YouTube managed to have enough on its site to keep her occupied until the next wave of distress hit at around a quarter to four. Then it was time to return between the sheets, with a toilet roll to hand for mopping up tears, until Finn had to get up for school.

So far today was going okay – until she received the post. She hit the switch on the small stainless-steel kettle and it whimpered for a moment before bursting with steam and shutting itself off again. She wondered how many times a day she did that – the kettle was the best workhorse in the house without a doubt. And it was always tea that Emma liked to drink. Hot and strong with a drop of milk. Paul knew just how to make it. It was one of the many things about him that she missed.

Finn was at school and never saw his mum in a state when she read the mail. He was at the age where he preferred to be with his friends. Although she realised that he adored her and was fiercely protective of her, she knew that she couldn't halt his progress in the normal rites of passage of a nine-year-old. Soon she would know all about the difficulties of being a single parent to a teenager and she hoped that she would be able to cope when the time came.

Emma picked up the kettle and added hot water to the teabag in the china mug. She pulled back a chair, grating it on the terracotta tiles, and sat down. Without any fuss she ripped open the envelope and took out another that had the setting-sun emblem of a travel company printed in the top left-hand corner.

Folded up inside it were three sheets of paper with neatly typed documentation. A leaflet fell out and rested on the table-top. It was brightly coloured with decorative edging and the word *CUBA* emblazoned across the top. More junk mail – Emma thought – almost dropping it in the bin. But instead she unfolded the other pages and let her eyes scan over the documents. Key words bounced off the page – *thank you – reservation – tickets – enclosed – travel – restrictions – visa*. She was reading a travel itinerary for two. These pages were all that were required for a ten-day holiday in sunny Cuba and the date of departure was only six days away.

Emma blinked and read the documents again – more carefully this time. The names printed across the top of the page were Mr P Condell and Ms S Owens. They had printed her initial incorrectly. She wished that they said Mr and Mrs Condell – she should have changed the name on her passport when renewing it after Finn was born – it was a tiny detail but now that she had lost Paul she wished she had his name on all of her documents. It hadn't mattered before. The date of booking was seven months ago – only a few days before Paul was taken so suddenly away from her. She picked up the outer envelope – it was addressed to Evans Graphics House. If Paul told them to send it to his work, then he must have wanted to keep it a secret to be a surprise – that was just the sort of attention to detail that Paul gave to everything that he did. In his work as a graphic designer he was more fastidious and precise than any of his colleagues and it was one of the things about his character that used to drive Emma mad. How happy she would be now to take all those times he was fussy and neat and hug him and his sweet ways, just to share some more time with him.

In recent years Emma had been longing to go to Cuba to see La Finca Vigía – Ernest Hemingway's home outside Havana where he reputedly spent some of the happiest years of his life. How wonderful of Paul to do this for her! But now he would never know how she felt about this lovely gift. She was engulfed by emotions that she hadn't felt since discovering him lying cold in the bed, that morning in September.

Suddenly the phone rang and she couldn't bring herself to answer it. All she could do was take her mug and ascend the stairs, seeking the comfort of bed before Finn got home from school.

Louise listened to the phone on the other end of the line ring out once, twice, three times before switching to the answering machine.

Hello, you've reached the Condells – we can't take your call but if you leave your name and number we'll get right back to you.

Louise was familiar with the deep West of Ireland tone of the man's voice. She hadn't suggested to Emma that she change Paul's voice from the answering machine but did wonder if leaving it was part of her sister's grieving process or just an oversight. Maybe her sister was not the best person to call – she was too caught up in her own pain to understand how shocked Louise was feeling after the short trip on the DART earlier.

She hung up the phone and tried to think about the next job on her list for the day. It was all becoming so tedious. She had given up work after the birth of her youngest child.

She and Donal had been happy with two children and doubly thrilled that Molly was a girl so Tom's arrival two years later was unplanned. It was difficult for Louise to work full time and co-ordinate a baby and a five-year-old starting school. She had tried job-sharing for a while but eventually took a career break to be a full-time mother. But with her new role she found it hard to fill her head with things that fed her brain. Shopping and cooking and cleaning had never been high on Louise's agenda – they didn't suit the lifestyle of a bohemian musician. But then again it was a very long time ago since she was either of those. The bohemian part of her personality was gradually smothered by the classroom in her role as a teacher. Now she didn't even play her piano any more.

Jack Duggan. Over the years she had forgotten about him as the children came along and she relished the role of mother, but seeing him a few hours earlier on the DART brought her right back to the first time that she realised she was in love with him. She hadn't felt this distressed since her wedding day.

She recalled her reflection in front of the long oak-framed mirror in her parents' house.

"You look beautiful," Emma had said with such sincerity that Louise almost believed her. But she didn't feel beautiful and a single tear had trickled down the side of her cheek.

Emma took a paper handkerchief and wiped it away. "We can't have you spoiling your make-up on your big day," she said sympathetically.

Louise had sighed with relief – knowing that there was somebody who understood what she was going through. She wondered if she would have been so empathetic towards Emma had the shoe been on the other foot.

She hadn't meant to fall into an affair with Jack Duggan six months before her wedding day – it had started out as a mild flirtation that was common enough in any workplace. But it subtly changed one evening in May when she knew that very soon Jack would be gone and she might never see him again. They both knew that what they were doing was wrong but neither could help it.

She had done the right thing by letting Jack go. She had done the right thing by Donal and held true to her vows for the last fourteen years and bore him three beautiful children who were the centre of both their worlds. So why did she feel so guilty for talking to Jack Duggan on the DART?

Damn, Louise thought. She was trembling inside. Her head was so full of thoughts of herself and Jack making love that she found it difficult to focus. Her stomach flipped as she recalled his eyes – the way that when he looked at her she felt as though he was reaching into her soul. If she stayed on her own until it was time to get the kids she could go out of her mind.

There was nobody else that she could speak to. Maybe Emma was at home but just hadn't answered the phone. She grabbed her handbag and car keys and slammed the door behind her. Luckily her sister was only a short ten-minute car ride away and she could tell her the incredible news before picking up Tom from school. She opened the doors of her Zafira MPV and slid onto the seat. Her heart pounded as she thought of Jack and the way he smiled at her. She felt in her pocket for the business card that he had handed her hours earlier. He was alive and well and living in Dublin – only a few miles away from her. Thoughts flooded her head and she had to be careful to focus on the road. She was so curious to know more about him and where he had spent the years that they had been apart. Did he have a wife? Kids? Did it matter? Of course not – hadn't she a husband and three children of her own? She had to speak to Emma and quickly or she would suffocate with her thoughts.

The roadworks on the Howth Road put an extra five minutes onto the journey and she cursed every second that it took her to get to Sutton.

Emma left the curtains open in the hope that the rays of spring sunshine might warm the room. She loved the fact that her bedroom looked out over Dublin Bay, with the familiar ESB chimneys in the distance marking the entrance to the Port of Dublin. The backdrop of the Dublin Mountains changed colour several times a day and had helped Paul and her to make up their minds to buy the house all those years ago.

"But isn't it too dear?" Emma had said at the time of the first viewing – two hundred thousand pounds was an enormous sum of money.

"Not as dear as it will be in two or three years!" Paul had assured her and of course he was right – as he had been about most things. Even with the collapse of prices in the housing market the house was still a bargain.

She missed his certainty and nose for predicting what was going to happen and his handling of the household finances.

That wasn't all that she missed. The scent of him on his pillow had gone even though she had put off washing the bed linen for as long as she could.

Suddenly the doorbell rang out – one loud and long ring that meant it could only be one person. At least Louise was used to seeing her in this state and wouldn't mind. But her impatient younger sister rang again even when she must have been able to see Emma's reflection through the glass door.

"Louise!" Emma said with a sigh. "Come in."

Louise barged past her and went straight into the kitchen where she hit the switch on the kettle. She looked as if she were about to burst. She propped herself up against the island in the middle of the room.

"Emma," she gasped, running her fingers through her long brown hair. "I had to tell someone – I saw him – today on the DART!"

Emma sighed because in typical Louise fashion she expected her older sister to know instinctively who she was talking about.

"Who?"

"Jack Duggan, of course!"

Louise's sureness brought a smile to Emma's face. "We haven't had a conversation about him in at least ten years so how in God's name did you expect me to know who you meant?"

"Who else would have me in such a state?" Louise raised her arms in the air and shook her wrists, the bangles on them jingling.

"Hey, I've seen you this worked up when talking about the state of your hair when it was cut shorter than you wanted!"

11

Louise closed her eyes and took a deep breath. "That's different – we are talking about Jack."

Emma didn't have much patience for her sister today. Anyway, Jack Duggan was someone from her very distant past. What was her problem?

"Were you talking to him?" Emma knew that it was always best to just listen to Louise when she was like this.

"Yeeesss!"

Emma shrugged. "Go on."

"You won't believe it but he's been living in Howth for two years and I never knew!"

"And what did he look like?" Emma proceeded to make tea while her sister elaborated.

"Just the same – God, he is so gorgeous – my heart was thumping as I spoke to him. His hair is much shorter and sandier than when I last saw him and he was wearing a really cool leather jacket and denim jeans."

"Is he married?"

"I didn't get a chance to ask – he got on at Connolly Station and I had to get off at Killester."

"Did he ask for your number?"

Louise shook her head. "He gave me his business card though. We were both in such shock we didn't say much – it was awkward. He did say that he'd been in the States for six years and was now a journalist for *The Times*."

Louise started to pace the tiles from the kitchen island to the table and back.

"So he didn't go on and become a rock star after all?"

"I guess not. I never thought he'd end up writing like you!"

"Come and sit down. I have something to tell you too." Placing the two mugs of tea on the table, Emma took a seat.

Louise joined her, looking a little impatient at Emma's announcement. She could think of nothing but Jack.

"I got a bit of a shock this morning in the post," said Emma.

Louise took the folded documents from Emma. "*Cuba*" was the first word that she read and then she scanned the travel documents one by one.

"God, Emma – that was so nice of him."

Emma nodded her head sadly.

Louise read on silently. "Hey, it says here that you'll be finishing the holiday with three days in Havana!"

Emma nodded. "I saw that – it would have been perfect."

"What do you mean 'would have'?" Louise said lifting her head. "What's stopping you from going?"

Emma shook her head. "I wouldn't want to go all that way on my own."

"Take Finn."

"You know how he complains about travel – he got cabin fever last summer in an airplane and we only flew to Bordeaux."

Louise thought for a moment. "What about me? I'd love to go."

"You have three kids and they'll be on school holidays for most of it."

Louise pondered for a moment. She could see Emma's mind race. She was always quiet when she was considering something and Louise felt that she knew instinctively what her older sister was thinking.

"I suppose you would want Finn to stay with me then?" Louise wondered why she was asking the question – the answer was obvious and Finn would rather stay with her than anyone.

A smile of relief washed over Emma's face. Louise's eldest son, being two years older than Finn, was his idol.

"Oh Louise, would you? He adores Matt. That would be brilliant – now all I need is someone to come with me. I bet Sophie would be on for it."

Louise felt the words like a blow. She wasn't surprised at the suggestion – life had a tendency to follow certain patterns and it was usually Sophie who landed on her feet. She never had to work hard to get approval or achieve anything and now she was going on a dream holiday with Emma – life was so unfair. But would she have the nerve to go? If she did, Louise didn't know if she could keep from telling Emma the truth. Surely Sophie's conscience would get the better of her?

"Why don't you call her?" she said, biting her lower lip.

"Okay. She's not away today?" Emma got up and went over to the phone.

"No. Not this week as far as I know!" Louise said, trying to hold back the angst in her voice.

She watched as Emma launched into conversation.

"It's me . . . how are you? . . . Sophie, I got a bit of a shock today – I got a letter in the post about a holiday to Cuba that Paul booked before he died . . . I know! . . . I'm still shaking . . . it was a surprise."

Louise watched silently as the one-sided conversation continued.

"Louise is here and she thinks I should go . . . it's in six days' time for ten days . . . Listen, Sophie, would you be interested in coming? . . . I wasn't going to use them but Louise has convinced me to go... come on, Sophie, you're the only person who can go off at the drop of a hat that I know . . . call around after work and we'll talk about it . . . bye."

"So I take it that's a yes from our little sister?" Louise said, unable to hide the disappointment in her voice.

"I had to twist her arm but I'd say she'll come. Are you sure you don't mind taking Finn?"

Louise smiled. However jealous she felt about Sophie going off on a holiday, she wanted Emma to enjoy her trip – after all that she had been through she deserved it and she would keep her reservations to herself. It was a strange twist that Paul would not be going now but his wife and lover would be going together.

"Sorry I haven't had a chance to talk to you about Jack –

14

maybe another day," said Emma. "I have to do some bits now before I pick Finn up from school."

"That's fine – no problem." Louise took the cue even though she was sorely disappointed that she hadn't got a chance to discuss what action she should take with her new information about Jack.

The thought of Sophie with Emma's husband brought her back to reality. She kissed Emma goodbye and got into her MPV, feeling her stomach churn as she recalled the awful moment of revelation of her younger sister's affair with her brother-in-law.

It was a few weeks before Paul's death that Louise had found them together. She had called around to collect a dress that she had lent Emma and needed to wear that night while Emma was away on a long-overdue spa weekend with a friend. Louise had let herself in with the key that Emma had given her. It was to be used only in case of emergency but Louise thought that the house was empty as Paul's car was not outside. Nothing could have prepared her for what she was about to see.

At first she thought the noises coming from upstairs was a burglar but she noticed a set of keys on the hall table and Paul's jacket resting on the end of the banisters. Then she realised someone was groaning and, thinking her brother-in-law must be in pain, she ran up the stairs. The bedroom door was open and she could see Paul's body rise and fall under the bedclothes. She felt awkward and embarrassed when she realised that he was not alone and presumed that Emma had come home early. But then the mass of strawberry curls on the pillow gave the woman's identity away.

Suddenly the couple stopped moving as Sophie realised that someone was present. She let out a yelp and pulled the sheet over her naked torso.

Paul jerked and turned around to see what had startled his lover.

"Louise!" Paul cried.

Louise was so shocked she turned and ran down the stairs as quickly as she could. She was out the front door before either Paul or Sophie had emerged from the bedroom. She still shivered to the bone every time she remembered that moment.

Sophie pressed *Save* on her computer screen and rolled her chair away from the desk. She didn't feel like doing any more designing today – she'd have to tell Rod that she needed the time off. It was just as well that the spring/summer ranges were all complete – it would be difficult for him to deny her the leave. She had brought in as many orders as last year and in such recessive times it was a major achievement. An early lunch was called for and she needed to clear her head.

She had wondered when her eldest sister would find out about the trip to Cuba. Paul had consulted her on every detail when they were planning it and now that she was getting to go on the holiday she felt a certain sense of satisfaction – a kind of compensation for losing him and the life with him she had been looking forward to.

It was all right for her eldest sister – she could mourn him openly – while she herself had to hide every trace of her anguish and there was much that she had to carry around silently and sadly since his death.

She decided to take the bull by the horns and go straight in and ask Rod for the leave. He wouldn't want to risk losing her now that she had made such good contacts with the UK buyers – they trusted her and for the last collection she was the only one that the larger stores wanted to deal with – a designer was much less threatening than a sales rep. If only they knew, she thought with smug satisfaction. Subtle manipulation was a game that Sophie was expert in – she had been doing her apprenticeship from before the time she could walk. The key to her success was her charm – nobody ever minded giving in to her – especially her father and her sisters.

Sophie flicked her long strawberry-blonde curls back off her face and strode into the corridor and past her colleagues – she was the first designer in the company to get her own office. But of course Sophie was worth it because she had assured Rod that she was special and he was so lucky to have her working for his company – and of course he believed her. Now he would be convinced that he simply had to let his golden employee take ten days off work. Even in this time of recession when designers were clamouring for work Sophie wasn't concerned. She would get the leave because she was Sophie Owens and she always got what she wanted.

"Hello?"

"Louise – it's Donal."

"Hi – will you be home for dinner?"

"Kevin wants me to take a look at a boat – he thinks it might suit us."

Louise sighed. The sailing season hadn't started yet but the preparation and excuses were well and truly back. "I thought you weren't going to change this year."

"We're just looking."

He was killing time before coming home and they both knew it.

"All right then – you can heat your dinner up in the microwave."

"I might get something in the club."

Louise wanted to scream. What was the purpose of her day? She had been to Superquinn – cooked the beef stroganoff from scratch – and now he wouldn't even be eating it. At least when she was at school she had papers to correct and classes to prepare which left her so busy she didn't have time to fret if Donal came home late from work. She found herself lately checking the time for *Desperate Housewives* or similar programmes once the kids were in bed.

"I'll see you later then," said Donal.

"Bye," she said abruptly and hung up.

If only she could find a balance: appreciation for the charmed life she had rearing her beautiful children and an interest that kept her fulfilled during her free time.

Her head was filled with thoughts of her encounter with Jack. She reached into her pocket and took out the small but slick business card that he had given her earlier that day. She wished that she was strong enough to chuck it in the bin – maybe rip it up beforehand. But she knew that she couldn't do that. After all, Jack had been nothing but gentleness itself towards her during all the time they had spent together. Hadn't she been the cruel one that had broken his heart and left him angry and hurt on that sad October afternoon fourteen years ago?

The trees were turning to all shades of orange, purple and brown as the chill in the air heralded the end of their affair. He had blamed her – told her that she was cold – he said she had planned this outcome all along. Her tears couldn't convince him otherwise, couldn't convince him that she held his future as a priority over her own feelings. But deep down she hoped that he hadn't meant it because they both knew that their love was the purest and most wondrous that either had experienced.

What was she going to do with his card now? Her head warned of the can of worms that she would be opening if she were to ring the number but her heart was egged on by the sureness in the pit of her stomach that she had to see him again – and soon!

She waited until the children were in bed – or in their rooms at least. Matt, the eldest at eleven, could often be heard pottering around his room until the small hours. Molly loved her sleep and often had to be shaken awake in the mornings. Tom was six and protested the most before going to bed but he could be bribed easily with a packet of *Match Attack* cards.

With the house to herself, she shut the kitchen door and,

using her mobile phone, she pressed the same numbers as those on the card that Jack had given her. She waited with bated breath as the phone rang out – each ring leaving her feeling more and more apprehensive. Finally the ringing stopped as the voicemail clicked in.

Jack here – leave a message and I'll get back to you.

Louise lost her nerve and turned off her phone quickly. Her heart pounded in her chest.

What would she have said if he had answered? There was so much she wanted to say to him, so much she needed to say, yet she couldn't put it all into words – she could barely put it into ordered thought – but she needed to speak to him like a junkie needed a fix.

Chapter 2

Six days later Emma was standing in a long line of people desperately trying to get through visa control in José Marti Airport, Havana.

Sophie's head was stuck deep inside a Dorling Kindersley guidebook.

"We can expect a delay of at least an hour getting through here," she said, shaking her curls in dismay.

Emma didn't need a guidebook to tell her that. There were twenty kiosks and as many people in each line approaching the customs guards. She didn't understand why people were taking so long to get through the checkpoint until she neared the desk herself.

A robust woman dressed in a short-sleeved shirt and tent-like skirt was asked to remove her spectacles so that the guard could be sure that she was the person photographed in her passport. The passport-control guard shook his head and stared at his computer screen for five minutes without speaking. Finally he handed the woman back her passport and told her rudely to step aside without gaining admittance. The next passenger was a young man with head shaved and a backpack slung over his shoulder. He got similar treatment before being told to stand aside. It was becoming apparent that the usual airport procedures were not followed in Havana. For a moment Emma was worried that they might not get through.

"It says here that we can expect anything up to another hour's wait before getting our bags off the carousel," Sophie said, looking up briefly from her guidebook.

The next two passengers had to pay the guard before getting their passports stamped to enter Havana.

Emma looked down at her swollen ankles – it was a hazard that accompanied travel on most long-haul flights. The stress of watching the antics of security didn't help the situation. She wished Paul was with her – he was always so calm in difficult situations.

"Your turn, Em," Sophie whispered in Emma's ear.

Emma wasn't surprised that when it was time to face a nerve-racking situation Sophie always left it up to her older sister to dive in first.

The passport-control officer slouched behind the glass window of the small wooden box that separated him from the public. He was wearing a khaki uniform that looked like it was left over from when the Russians were supplementing the state. He peered up over his wire-framed glasses and took Emma's passport through the slit in the box. He glanced at her and then back at the passport photograph. He couldn't have been any slower if he tried. He double-checked the tourist visa and put a few scribbles on a page and then looked at the photo again before pressing the buzzer to open the door that stood between her and the entrance to Cuba.

When she got to the other side boxes and suitcases were strewn everywhere. There didn't seem to be any particular method to the order in which the luggage was thrown and neither of the two long carousels were moving. It didn't help to know which flight you came off either. Emma figured that, as she had spent an hour and fifteen minutes getting through passport-control, her case had to be lying around somewhere.

"I need a shower and I need it quick," Sophie moaned as she stumbled through the door of passport control.

The temperature was at least thirty degrees. No air-con and even after locating their luggage they had to line up in yet another queue to go through customs that was as bad as the queue at passport control. Emma couldn't make out what was happening with the bags but they were getting pushed through some sort of security machine as each passenger was scrutinised before being let out one by one to Arrivals. Every now and again a passenger from the extremely haphazard queue was taken away to a private room with his bags. She was to find out later that the airport police liked to help themselves to certain contents found in cases brought back by their fellow Cubans. It was all slightly unnerving and Emma was glad that Sophie was distracted by the sweaty patches under her arms and not noticing any of the *Midnight Express* antics taking place.

Emma had been assured that the tour operator would have some sort of transport organised and waiting for them in Arrivals – but from her first impressions of Cuba things were done very differently to anywhere else she had ever been and she was concerned.

She needn't have worried because leaning against a pillar with a card in his hand with *Owens x 2* scribbled barely legibly across it was a man with dreamy Latin looks. He was wearing a white short-sleeved shirt and a pair of black shades. His hair was curly and dishevelled. He was slim and athletic and certainly didn't look as if he sat behind the wheel of a car all day.

"There's our man," Sophie nudged. "He's yum – a bit like Che Guevara!"

They edged up to him, laden with luggage. He stood much taller than the Irish girls.

"*Havana Tours?*" Emma asked in a strange Spanish accent that she hoped would help him to understand her better.

"*Señoras.* Owens?"

"*Sí,*" Emma grinned, hoping that her seven-day crash course of *Let's Speak Spanish* that came free with a newspaper would be enough to get her through the trip.

The driver took their cases and pointed them in the direction of the car park.

"Sol Melia Hotel?" he asked in husky tones. "I am your driver."

"*Sí.* In Varadero," Emma said as the driver closed the door of the Renault, locking them in.

The handles had been removed from the car door. Maybe they were broken and they hadn't been replaced. Emma had read before coming that Cubans didn't have access to spare car parts. She'd also read that they didn't have shops where the locals could buy the most basic toiletries. So, as internet sites advised, her suitcase was packed to the brim with packets of soap, little bottles of shampoo and boxes of tampons. She had read that the local women just loved a box of tampons because there is absolutely nowhere to get them on the entire island. Just in case, Emma had packed twelve boxes but wasn't too sure yet if she was going to have the nerve to give them to anyone.

Standing along the roadside were droves of people, mostly women.

"I wonder what they're waiting for?" Emma whispered in Sophie's ear.

"They are waiting for the bus," the driver informed them in perfect English.

Emma loved the sound of his accent. He would make a good character in a novel with his strong Latin looks, she thought. For the first time in months she felt inspired.

They were ten minutes on the road and so far had only passed two large blocks of tenements, lines of green trees and chicken-wired fencing. The buildings had been brightly painted once but were now dilapidated with peeling paint and dripping clothes hanging from makeshift washing-lines. Hungry dogs ran from building to building and barefoot children played along the side of the dust-covered motorway with makeshift balls and sticks. Emma was surprised by how happy they appeared in their abysmal surroundings and wondered how long Finn would last in this environment without his PlayStation and bike.

They passed some factories and what must have been a hospital. People dressed in uniform filed out through the gates onto buses.

The scenery started to change but still there was little traffic on the scantily covered roads. The motorways were more like very wide dirt tracks with potholes scattered here and there. Suddenly they were passed out by a 1950s' Chevrolet that looked like it had been riddled by bullets.

"Look at that car!" Emma exclaimed.

"Nice car?" The driver smiled into his rear-view mirror.

Emma laughed.

"How long will it take to get to Varadero?" Sophie asked as she jigged around on the sticky hot seats which were becoming increasingly uncomfortable.

"Two hours if we have luck!"

Sophie looked across at her sister in dismay. "Did you know it was that far away?"

Emma shrugged. "I gave you the inventory at the airport."

Sophie searched frantically through her bag and found it.

"Three hours! '*Transfer time is nearly three hours*'!" She sighed as she slipped the documents back into the slim white envelope.

"We'll just have to grin and bear it," said Emma.

"What does *Hasta la victoria siempre* mean?" was Sophie's next question as they passed a huge billboard at the side of the road with an image of Che Guevara painted along the side.

24

Emma looked over to where Sophie was pointing. "*Hasta* – that's 'until' '*siempre*' is 'always'and I suppose '*la victoria*' is 'the victory'?"

The driver was nodding in his rear-view mirror.

Sophie seemed satisfied and put her head back into her guidebook.

"You are from England?" the driver asked.

"Ireland," Emma replied.

"Che also had Irish ancestry," said the driver, smiling at Emma in the rear-view mirror. "His father's name was Ernesto Guevara Lynch. Che visited Ireland after the revolution."

Emma was impressed by the driver's knowledge and it struck her how good his English was.

"I'm a big fan of *The Motorcycle Diaries* – I read them when I was a teenager."

A broad smile appeared across the driver's face. "I enjoyed reading them very much also."

Emma leant back and let the road take her past the smoky factories and oil diggers scattered along the beach to their left. The sun started to go down and the scenery changed. Enjoying the peace, she watched the rich green landscape pass by.

She closed her eyes and tried to imagine how she would feel if Paul were sitting beside her instead of Sophie. It would certainly be different – he would be telling her all about the adventure before them and he would have read up on everything there was to know about the island. He would be the carer, but now instead she was going to have to mind Sophie. Her younger sister was able to pull the helpless card out of the bag for every situation. Even as kids, when the table had to be cleaned after dinner, she was first up to say that she would clear away – the easiest job by far – leaving the tougher jobs like washing-up for her sisters. If Emma or Louise protested they were berated by their mother for not offering to help first and told to take example from her instead. Sometimes she got out of doing any

25

jobs by virtue of getting in first – she always got in first and Emma always forgave her because she couldn't help the mothering instinct that hit her after the birth of her little sister. When Louise was born Emma was so hurt and jealous – the newly promised playmate was a nuisance and only took from the attention that Emma was used to receiving as an only child. When Sophie came along Emma was delighted. She was a wonderful replacement for the baby dolls that Emma no longer played with.

For Louise the new arrival was devastating – she'd had Emma and her mother all to herself and now she had to share them. Things were never going to be the same for any of them again.

"We're coming into Matanzas," Sophie said as they drove by a sign on the side of the road.

The last rays of light from the sun had disappeared. The depth of poverty in Cuba started to hit them as they realised that this was a big town – in Cuban terms a city – and not one street light illuminated the night. This was a third world country with deprivation that was difficult to contemplate coming from Western Europe.

Another half hour in the back of the taxi and the discomfort of the long flight from Dublin via Paris was beginning to take its toll.

"We are very near now – this is Varadero!" the driver exclaimed as the lights from distant hotels started to come into view. Street-lights were lining the long straight road that led along Varadero Beach.

Sophie pulled herself up and straightened her back with a stretch. "I'm starving – this place better be good!"

The driver turned off the long straight road into a driveway lined with lush cultivated vegetation on both sides. It led to a luxurious hotel entrance. Spotlights illuminated the tropical foliage and Emma wondered if the electricity would be better spent on the streets of Matanzas. The driver pulled up in front of a fountain with a statue in the middle that resembled Botticelli's Venus – beside it a sign read *Hotel Sol Melia*.

"This is more like it," Sophie said as the car came to an abrupt halt and the driver jumped out to open their doors.

"Have you any change for a tip?" Emma whispered.

"You've paid for this transfer already," Sophie said with a flick of her curls and stepped out of the opened door – giving the driver a smile as he helped her.

A porter dressed in a burgundy uniform complete with brass trims rushed to take the girls' luggage.

"*Benvenido a Varadero!*" he exclaimed with a wide smile.

In the distance salsa sounds drifted from the hotel bar.

"Can you hear that?" Emma said with a little gasp.

"I can hear my stomach louder – the dining room had better be open!" Sophie growled.

Emma turned to the driver – it was the first time that she had seen his eyes without the sunglasses – they were hazel, not brown as she expected – and they had a kind of smile attached.

"I hope you have a good holiday, *Señora* Owens."

"*Gracias,*" Emma replied.

He got back into the taxi and smiled up at her before he moved off. His hazel eyes twinkled and in that instant she hoped that it was not going to be the last time that she would see this man.

Chapter 3

"Wow!" Sophie exclaimed as she drew back the long and heavy curtains in their suite.

"Caribbean blue water, white sandy beach – there's someone sailing out there – look!"

Emma put her hand up to protect her eyes from the scorching sunlight, then sat up in the bed and looked out over the railings of their veranda. The sea had a band of turquoise running through the deep blue and tiny white caps rolled gently onto the beach.

"Not a cloud in the sky!" Emma proclaimed.

"This is one of the best rooms in the hotel apparently," Sophie said, pulling the door back and walking out to the balcony.

Emma felt a pang in her chest. This would have been so perfect with Paul, she thought sadly.

"Do you want to go down for breakfast?" Sophie said on re-entering the bedroom. "I'm starving."

"Okay, though I don't really feel hungry."

"Put your bikini on under your clothes. I want to catch a few rays of sun before the day gets too hot."

Sophie dressed quickly and waited impatiently as her sister did the same.

Emma threw her towel, novel and iPod into her stripey pink beachbag.

The walkway to the main buffet was shielded by towering palms. Emma spotted a couple romantically holding hands a few feet in front of them. She couldn't stop herself from thinking about Paul and imagining what it would be like if they were walking to breakfast together – but in hindsight they never held hands – it wasn't a Paul and Emma thing to do. That made her feel even worse and she berated herself for all the holidays they had been on when they should have held hands but hadn't.

"Look at this!" Sophie exclaimed as they entered the open-plan dining area.

Tropical fruits decorated the centre displays and every possible tantalising delicacy imaginable for breakfast was laid out on large platters. There were cold meats, French breads, pastries galore and a few feet away two chefs catered for those who would prefer hot food and pancakes.

"I don't think I've ever seen so much food!" Emma said.

She had read before coming that Cubans have ration books and restrictions with regard to what they were allowed to eat. They catered generously for the tourist industry judging from the display in front of her. With her conscience pricked she took a Danish pastry, a bowl of fruit and a cup of coffee before sitting down at the linen-covered table.

Sophie carried a tray with more food than she could possibly eat at one sitting.

"Are you going to eat all that?" Emma asked.

Sophie shrugged. "I'm just trying it all so I'll know what to have in the morning."

Emma began to eat her tropical fruit while Sophie took quick short bites from the array of food on the plates in front of her.

"They've a spa here – do you fancy going for a massage?" asked Sophie.

Emma shook her head. "I'm tired – I think I'll just get my bearings today."

Sophie nodded. "Okay – did you bring any good books?"

"I'm reading *Islands in the Stream* – Hemingway – at the moment, but I don't think it's your type of thing."

Sophie put a piece of pancake dribbling with maple syrup into her mouth and pulled a face when Emma wasn't looking. Her sister still had the ability to make her feel about six!

"I'm stuffed," Sophie said at last, leaning back on her chair as a pretty waitress with sparkling brown eyes and tanned sallow skin started to clean away the crockery covered with half-eaten food.

Emma helped clean up her space and put the used crockery into a neat pile to make it easier for the woman.

"Thank you," the waitress said with a smile.

Sophie grabbed her bag before the woman had finished her work. "Right, I'm off to get a good spot by the pool!" She stood up and left her sister to finish her tea.

"*Gracias*," Emma said to the waitress, returning her friendly smile.

Breakfast finished, Emma made her way through the dining area. Sophie only ever thought of what she wanted and needed to do and it had to be immediate but Emma had known what she was letting herself in for when she invited her along. She wondered what it would be like if Louise was there instead. In a way it could be worse if Louise was talking about Jack Duggan all of the time! Emma could barely stand to think of the guy that her sister had had an illicit affair with weeks before her wedding. At the time she had shown her sister compassion and sympathy but now, all of these years later, she felt that Louise needed to take a reality check. Donal was her husband and, although he could be anal about things like punctuality and neatness and he definitely took any chance he got to go off sailing, he was a good husband to her and a good father to their three gorgeous kids. He loved the role – unlike Paul who had taken a long time to get around to the idea of having a family and when he eventually did was happy with one child.

Emma slipped her sunglasses on her nose as she made her way out into the blistering sunshine. It had warmed up considerably in the short time they had taken to eat breakfast. She scoured the parasols and sun-beds beside the pool and spotted her sister pouring suntan oil over her fair skin.

A pool attendant dragged a bed for Emma over to where Sophie was.

"See how near we are to the bar!" Sophie exclaimed and pointed over Emma's shoulder to the sunken counter that lay between the bartenders and the pool. High stools stuck out of the turquoise water and one of the hotel patrons was enjoying his first mojito of the day.

"I think we're in paradise!" Sophie said, sliding her oily body down along the sun-bed and taking a chunky novel up into her hands.

Emma couldn't say exactly what was wrong but she felt an ache in her stomach and a desire to just be on her own.

"I might go for a walk if that's okay with you," she said and put her bag down on the bed beside Sophie's. "I'll leave my stuff here."

"Take as long as you like!" Sophie said, sinking her head into the book.

Emma took off her T-shirt to reveal her swimsuit and put it in her bag. She slapped some sun-cream on her arms and face, then tied her sarong tightly around her waist so that it would be comfortable and secure as she walked and set off to find the beach. The map she had looked at briefly the night before showed that it was a short stroll from the pool to the beach entrance. She wasn't in any hurry and decided to relish the experience of the warm sand creeping between her toes as the path changed from wooden planks to dunes. She spotted a gap in the dunes ahead and saw a Pico dinghy with brightly coloured sails breeze by on the blue Caribbean Sea. They were the same type of boat that the children in Sutton Dinghy Club sailed sometimes and for the first time since arriving in Cuba she felt a connection with home. She couldn't say that she missed Finn yet. Since Paul's death she had become disconnected with most people in her life. She often felt like she was swimming in the middle of an ocean – there was land all around on every side and she could swim comfortably to shore if she wanted but the fact that Paul wasn't going to be on any of those shores made her wonder what was the point. Sometimes she would see Finn in her dreams swim up to her in a life-raft but she always told him to go back to the shore because, although he understood how she felt, he couldn't possibly feel the same type of pain. That loss and emptiness that she had been carrying around for seven months now was becoming so comfortable that she didn't feel sad any more – it was just the way things would be from now on. Life would never be the same again and it was right that Finn was free to carry on and live a happy normal life and not carry the grief in the same way as his mother did.

She walked along the beach that went on for as far as the eye could see. The sand was almost white with only small groups of sun-seekers and sailors at the exits of the luxurious hotels dotting the coastline. It was all right to be on her own, now that she was here. She wondered if there were sharks out at sea and if so how far they would travel inland. This was the very same sea where Santiago must have fought so bravely with his fish in Hemingway's novel *The Old Man and the Sea*.

Many thoughts of Paul and her book filled her head on the return leg of the walk and she slipped in through the entrance gate to the hotel, unsure just how long she had been walking – the pink hue on her arms and shoulders warned that it must have been considerably longer than it had felt. She was parched and took refuge in the shade of the bar on the way into the hotel. The resort had five bars and seven restaurants and every meal and drink was included in the package. She only had to state her room number to refresh her palette with a cool glass of sparkling water.

The waitress was the same woman who had cleared their table at breakfast. Her black hair was tied neatly back in a ponytail off her face and she smiled showing perfectly straight white teeth. A gold chain around her neck spelt out the name *Dehannys*.

"*Hola*," Dehannys said with a friendly smile. "What you like?"

"*Agua con gas, por favor*," Emma said, nervously hoping that she hadn't set herself up for a fall by ordering in Spanish.

"Aah, *habla Español*?"

"*No – poco*," Emma said. "But I have been trying to learn."

"*Sí, bueno*," Dehannys smiled. "My English is not very good."

"We can learn from one another."

Dehannys nodded her head vehemently as she poured from a bottle of sparkling water into a glass. "That's good."

"*Gracias*," Emma said taking the glass from Dehannys. "Do you live nearby?"

"Matanzas – about half one hour."

"I think we drove by it last night – we came from José Marti Airport."

"*Sí*, I live with my mother and father and my son."

No mention of a husband, Emma thought as she drained the glass thirstily. She felt a kindred connection with this woman and something inside told her that she was meant to meet her.

"*Gracias! Vamos* and find my sister."

"*Adios!*" Dehannys said with a smile.

Emma felt good as she walked up the wooden boarding to the pool. The walk had energised her and she realised for the first time since Paul's death that she could feel really happy on her own just having a walk – of course the Caribbean sunshine and luminous turquoise sea did help.

Sophie looked up from her novel as Emma approached. "How did you get on?"

"The beach is fantastic – it goes on for miles."

"I'll check it out later," Sophie said, sticking her head into her book once more. "Oh, Finn rang while you were walking."

"Is he okay?"

"Of course – I bet it was Louise who made him call – I'd say she just wanted to find out what it was like here."

Emma recalled the look of disappointment across Louise's face as she dropped Finn off two nights before. Her son was delighted to be sharing his cousin's company but she realised that she had let her sister down again and was taking Sophie away on a junket that Louise probably wanted more.

Emma felt a compulsion to dive into the blue water in the swimming pool. She let her sarong slip from her waist and walked silently over to the water's edge.

Sophie looked up as the droplets of water from the splash Emma had made rained down her shins and feet. She could have warned me, she thought, as she turned on her side to ensure that her tan was perfectly even.

She was angry with Emma and had to hide her feelings at every turn. It was becoming unbearable. She had to come on the holiday or Emma would have smelt a rat – she knew her well enough. The irony of going on holiday with her lover's wife when she should have been sharing it with Paul! It was all right for Emma to go around moping and mourning – she didn't have to carry her breaking heart around in silence. Paul had agreed to tell Emma that he was leaving her a few days before he had died. They would have relocated to make it easier for Emma and Finn. Eventually Emma would have understood – Sophie was sure of it. Paul was her soul-mate and they were meant to be together for always. Now she would have to swallow her feelings and knowledge and watch Emma flaunt her grief for a whole ten days.

Chapter 4

Louise was finding it difficult to function. Two images were playing on her mind – one of her sisters lying in the Cuban sunshine and the other of Jack Duggan on his way into Dublin on the DART. It was too early in the morning for her sisters to be doing this and Jack was probably already sitting at his desk or out researching a scoop but both sounded better options than filling the washing machine with uniforms and underwear!

When she took her first career break from teaching music she felt as if it was richly deserved and such a relief, the second year was a mere continuation of her just desserts, the third year she dreaded the prospect of returning to employment, and Donal hadn't even asked if she was going back last year. She should be grateful – few women were able to afford the luxury of a husband bringing in a good wage that supported his family in this economic climate. She wondered if there was some sort of glitch in her make-up. Because deep down she had often wandered off in her imagination to the world where she was when she was in love with Jack Duggan. That was the place that she liked to escape to the most.

Now that she had actually seen him she felt numbed and torn. He was exactly the way she had imagined he would be all of these years later. In fact he looked even better as an adult than he had as a teenager.

A week had passed since she had dialled Jack's number and she felt the longer she left it to ring him the harder it would be. What would she say to him? What would she have said if he had answered his phone the other night? It was getting too much – becoming an obsession again. For the first year of her marriage she used to drive down Griffith Avenue just to pass by his house in case he came out of it. Of course he never did because he had become a college student and had found digs on the south side of the city, but even so on the off-chance that he was visiting his mother she would take the diversion. Donal never noticed and, together with the relief of that, came frustration that the man she had married didn't know her intimate thoughts or feelings at all. How could she spend the rest of her life with a man who was happy with only half of her because the other half was deeply in love with Jack?

But with time the obsession had ebbed, her life with Donal and the children and her teaching had taken over and her time with Jack Duggan seemed like a distant glorious dream.

Now, fourteen years later, she could see his face in the sink when she was washing the pans after dinner. She could see his face as she removed the crusts from her children's sandwiches. She could even smell his skin when she closed her eyes. His scent was the one thing that hadn't changed at all. His clothes were fashionable, his skin more rugged, his hair was several shades darker but his scent was undeniably the same. In frustration she slammed the door of the washing machine shut with a bang and broke down in a flood of tears. Her nose started to run so she grabbed a chunk of kitchen roll from the counter top and decided she had to do something.

Automatically she took the coffee canister down from the shelf where it rested and measured out two teaspoons of free-trade

Colombian rich roast. She had to pull herself together. She would be forty soon and she didn't want to feel that life had passed her by. The thought of going back to work scared her and the thought of staying home until her children reached college-going age scared her even more. What had happened to the carefree fun-loving Louise who had loved so passionately and so deeply in her twenties? How had she turned into this crazed compulsive mother of three with no real identity of her own? She took her mug and poured boiling water on top of the coffee granules. Nursing the warm black mug of coffee in her cupped hands. She walked into her sitting room. Her piano sat forlorn and unused in the corner of the room and for the first time in years she felt an overwhelming desire to strike a few chords.

When she worked as a teacher a day never went by without her playing on at least one occasion. At certain times of the year, like the lead-up to the Christmas carol service or the Battle of the Bands, she would be at her keyboard for several hours a day.

It was during the annual Battle of the Bands contest that Jack Duggan had made his first pass at his teacher. There wasn't a huge gap in age between them – she was only twenty-four and not long out of college – he was eighteen and technically an adult – but their status was a world apart.

She remembered the moment in every detail. They were in her classroom after all of the musical instruments had been put away. The school had a very different feel once the sun had set and although it was early summer there was a cloak of darkness to hide what was going on in the music room which had only one small window and was soundproofed. Where she and Jack stood by the large instrument cupboard it would have been impossible for anyone to see in from the outside. Besides, all of the participants and spectators of the show were still in the school hall which was one flight of stairs and several hundred feet away from where they were.

"Thank you, Jack," she had said as he handed her the amplifier and microphone to put into the corner of the press. She could still remember the instant when their eyes met and the transition of energy from her body to his.

Slowly he moved forward, confident that she felt the same way as he did.

The tension had been building slowly and eagerly like a pot roast for the last weeks of that school year and now that May had come and he would soon no longer be a schoolboy, he knew that the dark corner of the music room was the place to make his move.

The first kiss was very tender and clumsy in its innocence. It was only as she breathed in his scent that her desire for him made her crazy. He moved in towards her and she let her lips open hungrily to drink him in. He tasted so fresh, so new – not that her fiancé Donal was by any means an old man but, at twenty-eight, there were ten years between him and Jack.

Louise tried not to think of Donal as she let Jack grab her more forcefully and pull her onto the classroom floor. The roles were reversed. He was now the one in control and she was being guided on a route that could spell disaster at any instant if someone walked through the door. She had to use every ounce of self-control in her bones to stop them taking the kiss any further that night.

There had been that other time a couple of weeks before when she was perched on the ledge that ran around the walls of the classroom with her feet resting on top of the piano stool. At her side were a pile of essays on Debussy and Impressionist musicians. The bell hadn't rung yet for the start of class.

"You're early!" she had declared flippantly as her first student entered the room.

Jack came slowly over to where she sat – elevated on the ledge – and stopped that little bit too close for comfort – inches from the gap between her knees.

"It's my favourite class – I couldn't wait to get here."

And somehow they both knew at that moment that he wasn't referring to her tutorship.

Louise shuddered as she thought about it and took another

sip from her mug of coffee. She couldn't go back there but she could do something to bring the passion back into her life. She could do a few things. But for now she rested her mug on the coaster on top of the piano and sat down on the little-used stool. She lifted the cover that hid the ebony and ivory keys beneath like a vampire removing a coffin lid. It had been a while since she had played Debussy – she wondered if she could remember. As "Clair de Lune" rang gently from the piano-keys she felt her spirit lift and her heart. This was something that she had that wasn't Jack's or Donal's or anyone else's – maybe if she played it would help her find the answer to what it was she was missing and why her soul felt so empty.

"What did you do today?" Donal asked Louise.

He liked to hold court in front of his family on the evenings when he didn't go straight to the yacht club and Louise was always irritated by this conservative side of his personality. She looked over at her husband at the top of the kitchen table – still wearing his shirt and tie from work. His brown hair was thinning slightly but his skin looked remarkably youthful for someone who spent so much of his free time sailing.

"I did the washing then I dried and ironed everyone's clothes and put them back in the wardrobe!" Louise said snappily.

Donal hadn't meant to sound accusatory. He didn't know how to talk to her any more about the things that were important.

Matt and Finn were devouring their fish and chips and were anxious to go outside and play football.

"Have you called your mum yet?" Louise asked her nephew.

"I called on my way home from school but she wasn't there – Sophie answered. She'll probably ring later."

Louise nodded and started to slice her fish with delicacy and tenacity. Realising that she had been a bit harsh on Donal she changed her tack and tone.

"I spent a while on the piano actually, today – something I haven't done for years."

"That's good!" Donal said, genuinely pleased to hear she was doing something that she enjoyed. After all, he had his sailing. "I haven't heard you play in a long time."

Louise nodded. It was true and with the demise of her piano-playing had come the demise of her relationship with Donal. They seldom made love any more and he never complained. Sometimes she wanted him to just grab her passionately and tell her that he desired her badly. But Donal had never done that – not even in the first flushes of their relationship so why should he start now?

Suddenly Finn's mobile rang and the boy grabbed it clumsily and held it up to his ear.

"Mum, hi! . . . I'm having my dinner with everyone . . . What's it like?"

Louise watched as Finn hung on his mother's every word. She wished that Matt and she had a better relationship. She blamed herself for sending him to crèche when he was much too young – only a few months old. But those were the days when maternity leave was fourteen weeks and her work was everything to her and she was determined not to let the arrival of her first-born child change things in any way. But having children did change her and with it her priorities, and for the foreseeable future her children were her priority, which was why she felt so tortured over the last few days of thinking about Jack Duggan.

Finn hung up. "Mum says hi and she'll ring you tomorrow," he said to his aunt and tucked his head back into his fish and chips.

Louise smiled. "Thanks, Finn. Now would anyone like dessert?"

"Yes, please!" Molly and Tom said together.

Donal lifted his head. "We don't normally have dessert mid-week."

40

"It's a treat," Louise said, making her way to the fridge.

She was torn inside with feelings of guilt about her desire to see Jack again and the need to be a good wife and mother.

She trembled as she tapped the numbers from the business card into the phone. What if he didn't answer again? Would she leave a message this time? She didn't have to wait long to hear his unmistakable voice at the other end of the line.

"Hello?"

"Jack? Hi – it's Louise – Louise Scott – I mean Owens – from school!"

Damn she thought – why did I have to say "from school" – I'm such a fool!

"Hi, Louise, how are you?" he said.

Louise swallowed hard – she was feeling foolish for ringing at all now. "I'm fine – it was lovely seeing you the other day – on the DART."

"Yeah – a real blast from the past. Are you still up in the school?"

"I've been on career break for years – I have children now."

"Of course – how many?"

"Three – the eldest is eleven and the youngest six so I have my hands full."

"Great – sounds great!"

By his tone Louise could tell that he didn't think having a brood of children was great at all.

"You said you were living in Howth now – whereabouts?" she asked.

"I'm in an apartment on the harbour front – great view. I'm only renting! Just as well I didn't buy with the state of the property market."

Louise agreed with a loud "Hmm!" He was obviously free as a bird and enjoying it.

"There's a great farmers' market out here at the weekends," he said. "Do you ever come out?"

Louise paused – was he hinting for her to come out to Howth?

"Yes, my sister lives in Sutton and I often bring my kids out on a Sunday morning – they love the crêpes from the market stalls."

Why am I talking about my kids constantly, she berated herself. She could sense Jack's restlessness on the other end of the line.

"Look, I have to shoot here – I have to go to an award ceremony in the Burlington – great talking to you, Louise – maybe we can hook up sometime? We've got a lot of catching up to do."

Louise felt as if she had received a swift slap on the wrists.

"Great talking to you too!" she said as the line went dead.

What was that all about? He was totally distracted and so different from the way he had been on the DART. Maybe after the shock of seeing her initially he felt differently and didn't want to have anything more to do with her. Either way the phone call left her feeling empty and sad. She shouldn't have made it.

Chapter 5

"What do you want to do today?" Sophie asked.

"I'm really enjoying the rest." Emma stretched out her limbs on the bed and gave a loud yawn.

"I'm getting a bit bored – I wouldn't mind doing some sightseeing."

Emma sat up on the bed and smiled.

A knock came from the bedroom door.

"That's just the chambermaid – I'll get rid of her!" Sophie said, striding over to the door.

As she opened it the girl at the other side said apologetically, "I am sorry – I come later!"

"Hang on, Marina!" Emma called, remembering the pile of toiletries she had stashed in her suitcase.

She grabbed a tube of toothpaste and a packet of tampons and rushed out to give them to the girl who had been so lovely and looked after them so well by making little sculptures with their bath towels and sprinkling flower petals on their beds.

Sophie clicked the roof of her mouth with her tongue. She would have been embarrassed by Emma's behaviour had she cared what a Cuban chambermaid thought or felt.

"I've heard that these are difficult to get here?" Emma said, putting them into the girl's hands.

"Yes, thank you – *muchas gracias*!" the girl said, nodding her head vehemently.

Sophie chucked her bikini, book and sun lotion into her beach bag with a shake of her head.

Emma shut the door and walked over to Sophie.

"What's the matter with you?" she asked defensively.

"That girl has her hands on toiletries everyday – she works in the bloody hotel – I bet she has no problem getting anything she wants."

Emma wasn't sure if Sophie was right or not but she felt better for doing a good turn and it was mean of her sister to try and belittle her actions.

"I'm going into Varadero after breakfast – do you want to come? Maybe bring a few boxes of tampons to distribute to the general public?" Sophie said mockingly.

Emma ignored the remark and took her small white Apple laptop and slipped it into her bag.

"I might do a bit of writing instead – down by the pool."

Sophie tossed her hair back off her face and led the way out of the hotel bedroom.

Being in such close contact with her older sister for days and barely talking to another soul apart from the Cuban staff was beginning to take its toll on her. At least Emma wasn't talking about Paul. She decided that maybe she should put her true feelings aside and find a bit of fun. Men used to be a source of fun until she met Paul, the only man that had made her want to settle down. In Varadero she could check out if there was a good nightclub or a chance to meet some interesting people and get away from her sister!

Emma was surprised at the ease with which the words were appearing on the screen of her laptop. She had a bit of a job at first arranging her sun-bed in a shaded part of the pool area and lowering the parasol so that it cast enough shadow to see the screen properly but now that she was writing she felt as if she were on a roll. It was good to get away from Sophie – the solitude was just what she needed.

She didn't feel like she did when she was writing at home – it wasn't just the Cuban sunshine or the warm wind blowing up from the beach that made it feel different – Emma sensed another force helping her put down the words and show her what was going to happen next to her characters. She was writing about Martin – he was the hero in her novel and in every sense a Hemingway hero. Macho and strong with so much testosterone simmering around him that he sent the female characters crazy – these were two women, Jill and Ruth, who used to be friends until Martin came into their lives. He was in control of all of their destinies. So far she had given him dark hair but hadn't described his eyes – she considered giving him hazel eyes like those of the taxi driver who had brought them to Varadero. She often picked on a characteristic or feature of an actual person when she was trying to form her fictitious characters. Martin had started out his career as a regular policeman but had been elevated to the rank of detective quickly as his prowess became stronger. He had to have strength and again she thought of the taxi driver – there was something silent and strong about the man who had driven them from José Marti Airport.

Emma loved the control that she held over the characters in her novel – how different it was to real life where she felt that she had so little. Even Finn was becoming difficult to restrain when he wanted to do something that she felt might be dangerous or risky.

Life was much safer tapping away on the laptop and leaving your characters to make all of the mistakes and misjudgements. At least when a character in her novel died there would be no real tears shed – the funeral would be over in a couple of pages and the rest of the characters could continue on peacefully – even happily.

As she reached the 25,000-word mark that had taken her almost eight months to write she hit the save button, lay back and took a rest.

In the distance she saw Dehannys walk quickly up the path towards her with a bag slung over her shoulder.

The women were on first-name terms now and Dehannys had told Emma how to pronounce the days of the week and months of the year properly. She could now say *dos cervezas* with a Spanish accent.

"Are you finished work for today?" Emma asked as Dehannys drew near.

"*Hola,* Emma," she said with a smile. "I must take my break now."

"Come and sit with me," said Emma.

Dehannys looked embarrassed. "I don't think my manager would like. Staff are not allowed beside the pool when not working."

Emma chastised herself for being so thoughtless. "How is your son today?" Dehannys had told her the boy was unwell.

"He is *mucho* better, *gracias.*"

"Is he at home?"

"Yes, my mother she take care of him." She paused. "Would you like to visit my house – to see my family?"

Emma sat up on her sun-bed at the suggestion. What a wonderful idea! It would be lovely to see how a local family lived. "That's a very kind offer, Dehannys – are you sure you wouldn't mind?"

"Please, I would like it very much. My mother sometimes cooks for tourists – this is allowed by the government – it is called *paladar*, a small restaurant. I would like you to be our guest but, please, you must not say in the hotel to my boss!" Dehannys looked around as she spoke – afraid of anyone overhearing.

It was the first time that Emma realised the vulnerability of her new friend's position. "How can I get there – will the hotel get me a taxi?"

Dehannys nodded her head. "Of course – I will give you my address."

Emma searched around in her bag for a notebook and pen. "Write it down, please. Would you mind if my sister came too?"

Dehannys smiled and shook her head. "Your sister is very welcome in my home. I like this very much – you will see my boy."

"Have I shown you a photo of my son Finn?"

Dehannys shook her head. "Please! I very much like to see."

Emma proudly produced a picture of her son sitting on the edge of a Pico in Dublin Bay with the Dublin Mountains in the distance.

"This is where I live – in Dublin – in Ireland."

"It is very beautiful – he is fine boy. Come tomorrow night – I do not work Wednesday."

Emma smiled. "Thank you. What time?"

"Come at four o'clock and see Matanzas."

"Okay – see you at four."

"Yes – I see you then."

Emma watched as her friend walked off slowly and easily with that unmistakable rhythm she had noticed the Cubans displayed with each footstep.

In the opposite direction she could see her sister approaching, carrying two white plastic bags. Even at a distance Emma could see Sophie had a frown etched across her pretty brow. When she eventually reached Emma, she let out a loud sigh.

"That fecking bus is the pits! And there's nothing but a heap of junk in that market."

"Looks like you bought some junk!"

Sophie plopped down on the sun-lounger at Emma's side. She reached into the bag and took out a toy car made from an aluminium Coke can.

"I am going to get myself a mojito," she said. "Do you want one?"

"Why not?" Emma shrugged. Since arriving on Varadero Beach she had taken such a liking to the local cocktail that she usually had her first of the day before twelve o'clock.

As Sophie walked off towards the bar Emma bent over her laptop and continued working. She would tell her later about the trip to Dehannys' house.

"I don't see why I have to come along," Sophie whinged.

"You don't – you can stay here," Emma said as they walked up the steps from the gardens to the reception.

"This place is full of couples – I'm not sitting in the piano bar all night on my own." The fact that the hotel was a romantic retreat for adults only was part of the reason she and Paul had chosen it in the first place. Now their decision was coming back to haunt her.

"Well, it's up to you." Emma turned to speak to the concierge. "Could we have a taxi to take us to Matanzas?"

The man in the shiny grey suit with the pencil-thin moustache smiled a wide smile that said Emma had just asked for the impossible.

"Have you made a reservation?"

"No – I thought you could just call one?"

He showed his teeth with an even wider smile and shook his head. "I'm sorry, *Señora*, but we need to use official taxis from this hotel. They must be reserved."

Emma was dumbfounded. "What about car hire – could I get one?"

"It is clos-ed for today – very sorry!"

Suddenly a husky voice spoke above Emma's head in Spanish and after a few seconds she recognised the man who owned it. He spoke quickly and authoritatively and finally the concierge shrugged his shoulders.

"This man will take you to Matanzas," he said. "He has to go to Havana now and he can drop you on his way."

"Hello," Emma said with a smile. "You picked us up at the airport, didn't you?"

The taxi driver smiled back and in the light of day Emma could see his perfect white teeth more clearly than before. It was amazing for a nation of people with such problems getting toothpaste that they had such remarkable sets of teeth.

"Are you sure that isn't putting you out of your way?" she asked.

"No, I will be passing Matanzas – and I will bring you back tonight if you like."

"Thank you so much," Emma said.

Sophie threw her eyes heavenward as she followed her sister to the driver's Renault.

"How often do you travel to and from Havana?" Emma asked once they were settled comfortably in the taxi.

"Sometimes three but mostly two times in a day – I have to collect clients from the airport."

Emma noticed that the meter wasn't on and wondered if she should mention it. Perhaps he had some other way of calculating the fare? Eventually she decided she had better say something in case he had simply forgotten.

"Excuse me – but you don't have the meter on."

"There is no charge – I will be driving by Matanzas anyway."

Sophie leaned over and whispered in her sister's ear, "He's looking for a big tip, I bet!"

Emma felt very conscious of her younger sister's remarks and how they must sound to the man who had helped them out when he didn't have to. She glared at her to be quiet. In the rear-view mirror she could see the driver's reflection and his kind hazel eyes – not typically Cuban, she would previously have thought, but since arriving on the island she had realised that there was no such person as a typical Cuban. Skin colours varied from pallid cream to dark chocolate-brown and hair ranged from blonde to black as jet. But rhythm and a passionate nature was something that was universal to them all.

As they approached a small bridge an array of grand colonial houses came into view. They were now in need of repair and chalky pink and blue paint was peeling from all sides of the walls. In the distance several other small bridges of various design popped up – some with pillars at the side, others made from metal and more industrial than aesthetic in design. A colonial church rose above the low rooftops – casting a romantic shadow over the town. Emma had never been anywhere like this before. There was a rawness about the place that oozed character and charm.

"Do you have the address?" the driver asked.

Emma foraged in her bag for her notebook. "Yes, I have it here – sorry, I didn't get your name?"

"Felipe," the driver replied.

What a fabulous name, Emma thought. "Thanks, Felipe. I'm Emma and this is Sophie."

"Pleased to meet you, Emma and Sophie," he smiled.

"The address is *Cavadonga y Carnet* – or something like that."

Felipe nodded his head. "I know the place. My cousin lives in that street."

Sophie let out a shriek as Felipe pulled the car into a street with basic but inviting haciendas on both sides.

"These are good houses," Felipe said and Emma could see that he really meant it. "It was difficult after the hurricane to get cement to fix the damage but they are better now."

Most had tiny front yards with wrought-iron gates and wild flowers out front and the paint in all shades of green, blue and cream made the buildings look cheery.

Felipe stopped the car suddenly outside a turquoise-green door.

"This *paladar* is very good." He turned to look back at the girls. "What time will I collect you?"

Emma looked at Sophie and by her expression she could tell that her time would be limited here. "What time will you be back from Havana?"

"About three hours."

"That sounds good. Thanks, Felipe." Emma reached into her pocket and took out 20 CUC – the Cuban tourist currency and highly desired by the Cubans to buy goods that were only on offer to tourists.

"Thank you," Felipe said with a nod of his head as he got out of the car to open her door.

"See you later then," Emma said with a smile.

Sophie looked on with a mixture of amusement and impatience. As Felipe drove off she turned to her sister and frowned. "You do realise that was two months' wages you gave him as a tip!"

It was Emma's turn to frown. "I think he deserved it – he took us here when he didn't have to!"

"It was on his way!"

"Sophie, when someone does something like that to help why can't you just be grateful? The world isn't revolving for you alone."

Sophie raised her eyes heavenward and let her sister lead the way. She should have stayed at the hotel.

"This is delicious," Emma said, slicing into the roast pork.

"It is called *cerdo asado* and the beans and rice are *moros y cristianos*," Dehannys explained.

"What does that mean – *moros y cristianos*?"

"It is the black bean for the Moors and white rice for the Christians!"

Emma laughed. "I like that!"

"*Cerveza*?" Dehannys' father asked as he rose to his feet and lifted an empty bottle. He smiled cheerily and rubbed his stomach –

covered by a bright green shirt. He was sprightly and delighted to be entertaining the women with his wife and daughter.

"*No, gracias, Alberto*," Emma said, patting her stomach to show how satisfied and full she felt. It was difficult to converse with someone who hadn't a word of English but was bending over backwards to be kind and hospitable.

"*Mama, peudo que yo ahora juego?*" little Fernando asked his mother.

"*Sí*," Dehannys watched as her son skipped off through the kitchen at the back of the house.

"Your son is *mucho guapo* – he is like my boy!" Emma said.

"*Gracias*, Emma," Dehannys said with pride. "He is a good boy."

Emma was dying to know where the lad's father was but wasn't sure if she should ask in front of the family. Maybe it would be better to leave it for another day.

"Ahh, my brother!" Dehannys said excitedly as a handsome young man with coffee-coloured skin came into the house. "*José, estas son mis amigas, Emma y Sophie.*"

Emma watched as Sophie perked up in her seat for the first time all evening.

José was wearing a red shirt and black trousers with shiny black shoes and he would have looked very out of place in Dublin but, in the *paladar* in Matanzas with the dusky heat from the day still wafting in through the front door, he looked like he had stepped off a movie set.

"José is – how you say – music man – he plays piano in the Hotel Tryp in Varadero," Dehannys informed them proudly.

"Can you play for us?" Sophie asked, alluringly enough to ensure that she caught his attention.

"No piano in house – so sorry, but I play this," he said and picked up an old acoustic guitar that was resting against the whitewashed wall in the corner and started to strum.

Suddenly the room was lifted – he played and sang with such

emotion that everyone stopped what they were doing to listen. It was a soft Cuban ballad and it wrapped an atmosphere around the room that left the Irish girls in a kind of trance. His voice hovered over the emotional notes.

"Louise would love this," Emma whispered into Sophie's ear – but her sister wasn't listening.

José walked over to their table when he finished playing and pulled a stool out to sit beside Sophie.

"You stay in Cuba for how long?" he asked.

"We have three more days in Varadero and then we are going to Havana for three days."

"A La Habana," he said wistfully. "It is so beautiful."

"Do you go there much?" she asked.

He shook his head. "It is difficult to travel – I work in Varadero so I have no need to go. But I lived there for three years when I was a student in university."

"Where do you live, José?"

"I live here with my mother and father – it is difficult to get a house from the government."

The sun had now disappeared for the evening and Dehannys' mother had turned on the single bulb that hung in the centre of the room. Along the windowsill were small tea lights that she put a match to. They cast flickering shadows on the whitewashed walls and gave the room a cosy and intimate atmosphere.

"Coffee or *ron*?" Dehannys asked her guests.

"What is *ron*?" Emma asked.

"Rum – Havana Club – my father works in the factory," she said producing a long slender brown bottle with the distinctive red circle in the middle of the label.

José jumped to his feet and grabbed four tiny shot glasses that Dehannys proceeded to fill to the brim. He took his measure first and knocked it back in one go.

Sophie lifted her glass and took a sip – it brought water to her eyes and she coughed out loud.

José smiled and handed her the cloth napkin that was lying on the table.

"Thank you," she said and wiped her lips.

Suddenly the door opened and Felipe walked in, looking dishevelled from his day's driving. His eyes lit up once he spotted Emma sitting at the table and he gave her a gentle smile.

"*Amigo!*" José grunted, standing up to get an empty glass from the old wooden dresser in the corner. "*Ron?*"

"*Sí, gracias,*" Felipe said with a nod and took a stool next to Emma. "Did you enjoy the meal?"

"Great, thanks. You are back quickly."

He shrugged. "Sometimes I can drive quickly when there are no police." He lifted the shot of rum and raised it in the air before throwing it back in one gulp.

Suddenly the dim light in the centre of the room went out. Dehannys' mother started to shout at the bulb and flap about like a clucking hen.

"We have many power cuts in Cuba," Felipe whispered in Emma's ear.

Emma smiled at Felipe. She was glad that he had returned and was happy to stay on.

The darkness didn't seem to deter José.

"*Musica!*" he declared and got up to play his guitar.

Dehannys' granny and a couple of local women emerged from the scullery and everyone in the room started to clap along as José sang and strummed.

The gentle candlelight added to the atmosphere and Emma realised that for the first time in a very long time she was happy, with these strangers in this foreign land, and she wasn't sad or thinking about Paul at all.

Chapter 6

Louise packed up the younger children and made them put their coats on.

"It's too hot," Molly groaned.

"It's always cold on the pier and the north wind is blowing today!" Louise said, closing the buttons on Tom's jacket.

"They can leave them off in the car," Donal said in an attempt to hurry his wife.

Donal was standing at the open front door with six golf clubs and a bag of balls in his hands. The two older boys were becoming impatient. Donal had promised them all that on Sunday they would be brought to play pitch and putt in Deerpark.

Louise checked how she looked in the mirror one final time before setting the house alarm and following the others out to the car. She had put more thought than usual into her appearance for a Sunday trip to Howth. At the back of her mind was the prospect of meeting Jack Duggan.

She was left with an empty feeling in her stomach after she phoned him and now she needed to be sure that she looked her very best should she bump into him again. Donal seemed oblivious to the fact that she was wearing a low-cut top when she had insisted that her children should wear warm clothing.

The drive along the seafront was noisy with the four children in the back prodding and poking each other at every opportunity. Thankfully the traffic wasn't too bad and they had left early enough to avoid the post-one-o'clock rush.

As they drove up through the gates of Howth Castle and Demesne Louise could feel her heart pound. What if she did meet Jack today? What could she say to him after their awkward phone call?

"See you in about two hours and then we can get a bite to eat?" Donal said as he got out of the car with the two eldest boys.

"We'll take the kids to Casa Pasta or The Brass Monkey," Louise said as she slid over to take the wheel. "I'll be up for you before two thirty."

"Okay," Donal said, shutting the door firmly.

Louise watched in her rear-view mirror as her husband, son and nephew started to recede into the distance.

"Are we getting crêpes?" Molly and Tom chorused.

"In a few minutes now," Louise said with a sigh. She wasn't sure exactly what she was hoping to achieve by this expedition but Jack had said that he enjoyed the market on a Sunday. A long line of traffic awaited her once she turned out of the castle demesne and the car edged at a snail's pace all the way to the DART station.

"There's a space!" Tom cried as a car pulled out.

"Thanks, love," Louise said and reversed into the spot.

The sky had cleared and it was much warmer now than it had been when leaving Clontarf. With the brighter weather came the crowds and Louise knew that it would take them longer than usual to get the children their chocolate and marshmallow crêpes.

"Can we go watch the seals after we get our crêpes?" Molly begged.

"Okay – mind the traffic now – we have to cross here," Louise warned as they paraded along by the stalls packed with a cornucopia of goodies.

"There's the fudge Daddy loves – can we get him some?" Molly asked.

"All right," Louise sighed – it was as good a place to start as any.

The red and white striped canopy shielded them as they waited in line to buy their share. The fudge stall was a little bit removed from the rest of the market and a good vantage point to see the hustle and bustle of everybody milling about.

Louise let her eyes scan the busy area and suddenly she spotted a familiar face, but it was difficult to tell if it was him at such a distance. She waited as he proceeded to talk to the woman at his side. She felt a pang of realisation sweep over her as she watched the man put his arm around the woman and kiss her. Of course – it had been obvious all along. No wonder Jack was so short with her on the phone – he was in a relationship – maybe even married. Those emotions she had felt on the DART had been hers alone and she couldn't say that he felt anything for her – obviously he didn't or he would have called her back – how stupid she had been!

"Can we have chocolate as well?" Molly asked with a tug on Louise's jacket.

"Yes – I mean no!" she snapped distractedly.

She didn't know how she felt. Maybe she had been deluding herself. The young woman was beautiful – she could possibly be a model. Why on earth would a gorgeous young man like Jack with a fashionable job and the world at his feet be interested in his old schoolteacher any more? She couldn't feel any worse.

"Are we getting crêpes now?" Tom pleaded.

Louise looked around. "Okay – and then we can go down

and watch the seals if you like." At least then she would be far enough away from Jack and his girl.

The queue was much longer than usual and Louise wished she hadn't agreed to come to Howth. The boys could have played pitch and putt in St Anne's and she could have stayed home. On the other hand maybe it was better that she found the truth out now.

"Marshmallows and Nutella!" Molly instructed the crêpe-maker standing behind the stall.

"*Please*," Louise said firmly. It was difficult to hold it together as she kept looking over her shoulder.

"That's five euros, please," the crêpe-maker said politely.

Louise handed over the money. "Okay, kids, let's go and find the seals," she said, ushering the young ones over to the west pier where hopefully they could hide at the other side of the big blue-roofed ice-building and avoid bumping into Jack and his girlfriend.

"Great shot, Finn!" Donal said encouragingly. "Your turn, Matt."

Donal loved the time that he spent with his kids – maybe because he also got to spend so much time doing his own thing. He wished Louise was more fulfilled. She adored her children and was a good mother but sometimes Donal felt that she had sacrificed her own needs to keep the family ticking over and functioning well. When he met her she was so happy teaching – but the guilt of leaving their children with strangers was too much for both of them so Louise staying home seemed like the best option for everyone.

"Your turn, Dad," Matt said with delight after sinking his putt in two swift shots.

Donal focused on the ball and then back at the hole only ten feet away. He looked again before putting and watched it roll up to the edge and teeter before deciding not to drop into the hole.

"Hard luck, Dad!" Matt said with a smug grin. "Is this our last hole?"

"I think so – you have me on the run, son," Donal said with pride. His children were important to him – but his marriage mattered too. He had lost all sense of closeness with Louise – she seemed so distanced from him.

He knew that something had to happen but he felt hapless and sad with the state of his marriage. At least he had the yacht club and his sailing – maybe that was why he retreated there so often.

Louise leaned against a rail and watched her children giggle with joy as they fed the seals. The seagulls weren't having much luck today – the seals were too fast for them.

"Look, there's a baby seal!" squealed Molly.

It wasn't so long ago that you were a baby, Louise thought to herself. It was sad to see the baby stages pass so quickly but there was a sense of achievement in watching her children grow healthy and strong. Why isn't that enough for me? She berated herself for indulging in self-pity and didn't see the couple walk up beside her children to look at the seals.

"Louise!"

It was Jack.

"That's amazing, bumping into you again!" he said. His arm was resting around the waist of the girl at his side and he guided her over to where Louise stood perplexed and still.

"Jack, hi," she said awkwardly. "Come back from the edge, Tom!" She gestured towards the children. "These are my kids."

"This is Aoife – my fiancée." Jack showed no awkwardness which made Louise feel even worse. "And this is my old music teacher, Louise."

The girl smiled.

"Very nice to meet you," Louise said quickly – not sure

whether she found being introduced as his "old" or "music teacher" more insulting. But then again, how was he going to introduce her? *Louise was my lover when I was a school kid and she was my teacher!* It didn't sound good, even all of these years later.

"Oh, Jack told me about you – didn't you organise the Battle of the Bands?"

Louise wanted the ground to open up. "Yes, that was me. It's lovely to meet you – when are you getting married?"

"In the summer – July," Aoife answered. "Hopefully the weather will be nice – we are having it in Dublin – quite rare these days but, as we want both families and all of our friends at it, we decided not to go away."

Louise nodded her head. "Good idea. Well, best of luck with it all."

"Thanks!" said Aoife.

"Well, goodbye, then," Louise said, a little too abruptly for her own liking but she was anxious for the couple to move along and Jack was showing that was what he wanted to do.

"Bye, Louise," said Jack, ushering his bride-to-be along the quay.

Louise felt as if she had been winded. Luckily her children had been oblivious to the whole charade and hopefully Aoife was also. She couldn't help herself but when she saw him she became flustered. Maybe it was all the memories she had been carrying around inside for so long.

She could remember with clarity the first time she and Jack had consummated their affair. They had spent two years as student and teacher relishing their mutual love of music. He would often stay behind to discuss the more modern music that influenced him and wasn't on the exam syllabus. Louise loved the time they spent discussing the merits of Nirvana and Pearl Jam over the

Stone Roses. It would often take up half of lunch break or longer but neither would mind. He was so much more mature musically than the other students in her class and she was the only music teacher in the school so found it difficult to discuss her specialisation with her colleagues. He would bring in demos from his band and she would happily listen to the tapes as she drove to and from work. When Donal would ask about the noise that was coming from the stereo she would just smile because it made her feel young and in touch with the new generation. She didn't feel like there was a huge divide between them musically – although she had studied for four years in college she felt that he had a natural feel and knowledge of what music really meant that couldn't be learnt wading through manuals and scales. His natural talent was a gift and she envied him that. She had worked hard applying herself to her craft by reciting concertos and practising for hours on end. Jack just had to lift a guitar to make it strum in a way that she could never achieve with an endless amount of practice.

Then, shortly after the wind-up of term three, Louise offered to give Jack some revision tips for his Leaving Cert. They both knew that her offer had an ulterior motive – it was a means to scratching an itch that had been gnawing at them both since the first time he had stayed behind class to talk about music.

At the time Louise was renting a small terraced house in old Clontarf with Emma and it wasn't easy to deal with the cleaning, with Emma's high standards and her own lack of domesticity.

They generally compromised and Louise more often than not shoved her clothes and bits and bobs into trunks and cupboards to hide the mess and Emma turned a blind eye.

On this particular day when Jack was calling, she put flowers in a vase on the table in the small kitchen and put *Carmina Burana* from Carl Orff on the CD player in the front room where they were going to have the class. She changed her clothes several times in the half hour before he was due to call. She didn't want to come across as old and authoritative and yet she wasn't sure if they would cross the barrier again like they had in her classroom after the Battle of the Bands contest. It wasn't like they were going to suddenly become boyfriend and girlfriend – she had a solitaire ring on her finger that proclaimed to the world she was about to get married and he was waiting to finish his exams before he could truly say that he had moved out of secondary education. But still she couldn't help herself from preparing in the same way as she would have for a first date.

When he rang on the bell and she answered the door, all she could see were his translucent blue eyes and the feeling that there was a deep connection between them.

The smell of his skin was overpowering as she showed him into the front room and directed him towards the sofa. In front of it was a small coffee table where she had placed an array of curriculum books that they were going to study.

"Would you like a drink?"

"Have you got 7UP?"

It hit her suddenly that what she was feeling was terribly wrong. He might be eighteen but he was still just a schoolboy!

"Fine," she said rushing to the kitchen and searching frantically for a fizzy drink. At the back of the cupboard there was a bottle of diet 7UP, left over from a party they had thrown over Christmas – she hoped there was still a little fizz left in it. She poured and watched as a couple of bubbles floated to the top. It will have to do, she thought.

Jack was sitting upright on the sofa when she returned with the drink. His skin showed the signs of recent shaving and his hair had a newly washed shine.

"How are the studies going?"

"Okay," Jack shrugged. "English and Music are my best but that's because I like them the most."

"Are you still going for Arts?"

Jack nodded. "My mum wants me to do Science – she doesn't think I will get a job as a musician."

"She has a point!" Louise joked. "No, seriously, I think you are very talented and if you keep it up you never know – your band could make it."

"Already the guys have given up practice."

"They are probably anxious about the Leaving exams. When you all start college you can get into a routine again."

Jack shook his head. "I wish they were as committed as I am. I really hope we stay together."

Louise felt an awkward silence pass.

"Okay – so where do you want to start?" she asked.

Jack was speechless. He was fixed on Louise's hazel eyes.

The pause left a static electricity between them. Neither wanted to be the first to make the move but both wanted it to happen. How far they would go and where that kiss would take them they didn't know. It had to happen naturally.

Jack moved forward first and then stalled when his lips were a couple of inches from Louise's. Seeing the pleading in her eyes he moved closer again until they touched. It was very different to the kiss in the classroom. These kisses were more calculated – gentler than the first time. Jack had more confidence as he placed the kisses on her lips. Louise felt overcome with longing – for now all she wanted was Jack. She pulled her lips away and with a telling gaze she took his hand and led him out of the small living room. There was no need for words – both of them knew what was going to happen.

She led him up the stairs. A few feet behind her Jack took each step with caution. As they reached the small landing Louise paused outside a door and, still not speaking, she turned the handle and pushed the door open. In front of them was the newly made bed with clean linen. It was the first time Louise had made her bed in the morning since she and Emma had moved into the house. Secretly this was what she had wanted to happen.

Emma wouldn't be home until tonight and Donal never called without ringing first. The only other person with a key was her father and he was away – they wouldn't be disturbed.

On reaching the side of the bed Louise took control once more and put her hand up to Jack's face. His breathing was heavy with anticipation and she could sense his anxiety as once more their lips touched. This time he didn't hold back. The pent-up emotions that he had carried for two years at the back of Louise's classroom were ready to burst.

Louise felt her legs turn to jelly and her insides melt as their tongues felt around each other's mouths impatiently.

He took her firmly in his arms and forced her onto the bed, then was immediately contrite. "Oh sorry – I didn't mean . . .!"

"It's okay," Louise assured him. All too aware of his apprehension she urged him to continue.

They kissed slowly and gently until she grasped the hem of his rugby shirt and slid it up his torso until it was over his head. He then proceeded to take off his T-shirt and reveal a young trim body – exactly the way she had imagined him to be.

With trembling fingers he reached forward and started to open the buttons of her shirt. Louise could feel her nipples become erect with excitement and stick out through the lily-white lace bra. His hands slipped behind her back to find the absence of a clasp. She took his hands in hers and guided them to the front.

"The catch is right here," she said, guiding his fingers to where it nestled between her breasts. She gasped with delight at his expression once her breasts were released from the bra. The feelings of power and desire were different to any she had ever felt before with a man. His unbridled lust was overwhelming and she felt as if she could come without him laying a finger on her body. "Lie down," she urged as she expertly grabbed the buckle of his belt and pulled it open. She flipped the buttons on his jeans and pulled them down around his thighs and he followed her lead by opening hers. Both pushed their jeans off until they were lying with only underwear covering them and knowing that they would be taken off next.

As his hand cupped her breast she shivered with delight and they pressed their lips together.

Louise quivered with each stroke that his finger ran over her nipple and yelped as his hand slid over her panties. She desperately wanted him to touch her *there*. The fact that she was wearing underwear somehow made the experience even more thrilling.

"Please!" she begged.

He knew just what to do and slid his hand down between her legs and clumsily rubbed her. Within seconds she was coming with moans and groans that delighted Jack, giving him the confidence to expose his erection.

Louise wanted him more than she had ever wanted anyone in her life and she held him down and straddled him. She was the teacher again and she was going to show him how to make love.

He wanted her to show him exactly the way that she liked it. Every thrust was nirvana for him – he had only been inside one other girl and that time he wore a condom. Louise was so wet and firm around him, he felt as if he was having sex for the very first time. It felt too good and he didn't know how long he could last before bursting.

"It's okay – come now," she whispered as she started to jerk and fold her body onto his naked torso.

He let out a scream as he came and his eyes started to fill. "Oh God!" he cried.

Louise kissed him on the neck and breathed in his skin. He was so much fresher and sexier than Donal. It was the first time she had given her fiancé a thought since Jack entered the house. She didn't think that she would be able to face him when he called around later.

"Are we going to get Dad and the others?" Tom asked.

"Sure," Louise said distractedly. Recalling the memories were unsettling in her son's presence – even if he had no idea what his mother was thinking. "Let's get them now!"

As she drove up through the gates of Howth Demesne she felt unnerved. She had been deluding herself. Jack may have been a schoolboy when he fell in love with her but while she had been rearing her children and living a suburban life he had been off around the world experiencing adventures that she could only ever dream of now. She felt so envious of him. His girlfriend was beautiful – in a different league to the frumpy housewife that she felt she had become.

Chapter 7

"He was gorgeous!" Sophie gasped at breakfast.

She didn't need to elaborate. It was a general trait of the Owens sisters. They seldom needed to explain the details of what they were talking about to each other and often they would start a conversation mid-sentence and the others would follow it perfectly. It caused much annoyance to the men in their lives and was a habit that Paul detested the most. When he was with Sophie she would constantly remind him of his wife by starting to talk about a subject out of the blue and expecting him to know what she was speaking about. It wasn't the only thing that got to him by the end of his affair but Sophie was totally unaware that there could possibly have been anything wrong between herself and her lover. As far as she was concerned he was cruelly whipped away from her side in the very same way as fate had taken him away from her sister.

Thinking about Paul was very different to the day-dreaming she now indulged in on the sunny terrace of the five-star hotel on Varadero Beach. José was a fine example of manhood and Adonis-like in his proportions but her feelings for him would stay firmly several thousand miles across the Atlantic when she returned to Dublin. He had no prospects so was not a contender for a serious relationship but a holiday romance was a definite possibility. It was just a pity that she only met him as she was about to leave Varadero. She deserved some fun and flirtation after the silent grieving she'd had to endure after Paul's death.

"They were a very nice family," Emma said, picking up on Sophie's thoughts, "very hospitable. I felt so embarrassed when Dehannys' mother wouldn't let us pay for the meal."

Sophie waved her arm in the air. "She knows you'll be giving her daughter fat tips in the hotel so the dinner was a good investment."

Emma glared at her sister. "Do you have to see a twist in everything kind that people do?" she sighed. It was useless to argue.

Wide-eyed, Sophie innocently shook her long curls. "You're just not very streetwise, Emma – you never have been!"

Emma decided it was best to let it go. She had more time to get through with her sister on the largest island in the Caribbean and there was no point arguing. So far the holiday had gone well and Sophie had been surprisingly relaxed but after they had met Dehannys' brother the night before Emma realised that her sister would not be happy until she added him to her list of conquests.

"I told José that we might go to the hotel that he plays in later tonight?" Sophie stated in a tone that suggested she was asking Emma a question.

Emma nodded. The decision had been made for her and there was no point in trying to object. She cut a chunk off a large slice of pineapple and put it in her mouth. Her diet had been remarkably healthy since arriving in Cuba but she found the taste of white Cuban rum a little too likeable for her own good. She usually had her first mojito from the pool bar at twelve and continued drinking throughout the day. No matter how heavy-handed the bartender was she never felt drunk and started to consider that maybe she was building up a special kind of tolerance to the spirit. Her writing was flowing and so far she had reached forty thousand words. The change of environment was a definite plus and she realised, now that she was away from her home, she could happily work away without thinking of Paul every fifteen to twenty minutes. It was such a break and because Sophie was the only person around who knew her she didn't feel guilty either. Maybe she should travel more. Finn certainly wouldn't mind spending more time in his cousin's house.

Sophie stood up. "Right – I'm off to brush up on my tan."

"I'll be along in a little while – just going to take a short walk before I settle down to do some writing."

She watched Sophie stroll off with her beach bag swung loosely over her shoulder. She really was the very picture of beauty.

Emma had loved her little sister so much when she was a small girl. She was ready for a real live doll to mind and fetch for and feed when her mother would let her. It was her job to protect her from Louise and make sure that her middle sister didn't jeopardise her safety. Little did she realise that her youngest sister needed the least minding in the family. She had that knack of falling on her feet and getting everything easily no matter what she did. It was Louise who turned out to be the member of the family who needed the most care. Emma would never forget the day that she walked into the little house that they rented in Clontarf and found Louise on a chair in the kitchen stark naked and straddling a much younger man – a man who was not her fiancé.

But in true Emma fashion she didn't judge Louise and instead was a shoulder to cry on for her sister when she found it too much to cope with her situation and she finished the forbidden relationship. It was a great relief to Emma because she knew how conservative her parents were and everything had been arranged for Louise's wedding with Donal for a year before they were due to marry. Louise wasn't the type to up and leave Ireland either – she was always very much the home bird, so running away was not an option. In the end Emma felt that Louise had done the right thing but lately there were days when her incessant moaning – especially about Donal – was getting on her nerves.

Emma loved her brother-in-law. Donal was a rock and for a short while after Paul's death he was the only one that she could confide in.

"*Hola, Emma!*"

Emma turned around to see Dehannys starting to clear the breakfast china off the table.

"*Hola! Muchas gracias por la cena.*"

"*De nada,*" she smiled. "Fernando would like to write a letter to your son. He would like very much a friend in Ireland."

Emma nodded her head. "Of course – that would be great," she said enthusiastically. It would be good for her son to learn how others in the world lived and realise that not every little boy had a PSP or Wii to play with.

She said goodbye to Dehannys, assured that she would see her at lunch, and set off to find a quiet corner of the pool where she wouldn't be disturbed. She was on the brink of her hero Martin falling for a woman whose case he was investigating, and she felt that now was as good a time as any for her character to have loving feelings for another woman – after all his wife was dead over five years so he deserved to find love again. She felt very close to Martin – he had a lot of similar traits to her and he was someone that she really believed in. She had a clear picture of him now and Felipe the taxi driver had helped her to find his face.

"Are you sure this hotel is the next one down?" Emma asked as they walked down the long straight road, the lights seeming further and further apart.

"Yes, I am."

Emma wasn't so sure that Sophie knew where they were going. The road was very quiet and she would have been much happier if they had called a taxi to bring them to the Tryp hotel.

"See, there it is! The Tryp. I told you we could walk it!"

The surroundings were as opulent as the Sol and the staff at the reception desk as eager to please on the sighting of Europeans.

"Where is the piano bar?" Sophie asked the girl behind the desk.

"Downstairs to your right, madam," she replied in perfect English.

Sophie and Emma descended the staircase and surveyed all around until the sultry tones from José's piano led them the rest of the way.

Emma stood still and spoke to her sister with one ear on the strains coming from the piano bar.

"I thought he was good on the guitar but the piano is certainly his thing!"

"He is good, isn't he?" Sophie said with a smirk and continued to lead the way until José and his red shirt came clearly into view.

José changed tune immediately on seeing Sophie and started to play Cole Porter's classic "I Got You Under My Skin". After a few bars he started to sing. Sophie knew that he was singing it to her and she was loving every minute of it.

The sisters took seats next to José and he followed their moves with his gaze. He looked even better than he had in the modest surroundings of his mother's house.

"Be careful, Sophie," Emma warned.

"I'm a big girl!" Sophie replied.

José was only half an hour into his act and had to play for an hour and half more. Emma felt that she would have been better off in the small bar where Dehannys worked or back in her hotel room writing about Martin Leon.

"I might go back to our hotel – that okay with you?" she said.

Sophie glared and flicked her eyes heavenward. She wasn't really bothered! Emma was starting to annoy her anyway.

"Go then. I'm staying to talk with José when he finishes."

Emma knew that it wasn't talking that Sophie had in mind.

The concierge called a taxi and she was back in her hotel in five minutes. The solitude was blissful after spending so much time with her sister in recent days. She needed this peace to figure out how she felt now that she was out of her comfortable surroundings and a single woman again. She didn't mind the fact that she was no longer part of a couple. Finn was a constant reminder that she'd had a relationship that produced a wonderful human being. But there were still so many unanswered questions. The autopsy only told her so much. She was lucky that the pathologist never delved too much into her awareness of her husband's state of mind before he died – it was the sort of unfortunate circumstance that could open a murder file. But without a conclusive reason for his death she felt left in a kind of limbo. She thought that they were so happy. There were very few couples that they socialised with that had so much in common or who were able to communicate the way that she and Paul could. For Finn's sake it was better not to dwell on the details of his death too much. She was young and strong and had to get on with her life.

José sang the last song of his set to Sophie. "Got a Black Magic Woman . . ." he started to sing smoothly.

After Emma left, Sophie had perched herself on the edge of a stool right next to José and he had enjoyed the flirtation between them as he played each song. She listened avidly, lapping up the attention until he was finished.

He had taken a mojito with each of Sophie's and together they were relaxing into an intimacy that didn't include the rest of the audience in the bar. He didn't care. They would all be gone in a few days, just like Sophie, and he had to make the most of his youth and good looks to pull European and Canadian women that stayed in the hotel. He had it all worked out – even a spare room that his friend the chambermaid tipped him off about at the end of her shift each day. Maria relied on him to hit on women and get huge tips and then give her a cut when he scored. It was a mutually beneficial relationship and they weren't doing any harm – as long as none of the management in the hotel found out.

Sophie sipped on her mojito and stared into José's chocolate-brown eyes.

"Can we go somewhere after you finish?" she asked.

"I know a room in the hotel if you would like to be more alone."

"Excellent." Sophie grinned. She needed to be alone with a man again – she needed it so badly. She missed making love to Paul so much and José was just the sort of guy to take her mind off him – for a few hours anyway.

It was the response that José needed.

"I can't believe you took an empty room – what would have happened to him if the manager had found out and what about you if the police had found out? Don't forget we are in a foreign country!"

Sophie threw her eyes heavenward. "Relax, Em! Why do you have to be so paranoid? We are in his country and José knows exactly how to play the system!"

Emma was concerned because she knew how strict the regime in this country was and she didn't want her sister to land herself or anyone else in trouble.

"He was amazing!"

"Spare me the details," Emma said, burying her nose in her cup of English breakfast tea.

"Until you've had a Latin lover you really haven't lived," Sophie went on. "He didn't sleep all night long – it was six o'clock before he went for a snooze and then we were up at seven."

"How did you get back here?"

"He gave me a lift on the back of his motorbike."

Emma took another sip and closed her eyes.

"You know, you really need to move on, Em." Sophie shook her head.

Emma hated the condescending way she said this. How would she have any idea of the pain and anguish that she was carrying around inside every minute of every day?

"Even Dad thinks you should," Sophie continued.

It was one step too far. Emma couldn't stand the way Sophie wrapped her father around her little finger. The thought that they had been discussing her reaction to her husband's death was too much to take.

"I'm going for a walk."

Emma stood up abruptly and left her sister devouring her pancakes with maple syrup. She walked purposefully towards the entrance to the beach and breathed a sigh of relief on seeing the electric blue sea. Walking on the almost white sand she felt safe again – safe to think about Paul and her father and her family in any way that she wished.

Her father was always hard on her – he expected so much from her and held her up as an intellectual. She was the daughter who studied psychology and English literature – the others took artistic subjects and that was all right because Emma had led the way. It made her the envy of her sisters. Louise dealt with it by being naughty any chance that she got and Sophie clung to her role as the baby to get his attentions and sympathy – and it worked.

When Paul died Emma thought that her parents would be more supportive but they carried on in the same way as they had when Misty had died. Misty was the girls' only pet. He was a brown and white cocker spaniel and the whole family adored him. He was the sixth member of the Owens family – he was bought the Christmas when Emma had turned eight and the excitement of having a new baby sister had dwindled.

Larry Owens loved the fact that Misty was male and made him feel less outnumbered by the women that filled the house. Emma remembered him commenting during the BBC production of *Pride and Prejudice* that he knew exactly how Mr Bennet felt and in a way he was a modern-day version of the character himself.

The beach was almost empty today. She longed to talk to someone, so made her way back to the hotel beach bar where waiting behind the counter was Dehannys.

"Emma, buenos días!"

"Buenos días, Dehannys! Agua sin gas por favor."

"It is hot today?"

Emma nodded. *"Puis la playa esta linda."*

Dehannys put the glass of water on the counter top.

"Your brother and my sister were out very late last night!" said Emma.

Dehannys tilted her head, unsure if she had understood the insinuation correctly. *"José? Con Sophie?"*

"Sí." Emma could tell by the reaction she was getting that this was news she did not want to hear about her brother.

Dehannys took a glass off the counter and started to rub it vigorously with a tea towel.

"Dehannys, is everything okay?"

Dehannys shook her head. "My brother is a bad boy. He is to marry Gabriella but he is not good to her."

"Who is Gabriella?"

"She is my cousin and very kind girl."

"When are they going to be married?"

"Dos meses."

"In May?"

"Sí but . . ." Dehannys shook her head – she didn't need to explain.

Emma felt awful for mentioning the matter. "Look, Dehannys, we are going to Havana tomorrow so Sophie will never see him again."

Dehannys stopped cleaning the glass and rested her palms on the bar counter. "But tomorrow more women will come – tourists – and he will be taking them to his room in the Hotel Tryp." She sighed. "But I will be sad when you go, *amiga – ahora hablas mucho espanol!*"

"*Gracias – eres un professor muy bueno.* Will you write to me when I return? I could email you?"

Dehannys shrugged. "I have email address but is very difficult to use."

"Is there any way you could use the hotel's?"

"*Es difícil.*"

"I will give you my card before I go and if you get a chance please try and email me. I will post you some presents for Fernando when I return – is there anything he would like?"

Dehannys nodded. "He needs clothes and shoes."

Emma could tell by the way her eyes lit up that anything would be greatly appreciated.

How hard her new friend's life was, working for long hours at the hotel each day and she got to spend such little time with her son.

"Where are you working tonight?"

"*Aqui* – in this bar."

"Well then, I will spend my last night here with you and we can watch the sun go down and listen to the music and when you are not busy you can talk to me. Okay?"

Dehannys smiled.

"You're not walking to the Tryp on your own!"

"Are you asking me or telling me, Em?"

Emma wanted to shake her younger sister. She seemed to

ignore the fact that they were in a foreign country and anything could happen to a young woman on her own taking the long and isolated walk to the Tryp Hotel. Emma also felt that it was her job to protect her sister against the deceitful José even though she was capable of looking after herself.

"I was speaking to Dehannys today and she told me that José is engaged."

Sophie didn't move for an instant and then she grinned. "What difference does that make?"

Emma had had just about enough of her sister. "Are we going to eat first?"

"I've lost my appetite," Sophie said. "I'll get something later with José."

Emma grabbed the room key and her bag and left.

She set off down the familiar path to the small beach bar where Dehannys would be cleaning glasses and making drinks. The sun was setting in shades of vibrant red, pink and yellow and Emma wished with all her heart that Paul was with her. His choice of hotel was impeccable and she felt as if it was a gift he was giving her from the grave. Dusk would be on the beach soon and the stars would come out with clarity and sparkle like diamonds in a way that she would never see them in Dublin. Since coming to Varadero she had made it a ritual to go out onto the balcony every night and look up and see what ones she recognised.

Tonight the Port Royal beach bar was busier than usual and Dehannys was frantically crushing ice and mint together to make mojitos for the hotel patrons that sat at the counter. She waved at Emma when she saw her.

Emma took the last space at the end of the bar – near a trio of musicians who were setting up to play their guitars. She was in no hurry to be served and could order some bar food. It had been sheer indulgence eating every night in the many hotel restaurants and her stomach could do with some simple food. Lobster and fillet steak were overflowing at every sitting and

Emma often wondered what the average Cuban ate at night. There was a lot about this country that she would never know staying in the oasis of Varadero and she longed for her trip to Havana and a chance to see more of the real Cuba – like she had seen in Matanzas.

Dehannys slid a mojito along the bar to where Emma sat and winked. "Where is your sister?"

Emma gulped. She didn't want to tell the truth but she couldn't lie to her friend.

In the end Dehannys made it easier for her. "It is okay – she is with José, I guess."

Emma nodded.

"I hope he is not asking your sister for money."

Emma was shocked. It never occurred to her that he was selling himself as some sort of gigolo. That definitely did not sound like the type of guy that Sophie would be interested in. Emma let out a little giggle.

"What is funny?"

"You don't know my sister! He'd be lucky to get a drink out of her!"

"*Bueno*," Dehannys said, smiling now too.

Now that there was a lull in the bar and the band had started to play the mellow tones of Chan Chan, Emma felt this was her chance.

"Dehannys, do you mind me asking about Fernando's father?"

"It is okay – he is gone for a long time."

"Is he dead?"

Dehannys nodded. "*Sí*. We were young and very much in love. He worked in the Havana Club factory with my papa. He had accident in a big machine."

"Were you married?"

Dehannys shook her head. "Fernando come *tres mesos* after we bury him."

"I'm so sorry to hear that. Poor little Fernando never got to see his father!"

Suddenly she felt so relieved and privileged for all the photos and film she had of Paul with Finn. She had yet to get the courage to see any video footage but the photos were a great source of help late at night when she needed to remember what he looked like.

"But Fernando has my father – he loves him very much – he takes him fishing."

"And he has José?" Emma suggested.

Dehannys laughed. "Nobody has José – José has José for what he wants."

"I hope Sophie will be okay!" Emma said as she took a long and leisurely sip from her mojito and sat back to enjoy another classic from the serenading musicians.

Chapter 8

"Mum, I just need you to collect Molly and Tom from school – I won't be long," Louise wouldn't have called on her mother if she wasn't really stuck. In all the years that her children had been going to primary school she had only called on her five or six times and on each of those occasions she had received a similar response.

Even after Louise gave birth to her children Maggie expected her daughter to take care of herself and her new offspring without any extra help from her.

"I reared you three girls on my own," she said to Louise when she was only a few days home from the Rotunda. "Just your father and me – my mother came up from Cork for two days only and Larry's mother posted us a cardigan that she had knit for Emma with a packet of butterscotch for a present. I didn't see her until Emma was six months old."

Louise had heard it all many times over and at the end of the rant she always told her mother how grateful she was that she had given up so much by looking after her three girls so well. Emma often placated her mother by singing her praises too –

however, Sophie never indulged her but Sophie didn't indulge anyone.

Maggie made a tut-tut noise with her tongue and sighed. "All right! I can change the time of my golf lesson but don't be any later than three – okay?"

It was as good a deal as Louise could hope for.

"Thanks, Mum," Louise sighed and hung up the phone. She wondered how her mother managed to get her husband to adore her so much when she was usually so unreasonable and demanding. Sometimes she worried that she was becoming like her mother. It was a rare request, and unusual that none of her usual support group of friends were available to help her out instead.

At least now she would be able to meet Jack. With the children's welfare catered for, she went and searched for something to wear. Twin sets hung alongside smart fitted shirts with equally smart fitted trousers and lines of footwear. In the drawers were her comfortable clothes and tracksuits which she wore during her morning walks and were the dress code of the stay-at-home mum. Her wardrobe had turned into her mother's unbeknownst to herself.

It was a mild spring day so she could dress any way she chose. In the end she went for her one and only pair of blue denims and a fitted pin-striped shirt – she had a long necklace that would look good with it. And her raincoat – even though there was no forecast or sign of rain for the day.

Her heart started to race as she applied her favourite Mac make-up to her eyes.

The call from Jack had come like a thunderbolt. After the awkward meeting on the west pier she was shocked to get the text message asking her to meet him in the new Quay West restaurant in Howth.

She applied some of her newly purchased Benefit lipstick and popped it into her handbag. One of her friends had assured her that it was the trendiest make-up amongst the younger girls and if it was young and trendy then that was the product she wanted to use.

She jumped into her car – shaking with anticipation. Why on earth would Jack want to see her again? She had got a closed reception from him only a few days before but this invitation sounded hopeful.

She wished she didn't drive a people carrier – it said everything about her life now and the way she had become. Whatever happened to her aspirations to be a full-time musician or to compose? Those notions had floated away as each child was born and her role became more embedded in the family.

The free-flowing traffic had her parking up on the west pier in fifteen short minutes. She looked at her watch – it was exactly twelve thirty and she didn't want to appear too eager by being on time. Louise found it difficult to be fashionably late – it was a habit from working to the discipline of the school bell for so many years.

In her rear-view mirror she spotted him strolling confidently along the seafront. She ducked behind the steering wheel and watched from her side mirrors to check that he had entered the restaurant before getting out of the car.

Her stomach was in the same knot as it used to be before meeting Jack all of those years ago. She entered the stylish café with cosy leatherette booths, marble-topped tables and mosaic-tiled floors. In the corner booth, by the kitchen, she spied the back of Jack's head.

Louise braced herself as she made her way to where he was sitting.

He turned as she approached, feeling her presence before seeing her.

"Louise – thanks for coming," he said, standing and giving her a polite kiss on the cheek.

She smiled widely but noticed she wasn't getting the same reaction. Jack seemed nervous – almost shy.

"This is a nice place – I've never been before," she said lightly.

"It's new – nice to have somewhere different to go."

His voice was anxious and he didn't have the same air of confidence that he had shown a few days before when they met on the pier.

"Your fiancée is beautiful," she ventured.

"She's wonderful – the coolest girl I've ever been with."

Louise smiled nervously. What had she expected him to say?

"Time has certainly flown by, hasn't it?" she said as she sat into the booth.

Jack slid along the seat in front and rested his arms on the table. "It doesn't feel like fifteen years."

Louise nodded. She knew exactly what he meant. Now that it was just the two of them again they easily fell into the type of conversation that comes with those who have at one time been intimate.

He continued. "It's just been really bad timing running into you – a kind of omen."

He didn't look like he was about to marry the girl of his dreams. Instead Louise noticed the same anguish etched on his face as she had carried in the run-up to her own prenuptials.

"Is everything okay?" she asked.

He nodded but she wasn't convinced. The feeling that they could talk about anything like they used to as they lay on her bed in the little house in Clontarf came back to her and she asked him something that she regretted the minute the words left her mouth.

"Are you having cold feet?"

At that moment the waitress walked over and handed them both a menu card.

"Thanks," Louise said.

When the waitress was out of earshot Jack stared at Louise and said, "Is that what you had – cold feet? Is that why we had our affair?"

Louise was thrown. His tone was accusatory and she felt an uncomfortable heaviness in the space between them.

"Jack – it was a long time ago but what we had was special."

Jack's brow furrowed. His eyes were now fixed on the words on the menu but his brain was racing with thoughts of a different nature to the seafood listed. He looked up, then dipped his head behind the card again before saying very low, "You were able to finish it quickly enough!"

Louise took a deep breath. This was not the reaction she had expected – not the lunch she'd had in mind.

"Have you chosen some wine?" the waitress asked, popping up from nowhere.

"Just water for me, please," Jack said, eagerly brushing her off.

"A Pelegrino is fine," Louise said with a nod.

How was she expected to answer this man? He was definitely no longer a boy but he was still carrying emotions from the time they had spent together when he was one.

"Jack, I don't know what to say to you – but you remember on that day when I told you we had to stop seeing each other – I was just as upset as you were."

"But I was only a kid and had laid my heart on the line for you – you knew exactly what you were doing from the start."

"Hold on a minute here – I was just as vulnerable as you. I went up the aisle on my wedding day with you on my mind and I was sobbing my heart out only a few hours before it."

This was news to Jack. He didn't know if he believed her or not. "Then why did you go through with it?"

"Because it was the right thing to do."

"For you . . ."

"For all of us – you were only a school kid and I had done my time in college and was at a different stage of my life."

"You've proved my point."

"Jack, it wasn't that simple – you know it wasn't – what we

had was incredible and believe me I have thought about you so much over the years."

Jack nodded his head. "I thought of you too but I have to say there were many times when I felt really angry."

"Do you feel angry now?" she asked gently.

He shook his head. "Just sad."

"I'm sorry," she said, more softly this time, and put her hand on top of his.

He didn't move it.

"I did what I thought was the right thing," she said. "Nobody would notice the age difference now but at the time we were together it would have been shocking – and then there were our circumstances."

"I find it hard to believe that I have run into you just when I am about to get married to the most perfect girl in the world . . . and it feels wrong."

Louise understood what he was trying to say. "Now maybe you see where I was coming from all of those years ago. Donal is a good man but . . ."

"Don't tell me you wish you hadn't married him now!"

"I wouldn't say that but it is hard to know if the choices we make in life are the right ones."

"*Sliding Doors?*"

Louise smiled and nodded. "Something like that. If I hadn't been with you before I got married maybe I wouldn't have had any doubts but then again why was I with you?"

"That's what I'm trying to figure out!" Jack said, taking the glass that the waitress placed on the table and taking a sip.

"Are you ready to order?" she asked.

"I'll have the Dublin Bay prawns."

Louise scanned the menu. "Goat's cheese panini, please."

Jack took another drink. "I need to know how you really felt about Donal when we were together, because I thought you were going to break off your engagement and that we would get together."

Louise stared down at the table. There was no right answer. "To be honest I was in such a mess in my head those days I didn't know what I was going to do. I didn't want to stop seeing you and I didn't have the guts to cancel the wedding – I was carried along with the preparations and it was a bit like being on a rollercoaster – but believe me I never ever meant to hurt you."

"For the record you did."

Louise gulped.

"I had to tell you," he said. "It's been inside me for years, bubbling up."

"I'm really sorry," she whispered. "But I was hurting too."

"I spent four years in college sleeping with every girl I could and dumping them again just as quickly. I made sure that no one ever got the chance to dump me first – how messed up is that? When I lived in the States I was even worse – a one-night stand was the longest relationship I could hack. But then I met Aoife and she was different."

"How long have you been together?"

"Three years – we met in New York and she's from Dublin too – Malahide – so we had stuff in common. She had been modelling and wanted to get into PR work so she was ready to move back at the same time as me – both wanting a bite of the Celtic Tiger cherry."

"You didn't get long out of the boom then!"

"No, but thankfully we only rented the apartment and didn't buy – if we had it would have been at the peak of the boom."

"And are you home for good?"

Jack shrugged. "That was our plan but things are so bad here at the moment I'm not sure if we made the right choice coming home."

"And when did you get cold feet?"

"About two months ago – that's why I was so freaked when I met you on the train. The plans have been bombing along –

out of our control sometimes – her mother is so into the whole gig."

"That's a mother-in-law's job," Louise smiled.

"Anyway – I just wanted to know that it was normal."

"Jack, nothing is normal and everybody and every relationship is different. For me, I didn't have cold feet until after we got together."

"Did Donal get cold feet?"

"I have no idea. I am married nearly fourteen years and there are so many things I don't know about my husband. I guess there's lots he doesn't know about me either."

Jack shook his head. "See, that's not what I want from a relationship."

"There's no Mr or Miss Right out there but you have to make the most of it," she said, biting her tongue.

"Still trying to talk to me like a teacher, Louise?" he grinned.

Louise shook her head. "I don't mean to be harsh but I just don't know of any fairytale happy endings – that's all!"

Jack sighed. "I thought I'd feel better telling you how I felt – I've been practising what I was going to say for years but now that I've said it I don't know how I feel."

"I'm really truly sorry. I never meant to hurt you – or me."

"I guess we both knew what we were doing," he said with a smile. "It's surreal this, isn't it?"

Louise nodded. "A bit. I wondered where we would meet if we did but it wasn't like this!"

"I don't suppose we could be friends?"

Louise felt her heart beat faster. What a strange outcome!

"Would you like that?" he asked.

"I guess."

"Panini?" the waitress announced, putting the large white plate in front of Louise.

"Thanks."

"And the prawns," she said, putting the dish in front of Jack.

When she was gone Louise lifted her glass. "I don't know how we are going to manage it but here's to being friends!"

Jack lifted his and clinked it off hers. "To friends!"

Louise placed the bowl of cornflakes in front of Finn with a spring in her step.

"Just three more days to go – are you looking forward to seeing your mum?"

"Sure," he said, pouring the milk on top. "I thought she was home on Tuesday?"

"That's right – I should have said four days – but that will fly in. What do you all want to do today?"

"Can we go to Malahide Castle?" Molly asked.

It was a beautiful day and Louise felt happy with the secret she had carried since meeting Jack. He had texted her twice and she was feeling the excitement of her twenties all over again.

"I might come too," said Donal.

Louise couldn't believe it – it was not like him to miss Saturdays hanging out in the yacht club.

"Don't you want to put the boat in the water?"

It was that time of year again and there was a lot of maintenance work to be done to their cruiser.

"Kevin can't do it until tomorrow."

Louise nodded. The sailing season would soon be underway and Donal would be home late on a Tuesday, Wednesday and Thursday night and would be gone every Saturday afternoon. Sometimes he would do the brass monkeys to take up Sunday mornings during the winter.

"It's fine – I thought you might want to clean it or something."

"This way we can all do a family activity."

Louise sighed. What a brilliant opportunity! She had a full week of family activities with the kids – but it was good that

Donal was offering. "Maybe you could take the kids to Malahide and give me a chance to catch up on things in the house?"

"Okay," Donal said quietly. He had hoped that they would go as a family.

Emma had given Louise a voucher for Pangaea Day Spa in Sutton that she hadn't had a chance to use – if she was lucky they might fit her in for a Thai massage. It was a real treat and Louise usually floated for a week after the experience.

"Great," she said. "Try and wear them out a bit too."

Louise went out to the hall and picked her mobile off the table. She was about to hit the search button when a text came through from Jack.

Do u want to meet 4 coffee? J

Louise's heart raced. She texted back quickly.

Thinking of going for a massage! Louise

He responded equally fast.

I know where you can get a good one!!!

Louise smiled widely – not sure if she was taking him up correctly. One text could change everything in her life – did she really want to go down the road of falling in love with Jack all over again? She shook with excitement and anguish as she texted her reply – she couldn't resist.

How do I make an appointment?

"Where's Aoife?"

Jack took Louise's jacket and hung it on a hook behind the door.

"She's doing some promotion for Coca-Cola."

Louise walked around the apartment, scanning the pictures that hung on the walls.

"You've a terrific view."

"Thanks – yeah, that's why we took the place. It would be

89

better for both of us to be nearer town but when Aoife saw the harbour and Ireland's Eye she fell in love with it here."

"I've always loved Howth."

"Do you remember coming out here with me?"

Of course she remembered. They had climbed the perimeter of Howth Head and made love in the tall grasses on Upper Cliff Road. They had so much in common in those days – the hours they had spent in the classroom and after school playing music together had bound them into a harmonious double act. Then, when they took their relationship to a physical level, the emotion which they had put into music overflowed and enveloped their lovemaking. But now what had they, she wondered? Maybe it was only the memories of those passionate times that led them here on a Saturday afternoon when they couldn't be further away from the people they used to be.

Jack walked over to Louise and put his hand up to her face.

She felt a sudden awkwardness. Did she realise what she was doing? What were the implications for her marriage? If she had been dissatisfied before this, how would she feel if she were to thrust herself into a love affair?

Jack dropped his hand by his side, sensing her discomfort.

"Would you like to go for a walk?"

Louise couldn't speak. She shouldn't be here. This man standing in front of her was not her Jack – the one that she used to dream and wonder about as the years sped by and her children got older. This was a man with a life and love of his own who she couldn't just lift out of the annals of her memory to play beautiful music with.

"I'm sorry, Jack – I really think I should go."

"But you haven't even had a cup of coffee!"

"I've just thought of something I have to do – I'm sorry, Jack. Maybe another time."

She grabbed her jacket and fumbled with the latch on the door. She was on the verge of making the biggest mistake of her life and her better instinct wouldn't let her go through with it. She had done enough damage to her own emotions and Jack's before this – from now on she had to act responsibly.

Jack stood puzzled at the door as Louise stumbled down the stairs. He couldn't figure her out. He found it difficult enough to get to grips with his own emotions since bumping into her two weeks ago. Maybe those emotions weren't real. They were tortured with memories of their affair so long ago. It would be so easy to fall into her arms again and shed the missing years but maybe it would also ruin the marvellous memories. He wished he knew.

Chapter 9

Emma looked at her watch. It was typical Sophie behaviour. The taxi would be ready to collect them at ten and it was now a quarter to and she still had not returned from the night before, let alone packed.

Emma had said her goodbyes to Dehannys and was happy in the knowledge that sometime in the future she might see her friend again. Maybe when Cuba was no longer a communist state and Dehannys could leave easily – or she herself might even return to Varadero some day.

She snapped the lid of her suitcase shut and had a look under the bed to see if she had left anything behind. Her temper was fraying as each minute passed. Cuba was notorious for its Caribbean punctuality but she didn't want to leave the taxi driver waiting in case by any chance he was on time.

She wondered if Felipe would be asked to do the transfer. She had told him that she was due to be collected and brought to Havana at ten o'clock today.

He had been so chivalrous and kind in the *paladar* but had said nothing about ever seeing her again when he left her back to the hotel that night. She had felt guilty as she went out with him onto the porch to watch the stars – as if she were two-timing Paul – but a little voice spoke to her through the darkness that said it was all right to enjoy the company of somebody else. It didn't make her a bad person or her love for Paul any less.

Emma looked at the face of her watch again and sighed. It was time to ring room service and get the porter to take her luggage down to reception – but she couldn't go to Havana on her own. She took Sophie's suitcase out of the cupboard and started to fling her already tossed clothing into bundles. With one sweep of her hand she hurled Sophie's toiletries into her large pink make-up bag. Thankfully her sister hadn't taken the kitchen sink like she usually did when they went on holiday as kids.

As Emma closed the clasp on her sister's case she heard the lock in the bedroom door open.

Looking dishevelled and exhilarated, Sophie fell in through the door.

"You cut it bloody fine!"

"Relax, Em, we're on holidays."

"I've had to pack your case for you – or maybe that was your plan."

Sophie ran over to her bag and opened it. "You could have folded them as you put them in!"

"You've some cheek. Just get the rest of your stuff before I say something I might regret."

Sophie tossed her eyes heavenwards. She wanted to tell her sister how anal she had become – even worse than their mother – but then that might be one insult too far.

It was best to ignore her and put up with the silence on the long car journey to Havana. She might even get a couple of hours' sleep – she needed it!

Emma walked with the porter to reception.

She was at the concierge's desk when Felipe's familiar silhouette came into view.

"*Buenos días, Emma.*"

Emma blushed. It wasn't really a surprise to see him again – she'd had a hunch that he would be driving her to Havana. She wondered if he could have possibly orchestrated it.

"Felipe – are you taking us to Havana?"

"Yes, it is a good day for Havana."

"Every day is a good day for Havana," the concierge said with a hearty laugh.

"Would you like to sit in the front?" Felipe asked as they neared the car.

"Yes, thanks – I'll get to see more."

"I can be your guide."

Sophie shuffled along behind them – less than impressed that Felipe had shown up again and anxious to make herself comfortable along the seats in the back of the car.

They set off down the long straight strip that brought them on to the main road to Matanzas.

"If you like," Felipe suggested, "we can stop to see the birds of prey fly."

"That sounds good," Emma said, looking behind at the figure curled up on the back seat.

A few minutes later Sophie was sound asleep with her mouth open. Maybe it was just as well.

The drive to Havana in the light of day was so much more revealing than the journey after their arrival at José Marti Airport. The lush green vegetation all around reminded her of home.

Felipe took a sharp corner and ascended a steep narrow road to a viewing point. It marked the midway spot between Varadero and Havana. Felipe pulled up in the car park. In true Cuban fashion a group of locals were playing music outside a small bar and shop and taking donations from the tourists who had stopped to see the beautiful view. Wild birds of prey with huge wingspans soared and dived in the valley below.

"Coffee?" Felipe asked.

Emma nodded. She loved the way his voice sounded when he said the word. His mop of black hair and unshaven face gave him a wicked sex appeal.

Felipe said "*Dos,*" and the waitress behind the bar handed them out without looking for payment.

They took their espressos.

"Come and see the birds," he said.

She walked with him over to the blue railings in front of the café as one of the birds of prey swirled and spun in the air, putting on a display for them. Another joined in shortly and the backdrop of the viaduct and massive bridge that they had just crossed made spectacular viewing.

"I can see why so many people stop to see this."

"It is good for the government to get tourists to buy drinks at the café."

"Does the government own it?"

Felipe gave a little laugh. "The government owns everything!"

"Your English is excellent, Felipe – where did you study it?"

Felipe shrugged modestly. "At school and . . ." He hesitated. He didn't want to tell Emma too much about himself yet. "I practise talking with the people I drive."

He knocked back the last drop in his espresso cup and beckoned at Emma to follow him back to the car.

"How far are we from Havana now?"

"About one hour. You asked me about Cojimar – would you like to see it?"

It was like manna in the desert to Emma. Cojimar was the village where Hemingway used to take his boat out to fish.

"Is it out of your way?"

Felipe shrugged. "About twenty kilometres."

"Will you get into trouble?"

Felipe laughed. "I can say that my car broke down – it happens a lot!"

Emma realised that he was taking a chance to please her but she couldn't let this opportunity pass her by.

Sophie was still sound asleep in the back of the car – she'd obviously had her fun the night before. They could possibly get to Havana before she woke.

Felipe took a right off the main road when they had been travelling for about half an hour. The landscape they were passing was poor suburban. Emma was getting to see a sample of the sort of places where the majority of Cubans lived. The apartment blocks were dilapidated and neglected with brightly coloured paint peeling from their walls.

Felipe stopped at a petrol station and filled the tank. Nobody asked him for money – it had been the same in the café where they had come from. It was strange for a westerner to see how the system worked but obviously in his role as taxi driver the crest on the side of the car was enough to waiver payment.

"This station is owned by the –"

"Government!" Emma finished. "I think I'm getting the idea!"

Another ten minutes' drive and they were in sight of the sea once more. A gentle decline in the road brought them through a small and sleepy village much like the others they had passed en route. Here, however, there was a pretty bay with small fishing boats tied up and at the far end of the harbour a fortress left over from the island's colonial days. The tops of the wall and bollards were painted a bright powder blue – the shade Felipe had assured her that she would see plenty of in Havana.

"Would you like to see the statue of Hemingway?"

"Please – that would be great."

They left the windows slightly open so that Sophie could breathe in the back – Emma felt the need to check that she was still alive before they left her and set off for the short walk to the memorial.

"This is where Santiago lived – the old man in the Hemingway book," Felipe explained.

"Oh, *The Old Man and the Sea!* I love that book so much. I read it when I was in school."

"The fishermen were very proud of Hemingway – he was their friend. When he died they put together the metal parts of their boats – hooks, anchors – and made this statue."

The bust was coming into view now and together they walked up the few short steps to take a closer look.

In the distance an old American Pontiac drove by with a young couple cheering and waving from the back seat. The girl was dressed in white with flowers in her hair. It was followed by a mishmash of other types of cars blaring their horns.

"It is a Cuban wedding – it's good luck for you to see it!"

Emma watched as the local children ran along behind the cars singing and clapping for joy. There was something so beautiful about the whole scenario that Emma felt sad and happy at once. She wished that Paul was there – he would be taking photographs. She desperately wanted to remember the moment but didn't know how to record it. Then Felipe put his hand gently on her arm.

"Would you like me to take a photograph?" he asked and Emma wondered if he could read her mind.

"I left my camera in the car."

"Your phone?"

Emma had forgotten. She took it out of her bag and handed it to Felipe. He captured the young couple and their entourage just before they went up a narrow road and out of sight forever.

"Go up to Hemingway and I will take a photograph of you."

Emma did as she was told but felt foolish. She had taken hardly any reminders of the holiday so far by camera. Every time she thought of taking a photo she was reminded that Paul wasn't there – so it was just easier not to take any.

She tilted her head and smiled as he snapped. Then he came and handed the phone back to her.

"Stand beside me," she said – holding the phone out at arm's length with the castle and sea as background. She clicked and turned her phone to see the snapshot. Felipe was photogenic – and so was she! The contrast of her sun-kissed Irish skin against his tanned darkness was set against the clear blue sky.

Emma handed the phone to Felipe so that he could see what she had taken. He took a peek and looked up at Emma. Their gazes met. The moment was tense – both were thinking that same thought – how well they looked together.

"Maybe we should go?" he suggested.

"Yes, I think we need to check on Sophie," Emma said awkwardly. It was the first time for a long time she had seen herself in a photograph with a man other than Paul and it came as a shock – because she liked it.

They walked back silently as Emma gazed every few steps out at the harbour and the old men fixing their nets on the shore. When they were a few feet away from the car they realised that something was wrong as all of the windows were open wide.

My laptop! Emma thought.

Sophie was gone.

Felipe cursed in Spanish and quickly went to open the boot. He looked inside and breathed a loud sigh of relief.

"I thought your bags would be gone but you are lucky. And your laptop and camera are here."

"But where's Sophie?"

"She will not be far!" he said, slammed the boot shut and locked up the windows and doors. "Follow me!"

They started the slight incline up the road until they came to a beautifully maintained yellow building with mahogany shutters unlike any other in the village.

"This is *La Terraza*," he said, knowing that Emma would understand.

"Wow – it's gorgeous," she said, stepping into the restaurant. "So this is where Ernest Hemingway hung out with his fishing cronies."

Sitting up at the long mahogany counter was Sophie with a

tall glass filled with clear liquid in her hand. "I could have died, you know!" she moaned and took a long gulp from the glass.

"We left the windows open – there's no need to be so melodramatic!" said Emma. "And you left my laptop and our luggage unprotected!"

Sophie shrugged. As usual there was no point in arguing with her.

"I think I'll have a beer," said Emma. "Unless we have time to have something to eat?"

Felipe shook his head. "I would like to but I have to be at the airport to collect some people and bring them to Varadero."

Emma understood – a beer might even be pushing it but Felipe wanted a coffee so they sat at the bar beside Sophie and drank in the atmosphere.

"How long will you stay in Havana?"

"We have only two nights – is there anything you suggest we should see while we are there?"

"Tomorrow is my day off – if you like I can show you."

Emma liked the sound of this and, with the thought, she wondered if Felipe was single – he had said that he lived with his father but that didn't mean that there wasn't a Mrs Felipe. He did seem to be rather settled but when he had brought them to Matanzas he hadn't been in any rush to get home either.

"That would be really kind," she said. She could see from the corner of her eye that Sophie was about to butt in but she ignored her. "I would love to visit the Hemingway house."

"I can take you."

"Do you have your taxi on your day off?"

Felipe shook his head. "No, but my father has a car and we can take it."

"Can we just get to bloody Havana?" Sophie yelped. "I've no idea what we are doing here!"

The rest of the journey passed quickly, with Sophie again dozing in the back.

Emma absorbed the sights she passed along the way. It was totally different to anywhere else she had been. Over the years she and Paul had been to Thailand and South Africa and other exotic destinations but none were like this. It wasn't exactly the contrast with Ireland that made it this way – it was the energy that exuded from the people. While they drove through the outskirts of Havana Emma felt like she was in a film set. She was particularly struck by the extraordinary range of skin colour. The men standing at the street corners, the women strolling by with heavy bags and the children running with a makeshift ball were an astonishing variety of shades. She looked over at Felipe – he was a tanned Latin colour while many of his countrymen were black. It seemed to her that skin colour didn't matter to anyone in Cuba and she felt a wonderful kind of freedom.

"Felipe – is there racism in Cuba?"

Felipe laughed. "Fidel made it illegal to be racist – it was in his manifesto in the Revolution. What he did not say was that whatever colour your skin is everybody will be poor!"

"Surely there are people in this society who have more than others?"

"Not really. In this city I have the best job – my wages are ten CUC per month, but you can make that on tips in one day if you are lucky."

"What does a doctor get paid?"

Felipe shook his head. "About twenty-five CUC – you can understand why so many go to Canada or America. A teacher earns twenty but a worker in a factory can get ten plus all the black market stuff he can take home in his pockets – it is good to work in the rum factory."

Emma took all this information in – so maybe Dehannys didn't have it so bad with a father in the rum factory.

She sighted a very grand building. "Look at that building!"

"Yes, it is the Capitolio. A very big museum – you must visit it."

"I have so little time to see so much now that I am here." Emma didn't try to hide her excitement.

"It's much hotter here than Varadero," a voice piped up from the back of the car.

Sophie was awake.

"We are nearly at your hotel," said Felipe, glancing back at her.

And they were only two more minutes on the bumpy roads until they came to a tall hotel that had been freshly painted yellow with bright blue window and door-frames.

Emma didn't want Felipe to go. It was so nice to have a man to talk to and she loved his company.

"I will see you tomorrow," he said. "Ten o'clock?"

"That would be great – thanks for everything, Felipe."

"Where's a good nightclub to go to tonight?" Sophie asked. "I fancy a bit of action after Varadero."

"You want to dance?" Felipe asked.

"Yeah."

"Casa de la Musica – you can walk from here. It is the best."

"Thanks so much for all of your help, Felipe," said Emma again, "especially for taking me to Cojimar."

"I am glad you liked it," he said with a smile.

Emma went to give him a tip but he wouldn't take it.

"Please," she said, "it's the least I can do for taking you out of your way."

"The government paid!"

Then quick as a flash Felipe jumped into his car.

Emma waved at him from the top of the steps as he drove away. He was a good man and she enjoyed his company – he was shy in a way but also very self-assured – a complete Cuban enigma. She grabbed her suitcase and made her way into the reception. The concierge rushed to get their bags and beckoned to the staff to check the European women in.

The porter in the Hotel Telegrafo was very different to the

squeaky-clean-shaven youth who had taken their bags in Varadero. This porter was grubbier and more anxious with his clients. When he was sure that the door of the lift was shut he started.

"You want good cigar in Havana – you come to me – I can get very cheap. Authentic Coheba – like Castro smoke. Havana Club – seven *años* – very good."

"Thank you very much," Sophie said curtly. "We don't smoke but I'll get back to you on the rum."

The corridors were dark and the ceilings extraordinarily high. When the porter opened the door of their room a ray of bright light was streaming in through the curtains. He rushed over and pulled them back to reveal the huge French windows.

"Parque Central! Come and see!" he urged them.

They crossed the room to join him on the small railed balcony.

Below all the life of Havana buzzed by – some on mopeds – others in the fantastic old American cars that were put together like patchwork quilts. On the adjacent street a huge odd-looking vehicle filled with a couple of hundred people roared past. The girls were later to find out that these acted as buses for the general public and were called *camellos* because of the hump-backed eighteen-wheeler cabin being pulled along behind the truck.

"Look at that for an ingenious form of transport!" Emma said, pointing to a guy sitting on a bicycle-pulled rickshaw covered in an old square of tarpaulin that was once used to advertise beer. Then in the middle of it all was a line of Renault taxis like Felipe drove – representing the modern Cuba.

Emma felt it was fate that Felipe had collected them from the airport on the first day and she knew that he was meant to show her all the places that she wanted to see. It was fortuitous that he would be off the next day. Meanwhile she had twenty-four hours to get her bearings and there was one place she desperately wanted to see after they had lunch.

Emma handed the porter two CUC for a tip and he left the room as if walking on air.

Sophie threw herself on the bed.

"You wouldn't get us some water, Em?" she groaned.

Emma went over to the minibar which was discreetly hidden in a small locker and opened the door. She threw a bottle of water on the bed beside her sister.

The journey from Varadero had been hot and sweaty. She showered quickly and changed into comfortable walking shorts and a T-shirt.

"Where are you going?" Sophie asked.

"I'm going to explore the old town – it's only a ten-minute walk from here."

"On your own?"

"Well, you don't look like you're fit to go anywhere."

"Give me twenty minutes –"

"You're going to be longer than that – call me when you surface."

Sophie wasn't in any fit state to argue. She pulled the starched linen sheet back on the bed and crept under it.

Emma put her sunglasses on her head – she would need them.

She took her small map of the city and started her walk across the park. It was considerably more humid in the city with the buildings retaining heat all around. It was amazing how the locals, called *Habaneros,* lolled about in large groups watching the world go by. Young people who she would have thought would be busy working at this time of the day were embracing openly and drinking home-made lemonade sold from carts. The price was two cents – Cuban pesos, not the tourist currency.

It was starting to get to Emma, the idea that certain items were accessible only to tourists or people that could get their hands on CUCs and the rest of the population just had to accept that they were excluded. They weren't exactly luxuries either – certain cosmetics, electrical goods, all sorts of things that were cheap and taken for granted in any store in Dublin were forbidden to the average Cuban. Yes, she thought again, if she were still a journalist she would have a lot to report. She could understand why so many risked their lives and set off on the treacherous 90-kilometre journey across the sea to Florida. But for now she was on a voyage of discovery to see what Cuba had to offer that the rest of the world didn't.

Sophie groaned and got out of the bed. She had left some Panadol in her toilet bag – she always kept a full pack handy. She was glad to be away from Varadero now. José was a cad. He had the cheek to ask her if she could change some money for him and he would send her the euros when he earned them in tips. She wasn't going to fall for that one. He had waited until they were getting on his moped to go back to her hotel before asking. She knew he was a bit of a rogue – that was what had attracted her – but she never thought that he would have the audacity to touch her up for cash.

She scanned the room and the shiny tiled floor. The headboard was easily ten feet tall. She went onto the balcony and watched the cars, trucks and bikes move in free flow in all directions. There wasn't a lot of order on the streets and she guessed there wasn't much order anywhere in this city.

She felt she was looking at the real Cuba now – not the perfectly polished hotels and sandy beach of Varadero. She was ready to see the real Havana – the one in which all the famous musicians, like those that had played with the Buena Vista Social Club, had their roots.

It was what Paul had planned for them. After all, he was taking *her* on this trip, not Emma. She was lucky that Emma had handed the holiday details over to her that day and not commented on the initial of the Owens sister who was meant to be travelling: the initial 'S'. Emma had noticed it of course but thought it was a simple typing error. Sophie had claimed that ticket and managed to change Paul's name to Emma's on the other one, successfully using her usual charm with the guy in the travel agent's, although he wasn't supposed to change it without a huge penalty. Louise had spotted the initial 'S' detail too which had made Sophie very nervous – Louise could have blown it – she was always looking out for Emma. She shuddered when she thought of how Emma would react if she found out that this wasn't a surprise planned for her at all but a celebration of the three-year relationship Sophie had had with her brother-in-law.

It was only days before Paul's seventh wedding anniversary that he had bumped into Sophie in town and taken her for lunch in Cooke's Bistro. Sitting in the Dublin sunshine under the dark green awnings, they could have been in Paris or Rome. She had recently finished a relationship with a nightclub owner who was flash and brash and she wanted someone she could talk to about art and design and culture. Sophie had never realised how attractive Paul was when he had Emma by his side. It hit them both like a thunderbolt. Paul called her his "seven-year itch" and she would always respond. "Would you like me to scratch it for you?"

Sometimes they met in his office – sometimes in hers. It was easy to pull the blinds on his office and lock the door from the inside. Sometimes she got carpet burns from the floor covering but they always laughed about it afterwards.

On the very odd occasion when Sophie felt bad for what they were both doing behind Emma's back Paul would scoff. "Do you realise how nice I am to your sister? I was a bastard to live with before we started having this affair. *You* are responsible for making me a much nicer person!"

Sophie didn't believe it. She would never use an adjective like "nice" to describe him. Pernickety, precise, compulsive, energetic and definitely talented but "nice" was not Paul. The awful thing was that it was the word Emma had used in church to describe her husband at his funeral. It showed how little she really knew him.

Sophie took a drink from the bottle of water and swallowed

back the Panadol. Another couple of hours in bed and then she would be able to face Havana.

As Emma left the large public square of Parque Central and her feet touched the cobblestones of Calle Obispo she knew that she wasn't far from her destination. The buildings were colonial and crumbling and it was the Habana Vieja that she had expected. The touch-ups here and there with pink and blue paint brightened the aging buildings. Some of the doors were sculpted from metal, intricate and ornate, and must have been beautiful in their heyday.

Behind some of the doorways old people sat peering out – shielded from the heat of the sun. A few children ran out in front of her path, oblivious to her presence in their game of chasing. Two of them were not wearing shoes. The stench from the sewers or garbage tips – Emma wasn't quite sure which – wafted from the sidewalks. Suddenly the large pink façade described perfectly in her Dorling Kindersley guidebook appeared at the end of the street and she knew that she was at the next destination on her Hemingway pilgrimage.

Ernest Hemingway had lived in the Ambos Mundos Hotel for some time before settling in La Finca Vigía and she desperately wanted to feel his presence as she stepped through the doors of the airy boutique hotel. She wasn't disappointed.

A few steps into the foyer and she was in a brightly lit bar area. The bartender wore a crisp white shirt and a black bow tie that brought him back to the middle of the twentieth century. Skinny blinds let dappled light through the tall windows and occasional palms in large ceramic pots divided up the space between bar and foyer.

Emma smiled at the bartender and walked over to a wall covered with photographs of Ernest Hemingway. The images were all in shades of black, grey and sepia and were framed against olive green wallpaper. Hemingway was reeling in a fish in one of the pictures, shaking hands with Castro in another and eating lobster with a group of friends – making Emma envy the exotic and cultural life that he had led. A small sign on the wall explained that for two dollars tourists could visit the room where he lived for some time in the 1930s. But first she wanted to have a drink. It was hot and dusty outside and the bar and smiling face of the tender were welcoming.

"*Buenas tardes, señorita*," he said with a smile as Emma perched herself on a high stool. "You like?"

"A mineral water – *con gas por favor*."

He poured it steadily and added ice and lime.

"*Gracias*," she said and took a sip with relish.

"You come to see Hemingway room?"

"*Sí*," she nodded.

As she spoke a tall slim figure walked over to the bar. He was wearing a white aertex T-shirt and his skin resembled smooth milk chocolate. His dark brown eyes glistened and widened as a smile appeared on his face.

He was the most beautiful man Emma had ever laid eyes on.

"*Buenas tardes, Marco!*" he addressed the bartender. "*Una cerveza, por favor!*"

"*Sí*, Señor Adams – you have a good day?"

"Very good, Marco." His accent changed when he spoke English and there was a definite American twang in there somewhere.

The man turned to Emma and nodded courteously before taking a seat on the stool beside her.

"Your friend, eh?" he said to the bartender who slid a bottle of beer across the counter to him.

Emma felt oddly comfortable in the strange surroundings with two foreign men beside her. The fact that the hotel was so sparsely populated brought a homeliness to the meeting with this man and under normal circumstances she might have felt ill at ease but at that moment she felt as if she was exactly where she was meant to be.

"I'm Emma," she said, holding out her right hand. "From Ireland."

"Well, Emma from Ireland," he replied, taking her hand, "I am very pleased to meet you. I'm Greg from Canada but I've got a lot of mixed blood so I guess I could call myself a citizen of the world!"

Emma's attraction to this handsome man was like a pin to a magnet. It was all right to be attracted to him – she was out of her comfort zone, thousands of miles from home. She wasn't Paul's widow – she wasn't Finn's mum – she felt like a character in one of her novels and Mr Greg Adams was so delicious she had a notion to put him into her book with Felipe.

"Are you on holiday?" she said in a slightly flirtatious tone.

"I call these trips business but you cannot visit Cuba without pleasure. My mother is Cuban and she met my father here – but he took her back to Nova Scotia over forty years ago and she hasn't returned since."

Emma was intrigued – she could feel her journalistic inquisitiveness take over. "My, what a great story! So you have relatives here?"

He nodded. "Cousins and aunts – I see them sometimes. My grandfather is still alive, believe it or not, but he lives in Cardenes and it is difficult to get there – my visits are generally not long enough to go trekking the country."

This guy was so open and frank she liked him instantly.

"What business are you in – if you don't mind me asking?"

"Emma from Ireland – you can ask me anything you like!" he grinned cheekily. "I buy art and sell it back in Canada. There's big demand for Cuban artists there. Have you been to any of the markets here yet?"

Emma shook her head. "I only got into Havana this morning."

Greg's smile widened. "Well, then you are in for a very special treat. Have you had lunch?"

Emma shook her head.

"I hate to eat alone," he said. "Would you like to join me in *La Bodegita del Medio*? I'm a Hemingway fan – that's why I always stay here."

Now at last Emma felt slightly unnerved. Greg seemed genuine but it wasn't a good idea for a foreign woman to go off with a stranger in any city – she imagined Havana not to be any different.

Greg sensed her reservation. He beckoned to the bartender. "Marco, tell Emma from Ireland that I don't bite, eh!"

"Señor Adams stay here many times – he very good customer," Marco said, holding his hand out to Greg for a tip in jest.

Greg smiled and duly planted five CUCs in his palm.

Emma's desire to find out more about this gorgeous man took over. She had nothing to lose – Sophie was probably still asleep and she knew from the research she had put in with her guidebook that the bar he was talking about was only a couple of blocks away.

"Okay – thanks," she said and stood up to pay Marco for her water.

"It is okay you no pay!," he smiled. Greg would tip him again later!

Greg offered her his arm chivalrously and Emma linked it.

They walked with ease up Calle Mercaderes until they came to the Plaza de la Catedral. The Baroque façade of San Cristóbal shone like a glittering prize of colonial architecture. An old woman dressed in traditional colonial costume – complete with white lace and a red rose – sat smoking a cigar on its steps. She was surrounded by tourists taking photographs and a small dog was yapping at her feet. An old man by her side was selling peanuts wrapped in white paper cones.

"It's marvellous here!" Emma gasped.

"It is good for tourists but I like it – I never get tired of the atmosphere in La Habana Vieja. Now that is a nice place for dinner when the sun goes down," he said pointing at a very

European-styled courtyard restaurant. "El Patio – the government own it of course – like everything else – it must have been pretty spectacular in its heyday over a century ago."

"Yes – it's strange the way the government own everything. But I was in Eastern Europe before the Iron Curtain fell and although it was communist it felt very different to this."

"There's nowhere in the world like Cuba – Castro made the biggest island in the Caribbean his own. Not everything he did was good but he didn't do all bad either – just can't let my mom hear me say that."

"Does she ever want to come back – even to visit?"

"No. She hates it that she can and so many people haven't got the choice. She says that she was lucky because she met my father – a tall White Canadian who took her off to a better life. Secretly I think her soul misses it here."

Emma loved the way he spoke – not many men would be so open to a woman they had only met a few minutes before – but then these weren't normal circumstances and she could tell already that Greg was no ordinary man.

The yellow sign with Bodeguita del Medio painted on it in bold black letters stood out on the Calle Emperado like a vision.

"This is where Hemingway liked to have his first mojito of the day," Greg explained. He opened the louvre-doors that led into the cramped bar heaving with tourists.

At first Emma thought that the vibrant blue walls were covered in a script-type wallpaper but on closer inspection she could see that the autographs in dark-blue felt pen were of the restaurant's patrons.

"Come on," Greg said, leading her into the eating area at the back of the building. "You can write your name later, eh?"

The eating area seemed to be made up of several small rooms all joined by tall open arches. Even at the very highest point of the walls patrons had signed their names. Miguel from Venezuala was there in 2001. Maria Cruz from Madrid was there in 2004 and many other names that were scribbled over in so many languages and layers they had merged into irregular patterns on the wall.

They took a seat at the only table for two available and the waiter pounced on them instantly.

"*Buenas tardes*. To drink?"

"*Dos mojitos, por favor*," Greg said.

Emma looked down at her paper placemat which doubled as the menu. The letters B del M were printed across the top in the same naïve style in which they were painted above the bar they had passed on the way in. There was a mixture of dark woods and bright blue paint everywhere with chandeliers hanging from the vault-like ceilings.

"I love it here," Emma exclaimed as a trio in the corner piped up with music.

"We have to sign the wall before we leave."

"If we can find a spot," Emma ran her fingers over the hundreds of signatures on the wall beside where she sat. "People must have used ladders to get to the top of the wall!"

Greg lifted a blue marker from the pot in the middle of the table.

"I bet you can squeeze Emma from Ireland in there somewhere."

"Thanks," she replied, taking the marker in her hand and searching for a space on the wall to scribble. "I've never been anywhere like this – I'm glad I bumped into you."

"Cuba is a great place," said Greg. "People are so friendly – I wouldn't ask a stranger in a hotel in Canada out for lunch and she would probably not accept the way that you did but when I'm in Havana this strange vibe sweeps over me."

Emma knew what he meant but she couldn't imagine any woman turning down Greg's offer of lunch or anything else. She felt as though she were on the edge of a precipice – a different kind of hanging on to the way she had been for the last seven months.

Greg surveyed her pretty face as she printed her name over the layers of letters.

"So where is Mr Emma from Ireland – or is there one?"

"He's in Ireland," she replied – well, it was partly true. Anyway she hardly knew Greg – she wasn't going to tell him that Paul was in Balgriffin Cemetery.

Greg didn't flinch. It didn't seem to bother him that she had a husband.

"And what about Mrs Greg from Canada?"

"Both of them are in Canada and they are both *ex* Mrs Gregs. I'm a great boyfriend – everything goes along really well with the women in my life until we get married – and then . . ."

"Have you any kids?"

"A daughter from my first marriage – I didn't have any with my second wife. What about you?"

"I've a son, Finn – he's nine."

"Great name."

Emma nodded. It was the only one that she and Paul would agree on.

"Do you like Creole food?" he asked.

"I haven't really tried it. The hotel in Varadero had all kinds of different restaurants and apart from one meal in Matanzas we haven't tried much ethnic food."

"We? You mean there are two Emmas from Ireland?"

Emma smiled. "Kind of – there's a Sophie from Ireland – she's my sister."

"And does she look anything like you?" he said, smiling wickedly.

"Not remotely – she has strawberry blonde hair and green eyes – very Irish."

"But you've got a great Celtic look, Emma from Ireland. I visited Dublin many years ago and lost my heart several times, all to women with blue eyes and black hair."

Emma flushed – it was a direct compliment and she felt flattered that it was coming from such a divine man.

"How long were you in Varadero?" he asked.

"Seven days and we will be three in Havana."

"I think I'd have done it the other way around – don't get me wrong – Varadero is cool but you could be anywhere in the Caribbean. Now Havana is different – there's no place like it in the world."

Already Emma felt she could agree with him. "So tell me more about Cuban art?"

"Yes – everyone in the world knows of Cuba's famous musicians but their artists are just as special – I have been co-ordinating exhibitions of Cuban art all over Europe and the US. It's cheap and they are masters of the figurative – good news now that people see through all that conceptual nonsense – it was in vogue far too long."

"Really – I guess I always associate Cuba with music and dance now that you mention it."

"It's a melting pot for artists. And look at the writers it has inspired – especially our friend Hemingway, eh?"

"How do you know I'm a Hemingway fan?"

"Why else would you be sitting in the Ambos Mundos hotel on your own when you aren't a guest?"

"Maybe I am a guest?"

"I was there for breakfast and if you were I would definitely have noticed you!"

Emma fanned herself with her street map of Havana. With relief she accepted the mojito that the waiter put down in front of her. She needed to cool down. He was making his intentions clear with his indirect compliments.

Greg's features were fine and sculpted – more Caucasian than African. He would be a perfect model for Armani clothing. But that was the nice thing about him – he didn't seem to realise it himself.

"How long are you staying?"

"Just two more days and then my work will be done. I have artists who paint commissions for me between trips but I am always looking out for new talent."

"I passed a gallery in Calle Obispo on my way here but it was more like someone's living room with a few paintings hanging on the wall."

"It's good, isn't it," Greg smiled. "Just think, all of this talent on sale for a few dollars. If you like we can go to the market after lunch – it's beside Plaza de la Catedral."

Emma took a sip from her mojito. "Okay – that would be nice."

Sophie sat up in the bed and looked out through the huge windows at the rain falling in sheets from the sky. She opened the windows to view the *Habaneros* swarm like ants for cover from the shower. As long as she didn't step out onto the balcony she would remain perfectly dry because the rain was falling in straight lines.

A bicitaxi with passengers passed by through the puddles, its driver drenched from the spray left behind by a Cadillac. Pedestrians held plastic bags up over their heads as makeshift umbrellas. A couple of *Habaneros* didn't seem bothered by the shower and happily stood underneath the palms in the middle of the park.

She wondered where Emma had got to. She could always try her mobile phone but another part of her was happy with the peace. It had been full on by the pool every day in Varadero. At times Emma had annoyed her with her talk of how perfect her dead husband used to be. She wanted so badly to tell her that she loved him too but knew that Louise would kill her if she ever told the truth. To say nothing of what Emma would do to her.

The sticky heat of the day was cooled by the rain momentarily. She decided to have a quick shower before she ventured out.

By the time she was drying off, the rain had stopped and the heat and dust of Havana was back. She took the stairs down to reception and picked up a map of the old town. She was travelling light – with a shoulder bag containing a few CUC and her mobile phone. Lines of government taxis like the one Felipe drove parked up in the middle of the square.

114

She felt a kind of unease as she crossed Parque Central and entered the old town. The narrow streets were dirty and dilapidated and Sophie didn't like the way the locals were looking at her. She held tightly to her bag in case anyone should grab it. Already she could feel her armpits moisten with perspiration. She stopped at a small café on a corner where a group of tourists were having a drink. She felt it safe to take her phone out in the company of people that looked familiar.

She dialled Emma's number and waited.

"Hello?"

"Emma, it's me – I'm in the old town."

Emma looked forlornly at Greg. Their private time together was over.

"So am I – what street are you on?"

"God, I don't know – there are all these goddam awful pink and blue buildings. The place is falling down around my ears."

"Can you find Plaza de la Catedral?"

Sophie opened the small map that the hotel receptionist had given her.

"Got it – Cristóbal church."

"Yes – well, take the furthermost corner to the right of the cathedral out to Calle Tacón – cross the road, towards the sea – there's a park and you can see stalls of artwork. I am in the middle of the market."

"I'll do my best."

An old lady stopped and looked at her. She moved as if she was dancing and she smiled gently at the stranger with the unusual red hues in her hair. Sophie brushed by her, oblivious to the woman's welcoming attitude.

She found the cathedral with ease and took a right as Emma had directed. She walked until she found a sign for Calle Tacón. It was less daunting than the side streets from where she had come.

The stalls of a market came into view as she crossed the road and she craned her neck in search of her sister. It wasn't Emma's figure that she spotted first but a tall and handsome coffee-skinned man who resembled Barack Obama. He was gorgeous and she felt compelled to walk in his direction to take a closer look.

As she neared she got more than a shock when she saw her sister walking with ease at his side. They were laughing and brushing gently off each other's arms as they strolled.

It was an image so out of context with how Sophie viewed her sister that she felt like laughing out loud. She quickened her step and caught up with them.

"Emma!" she called.

The couple stopped and looked around.

"Hi, Sophie! This is Greg. Greg, this is Sophie."

Greg held out his hand. "Greetings, Sophie from Ireland."

Emma and Greg chuckled out loud at the same time.

Sophie didn't like being the focus of a joke. "So, Greg – how do you know my sister?"

"I met her at my hotel – I'll have to give them a tip when I get back. Your sister's very good company – we've had a very good lunch."

Sophie frowned. She didn't like seeing her sister being the centre of attention. That was *her* role.

Emma was glowing from the flattery and Sophie could see that she was smitten.

"Where are you ladies staying?"

"*El Telegrafo*," Emma said.

"I have to do some work now but would you let me join you for dinner? I hate to eat alone and I know some good restaurants in Havana."

"That sounds great, Greg," said Emma. "We are only finding our way around and it would be good to be shown by someone who knows the place."

"How about seven thirty? I can call by and pick you up, eh?"

"Okay," Emma said, looking over at Sophie who shrugged her approval.

"Enjoy the rest of the afternoon, ladies," he said with a wink at Emma as he strolled off.

Emma was visibly flushed as she watched him walk away.

"Oh my god, Emma – could you be more obvious?"

"What do you mean?"

"You were gushing all over him – and you only lost your husband a few months ago!"

Emma gasped. "Fuck off, Sophie!" She felt as though she had received a physical blow. "I was only talking to the guy."

Sophie gave a look that said she knew what was going on in her sister's head. She had been thinking the same thoughts about the gorgeous stranger too.

Emma stomped off in the direction of the Plaza de la Catedral as she tried to hold back the tears. She was so confused – first by the kind attentions that Felipe had shown her and now by the flattery of the Canadian. They had helped her forget the pain of the past seven months and she didn't need to be made to feel guilty by her younger sister.

Sophie followed behind with enough distance not to lose sight of her but at the same time not to be too close. She felt so hard done by – Emma got to be the mourning wife while she had to do her mourning alone and now Emma was allowing herself to flirt too!

Greg tipped the courier off generously. Two CUCs was a lot of money in a young boy's hands.

Greg had made some astute purchases and was very pleased with the way the trip was going. It was a real treat running into the intriguing Irishwoman and her sister. He could have some fun tonight. Life couldn't get much better than this. He really did have the best of both worlds.

Chapter 10

Donal picked up a hose and started to spray underneath the hull of his boat. He hoped that Emma was having a nice time. She deserved a break. He had been the only man that she could turn to for help after Paul died. Mr and Mrs Owens were a law unto themselves and were useless as a support to her. They felt that after putting their daughters through college their work had been done and their family reared and it was now time for their children to look after them – so the dinners on Christmas Day and other festive occasions were passed onto Emma's and Louise's shoulders and now that he was the only son-in-law he had visions of her parents making more demands on Louise and him for the foreseeable future.

Emma would continue to pander to her parents, like Louise did. It was unfair, but that was the way responsibilities fell in the family.

Sophie, he didn't have much time for. She was always the cause of any family arguments between the sisters. She knew exactly how to wind Louise up the wrong way and that made his life all the more difficult.

But it was he who had chosen the most highly strung sister. Their meeting was pure chance but he knew from the first time he laid eyes on her that Louise was his wife-to-be. Such a contradiction at the time – the vivacious music teacher and the pragmatic accountant – but he always believed that it was fate that had thrown them together. He was a young associate and happened to be sent to do an audit at the school where she worked. He remembered how annoyed he was when he was given the boring school project. Later on that week when he started the job and went into the staff room and saw Louise sitting at a table and waving her bangle-laden arms in the air he thanked his lucky stars.

She hardly noticed him at first but it was while she was having problems with the photocopier and kicking and cursing it that he rushed to her aid. He helped her remove the jammed paper and staple the sheets together. She was so pleased that she spontaneously hugged him – then rushed off to her class.

It was that sort of impulsiveness that he missed about her now that they were married fourteen years. It was that lack of spontaneity that caused him to spend so much time in the yacht club.

Kevin strolled over to where Donal was hosing down their boat.

"Sorry I'm late!"

Donal nodded. Kevin was always late. "The boys were giving me a hand but they seem to have run off to get change for the vending machine. Grab a hose – we've only got the crane for another twenty minutes."

Kevin had chosen Donal as his partner for his reliable qualities. They had met in college and lost touch when they had gone in different directions – Donal was always going to get an apprenticeship with one of the big companies with his grades. Kevin however was happier just to get his degree and get out into the world of sales and he had made his mark during the Celtic Tiger period. Business now however was not as it had been and he was glad that he had Donal for a partner – he had yet to tell him that he would have problems paying his half of the marina fees and boat maintenance this year.

"Have you any plans for Saturday night? Judy was wondering if you fancied trying out the new menu in the restaurant and she hasn't seen Louise since Santa Sunday."

Santa Sunday was a family day in Howth Yacht Club and the Scotts and Harleys always got together with their children who were of similar ages. But Judy Harley was a hands-on sailing mother who loved the outdoor life – very different from Louise who didn't care for sailing and begrudgingly went on the annual excursions to Ireland's Eye and only on sunny summer days.

"I'll ask – that would be good."

"Kick the year off – that chap Tony is keen to crew and I'd say he's reliable."

"So is Jeremy not sailing with us this year?"

"He's after getting an etchell," Kevin informed him. "He's keen to helm and Frank has bought half with him."

"Oh!" Donal continued to clean. Most decisions were made by Kevin and sometimes he felt like a hired help. But then again it was easier not to cause hassle. But he didn't like Tony – he was flash and brash and would be trying to helm any chance he got.

"Is there anyone else apart from Tony looking to crew?"

Kevin wasn't surprised at Donal's reaction – he knew how fussy he could be about who sailed on his boat. "If you've got a problem I can put a notice on HYC website but the season starts next week and we'd be mad to turn down someone who knows how to sail."

Donal knew that he was right. He picked up a brush and started to rub away harder at the last bits of seaweed that stuck to the keel. He wanted to make a stand but maybe this wasn't the matter that he needed to make a stand on.

Jack was sent to Stephen's Green to cover an Easter street festival that would take up most of the day. He really didn't want to be there. Aoife was delighted that he was going to be so near her and they had arranged to meet for lunch in restaurant Sixty Six on George's Street after she finished working on a shoot in Dublin Castle. Weekend work was a pain and although he didn't have to do it often he would much rather have time to himself.

Aoife on the other hand loved her job so much she was quite happy to take whatever work she was given.

Jack looked at his watch. Almost time to meet her. He put his notebook away and strolled the short walk through Grafton Street to George's Street. She would be late – she always was. But he was hungry and wanted to take the weight off his feet. The restaurant was trendy and Aoife loved it because the décor reminded her of New York – it could just as easily be in downtown SoHo as Dublin.

He took a table in the corner and surveyed his Blackberry. There were no messages. Secretly he had hoped that Louise would contact him after running out the day before but in his gut he knew that she wouldn't. Aoife was driving him mad with fabric samples and talk of menus and holiday brochures for their big romantic honeymoon. He wished they could just pack up and go back to New York and forget about weddings and Louise.

But he couldn't forget about Louise. She was his first real sexual experience. It was so much more meaningful than he had realised at the time. Now when he saw her he longed to feel eighteen again with the same sense of wonder about sex as he had when he was with her. He had tried to find it with every woman since but it escaped him and he knew that he probably never would have it again.

"Hi, hon, sorry I'm late," Aoife said as she leaned down to kiss her fiancé. "Have you ordered a drink yet?"

"I'm not here long."

"I've been drinking so much champagne I feel sick. I think I'll have a fruit juice."

Jack beckoned the waitress over. "Two freshly squeezed orange juices, please."

"Aren't you having a coffee?" asked Aoife.

"I've been drinking it all morning – trying to warm up – are you hungry?"

"Think I'll have a sandwich – they're serving food at the castle later. Why don't you get dinner?"

Jack was right off his food. "I'll just have a sandwich too."

"I was talking to Monica and she went to a tropical island in Malaysia for her honeymoon where the villas are totally private with four staff for every couple staying. It sounds divine and we can spend a few days in KL – I've always wanted to go there."

Jack smiled. "Sounds nice – but how much is this exclusive place?"

"Don't worry about that – I get ten percent off with Cassidy Travel."

"It depends on how much the holiday costs – our jobs are pretty precarious at the moment. They let five staff go from my department – good guys who had been there longer than me."

"They were probably too expensive to keep – anyway, don't worry, my dad said he would help us with the honeymoon."

"He's already paying for our wedding and the dresses and the photographers – we can't be taking handouts from him all the time when we're married."

Aoife waved her hands in the air. "Relax, Jack! Why are you all bothered suddenly?"

The truth was something he couldn't tell her. "I think these arrangements have got out of hand. Can't we cut back a bit on all the expense? I thought the cost was why you didn't want to get married abroad."

Aoife pouted. She really had no idea where this was coming from. Jack usually was happy to go along with whatever decisions she made. Her eyes welled up and she reached for a tissue in her bag.

"This is really bad timing to come out with all this about cutting costs." She threw her eyes heavenward to fight back the tears. "We haven't even bought a place to live."

"We agreed that it's not a good time."

"Daddy says it's the perfect time – when property prices are falling."

"I'd like it to be our decision and not your father's. Since we got back from the States we can't seem to make a decision about anything without involving your family. I thought we were free spirits – we were both the same when we met in New York but all of a sudden you've changed."

Aoife couldn't fight the tears any more. She stood up. "I don't have to be spoken to like this! What's got into you all of a sudden, Jack Duggan? It's you that's changed not me!"

He let her stomp out of the restaurant and buried his head in the palms of his hands. She was right. Her family were nothing but kindness itself and up until now he had always appreciated her father and his advice. He was the one that was changing. Suddenly he didn't know what he wanted any more.

Louise's parents were coming for dinner. She put the large joint of dressed beef into the oven and adjusted the heat. She could leave it for two hours and that would be plenty of time. The table was set and the vegetables chopped, ready to put on in over an hour's time.

How was she going to fill in the time while the roast cooked? The younger children were outside with the neighbours' kids, Matt and Finn were at the Yacht Club with Donal and she had to fill the space and time before dinner to prevent ringing Jack. She had been so tempted to call him after making a fool of herself in his apartment but she wouldn't have known what to say if she had.

Suddenly she had the perfect solution.

Louise braced herself before hitting the ebony and ivory keys. She hadn't played Chopin in a very long time but the *Prelude in A Minor* was perfect for how she felt. She needed to release some of the pent-up emotions that she was carrying inside. She let herself fall into the music. It was perfect – a sense of peace and balance filled her. She wasn't sure how long she was playing but when she stopped she felt exhausted.

She went to the kitchen and put the vegetables on a low heat to cook, then returned to the piano. Picking up a piece of sheet music by Mozart, she decided to play on for the practice but soon her concentration was disturbed by the front door banging.

"We're home!"

Louise stopped and got up to see Donal and the boys standing in the hallway covered with muddy marks and wet patches.

"Hi – did you have fun?"

"Great – yeah. We're calling for the guys – playing footie," Matt said and went back out the front door with Finn.

"Did you have a nice afternoon?" Donal asked.

"I was just playing the piano."

"That's good – I'm glad you're back playing."

Louise knew what he meant – playing music again had improved her mood.

"Do you fancy going out with Kevin and Judy on Saturday?"

Louise made a funny face.

Donal stared at her – waiting for her protests. But instead she surprised him.

"Okay – we can, I suppose."

What was a dinner with Kevin's sailing friends when she had almost committed adultery?

"When are your parents here?" Donal asked.

Louise looked at her watch. "Not for another half an hour." The aroma from the beef was wafting out of the kitchen.

"I'll go up and change."

With a sigh Louise abandoned Mozart and went to tend to the vegetables. She lifted the roast beef out of the oven and let it rest next to the hob. The phone rang and she slipped her oven gloves off and lifted it.

"Hello."

"Louise." Her mother was sobbing. "Your dad – it's too awful!"

"Slow down, Mum – what's happened?"

"Your father has been attacked. Burglars! I just went out to get the papers and when I came back he was –" Maggie broke down in uncontrollable tears.

"Did you call the police?"

"I don't know the number."

"I'll call them – just stay there – I'm on my way."

"Get Donal to come – I'm scared that the burglars are still in the house."

Louise dialled the emergency services and hit the switch on any electrical appliances in the kitchen.

Donal was filled in on the situation as he pulled on some fresh clothes.

"Let's go," she said.

"Who's going to look after the kids?"

"Matt will have to. I'll ring Marie next door when we get in the car and tell her to keep an eye on them all."

Donal drove as if the road was on fire until they got to Raheny. Maggie was waiting at the front door, still wearing her coat. A police car was parked outside and an ambulance was approaching, blaring in the distance.

Louise rushed up the driveway and put her arm around her mother who collapsed in tears with relief on seeing her daughter.

"How's Daddy?"

"He's unconscious. The police are with him."

"Did you see anyone?"

Maggie shook her head. "I thought it was strange that the door was open but you know your father – he could have been doing something in the garden – but when I called him there was no reply. Then I went into the kitchen and he was lying face down on the floor with blood all over the side of his face."

"Here's the ambulance crew now," Donal said as the men in bright yellow jackets pushed by with an array of accoutrements.

They followed them in. Larry was rolled onto his side. The blood was red and still flowing from the gash on the side of his head. His mouth was open and his eyes closed.

"Oh my God, he's dead!" Maggie sobbed.

"He's going to be fine – he's just had a bad knock," the tall guard standing at her side assured her.

"Are you sure?"

The ambulance men put Larry on a stretcher and carried him out to the ambulance.

"Donal, will you go with Dad? I'll follow with Mum."

"I'm not going to Beaumont Hospital," said her mother. "That place is covered in germs – they've got that MRSA thing!"

"Take your mum home to our house and check on the kids," said Donal. "I'll go to the hospital and let you know when anything develops."

Louise smiled gratefully at her husband – he seemed to have a calmness that soothed all those around.

"Thanks," she said.

Donal handed her the keys of the car and followed the crew and Larry out to the ambulance.

"I really don't feel like I could eat a thing after what's happened to your father but I suppose I should keep my strength up," Maggie said dolefully.

Louise couldn't understand how her mother could eat after seeing her husband in such a state but she knew her well enough by now to slice up the beef and serve her some food.

"You wouldn't have some horseradish sauce with that?" Maggie said as she started to cut into the thin slivers of meat.

"Of course," Louise said, taking the jar out of the fridge before hollering out to the children. "Kids! Your dinner's on the table!"

The four children gathered around their grandmother at the kitchen table.

"Keep it down, children – I've had a terrible shock," Maggie said sharply.

Not to mention my poor father! Louise thought but refrained from saying anything. There was no point in making matters worse and her mother could be so intolerant when she wanted.

Suddenly Louise's mobile phone rang out with her husband's name on the screen.

"Donal, how is he?"

"He's come around but they said he was very lucky – whoever did this could have killed him if they had hit him a few inches further back on the head. They expect him to make a full recovery but it will take some time. How's your mother?"

"Unbearable," she whispered into the phone.

"I'll come home and let you come in here – I suppose your mother's going to stay with us?"

Louise didn't fancy having her mother to stay any more than her husband did but she knew that she would have to look after her.

"Do you mind?"

"Of course not."

"You've been so good – thanks, Donal."

"It's okay. I'll see you soon."

Louise felt so grateful to her husband. He might be away sailing any chance he got but, when the chips were down and she needed him, he was there.

Chapter 11

"I'm going to take a look at the Malecón – you can come or you can stay!" said Emma to Sophie.

"Why don't you just relax before dinner?"

Emma sighed. "I just want to see it – that's all."

"This mood you're in – it's about that guy Greg, isn't it?"

"You can be so insensitive, Sophie – I was only talking to Greg – he's a nice man and he asked me to lunch, but I don't like you tossing Paul's name around in the way you did."

"I was only joking with you at the market!"

Emma frowned. They both knew that she wasn't. "If I want to have lunch with a stranger then I will – okay?"

Sophie tossed her eyes heavenward. "Come on, let's go for a walk!"

They stepped out onto the street. Sophie surveyed her map while Emma stood at her side. "If we keep walking up the Paseo del Prado we'll end at the Malecón – it's nearly time for sunset and that's when all the locals take a stroll along it."

Emma looked at her watch. They had an hour and a half to kill before meeting Greg.

They crossed the street to the pedestrian strip shielded by tall trees on both sides. There were two huge sculptures of majestic lions cast in bronze in the middle of the thoroughfare. Some young boys were laughing and climbing on their backs. They were tall and lanky and wearing trousers that were centimetres too short. Their shoes were cut at the toes to fit their growing feet. Other children made their own amusement by dancing to the music being made by one of the youngsters with a box and a spoon.

It wasn't windy when they reached the promenade and seafront but the rolling tide brought with it ferocious waves that crashed against the wall. Young men with bare chests and wearing scraggy long shorts lined the wall. Some were drinking rum – others dancing to an invisible beat – others standing on the edge of the wall debating whether or not to dive in for a swim.

An array of attractive buildings lined the road on the other side. Each building was painted in a different pastel shade that had faded from the direct sunlight beating against its façade. In the distance the sun was dipping lower over the stretch of high-rise buildings in the Vedado neighbourhood.

"It's everything I imagined."

"Me too!" Sophie sighed.

Emma turned to her suddenly. "I never realised that you had a hankering to visit Havana?"

"I've always fancied coming here – Paul knew that!"

Emma shook her head. "What's Paul got to do with you wanting to come here?"

Sophie stared at her sister. She longed to tell her. She wouldn't though – instead she would lie.

"Paul talked to me when he was planning this trip – he wanted to be sure that it was what you wanted." The words cut her throat.

"Oh!" Emma turned to look at the sun and watched it become a darker shade as the sky filled with hues of orange and yellow but her thoughts were elsewhere.

Why had Paul done that? Why had he discussed his plans

with her youngest sister? It didn't make sense. But then there was a lot about the last few weeks of Paul's life that didn't make sense. Like the visit to his doctor complaining of depression and the prescription for extra-strong sleeping tablets and anti-depressants that she had found in the pocket of his jacket.

"Come on – we don't want that hunky Canadian to slip away," Sophie said, with a nudge to her sister's arm. "We could always try one of those funny little yellow taxis if you don't want to walk back." She was talking about the 'coco taxis' that scooted up and down the Malecón.

"They do look like fun!" Emma agreed. She had to stop torturing herself – she would probably never find the real cause of Paul's death.

Sophie hailed one of the small egg-shaped scooters that were just big enough to carry the driver and two passengers. The girls sat precariously on the red plastic seats and let the wind blow around them on the journey back to their hotel. They felt every bump on the road along the way.

As the evening drew in, Parque Central came to life. The young people who had been lazing around earlier had multiplied and were now outnumbering the palms and decorations in the square. Some were making their own music with makeshift instruments. A cacophony of life and vibrancy rang around the square – percussion provided by car horns and engines.

They got out of the coco taxi and slowly ascended the hotel steps. Sitting in the marble-floored foyer with a newspaper in his hands was Greg. He was wearing a grey shirt and cream trousers and would have looked well on the pages of a fashion magazine. He jumped up as the girls neared.

"Hi, Greg! You're early – we aren't dressed for dinner yet," Emma said.

"Don't worry – I'm catching up on world news. I know we said seven thirty but I wanted to check out your hotel – it's very nice but I have to admit I prefer my little place."

Sophie gushed with big smiles and twiddled with her hair.

"We'll be down as quickly as we can," Emma said.

"Don't rush for me, ladies – I like sitting here!"

When they got into the lift Sophie wouldn't make eye contact with Emma. It was a difficult situation. They both were flattered by and attracted to this handsome man. Emma felt as if Sophie was constantly looking over her shoulder as though she was doing something wrong. Was seven months enough time and distance to consider a relationship with another man after Paul's death? She couldn't say – time had taken on a whole new dimension since Paul's death and days felt like hours and minutes felt like weeks and sometimes she honestly couldn't tell anyone how she really felt inside.

"Look," said Sophie, "I know you saw him first but I guess you're not ready to meet someone – I mean it's too soon after Paul, right?"

Emma couldn't believe she was being pulled into this conversation. "Of course – if he likes you then go for him," she said curtly.

Sophie smiled. Sophie felt vindicated. She needed compensation for the fact that she had lost Paul. She was young – she needed to find a life for herself. Emma had the luxury of grieving publicly and she was well catered for financially and had her son to show for her union with Paul. But Sophie was left with nothing but feelings of loss after Paul's death. Now she would enjoy Greg's company and Emma would have to watch like she used to at family occasions and festive times of the year.

Greg opened the door of the Floridita and the girls entered – feeling as if they were stepping back in time. The waiters rushed around wearing the trademark scarlet blazers with white trims along the collar. In the corner a trio were playing bass, guitar and drums. Emma could smell the aged instruments in the air. She

spotted a huge brass statue of Hemingway propping up the bar –
the head not unlike the one she had seen in Cojimar earlier that day.

"Is that who I think it is?"

"Yes." Greg laughed at Emma. "You'll find he crops up in
lots of places the more you get around this city!"

The letters *Home of the Daiquiri* were embossed along the
bar under the red leather trims.

"Okay ladies – this is where Hemingway mixed up the special
recipe for the daiquiri way back in the 1930s."

"What's in it?" Sophie asked with a flutter of her eyelashes.
She had been working Greg since they had left *El Telegrafo*.

"It's a blend of white rum – of course – and lemon, sugar and
a few drops of maraschino on crushed ice."

"Yum – I'll have one of them," Sophie said, licking her lips
suggestively.

"And will you try, Emma?" Greg asked.

"Lovely – sounds good."

Greg ushered them to a small round plastic table that would
look out of place in the newly refurbished Ireland of the twenty-
first century but in Havana it felt authentic and right.

A waiter rushed over – his trousers covered by a long white
apron to match his starched white shirt. He had brilliant blue
eyes that contrasted with his coffee-coloured skin.

"You like?" he said, putting small paper coasters in front of
each of them.

"*Tres daiquiri, por favor*," Greg said and sat back on his
plastic chair, crossing one leg over the other. "So, ladies, do you
fancy eating here? It's full of tourists but it's good."

"I like it," said Emma.

"We actually had a Floridita in Dublin up to recently but it
was nothing like this," said Sophie.

"You'll find that with anything under the Cuban brand that's
outside the country. I bet it's all polished and shiny."

Sophie nodded. "Yes – like any trendy bar in Dublin city. I

was there at the launch of a product that my boyfriend was doing the advertising and promotion for."

"Which boyfriend of yours was in advertising?" Emma butted in. Sophie had never before mentioned a guy in advertising.

"Oh you never met him," Sophie said hurriedly. "He was just a guy I went out with for a couple of weeks."

"Did Paul know him? He mentioned something about that, some promotion they had in the Floridita, in passing – I'm sure Evans covered that."

"He was very junior – I don't think he was in Evans for long." The waiter placed three cocktail glasses on the table.

Sophie grabbed hers quickly and hid behind it. "Do you have a menu – we're going to eat here!" she said to the waiter.

Emma frowned. This was the first time she had heard of Sophie having a boyfriend in Paul's company – why hadn't he ever told her?

"So, Emma from Ireland, what do you want to do later?"

Emma was still reeling with thoughts of her sister and Paul's colleague. She longed to fill in the blanks and weeks that led up to Paul's untimely death. But Donal had warned her against looking for clues and searching for things that weren't there. He had said that they would probably never know why Paul had done the things that he did.

"I don't mind," she shrugged. "Well, I want to go dancing – what about the Casa de la Musica that our taxi driver Felipe told us about?"

"The Casa de la Musica it is!" Greg declared.

When they had filled their bellies with the huge variety of lobster and shellfish on the Floridita's menu, they took the short walk through Parque Central and Calle Neptuno to Casa de la Musica. When they reached the entrance the two sisters looked at each other – both thinking the same thing.

"This is like that hall in Longford we used to visit as kids when we stayed with Auntie Joan."

Sophie had taken the words out of Emma's mouth. The bleak corridor with a scruffy window box just inside the door could have been leading to a disco in 1980s rural Ireland.

Greg paid the fifteen CUC entrance fee for the three of them and they walked down to a huge pair of swing doors – from behind it came the rhythm of a modern dance mix fused with a salsa beat.

"The bar could do with refurbishment!" Sophie whispered in Emma's ear.

Emma scanned the bleak counter with five dim lights illuminating the drinks behind the barmen. There wasn't a wide range of brands or drinks but there was row upon row of Havana Club bottles. No wonder the menu had so many rum cocktails on offer.

"Would you like to take a seat, ladies, and I'll get us some drinks?" Greg asked.

"Thanks," Sophie said with a flirtatious smile and led her sister down to a table by the dance floor.

"The last time I sat on these, I was in school," Emma said, pulling back an orange plastic chair. "It's kind of nice to be in a different sort of place to the usual nightclubs you get when you go on holiday."

"This place stinks – and I need to go to the toilet – I bet they are grim."

"Oh, it's just old – we've got used to everything being shiny and new in Ireland."

Sophie tossed her eyes heavenward as she stomped off to find the toilets.

Greg returned with three mojitos in his strong hands and placed them down on the table.

"Thanks, Greg," Emma said, lifting hers to take a sip.

"Where's Sophie?"

"She'll be back in a minute."

"Sophie's good fun, Emma from Ireland, but she doesn't have the sophistication of her older sister!" he winked.

Emma blushed and took a sip from her glass – there was something not quite as sincere about him as she had first thought. The dance floor was empty and there were only a handful of people scattered around the railings and chairs on the dance floor.

"There's a singer playing tonight – he's big in Cuba – then the real dancing will start when he finishes."

Gabriel Martinez was a superb performer and he sang for over an hour and a half. Some of the locals got up and danced while he sang. The tourists – mostly South American and Canadian – sat on the sidelines and watched how salsa was done.

When the DJ came out on stage there was a rush onto the dance floor – it was different to anything the Irish girls had seen before. A young Cuban couple stood out from the crowd. He was wearing a baseball hat and tight-fitting wine-coloured shirt which complemented his dark skin. He was as nimble and flexible as an elastic band. His dance partner was exotic and wore a pink frilly mini-skirt with low-cut blouse. Her silver sandals were constantly in the air as her partner spun her and tossed her around to the beat of the music. They moved better than any of the participants on the dance shows on TV back home.

"Come on, Greg – I bet you can move – let's give it a go?" Sophie said, standing up.

Greg stood up and took her hand.

Emma watched enviously as Greg – who was a proficient dancer – spun her sister and led with a couple of salsa moves. They laughed and appeared to be really enjoying themselves.

Emma wondered how genuine Greg was – he was saying one thing to her and then flirting with Sophie the next minute. Did she really need her emotions to be tossed around? Her head had been melting since Paul's death. It wasn't like he had been knocked down by a car – or drowned at sea – or dying of an illness for months. The inquest was harrowing and, although it was only a formality and Donal had assured her that she didn't need to attend, she hated the questions that hung over her husband's death. Yes, he had a heart attack and that was what killed him but the fact that there were two empty bottles, one of anti-depressants and another of sleeping tablets, left the cause as inconclusive. She had no idea why her husband would need anti-depressants. And finding out that he was taking them in the lead-up to his death was even more upsetting.

She took a drink and tried to forget about everything when a familiar figure appeared in front of her.

"Emma!"

It was Felipe. He was standing, wearing a white shirt and black trousers – coming straight from work no doubt – and he had a shot of rum in his hand. His hair was dishevelled and his jaw showing signs of early-morning shadow – but he looked gorgeous.

"Felipe – how nice to see you!" Emma was glad of the company – there was something safe about him that she didn't feel in Greg's company. "Did you know I'd be here?"

"I hoped that you would come here. It is good?"

"Yes – brilliant music – you were right."

Felipe pulled up a plastic chair and sat beside her. "Did you have a nice day?"

"Great, thanks – we ran into this Canadian man and he joined us for dinner."

Felipe looked out onto the dance floor at Sophie and her partner. He didn't usually try to get to know tourists – he had lost his wife by befriending a Mexican man three years before. Now he was very careful about whom he made friends with. But he really liked Emma – he had been attracted to her blue eyes from the first time he saw her in Arrivals at the airport. When he came back to the hotel the next day to do a collection, he had walked out to the balcony that overlooked the pool and scanned the sun-beds until he found her sitting under the shade of an umbrella working on her laptop. It was fate and good fortune that brought him to the hotel the night that she needed a taxi and she hadn't been far from his thoughts for a moment since. But Felipe was deep down a shy person who kept his feelings very much to himself.

"Where did you go today?"

"Oh, I was all around old Havana and I went to see the Ambos Mundos and the Catedral. But I'm looking forward to tomorrow."

"Yes, that will be very good. Would you like to dance?"

Emma could feel herself blush. However, she liked the thought of dancing with Felipe.

Felipe led with such assurance that he made her feel safe and confident with her moves.

They brushed against Greg and Sophie.

Greg was put out by the presence of another man but hid it perfectly.

"Greg Adams," he said, and held out his hand.

"Felipe," the Cuban man said, shaking it firmly.

"So how do you know the ladies?"

"I drove them from Varadero."

Greg smiled widely. A taxi driver – not much competition.

"Why don't I get some drinks," Emma said. "Sophie, will you help me?"

"A lady shouldn't be at the bar – please let me – what would you like to drink, Felipe?" Greg asked.

"I am fine."

The girls went back to their seats with Felipe. Sophie couldn't hide the grin on her face. Felipe was the perfect distraction for her sister and she would have Greg all to herself.

"It's great that you called by, Felipe!" she gushed.

Felipe felt embarrassed by her enthusiasm – he knew perfectly well that she wasn't in the slightest bit interested in his company and he could see her agenda perfectly.

Emma smiled at Felipe. The four were suddenly arranged into couples and when the disco started up Sophie used every move she could to mark out Greg as her territory. Emma let Felipe take her around the floor until she needed refreshment.

"Are you tired? Do you want to go?" Felipe asked.

Emma picked up her drink and shook her head. "No – I was just day-dreaming – or night-dreaming!" she said lightly – looking at her watch. "Oh! I didn't realise it was nearly three o'clock."

"If you like I can take you back to the hotel?"

"Why don't we all go?" she said briskly and called to the others. "Will we go back to the bar of El Telegrafo? They're bound to have residents' hours."

"Sounds good!" Greg said taking up his mojito and finishing off the contents.

"Okay," Sophie said, turning to Greg and giving him the unbearably flirtatious look that was grating on Emma's skin.

Felipe drove the couple of blocks back to Parque Central and as they got to the door he stopped suddenly. "I will see you tomorrow – at ten o'clock?"

"Aren't you coming in for a drink?" Sophie asked.

Felipe shook his head. "No, I will see you tomorrow."

Greg led the two girls into the bar as Felipe disappeared into the night.

"I wonder why he wouldn't come in?" Emma sighed.

Greg shrugged. He was pleased to have the two women to himself. He'd had a wonderful threesome with two Swedish women in Miami a couple of years before and wouldn't mind the same experience with two Irishwomen.

Emma wished Felipe was still there. She couldn't look at Sophie drooling all over Greg any longer.

"I think I'll go to my room actually – I'm feeling really tired and I've a lot to see tomorrow."

Sophie's eyes brightened. "Okay, see you later – we won't be long – will we, Greg?"

"Not at all – see you tomorrow I hope." He handed her his business card. "My cell phone is on that if you want to hook up tomorrow."

"Thanks," Emma said and went over to the elevator without looking back. Good luck to Sophie – she could have Greg – she could have anyone she wanted. She didn't care any more. The risk of falling for another man was too great. Look what she had done to her husband – who had so much to live for.

"Do you want to go somewhere?" Greg suggested to Sophie.

Sophie's eyebrows rose. "Okay – I would like to see your hotel."

Greg shrugged. He would have to settle for one sister.

They went out into Parque Central and the hive of activity that buzzed all around.

"Tell me about Canada – I've always wanted to go."

"It's a good place to call home – damn cold in winter. I like to take my trips to Cuba during the winter months."

"But you probably have snow?"

"Plenty of snow. What do you work at, Sophie?"

"I'm a designer – I design knitwear for an Irish company but we have a skeleton staff now as most of our production is outsourced to China."

"It's the same world over – a difficult time for the clothing business."

Sophie didn't seem perturbed. "I'm a very good designer!"

Greg smiled. He liked this Irish girl's cockiness. "Almost here – see that building on the corner?"

Sophie nodded. They ascended the couple of steps and entered the foyer which was almost empty apart from one very old patron and Marco behind the bar.

"Long shift today, Marco?"

Marco smiled but the tiredness lifted from his face when he saw Greg's partner. She really was stunningly beautiful and exotic, the red hues in her hair causing him to stare. He was used to seeing Greg enter the hotel with different beautiful women.

"Fancy a drink in my room?" Greg whispered in her ear.

Sophie nodded. It was what she wanted.

The lift was ancient and Greg steered her over to the stairs. "I'm on the next floor."

The room was clean and bright when Greg put on the lamps. He had made it his own and his personal items were scattered all around.

Sophie was drawn to a small mahogany games table in the corner. It was inlaid with squares in a lighter wood.

"Can you play chess on this table?"

Greg went over and ran his long fingers along the smooth wood.

"We could if we had chess pieces – but we could always play with something else – what about bottles from the mini bar?"

Sophie giggled. The idea appealed.

Greg took out a mixture of whiskey, vodka, gin and rum and set them up on the table.

"How will we know what each piece is?"

"That's complicated," Greg agreed. "We could always play checkers, eh?"

"You mean draughts?"

Greg shrugged. "We could play Canadian rules but that might involve too many bottles – so English draughts it is – would you like to be whiskey and gin?"

"Would you mind if I was rum and gin?"

"Of course not – the lady's choice. I am whiskey and vodka then. Why don't we spice it up a bit – when you take your opponent's piece you have to drink the bottle, eh?"

Sophie giggled again. "All right." She had sobered considerably with all of the dancing.

Greg set up the chairs at the table. Then he made his first move. The game had begun.

Sophie was overly anxious and took one of Greg's pieces as soon as possible – then she realised that she would have to drink first.

"Can I have some Coke or juice with it?"

"That would be cheating – don't you think?"

Sophie smiled weakly and threw the vodka back. Her face grimaced with the sharpness on her tongue. The warmth from the liquid ran down her throat and she felt the buzz from the alcohol start to take effect.

Greg laughed and set up the next move. He wanted her to take another of his pieces.

"Oh no," she protested. "Look, if you move here you can take two of mine!"

Greg did as she suggested and knocked back two bottles quickly. He was tall and strong – he could handle his alcohol.

"This one is mine," Sophie said, taking another bottle of vodka and unscrewing the cap.

Greg smiled a delicious soft smile as he surveyed Sophie. When she made her next move he placed his hand on top of hers. "Let me open it for you, eh?"

"I can manage," she said. But the alcohol was affecting her dexterity. She handed the bottle over and he took the top off. She sipped and licked her lips.

"Mind if I join you?" he asked.

"Of course not!" The game was only a folly anyway – a prelude to something that they both wanted.

Greg knocked a rum back and stood up. He held out his hand and Sophie took it.

They walked over to his bed – covered with a white bedspread. The fan above their heads spun around – circulating the humidity in the air.

Greg put his hand up to her face and kissed her cheek.

Sophie could feel the tension and excitement build between them. She couldn't wait to see his beautiful coloured skin – hidden underneath his grey shirt.

But he wanted her to be ready. He gently lowered her onto the bed and ran his dark smooth fingers along her body –

unbuttoning her top and peeling it from her shoulders. His eyes widened as he spotted the front-opening bra – he would leave that for later. He slipped his fingers under the elastic in her skirt and pulled it down gently, taking her underwear with it. Then kneeling down on the ground he slid his palms along her thighs to open her legs.

Sophie ached inside. She longed to feel his tongue run along her most sensitive spot. She didn't have to wait. He was an expert and knew how to bring a woman to orgasm quickly but without taking away the enjoyment of anticipation. Sophie yelped as he put his fingers inside to increase her pleasure.

Sophie put her hands on the back of his neck and pulled him up to her breasts.

He opened the catch and momentarily put his lips on her nipples, then hungrily licked them with his tongue. He had to take off his shirt, now wet and sticky with sweat.

Sophie helped him off with his chinos – he wasn't wearing any underwear and her eyes widened as she saw his erection for the first time. She couldn't contain the desire to hold it and feel its length and girth. She hadn't been so turned on since the first time she had made love with Paul on the floor of his office. The sheer physicality of the beautiful man in front of her had her in a frenzy. She felt him enter – her face melted with the pleasure of each thrust. It was euphoria on a level that made Sophie scream. Had she finally found the man to replace Paul?

Chapter 12

The alarm clock rang out and Donal jumped up in the bed. He hit it off and then slowly lay back down.

"I'm sorry," he said to Louise. "I must have put it on last night. We were both so distracted going to bed."

"It's okay – we need to check on Mum and I want to go back into the hospital."

Donal looked his wife up and down. She always smelt so good first thing in the morning. It had been three months since they had made love.

Louise slid out of the bed and pulled her dressing-gown on – oblivious to the emotions she was arousing in her husband. She went straight to the spare room where her mother lay prostrate on the bed with her mouth open and a loud snoring noise coming from her nose.

She'd had a terrible shock but was still composed enough the night before to call Louise before she left the hospital and ask her to stop off at her house and get her face cream and a few other things that she would need to get a night's sleep.

Maggie Owens was a remarkable woman – so conservative,

so religious and so self-righteous. But Louise admired her for the way she looked and held herself. She could pass for a woman ten years younger with ease but there was a reason why she didn't have so many lines on her face and it wasn't botox or the hat she wore to shield her skin from the sun. Maggie left any worries financial or emotional to her husband. He was a man and all matters like that were his affair. She had a job to look good and be an upstanding albeit judgemental member of society.

Louise knew that Maggie would turn this tragic event where her father had been beaten up into a personal assault on herself.

She considered ringing the girls in Havana but there was no point in telling them – why cut Emma's holiday short by just one day? She deserved the break. Louise wouldn't mind cutting Sophie's holiday short but that would not serve any purpose either.

Finn came out of his room, scratching his head.

"How's Grandad?"

"He's going to be fine, love," Louise assured him. After losing his father so tragically she realised how important male role models were in the young lad's life.

"That's good," he said sheepishly and went into the bathroom.

Louise went back into the bedroom to dress.

"I'll go to the hospital and see how Dad is," she said to Donal. "Will you give the kids breakfast and see that Mum is okay?"

"I was meant to go to the club."

Louise looked at her husband in despair.

"Okay," said Donal. "It's unusual circumstances."

Louise grabbed her bag and ran down the stairs. She took a banana from the fruit bowl and lifted her car keys from the hook where they always rested beside the phone. Then she got into her people carrier and drove to Beaumont Hospital.

She wasn't on the road long before her phone bleeped with a message. She decided it was better to check in case there was something wrong at home. But the message wasn't from Donal – it was from Jack.

I need 2 c u J

She trembled as she looked at the screen. She had been thinking about the fool she had made of herself on Saturday until all this happened. He was a single guy without commitments – it was normal that he should expect her to see or talk to him at a moment's notice. But this was not the time. She had to prioritise her family.

She drove steadily along Sybil Hill, trying not to think about Jack but he invaded her head all the way to the Artane roundabout.

She couldn't resist the temptation. She hit the Bluetooth function on her steering wheel and dialled Jack's number.

He answered quickly.

"Hello, Louise, is that you?"

"Hi, Jack – look, I've a family crisis at the moment – my dad's in hospital – he was beaten up by a burglar."

"That's awful. I'm sorry to hear it. Is he going to be okay?"

"I think so. But something else has shown up when they took him in for observation. Are you okay?"

Jack suddenly felt like a student again – looking to his teacher for reassurance while she dealt with a real adult crisis.

"I'm fine. I just needed to talk to you after the way you ran out – I'm sorry."

"Jack, you did nothing wrong – I'm married and in a different position to you!"

"I have the knack of upsetting people at the moment. Especially Aoife!"

"What happened between you and Aoife?"

"I wasn't very nice to her – I suppose it's the cold-feet thing we discussed."

"Jack, you have to pretend you haven't met me again. It's not good for either of us."

"I'm trying but it doesn't seem to be working. I'm really sorry for what I said to you in the café that day too."

"Look, you needed to get that off your chest. I'm fine – but

I'm married and you have to remember that it's only cold feet that you're having."

Jack sighed. What was he expecting her to do? "Thanks for ringing me back, Louise – I just wanted to be sure that everything was okay between us."

"Of course, Jack, but I am going to be up to my eyes for a while with this awful thing that's after happening with my parents."

"I understand. I'll let you go – keep me posted."

"Mind yourself, Jack. I'll be in touch."

Louise hung up. For the first time since meeting Jack again she was glad that she'd had the strength not to be dragged into a love affair. Her life was complicated enough.

Jack didn't feel much better after hearing Louise's voice. He had hoped that maybe they could meet and she would sort out his feelings but things were very different now for her.

He needed to speak to Aoife. What was he feeling? Why was he so confused?

He picked up his mobile phone and dialled her number. He had to do something.

Aoife had spent the night in Malahide. She rang her friend Cathy and they went down to Gibneys which was always lively on a Sunday night and drank bottle after bottle of Smirnoff Ice. They got a bag of chips in the Beachcomber and drank tea in her mother's kitchen until four o'clock in the morning. But when she woke she didn't feel any better. Although she had flirted with lots of guys in Gibneys and been assured by her best friend that she was totally in the right and Jack needed to be taught a few lessons – she felt bad – bad for Jack and bad for herself.

Why was he like this all of a sudden? Something had changed! She went into the bathroom and looked at her reflection. She usually took her make-up off before going to bed – but then she wasn't in good form after the long chat with Cathy and remembered the tears she had shed, wiped away with coarse kitchen roll. She needed to talk to Jack. She wiped her face with a cloth and went back to her old room to get dressed. She would confront him head on. She didn't have to make the first move either.

Suddenly her phone rang. She recognised the number and let it ring until it almost went to voicemail.

"Yes."

"It's me – I need to see you."

"I'm not sure I want to see you."

"Aoife – I'm really sorry for all the things I said yesterday."

"Why did you say them if you didn't mean them?"

"I did – I mean I didn't mean them to come out the way they sounded."

"You've got a lot of explaining to do, Jack Duggan."

"I know – can we meet?"

Aoife sighed. "I'll come out to Howth – I want to change my clothes."

"Let's go for a walk around the cliffs – it's a good day."

"I'm exhausted – I had a late night."

"Oh!" Jack wondered who she had been with. "Okay – we can talk in the apartment. I'm here."

"Fine," Aoife said and hung up abruptly.

She drove with her angst bubbling inside like a pressure cooker. She hadn't had the nerve to tell her parents about the row. As far as they were concerned she had been having an overdue girlie night out with Cathy the night before. She was much too ashamed to tell them the hurtful things that Jack had said.

The gates of St Lawrence's Quay Apartments opened and she parked her car. She looked at her hands and they were shaking. It wasn't the effects of alcohol from the night before that was causing them to do so either.

The lift ride was brief. She stood outside the apartment door and put her key in the lock. Before she could turn it Jack had opened it.

"Hi," he said sheepishly.

She looked at his boyish blue eyes and fine features and could feel herself melt. She loved him so much. But for now she had a duty to herself not to show it.

"I want to get something in the bedroom – I'll be out to talk to you in a minute."

She brushed by him and threw her handbag onto the couch. She slammed the door behind her when she got into the bedroom and fell onto the bed – burying her face into her hands. Her gut told her something terrible was about to happen. She couldn't bear the thought of telling her parents that the wedding was postponed – or even worse cancelled.

She had to pull herself together. She changed her clothes and left Jack sitting apprehensively outside on the living-room couch while she fixed her make-up and brushed her hair. She checked how she looked in the mirror and felt much better able to face her fiancé.

"So – what is it that you want to talk about?" she said, standing firmly on the shag-pile rug.

"Come and sit down beside me."

She stood firm. "I'd rather stand, thanks."

"Aoife, this is the hardest thing I have ever had to do."

"Well, it's pretty hard for me too. I think you should say what you have to say."

Jack stood up to be at eye level with his fiancée.

She took a few steps backwards.

He moved forward and reached his hand out to stroke the side of her face but she winced.

"I think we should postpone the wedding."

Aoife gasped. "Have you met someone else?"

"There's no one else," he said, too quickly to sound convincing.

"That's it, isn't it – you're having an affair?"

Jack shook his head adamantly. "I'm not having an affair –

148

please believe me – and I want us to stay living together – but it's all got out of hand. Your family – the wedding plans – the honeymoon – I'd rather we did something small and simple – just us."

"But you never said before."

"It just snowballed. We were only going to have family first and then a few friends and then it was some from work and before we knew it we were inviting everyone we know and now you need a designer wedding dress and . . . the list goes on."

"Every girl dreams about her wedding day and I want it to be really special."

"And so do I but it's got to be about the marriage – not the wedding."

Aoife's looked at him earnestly. "I thought it was!"

Jack hadn't done a good job of explaining his true feelings because he wasn't being true. The thought of a life with just one woman frightened him. Seeing Louise and having feelings that he didn't realise he still felt scared him and now the thought of losing Aoife scared him too.

"Please, can we just postpone the wedding and bring it back to basics. It's not good to be showy with so many people losing jobs and the economy in the state it's in."

Aoife took a sharp intake of breath. "I'm going to pack a bag and go home for a few days. I don't know how I feel. You're not being very fair throwing this at me so suddenly."

"I know. You will come back?"

She shook her head. "I don't know."

Jack suddenly realised what he had done. "Don't go then – I'm sorry, Aoife – I don't want to lose you."

Aoife was trying hard to fight back the tears. "I feel like something has been broken between us. I loved you so much – I was so sure that I had found my perfect mate."

"I am – you are – we are," Jack insisted.

"If you felt the way I did then we wouldn't be having this conversation."

She was right and Jack had brought all this about.

"What do I have to do to make it up to you?"

"You can't undo what's been said. I think it's best if I go back to my mum's – for a few days at least."

Jack nodded. He needed time to digest what he had started. He needed to be sure what he really wanted.

"There were at least three little bastards responsible for beating Dad," Louise said, throwing her handbag down on the kitchen table.

"Are you okay?" Donal said. "Now relax and tell me again but more slowly."

Louise was shaking but appreciated Donal's calming concern.

"Dad was interviewed by the police while I was with him and he said they were young fellas in hoodies – they couldn't have been more than fifteen or sixteen."

"Is he sure? That sounds very young."

Louise nodded. "The police confirmed it. They're looking for a pack of youths from decent homes in Raheny that are going around terrorising older people and stealing from them and then beating them up – they aren't even scared enough to disguise their appearance. The police say it's hard to catch them and even harder to convict them because of their age. What is the world coming to, Donal?"

Donal scratched his head. "It's bad all right."

"They could have killed him and probably would have if Mum hadn't disturbed them."

"Surely not?"

"Donal, they used sticks to beat him and part of their fun is doing bodily harm to their victims. They nearly killed a young guy walking home with his girlfriend at eight o'clock in the evening a few weeks ago. I couldn't believe what the police were telling me."

"Well, at least your dad is going to be okay."

"He's terribly shook and they are worried about his heart – they said it was very weak."

"Is this from the attack?"

Louise shrugged. "I'm not sure – it might be induced by the attack but he had a weakness there anyway – three of the valves are blocked."

"What are they going to do?"

"It looks like he's going to need a triple bypass."

"That's not good – especially at his age."

Louise nodded her head – her thoughts precisely.

"Did they take anything?"

"His wallet – he only had twenty euros in it. There was really only Mum's jewellery that might have been of any value to them but they weren't there long enough to find it."

"It's all so pointless."

"I know, but when I was sitting in there I couldn't help wonder if it was a kind of blessing in disguise – if he has something wrong with his heart this operation could save his life and we would never have known if he wasn't sent to hospital for observation after the burglary."

Donal raised his eyebrows. "That would be a strange twist of fate." Suddenly his expression turned to one of panic. "Hold on – what will happen to your mother if he has to have surgery?"

Louise's face dropped. She relished the thought of minding her mother as little as Donal did. "At least Emma's home on Tuesday and we can share her!"

Chapter 13

The first thing Emma noticed when she woke was the empty bed beside hers. She wasn't surprised. Sophie had set her sights on Greg from the moment she laid eyes on him and she always got what she wanted.

She looked at her watch. It was a good time to call Finn and see how he was getting on. She reached across to the bedside table and took up her phone.

"Finn?"

"Hello, Mum."

"Darling – how are you? I'm missing you so much."

"It's been mad here. Granddad got beaten up by a burglar and Granny was staying over here last night. Louise has gone to the hospital and Donal's trying to keep Granny happy!"

Emma sat upright in the bed with the shock. Her heart was pounding.

"Is Granddad all right?"

"I think so – Louise hasn't come back yet. There was blood on his head and everything."

"Oh my God! Can I speak to Donal?"

"Sure – I'll get him."

Emma's mind raced. Her father was a big man but he had become frail since turning seventy and wasn't aware of the restrictions his own body had put on him.

"Emma – Donal here."

"Hi, Donal – Finn was just telling me about Dad. How is he?"

"Louise didn't want to upset you because you were on your holidays and you will be coming home tomorrow anyway."

"I could try to get home today."

"Honestly, there is no need. Your dad is going to be fine. He's shook up and they are keeping him in for observation." There was no need to worry her with details of his impending heart surgery. "I think they were concerned about his age and that's why they've kept him in."

"She should have told me!"

"You have me to blame for that – really, Emma, we're fine."

"I'm so lucky to have you for a brother-in-law – I hope Louise realises how lucky she is too. It can't be easy placating Mum."

"I have a handle on your mum – she's okay."

"Thanks for everything."

"We are family, Emma."

That's what he had said to her when he had accompanied her to Paul's inquest. He had arranged for his good friend John, a solicitor, to handle the case and it had been closed with the greatest of sensitivity. Nobody needed to know why he had died. It wouldn't serve any purpose. And Finn would never need to know, nor any other member of the Owens or Condell family, that there even was an inquest. Emma knew that if she could trust Donal over this then she could trust him over any other matter imaginable.

"Thanks so much, Donal."

Donal sometimes wondered if he had married the wrong sister. Emma was so calm and stable – everything that Louise wasn't. But then again maybe he and Emma were too alike – wasn't it opposites attracting that had drawn him to Louise in the first place?

"I'll see you Tuesday. Enjoy the rest of your holiday."

"See you then."

Emma hung up and contemplated ringing Sophie. No, she didn't want Greg to think that she was checking up on him. Instead she wrote her a note on the hotel writing paper.

Mum and Dad burgled. Dad in hospital but okay.

Emma had a shower and decided she had plenty of time for breakfast before meeting Felipe. She didn't want to see Sophie and she didn't want to hear the details of how her night with the handsome Greg had gone.

"Oh my God – you are unbelievable!" Sophie cried as she collapsed in a heap by Greg's side and rested her head on his glistening chest. Beads of sweat streamed down her sun-kissed freckled face and landed on his coffee skin. She wanted to lick them off. He brought animal instincts out in her that she didn't know she had.

"Will your sister be wondering where you are?" he asked as coolly as if he had just made a cup of coffee instead of performing sexual gymnastics a few moments before.

"She'll know where I am."

Greg knew that too and was sorry. He had really liked Emma better but Sophie had seemed the most playful. He was right. But liaisons like this one with Sophie were common for Greg and he liked the way Emma's head worked. He probably shouldn't have taken the easy option. But the girls would be in town for one more night. He could always try his luck with Emma later.

"What are your plans for today?"

"Emma is meeting that taxi driver and they are going to some Hemingway place – so I am free!" Sophie grinned. "I'm so glad to be getting a break from her – it's heavy going being with your sister day-in day-out. Especially after the whole Paul episode."

"Is Paul her husband?"

"Was – he's dead."

Greg wondered why Emma had omitted that information when she was telling him about her husband.

"I'm sorry to hear that – when did he die?"

"Last September. Emma can't seem to pull herself together since."

"It must be very difficult. How did he die?"

"Heart attack."

"He must have been young?"

"Forty – he was really cool."

Greg was intrigued by her tone of voice and expression. "Sounds like you fancied him a little?"

Sophie nodded. She could tell Greg – she had nothing to lose. She would never see him again after all and it would be good to tell someone that she loved Paul too. "I did love him actually and he loved me – we were lovers for the last three years of his life."

Greg took a sharp intake of breath. "That was playing with fire, don't you think?"

"We can't always choose who we fall in love with."

"It could have gone terribly wrong though if your sister had found out."

"He was only a few days from telling her about us. We had booked this holiday as a celebration. He was going to let her stay in the house and then he was going to move in with me."

"Wow!" Greg had fallen into precarious relationships himself over the years but this girl had balls of steel. "So Emma doesn't have a clue?"

Sophie shook her head. "And you won't tell her either, sure you won't?"

"I've done some pretty dangerous things over the years but I couldn't compete with that. I think Emma is better off not knowing – and if I were you I wouldn't tell anyone else either."

Sophie didn't like the change in Greg's tone. She wouldn't be lectured by anyone about morals.

"Take a chill pill, Greg. A man like you is bound to have a couple of skeletons at least in his cupboard. Where's *your* wife?"

"I'm divorced. Single now so I'm a free spirit."

Sophie's eyes widened. She regretted revealing so much to Greg now – maybe he was someone that she could have a future with? Since losing Paul she desperately wanted to find love again – she wanted a family – a chance to experience the things her sisters had.

She wouldn't mention Paul again. Maybe she should take a different approach with Greg.

Emma stood in the foyer of El Telegrafo where the night before she had left Sophie and Greg. The reception desk was thronged with visitors seeking help and information before they set off on their day's explorations. She looked at her watch – it was exactly ten o'clock when Felipe appeared, dressed in a casual black T-shirt and pair of khaki shorts – and wearing a leather strap on his wrist. He looked totally different out of the familiar black and white uniform – more like a rebel than a taxi driver.

"Good morning, Emma – did you sleep well?"

"Yes, thanks, Felipe." She hesitated for a moment. The stress of her phone call from home had her mind in a spin.

"Are you okay?"

"I've just had some bad news from home – my father was attacked by burglars yesterday. I feel bad that I can't do anything from so far away."

"That is not good. Is he in hospital?"

Emma nodded. "I think he will be fine and I don't suppose I can do anything until I get home." She smiled at him. "I guess we should get on with our outing. It's good of you to take me around on your day off."

Felipe smiled. "It's nice for me."

And Emma felt it was nice to have someone to take her mind away from the worries of home.

"What do you usually do on your day off?" Emma asked.

He shrugged. "I sometimes visit my mother in Pinar del Rio."

He led her down the steps to a red Buick convertible.

"Is this yours?" she asked.

Felipe nodded. "My father and I made it with parts. The engine is Lada but it works well."

Emma let Felipe open the door for her and she sat down on the hot leather seats with excitement and anticipation.

Felipe slipped a pair of black sunglasses on and started up the engine. The fumes from a gigantic *Camello* bus blew into the car but Emma wasn't phased – this was the most stylish way to travel around Cuba.

The road was unmarked like all of the roads she had travelled in Cuba. The hustle and bustle of Havana was wonderful to view from inside the romantic vintage car. She looked across at Felipe and he looked different too. Out of his taxi driver's clothing he was more himself. Emma felt that there was a lot hidden under the surface of the enigmatic character that sat beside her. He wasn't like the other Cubans who worked in the hotels and bars and he was different to Dehannys' family too. She couldn't figure out what it was but his silences left her curious.

"Did you drive from Matanzas this morning?"

"I spent the night with my cousin in Vedado – my father brought in the car today – he is visiting his sister."

"I'm glad to hear that – I'd hate to put you out of your way."

"It is nice to spend the day like this. I like Hemingway."

Emma was surprised. "Oh, have you read him?"

"Only two novels. It is difficult to get books that are not about the revolution!"

"I could send you some – in Spanish – I can get them on Amazon."

Felipe smiled. "Thank you. But in English – then I can practise."

"I'll get some Hemingway books and send them to you as soon as I get home!"

They travelled to the outskirts of the city where the roads became even bumpier than they had been in Havana. The car started to ascend as they came to a narrower road and in the distance Emma could see the sign for the Finca Vigía.

They ascended a set of steps that led up to the entrance of the house and Emma felt like she was stepping back in time to 1960 and the last time Hemingway had been there.

Half-empty bottles of spirits sat next to the writer's favourite chair. Hunting trophies lined the walls and she and Felipe stopped to stare at the beautiful gazelle that had been killed in Africa and brought all the way across the Atlantic Ocean.

"It's so cruel but so much a part of who he was," Emma said.

"Come," Felipe beckoned.

They went on to his study where thousands of books in the English language lined the walls. Emma surveyed their spines and longed to grab them and feel the very words that at some stage must have inspired the great man himself. The museum curator was watching her carefully. In his study, Hemingway's battered black typewriter rested on a thick hardback book – raised so that he could write standing up.

"Do you like it?" Felipe asked.

"Oh, it's wonderful. More than I ever imagined it to be. Thank you so much for bringing me here."

"I like it here. I like books but for some time after I finished university I didn't want to read another."

"What did you study?"

"I studied law."

"And did you finish?"

"*Yes*. And I practised law but I stopped two years ago. Now I make more money."

"Oh! You gave up being a lawyer to drive a taxi?"

Emma was gobsmacked at the idea of Felipe giving up a good profession to drive tourists so that he could support himself better. She'd always felt that there was more to Felipe but this revelation confirmed it.

Felipe had held off telling her too much about himself – he felt that it was all right to tell her personal details now. From his previous experiences he was slow to trust people – especially people from other countries. But he really liked Emma and the fact that she didn't quiz him or want to know more about his other profession pleased him.

They surveyed the rest of the residence which didn't take long and when Emma looked at her watch it was only eleven thirty and they still had the whole day ahead.

"Would you like to take lunch in Habana? I will show you a good place."

"Thanks, Felipe – I think we have seen everything here."

He opened the door of his car which was like a furnace after sitting in the hot sunshine. A warm breeze blew into the car as they drove the return journey to Havana.

"My wife loved that house – she always wanted to live in a house like that."

Emma was startled. "Were you married?"

"I was for four years. My friend from Mexico liked my wife. He was a lawyer too but in Mexico a lawyer can make a lot of money. My wife liked nice things and she liked him too." He smiled ironically at her.

"I'm sorry to hear that, Felipe – it must have been awful."

"It was difficult but now I am happy. My mother never liked her – my wife did not like children."

"Do you have any children?"

"No. It is my regret."

"I have a son – Finn is his name and he is nine."

"And your husband?"

"My husband is dead." Emma took a deep breath. Until now it was horrible giving away this information. It was like she was

159

revealing her soul – but saying it to Felipe, in the front of his car while driving through Havana, it felt all right. "He died seven months ago."

Felipe slowed down and glanced at Emma. "I am very sorry."

She knew that he really meant it. "Thank you."

"How did he die?" He wouldn't have asked her if he didn't feel that she wanted to talk about it.

"He had a heart attack."

"That is very bad."

"Yes, but it wasn't a normal heart attack – he suffered it after taking too many pills. He meant to kill himself."

Felipe didn't know how to react. "Are you sure that he did not take them by mistake?"

"The autopsy was inconclusive but I think he knew exactly what he was doing. The date on the bottle of pills was the same as the day that he took them."

Felipe was driving and had to keep his eyes on the road but this was a conversation that needed his full attention. He would take her to a place where they could talk and she would say everything that she needed to say.

Emma didn't flinch – she stared straight ahead at the oncoming traffic. There, she had said it, and to a total stranger. She felt relief. Until now Donal was the only person in the world she could confide in. But now she had Felipe and after tomorrow she would never see him again so it was okay to tell him her shame. How could someone be so unhappy with their life and family that they would want to kill themselves? She asked herself this several times a day and still couldn't find a conclusive answer.

"We really have to get up," Greg insisted. "Breakfast is finished."

Sophie had enticed Greg into one more session of lovemaking and he was anxious that he would be later for his appointment with an art dealer than he had arranged.

"I couldn't eat a thing!" Sophie said as she sat up in the bed and fluffed the pillows behind her. "What are we going to do today?"

"I have to visit a dealer at twelve o'clock so you can come with me and then we can get something to eat if you want, eh?"

"Okay."

Greg got out of the bed and went into the small but adequate shower room. The heat from outside was wafting in through the open window and the fan in the middle of the room was no longer doing the job it was able to the night before.

Sophie slid into the shower but Greg insisted that it really wasn't big enough. He grabbed a towel and started to dry off while she let the water cool her down momentarily.

Sophie's head was abuzz after making love to Greg and learning he was single. She would see what other information she could drag out of him as the day progressed.

She looked at her crumpled skirt and shirt from the night before – now lying in a pile on the floor. She didn't have a hairbrush. She would have to be resourceful – she was Sophie Owens and she would make herself look fabulous. She slipped an elastic band from inside her tiny handbag, then turned her head upside down and tied her hair into a ponytail. She knotted her shirt and pulled it up under her bra to make it more casual and suitable for daytime. Her skirt was made of chiffon and the creases would fall out as she walked.

"Okay, are we ready?" Greg was wearing a cream polo shirt and brown trousers with creases running down the front.

"Sure," Sophie said with a smile. She was ready for anything with this guy.

They stepped out onto Calle Obispo and Greg took her hand. Sophie grinned to herself. She was so full of lust for this gorgeous man at her side that she felt heady with excitement. They walked along Calle Mercaderes and took a left turn onto Calle O'Reilly.

"Hey, this street must be named after an Irishman!"

"We all have a little Irish in us – my grandfather was from Belfast."

"Really!"

"This way," he said, leading her into the doorway of a tenement.

"*Hola, Señor!*" An old woman nodded at Greg as he walked through her small and meagre living space with only a table and chair for furniture.

They continued out through the back of the house and entered another tenement with a stairway running up the side.

"Take care – the steps are not safe."

Greg knocked on a door so crooked and eaten by time it barely performed the function for which it was built. The bottom of it grated on the floor as it opened.

From behind, a *mulatto* woman smiled at Greg. She knew him well.

"*Hola, Señor Greg.*"

They broke into conversation in Spanish and Sophie was left feeling like an outsider.

Greg surveyed painting after painting that the woman showed him and they spoke numbers for a good hour. Sophie's patience was starting to wear thin and she was beginning to feel hungry, having missed out on breakfast. She had never been treated like this before by any man. Eventually she interrupted.

"Look, Greg, I'm starving – can we just go?"

"I'm sorry, honey, but I'm working here. You can go back down – there's a tourist café on the corner of Obispo and the street we came off. I'll meet you in it when I'm finished." He turned back to speak to the mulatto woman as if Sophie was already gone.

She was incensed with his treatment but knew that she didn't have any great options other than going back to her sister.

She descended the stairs with shaky steps and went back the way she had come. The old lady was now accompanied by an old man who was chewing on a massive cigar. They were unperturbed by her presence and nodded genially as she passed.

Back on Calle Obispo she spotted a café that had a tourist menu and currency on a card in the window. She took a seat near the open window. She was still angry with Greg for leaving her just sitting there while he did his business. But she wanted him and maybe they could have something more than a holiday romance.

Felipe had a plan to take Emma to Vedado. If he could distract her with sightseeing she might relax. But still she stared at the road ahead as if she were searching for somewhere specific.

"Would you like to see the Plaza de la Revolución?"

"Thanks, I don't mind – it's all new to me."

They were on the edge of Vedado and didn't have far to travel.

Felipe parked up at the side of the road, off Revolution Square.

Emma opened the door and slid out of the car. She wanted to take in the sight before her but she could only think of Paul and wonder and wish she knew why he had killed himself.

"You see there – it is Che," Felipe pointed at a large official building with a bronze wire sculpture of Che Guevara imprinted across it – so big it spanned the entire floors of the highrise building. *Hasta la victoria siempre* was written underneath. "That is the Ministerio del Interior."

"I saw that slogan on a poster on the way to Varadero – is this where Fidel used to speak to the people?"

"I saw him here many times."

Felipe looked at Emma's pretty face as she – oblivious to his attention – surveyed the square. He loved blue eyes. They were so unusual in his country. She was wearing a simple pink T-shirt and white skirt. Her dark hair was held back by her sunglasses and in that instant he longed to kiss her.

"I hope I haven't shocked you," she said suddenly, "by what I said about Paul." She dipped her head and slipped her sunglasses on to cover her eyes from the glaring sunshine.

"My wife ran away from me – with another man. Your husband left you for himself. No one knows what is in another's heart."

He had just described perfectly how she felt and had never been able to put into words. She wanted to hug him then and there. But she wouldn't.

"Thank you, Felipe."

He smiled. He had connected with the beautiful Irishwoman. "Come – I will take you to a very good place for your lunch."

Emma jumped inside the car and let the wind blow through her hair as they drove along La Rampa. The streets in Vedado were laid out in perfect grids and stretched all the way to the Malecón. In the distance Emma saw a large building that she recognised from images she had seen of Havana.

"Is that where we're going?"

"Yes," Felipe smiled.

Emma felt freedom like never before. She was emancipated after confiding in Felipe about Paul and he had shared his sad story of desertion by his wife. In a way they were similar.

As they drove up the palm-tree-lined road that led to the Hotel Nacional Emma couldn't hide the smile across her face. She felt like a character in one of her books. Could Felipe possibly have been sent to her to inspire her to write and live in a new way? She felt giddy as he opened the door of the Buick.

Felipe reached out to take her hand and help her out of the car.

"Thank you," she blushed. "That was without a doubt the best car ride I have ever had."

"You will like it here."

The five-star hotel exuded excellence and opulence. A corridor of arches in classic art-deco style filled the foyer. The building had changed little since the days of Frank Sinatra and Batista.

"Come see the view," Felipe said, gently taking Emma by the arm and guiding her to the garden where residents lounged on the wicker armchairs and surveyed the expansive Malecón and Caribbean Sea. "What would you like to drink?"

"I'd love a cold drink – Coke please."

Felipe went up to the bartender who stood under the shade of a thatched canopy. Emma sat in one of the comfortable chairs and watched the sea crash against the walls of the Malecón. Suddenly her phone rang. She had wondered when it would.

"Sophie," she sighed, "I have some bad news from home."

"I know. I've just read your message."

"Well, there is nothing we can do – according to Donal. Dad is doing well but they have kept him in hospital."

"Typical – there's always some drama with Mum when you go away."

Emma didn't understand what her sister was saying. "What do you mean?"

"I bet all the fuss is over Mum – it's Dad that's been attacked."

Emma knew that she was right. She wished that she was there to ease the tensions that must surely be rising between Louise and their mother.

"Where are you?"

"I'm in the hotel room."

"On your own?"

"I left Greg downstairs. I came back to get changed – we are going to El Patio for lunch. Greg asked me to invite you but we are getting on really well so will you stay away from that restaurant?"

"By all means – don't let me ruin your party!"

"I don't know when I'll see you."

"Just be sure that you are in our hotel by twelve o'clock

tomorrow morning with your bags packed – I don't want to miss our flight!"

Sophie clicked the roof of her mouth with her tongue. "Give me a break. I'll ring Dad later – I wish he'd use that bloody mobile phone I got him for Christmas."

"Mind yourself, Sophie," Emma said and hung up. She really wished that there was something she could do for her family back home. She would ring her mother later and check.

"The waiter is bringing drinks and I asked for some sandwiches."

"Thanks, Felipe."

"Are you all right?"

"Yes, thanks – that was Sophie on the phone – she's tied up for the day."

Felipe nodded. She didn't need to explain. He was delighted with the outcome but hid his feelings discreetly.

"Have you forgiven me for taking so long with the *mulatto* woman?"

"Just about." Sophie batted her eyelids and pushed his arm playfully.

"I have been negotiating with her over a particular painting for some time now and I clinched the deal today. You must be my lucky charm, eh!"

"Glad to be of assistance but this is my last day in Cuba and I need a bit of attention now – especially when I don't know when or if I will ever see you again!"

Greg eyeballed her carefully. "I hope we will meet somewhere. Do you ever go to New York?"

Sophie shook her head. "There was a time when our company did mad things like send me there on research but at the moment we are lucky to stay afloat and the only travel allowed is to China and I don't know for how much longer that will be a runner."

"Things are changing in every aspect of business. A new era is dawning. Art like most commodities is finding it difficult to hold its value."

"Do you ever come to Europe?"

"London about once or twice a year but most of my business is in New York. The UK has been hit hard by recession."

"Don't I know it! I'd love to open up a line of my own."

"Why not? If you can set up a business when times are hard just imagine what will happen when the economy improves."

"I've been toying with the idea of recycling knitwear – literally unravelling and remaking in a different form and mixing wools and tweeds."

"Sounds good. You should go for it."

"Do you really think so?"

"I think everyone should follow their dream – I followed mine."

"Did you always want to deal in art?"

"I wanted to be an artist but my father insisted that I went into a profession that paid – I didn't want to be a doctor like him so I chose banking – and hated it. After he died I invested the money that he left me into art and fell into the business of dealing. My mother told me about all the wonderful artists in Cuba and when I came here that was confirmed. I have luckily fallen into my perfect career."

Sophie watched as he spoke – so gentle and mellow and how his voice soothed her! She really was in danger of falling for this exotic creature.

Greg put his arm around her waist and guided her through the narrow streets of La Habana Vieja. She felt as though she could breathe him in through the heat and dust. If only she had more time with him. She needed to make him want her more – but she was in unknown territory. With all of her other relationships she'd held the trump card and kept her lovers on a string. With Greg, however, she felt vulnerable and unsure of how he felt about her.

The façade of Catedral de San Cristóbal came into view as they left Calle San Ignacio and entered the Plaza. Some wrought-iron tables and chairs were scattered outside an old colonial building where tourists gathered to sip on iced tea and water to cool down from the heat of the afternoon sun.

"This is El Patio – I think you will be impressed."

The maître d' rushed out to welcome Greg. He spoke in Spanish and with an abundance of regard that Sophie had not yet seen in any establishment so far in Havana.

"Shall we eat *al fresco*?"

"Absolutely."

Greg sat so comfortably and confidently in his own skin. He was the most incredible lover. Sophie felt even more insecure and desired some sort of reassurance that today would not be the last time that she would see him.

"Why don't we make a date to meet in – let's say six weeks?"

Greg smiled. "It's difficult for me to think where I will in six weeks – I need to check my diary."

"Go on then – do it now. I've seen you checking your Blackberry for emails."

"Sometimes I have to change plans quickly if a piece of art comes up unexpectedly."

"Well, can you give me a date in two months?"

"I've told you I will be in New York."

"I will have trouble getting more leave after this trip."

"Okay – why don't we email and see what we can do, eh?"

Sophie realised that it was as much commitment as she could expect – she needed to play it cooler. Her head was all over the place – maybe it was the heat of Havana causing her to behave so needily – but deep down she knew that it was the passion and strength of the beautiful man at her side and her desire to have him.

Sophie was always determined to get what she wanted. She recalled having the same feelings of want and need as a child when Louise had her ears pierced. Emma had had hers done when she turned ten. Louise was only eight when her mother gave in to her pleadings. Sophie was four and although half Louise's age she felt it was her birthright to have whatever her older sisters had. Her mother had other ideas. No matter how much Larry Owens begged on his youngest daughter's behalf Maggie wouldn't budge.

"I should never have let Louise get hers pierced and I wouldn't have if I knew I'd have to put up with this whingeing!" she shouted at Sophie. "If you can't wait until you are eight then you can go and live with your Granny Owens!"

Sophie burst into uncontrollable tears. She was in such convulsions that she did have to be sent to her Granny Owens so that Maggie could go ahead with Louise's birthday party with some semblance of peace.

The tears didn't stop though and for seven days Sophie moaned and roared her way around the house with such a temper that Maggie herself brought her to the jeweller's to get a pair of gold studs. That was when Sophie knew that she had broken her parents. There was no turning back after that.

She was so young but she had managed to get exactly what she had wanted.

She was going to get Greg too – she only had a few more hours but knew that she could do it!

"Come," Felipe said as he stood up. "I will show you the hotel."

Photographs of Sammy Davis Junior, Fred Astaire and other American entertainers lined the walls of the hallway.

"I feel like I have been transported back in time today. Your car is gorgeous, Felipe. It must be some prize to have."

"It is difficult to own a car – if you inherited it and it was bought before the revolution then you can keep it. There are many unusual laws in place here. Since Raul took over from Fidel he has tried to make some changes but the older ministers do not want change. For example it is not so difficult to have a phone now."

"I've noticed some people on the streets with them – surely that is a good advancement?"

"There is so much to do – and food is a problem since the hurricane. There is not enough for all the people in the country – more rationing."

"Is there anything you could have done to help if you had stayed a lawyer?"

He shook his head. "It is very difficult to move forward in this country."

"Would you ever consider leaving Cuba?"

"I would like to see the world. Maybe some day."

"If you ever get to visit Ireland you would be very welcome to stay with me."

Felipe laughed.

"Why is that so funny?"

"It is not easy to leave Cuba – so many documents are needed. *Mucho dinero* is needed also."

Emma felt insensitive. "Well, I'll leave you my email address and if you ever get the chance to come to Ireland I would like to show you the hospitality that you have shown me."

Felipe seemed embarrassed. "Would you like to go back to the old town? Or maybe the beach?"

"I'd love to stay in the city – as I only have this one full day."

They walked out of the hotel and back to the Buick which gleamed in the sunlight.

Driving along the Malecón with the wind brushing off her face, Emma felt again as if she had stepped into the pages of her novel. Maybe she could change her plot – why not write something romantic for a change? After all there was nothing more romantic than cruising the Malecón in a vintage American sports car with an attractive Cuban man.

She was definitely more in the frame of mind to write about love at the moment than death. It was death that had been hanging over her for the last seven months.

Chapter 14

Jack sat in the corner of the Quay West restaurant and sipped on his cappuccino. He felt very different sitting on his own to the way he had felt when sharing lunch with Louise.

He wished he could turn the clock back to the day on the DART when he had first seen her again after fourteen years. If he could do that, he would make a point of getting the next train. If he hadn't bumped into her again he would be forging ahead with the plans for his wedding with Aoife and they would be happy – like they were in New York. But as he took his spoon and stirred the hot coffee he recalled the same feeling of doubt that he had felt when they had first purchased the solitaire engagement ring. There were lots of times when he had heard a little voice niggling in his head and asking if he was sure that he was happy with the arrangements. Meeting Louise had only confirmed the doubts that he had hidden.

Jack's phone rang and he answered.

"Hello?"

"Jack – it's Peter."

Jack had to think for a moment – he recognised the voice but wasn't sure where to place it.

"Peter Kelly – from school."

"Peter!" Jack recalled. "How are you doing – it's been years! How did you get my number?"

"I ran into your mother in Killester and she told me all your news. Do you fancy meeting for a beer?"

"Sure – I can't believe it – where are you living?"

"I'm in Glasnevin – I've been home for three years and didn't know you were back too – do you want to meet in town – or we could go local to Harry Byrne's?"

Jack smiled on hearing the name. He hadn't been in Harry's for years and as kids they were always trying to get served there.

"Going local sounds good – what are you doing tonight?"

"I've no plans – tonight is good."

"Okay – about nine?"

"Sounds good – see you then, Jack."

Jack returned to his drink with a smile. He had shared some good times with Peter. They were always close in school. Even though they had been to different colleges they remained good friends. It wasn't until Jack went to the States that they lost touch and men aren't good at maintaining old friendships with Christmas and birthday cards like women are.

He would enjoy catching up on old times.

Aoife went home with her bag full of clothes and toiletries. She was sobbing but didn't know if or what she would tell her mother and father. She didn't think that she could hide her emotions for much longer. Maybe her mother would have some good advice.

She parked up in the driveway and came into the house through the back door.

Her mother sat at the kitchen table with a magazine and mug of tea in front of her.

"Hello, love – are you coming back for another night?"

Aoife nodded but wasn't able to open her mouth for fear of bursting into tears.

Her mother's intuition told her that there was something wrong.

"Aoife, is everything all right, love?"

Aoife shook her head.

Her mother stood up and went over to her and gently brought her over to a chair at the table.

"Sit down and tell me what's wrong."

Aoife burst into tears – covering her stained face with the palm of her hands.

Her mother grabbed some kitchen roll and handed it to her.

Aoife sobbed into the tissue. "It's Jack – something's happened, Mum, but I don't know what – he's gone all funny about the wedding."

"Has he called it off?"

"No, but he doesn't want a big affair. He thinks we are getting too caught up in the whole thing and he wants to postpone it."

"Is he having cold feet?"

"What?"

"Sometimes guys just go through a phase – it's common enough. Your father wasn't great with all the wedding preparations when we were getting married and we only had a small do in the North Star Hotel."

"I don't know what it is."

"What does he want to do?" Eileen's tone was becoming firmer – she couldn't conceal the anger she was feeling towards her daughter's fiancé.

"He wants us to stay living together and postpone the wedding."

"And you told him?"

"I said that I needed to come home and think about it."

"Good girl – the cheek of the pup! Some guys just have it too good. Does he realise how lucky he is to have such a beautiful girl like you – and all your father and I have done to help him!

I tell you – I'd let him sweat a bit. You have plenty of friends here in Malahide still. Go out and enjoy yourself and give him something to worry about."

Aoife took another piece of kitchen roll from her mother and wiped her nose.

"Thanks, Mum."

"It will be okay, you know – everything works out for the best."

"I know," Aoife nodded.

Eileen went over to turn the kettle on and hide the anger etched on her face. If she could get her hands on Jack Duggan she could happily kill him.

Maggie Owens decided that she would like to be brought home.

"Thanks for putting me up but the children are very noisy."

Louise knew that her kids weren't saints but they weren't badly behaved. It was her mother's way of making her feel bad.

"Will you be okay in the house on your own?"

"I'll use the alarm tonight."

"You and Dad should be using it every night – I don't know why you got it fitted if you don't use it."

"I will – I might see if Adele Harris from up the road will stay with me for company – she likes to play a game of cards."

Louise breathed a sigh of relief. It would be wonderful if her mother went home – it had been tense running from the hospital to the house and managing the kids and her mother. Donal had been really helpful – she was feeling more guilty each day about the thoughts she had of Jack. Her life was with her family and it was up to her to keep everything together. It was nice though to think that he still found her attractive.

Jack scanned the back room of Harry Byrne's Bar. It was crowded for a Monday but it was still technically Easter so some people were probably prolonging the holiday. Others had no jobs to go to. He ordered a pint of Heineken while he threw his eyes over the rest of the room.

Peter sat in the corner on a high stool. Jack recognised him instantly – even with the small goatie and thinning hair.

"Hey, good to see you!" Jack held out his hand and they shook vigorously.

"Great to see you, Jack – you haven't changed a bit."

"I was going to say the same about you. It's been a long time."

"I was trying to figure out how long on my way here – it must be seven years."

"I'd say you're about right – there was that Christmas we had drinks up here with Ray and the boys."

"Yeah, did you hear about Ray?" asked Peter.

"No – where is he?"

"He's retired – a dot com millionaire – living in Australia now."

"Well, good for him. Do you ever see anyone else?"

"Conor from our band is still around – living on the southside and working in the car trade – at least he's working."

"I haven't thought of him in years."

"Sometimes I think we did the wrong thing going to college," said Peter, "and we should have stuck together and made our fortune."

"Well, there's only one U2 – how many other bands have tried and never come to anything?"

"That's not like the Jack Duggan I knew in school – you tried to get us to stay together – you were the one that believed we were the next big thing."

"Well, sometimes age and good sense catch up on you."

"Wow, Jack – what's gone wrong? I always relied on you to be upbeat and tell me that I was invincible."

"You've called me on a bad day – woman trouble."

"Your mother said that you were engaged."

"Yes. But – it's a long story really."

"I've plenty of time!"

Jack wondered if he could tell Peter – who was almost a stranger to him now – how he was feeling. It wasn't something he would normally do.

"Let's talk about the good times – do you see Niall?"

"I'm not sure where Niall is – he was crazy about Miss Owens – do you remember her?"

Jack took a sip of his pint. "Eh, yeah – saw her only the other day."

"You're joking – what was she like?"

"Much the same," he shrugged.

"I remember you had a huge crush on her too – I thought she fancied you – it was always 'Jack, will you help me with this?' or 'Jack, could you read that?', or my favourite was 'Jack, could you get the window pole?'!"

Peter laughed heartily but Jack could only manage a whimper of amusement.

"Sometimes it was like you were the only one in the class!"

Jack took a gulp from his pint. "Yeah, well, she was into our band and our music and I guess she was trying to encourage us."

"So tell us – where did you see her?"

"On the DART – and then she was out in Howth with her kids one Sunday."

"She probably wasn't much older than us, thinking about it now. Is she still teaching?"

"No."

"That's a shame – why do the cool teachers always leave? Remember old Hackett – I bet he's still bellowing and putting kids off science for life."

"Yeah – we had good times though. So what about you – hitched, divorced or looking?"

"I'm just happy to be single – had a lucky escape. I was living with a girl for five years. We nearly got married but – it didn't work out – you know how it is."

Jack knew by his tone that there was a story there but it was too early in their re-acquaintance to be informed.

"Are you still doing painting and decorating?"

Peter laughed into his pint. "Is that what I was doing when you last saw me? No, I have moved on, thank God. I trained in advertising when I was in London and I've been working for a graphics company since I came back. It's interesting times at the moment – the recession has made each brief even more challenging."

"That sounds really good."

"And what are you doing yourself?"

"I'm writing – I got a slot in *The Irish Times* and I'm just hanging in there while lots of much more experienced and higher paid guys seem to be getting the chop."

"I bet you are a really good writer. Do you play the guitar still?"

Jack laughed and shook his head. He never thought that he would stop but it had been three years at least since he had strummed a chord. "I'm finished with all that."

"I really miss it – I even bought a set of drums last year but when I split up from my girlfriend I had nowhere to put them so they're in my mother's shed."

"You're crazy – and back living with your mum?"

"Yeah – had to after I finished with Melanie. She took over the apartment we bought – thank God – it's in negative equity now."

"Maybe we should start busking – remember we did it after school a couple of times."

"They were good days, Jack."

Jack grinned. They were very good days. But for a very different reason to the ones Peter was thinking. "Listen, can I tell you a secret? I really don't want you to breathe a word to anyone – ever!"

Peter was intrigued. He had to say yes to find out more.

"It's mad you calling me up like this out of the blue," Jack went on, "because I really need to talk to someone – do you believe in the power of coincidences?"

Peter shrugged.

"Well, I told you that I ran into Miss Owens – the timing has been shit – I'm not sure but I think I was having cold feet about Aoife – my fiancée – then I met Miss Owens for lunch and the truth is – we have a history."

"Explain history?"

"This sounds crazy but before we sat the Leaving I went to her house for some grinds – only the type of grinding we were doing didn't involve books if you know what I mean."

Peter's face dropped. "You didn't?"

"I did." Jack's face was deadpan.

"You dog," Peter grinned. "You total dog – why did you never say anything?"

"Because of the very reaction you've just had!"

"Wow – pretty cool!"

"It was and well the truth is she kind of messed me up for the college girls that I went out with after we split – I couldn't trust a woman for ages."

"What a training – and if you got it wrong did she make you do it over and over again?"

"I was hoping you could be serious about this!" Jack said.

"I am – sorry – just a bit of a shock. I am so jealous – no wonder your head is blown away after meeting her again."

"It's all over the place."

"And what's Aoife like?"

"She's hot."

"I'm going to be sick into my pint. I haven't had a shag in four months – I should have known better than to come here and meet you."

"Sorry, mate. I just have to tell it like it is."

"Well, I'm going to start hanging out where you're going."

Jack laughed. "I don't know what to do!"

"Can't you shag both of them – I mean one is already hitched and the other will be there on tap."

Jack wasn't going to get through to Peter. "Just forget it."

"I won't be able to sleep tonight thinking of you and Miss Owens. I still can't believe you never told any of us."

"I really liked her."

Peter shut up and took a sip from his pint. This was not the sort of conversation he usually had with his mates. "Sorry, Jack, I'm not a good one to give advice. I never had the knack with women – not like you."

Jack didn't agree – if he had the knack he wouldn't be in the state he was now.

Chapter 15

Greg stood up and shook the sand from his body. The sun was going down and the waves were lashing harder against the shore of Playa Santa Maria.

"Hungry, eh?"

"Starving," Sophie replied, eyeing up the lean and muscular body before her.

"Good. I'm meeting a man from the government in an hour in one of the restaurants near Plaza de Armas."

Sophie sat up on her elbows and frowned. She'd presumed that she had the handsome Canadian all to herself. This didn't suit her plans at all.

"I need to go back to the hotel before we go out to dinner," she said.

"We haven't got much time for that. Why don't you go back to your hotel and follow me on? You could see if Emma wants to join us, eh?"

Sophie huffed. This was not the plan she had in mind for the evening. "How are we getting back to Parque Central?"

"We can take a cab – you can drop me off near my hotel on the way – I'll have a shave and quick change."

Sophie pulled on her clothes and tidied up the small bundle of towels and beach gear.

She was silent all the way back in the taxi and as it dropped Greg off at the corner of Plaza de Armas and Obispo she could only manage a fake smile.

"See you in about an hour. The restaurant is painted green – just over there . . ." He pointed.

"Okay," she replied and let the taxi take her back to the Telegrafo.

She was surprised to see that Emma had not returned all day. She wondered what sort of time her sister was having with the taxi driver – as far as she was concerned all native Cubans were on the make – like José in Varadero and she hoped that her naïve sister wasn't getting taken for a ride!

She looked at her watch – it was too late now to ring her father – she should have done it earlier. But it wasn't too late to call Louise.

The dial tone was louder and slower than usual.

"Hello?"

"Oh, hi, Sophie," Louise said in a quiet voice. "What time is it? We're all in bed!"

"It's about half six here. How is Daddy?"

Louise pulled on her dressing-gown and went out to the landing so as not to disturb her sleeping husband.

"He's okay. Mum has gone home tonight."

"I bet that's a relief."

"It will be good when you two get home. It's tough doing the hospital visits on my own."

"I'm going to be very busy when I get back with work."

"Don't push it – you've just had ten days in the sun. I don't begrudge Emma getting the break but you are always going away."

"Are you still mad with me?"

"I can't believe that you went off on holiday with her – after everything you did behind her back!"

181

"That's rich coming from you – like you're some kind of saint."

"I wouldn't do that to my sister!"

Sophie laughed down the phone. "Take a chill pill, Louise. Just be sure to tell Dad when you see him tomorrow that I rang to see how he was. Gotta go here."

She hung up without waiting for a reply. Louise had become so uptight. She certainly wasn't an advertisement for matrimony and parenthood.

She thought of Paul and her heart ached – her perfect life plans shattered. But maybe she could have a fulfilled future – a good marriage with someone who enthralled her – like Greg. They had one more night together but she would make sure that he adored her enough to see her again.

"It's been a lovely day, Felipe," Emma said. "Thanks for showing me so many nice places."

"The sun is setting now – this is the best time in Havana."

"I've taken up so much of your day."

"I had a good time. I want to take you somewhere special to see the sunset. It is a tradition for *Habaneros* to go to La Cabaña."

"Beside the Moors' Castle?"

"Yes, you are learning your way around Habana very fast."

Emma really appreciated having her very own tour guide who was the ultimate gentleman. She wasn't sure how he felt about her. He was by nature a reserved person but feminine intuition told her that he wouldn't be hanging around since ten o'clock in the morning if he didn't have some sort of attraction to her.

"Thanks for staying with me today and showing me all of the sights – it wouldn't be the same on my own."

"I get lonely sometimes also. We can get something to eat and then visit the castle to see *el cañonazo*."

"What is that?"

"Every evening at nine o'clock some Guards of the Revolution dress in the costume of English soldiers and they shoot from *el cañón*."

"Great – it sounds like something I should see."

After eating tasty crab rolls and rice in a small *paladar* that Felipe knew to be the best in Havana they drove along the winding bay to view the city from the other side and see the spectacle of *el cañonazo*. Several tourists and some locals had the same idea and were waiting patiently around the perimeter of an extensive square that gave panoramic views of the rest of the city. They sat on the old eighteenth-century walls and watched as the crowd grew.

"Very soon the soldier will shout '*Silencio!*' to tell the people of the city that the walls are closed for the night," Felipe whispered in Emma's ear.

He did a few seconds later and was followed by six others – one of the soldiers holding a flag and another beating a slow steady march on a drum. Their red costumes and black tricorne hats were dishevelled and unlike those Emma had seen before in movies and museums.

The leading guard took a torch and lit a strip of torches behind the large black cannon. The ceremony was brief and when the flare flew out and a large bang erupted around the bay everyone cheered.

"I've never seen anything like that before – it was really good – thanks for showing me!" Emma said and turned to see the flickering from the torchlight reflect in Felipe's eyes.

"I am glad that you liked it." He smiled and turned his head to watch the end of the spectacle.

It was so romantic sitting with the warm night-time breeze wafting around them. Felipe looked so different from the night before. Emma studied his profile as he looked on – she couldn't tell if he knew that she was staring at him or not. The rebel lawyer who had chucked it all to drive a taxi – how she wished she knew more about him. She wanted to know him better and she only had a few more hours in Havana. In fact, she suddenly realised that she desperately wanted to see him again. If only it was a few months from now! She needed more time to grieve for Paul. But, nevertheless, when she was with Felipe she felt so happy and warm – much more exhilarated than she had felt with Paul for a long time before his death if she were to be honest.

Felipe turned and looked at her. "Would you like to hear some jazz now? I can take you to a good place."

How amazing he is, thought Emma – a cosy jazz club was exactly what she fancied at the end of a perfect day.

"Sounds great."

The drive back around the bay and along the Malecón was electric, with more Habaneros than usual lining the streets.

Emma was recognising her way around. "We are in Vedado now?"

"Yes – you can work in my job soon."

Emma laughed. She would try and remember this moment – how she felt – and put some of these good emotions into her novel.

Felipe took a left turn onto Calle 23 and slowed down. He searched for a space that was near a policed corner and parked up the Buick.

The street was alive with Cubans and tourists heading out for a night of entertainment.

Felipe guided Emma to what looked like an old telephone kiosk – painted red like she used to see in London in the 1980s. The kiosk was adjoined to the doorway of the underground club.

"We are going into that?"

"Yes," Felipe said with a smile at the shock on Emma's face. "This is *La Zorra y el Cuervo* – the best jazz club in Havana."

A tall man with a shaven head and black sunglasses stood just outside the telephone kiosk. He was too handsome to be a bouncer in any other city in the world and also too friendly. He led them into the tight space beyond and down a flight of stairs where hidden underneath was the cave-like bar. The strains of a saxophone and percussion rang in the air before the couple reached the cosy bar area. Pictures and photographs of the many musicians who had played there framed the walls and the usual array of spirits and rum lined the back of the bar. In the corner a large glass case advertised the finest range of Cuban cigars and the smoke from those who were partaking in a Cohiba wafted through the air.

"What would you like?" Felipe asked.

Emma was feeling embarrassed by Felipe's kindness and generosity – he might have the best-paid job in the city but even his tips couldn't maintain the amount that he was spending on entertaining her as his guest.

"Please let me pay."

"It is a different price for me – you pay more because you are a tourist."

"Well, if you insist, but let me pay you back for something – you have been driving me around and looking after me so well all day."

"It is so nice to have your company."

Then Emma saw a glimmer in his eye that confirmed what she had suspected. He was attracted to her.

"Please, sit down," he said.

Emma took a table beside a pillar with a good view of the small stage. A mural decorated the wall behind the musicians. She looked around at the eclectic mix of individuals – some definitely were local. She had seen a type of Cuban man the night before wearing bright white shirt, trousers and beret – the contrast with their dark skin made them stand out amongst the other locals who preferred to dress more colourfully.

Felipe put two glasses of mojito down on the small round table. He pulled back a chair and sat.

"You like it here?"

"It's great – so different to anywhere I've been."

"Very good musicians play here – students from the music school in Habana also."

"It's the perfect way to end the day," Emma said, raising her glass to say cheers.

Felipe smiled. He had enjoyed the day every bit as much. It had been a long time since he had spent so much time entertaining a woman. She wasn't just any woman either – she was so exotic with her black hair and piercing blue eyes – so unlike his wife and most of the women that he'd had brief encounters with since she left. He felt his heart fill with an overwhelming desire to kiss her but the fear of rejection stopped him. His wife had left some bruises on his heart and he would have to be careful because there was a grim reality that after tonight he might never see Emma again.

Sophie made her way cautiously along Calle Obispo – she should have got a taxi. For some reason she thought that the stroll from her hotel to Greg's was much shorter – it had been the night before but that was in his company.

She pushed through the crowd that gathered outside a café where salsa music poured out onto the street.

In the distance she could see the restaurant that Greg had pointed out earlier. He was sitting at a table outside with a man wearing a dark grey suit who was much shorter than Greg and whose belly fell out over the belt of his trousers. His head was shaven and he was chewing on the end of a Cohiba.

Greg stood up as Sophie arrived and he introduced her to his companion, Don Carlos, with his inimitable charm.

"You look beautiful, Sophie!" said Greg.

She allowed him to kiss her on both cheeks and took the chair nearest to him. She wanted to be as far away from Don Carlos as possible – he gave her creeps.

"I hear from Señor Adams that you are Irlandesa?"

"Yes."

"You like our country?"

"It's very nice."

"What you like to drink?"

"I'll have a glass of wine – red – Chilean if you have it."

Don Carlos clapped his hands and the waiter rushed out. He spoke quickly and condescendingly to the young man.

Sophie wished that the horrible little man wasn't there.

Don Carlos continued speaking in Spanish as he addressed Greg – after five minutes Sophie felt as if she was invisible. She wouldn't put up with treatment like this from anyone at home – so why should she do it on her holidays?

The waiter arrived back with a glass of wine and put it down in front of her. She sipped it and decided that she would do something about her situation. She took her phone out of her bag and stood up.

Greg looked up. "Where are you off to?"

"I'm making a call."

Greg went back to his conversation with Don Carlos immediately which irritated Sophie.

She dialled Emma's phone but couldn't get a dial tone. She tried a few times but cursed when the same voice in Spanish told her that the number she had dialled was unreachable. Where could Emma have got to?

Emma drank three mojitos before the band played an encore. The club was casual and nobody minded the patrons chatting while the musicians performed.

"It's been so nice – thank you for bringing me here."

"It is good. Would you like me to take you back to the hotel?"

Emma nodded.

The mojitos had made her heady and giddy and she tripped on the steps as they came up onto La Rampa.

"You know, I don't feel at all tired."

"We can just drive – if you like?"

Emma nodded. The Malecón was alive with young people drinking from bottles of Havana Club. Some were making music. One man sat on the wall and was holding a makeshift fishing rod. Emma looked at her watch – she couldn't imagine any other city in the world with such an abundance of diversity lining its streets at one o'clock in the morning.

It had cooled considerably but the open-top Buick was still the best way to travel.

"Would you like to see the beach?"

"Okay."

Felipe did a U-turn on the road.

"We will go and see Miramar – there are many beautiful houses there. I will show you where dolphins swim."

The streets were straight like those in Vedado and there were several Embassy villas with the flags of different nations hanging from them. The seafront wasn't as spectacular as the winding Malecón but it was more secluded and there were fewer passersby.

Felipe parked up at a quiet spot on Avenida 1 where they had a good view of the sea and could hear it crash against the shore. The moon hung like a disc in the sky – casting droplets of light on the waves which rolled like silver ribbons.

"It's lovely here."

"I like it. Matanzas is not like Habana."

"I'll be sorry to go – although I'll be happy to see my father – I hope he is all right."

Felipe opened the glove compartment and took out a slip of paper – then with a stub of a pencil that he kept in the side of the door he wrote down his phone number and address.

He handed it to Emma. "Please, can you write to me from your country?"

Emma smiled. "Of course – do you have email?"

Felipe shook his head.

Emma reached into her bag and took out her business card. She had printed up two thousand of them a few years ago and so far had given out about fifty.

"Please write to me. I would like to keep in touch. I've shared more with you in the past couple of days than I could ever say to my own family. My parents and my sisters wouldn't understand the pain I carry over my husband's suicide."

"You must not blame yourself. For a long time I took the blame when my wife left – you are a good woman, Emma, and the problem is something that your husband only knew."

Emma could feel her eyes water. She was overcome with the emotion of the beautiful setting, heady with the effects of three mojitos and moved by Felipe's thoughtfulness and care.

"Thank you," she said, leaning back on her seat.

The moonlight touched the side of Felipe's face and the rim of the windscreen.

He turned his head and looked at Emma. He was unable to free his gaze from her eyes. She was exposing her soul and all the hurt that she had been carrying in them. He longed to move forward and kiss her lips – sprinkled with moonlight.

Emma could feel him look right through her – she felt exposed and naked. His wild black hair and dark eyebrows that framed his hazel eyes were transformed by the moonlight. Instead of the quiet mild-mannered man who had been so kind to her she saw a strong figure full of passion and emotion. She was overcome by the desire to feel his lips on hers.

Felipe leaned over until his face was only an inch away from Emma's. Their eyes were locked upon each other – both afraid to make the first move.

And then it happened – their lips met – bathed in moonlight – the kiss was magical.

At exactly the same moment they could feel all the love and hurt inside each other. Their lips merged for what felt like minutes but must only have been a few seconds.

Suddenly Emma pulled away from Felipe – and the handsome man's face became clouded by an image of her dead husband's. The energy she had gained from the kiss was dissipating and all she was left with was a cold empty feeling in her heart. Her grief erupted with huge tears falling down her cheeks.

Felipe took her in his arms and let her head rest on his solid and strong shoulder. His heart was swaying between hers and his own grief. He held her for a long time, stroking her hair and the side of her face, while she released as much hurt as she was able to.

"Maybe you will come back some day?" he whispered in her ear.

Emma sat up – pulling reluctantly away from Felipe's embrace.

"Maybe, Felipe. I would love to visit Cuba again – to see *you* again. But, you know, it might be easier for you to visit me in Ireland."

Felipe laughed.

"Why is it so funny? I would like you to see where I live – it is an island too."

"It is very difficult to leave my country – and very expensive – even for a taxi driver."

Felipe turned the key in the car.

She felt suddenly very naïve and hated herself for being so insensitive – she really had learned very little about Cuba or the restrictions its people lived with.

They drove silently back to Parque Central and Felipe pulled up at the door of the Hotel Telegrafo.

"Would you like me to take you to the airport?"

Emma was thrown by the simple question. She hadn't thought about it. "I don't know – what's the arrangement? It will be organised by the tour operator, won't it?"

Felipe shook his head. Her hesitation hurt. He had to protect himself – he didn't want to fall in love and was treading dangerous territory.

"Maybe it is best to say goodbye now," he said.

Emma was racked with the guilt of the kiss but aching to see him again. She got out of the car and stood on the pavement.

"Thank you so much for all that you have done."

She felt like a little girl lost – standing on the side of the road.

"I have done nothing." He nodded his head gently. "I had a good time – I hope you have a good voyage home, Emma."

Then he turned and put his foot on the accelerator pedal and drove the Buick out onto the road without looking back.

Emma felt that he was taking a part of her with him in his car. She didn't want to go back to her hotel room on her own. She looked at her watch – it was nearly two o'clock in the morning. Time had passed so quickly in Felipe's company. She turned and went into the hotel and took the stairs instead of the lift. Her heart was heavy with each step that she took. Inside she was aching with a mixture of emotions that left her feeling confused. She wasn't expecting to find Sophie in the room when she arrived but there she was, curled up in a ball with a sheet over her body as she slept soundly. She was curious to know what had happened with Greg but would have to wait until the morning to find out.

Sophie threw her luggage onto the check-in carousel with such awkwardness that Emma was tempted to lean in and fix it – but Sophie was a big girl and maybe it was time that she took responsibility for herself.

Emma handed the tickets over to the Air France steward who checked their passports and documents for the flight.

"*Merci, madames*. Your flight departs from Gate Two."

Emma smiled and thanked the air steward and followed Sophie who had already stomped off.

"Wait a minute!" she called.

Sophie stopped.

"Sophie, if you don't talk to me then how will I know what's the matter?"

"I told you I don't want to talk about it. I just want a drink of juice."

"You should have come down for breakfast with me."

"I told you I wasn't in the mood."

They passed through security and set off for duty free.

"This is a long flight and if you are going to sulk then we can change seats and you can sit next to someone else."

"That's fine by me!" Sophie snapped.

They boarded the plane and took their seats silently. Sophie stuck her head into the in-flight magazine.

They were over the Atlantic Ocean before Emma started the conversation.

"So what happened with Greg?"

"He was so selfish – he arranged to meet this really rude little man who is a state official. I was bored out of my brain for almost three hours. And where were you? I was trying to call you?"

"You made it perfectly clear that you didn't want to see me until we were on our way to the airport."

"You were probably with that taxi driver."

"Felipe was very charming and don't call him 'that taxi driver' – anyway, he is a lawyer."

Sophie's ears pricked up. "You're joking!"

"What does it matter what his profession is? He was good company and fun."

"I suppose it's about time you moved on. Paul is gone and it's time to get over it."

"He was my husband – you wouldn't understand."

Sophie glared at Emma. The cheek of her – she always put her down with little one-liners like that.

"Just because there were a few years between us as kids," she said, "doesn't mean that you are the oracle now. I know a damn sight more about loss than you could imagine."

The chief steward was handing out pillows and blankets to passengers who wanted to go to sleep. The two sisters' voices were becoming more animated and louder as the conversation was progressing and those sitting around were taking notice.

"What loss have you ever known? You didn't even come to Granny's funeral because you were going to Amsterdam for the weekend to smoke joints with your friends – that's the kind of priorities you have!"

An old lady sitting in front of the sisters turned to see who was making such a racket. The two carried on their conversation regardless.

Sophie turned the overhead light on. "She hated funerals – she always said so – and I'd have lost my flight and the hotel was pre-paid. Anyway I don't have to answer to you."

"You don't answer to anybody – you just run to Dad and he always gives in and bails you out – no matter what it is!"

"I pay my way."

"How come Dad paid for your car insurance then this year? Mum told me so don't deny it. Louise and I have families to look after and you still run off sponging whatever you can from him – and he's only got his pension now."

"You're just jealous. You've always been jealous of me – I suppose you have good reason to be."

Emma's brows furrowed and she shook her head with disgust. "Give me a break – why on earth would I ever be jealous of you?"

"Because I can have any man that I want."

Emma's frown turned to a smile. "Because you nabbed some Canadian on holiday? You probably only wanted him because he chatted me up first – he bought me lunch."

"But he shagged me!"

"Like that's something to be proud of?"

Sophie turned pink with fury. "Fuck off!" she screamed – loud enough for an air steward to hear and look to see who was making the din.

"It's time you grew up and found a real man to have a mature relationship with," Emma said coldly.

"But I *was* having a mature relationship – a very real relationship that was going to be permanent – *who* do you think your husband was sleeping with for three years before he died?"

The air steward had identified the culprits and was walking up the aisle to where the two sisters sat.

Emma's eyes widened. She could not believe what she was hearing – she felt as if she was about to vomit.

"Tell me that you are lying."

"I won't – I was sleeping with Paul – we were lovers and he was about to leave you before he had his heart attack!"

Emma started to shake – unable to speak.

"Is everything all right, Madame?" the steward asked, realising full well that everything was not.

"I need another seat," Sophie demanded.

"We are very full tonight, Madame."

"Just get me away from her!" Sophie said as she stood up and reached to the overhead locker for her bag.

Emma put her head into her hands – she was trembling from her very core.

"Come with me," the air steward said, leading Sophie to a seat at the very back of the plane.

Emma was hyperventilating and about to erupt into a cascade of tears. This couldn't be. How could her husband be so deceitful? How could she never have guessed that he was with another woman – and that that woman could be her sister? Her mind spun around like a spinning top. She longed to touch Irish soil. To be home again where she could try and make sense of this new revelation. For now she needed a brandy to calm her nerves. She reached up to the call button and hit it.

Chapter 16

Finn stood at the barriers of Dublin Airport beside his Aunt.

"Is her plane in yet?"

Louise looked up at the screen. "She landed about five minutes ago so she should be through in about twenty minutes."

Finn jigged around – full of anticipation – Louise had never seen him so excited.

"Do you want to sit down while we're waiting?" she asked.

He just shook his head.

Sophie appeared first. She was pushing a trolley but Emma was nowhere in sight.

Louise rushed up to give her a kiss. Sophie let Louise brush her lips briefly off her cheek. "Where's Emma?"

"Still inside. I'm not sitting in the same car as her – I can't stand another minute with her – I'm getting a taxi."

Louise's stomach muscles clenched – Emma and Sophie seldom fought but when they did it was usually apocalyptic.

"What happened?"

"I don't want to talk about it. I'm going now."

Sophie stomped off in search of a taxi rank leaving Louise speechless and confused.

Louise looked around to see Emma hugging her son warmly. She rushed up to her sister and when she was finished hugging Finn threw her arms around her.

"Emma – did you have a nice time?"

Emma gave her sister a kiss on the cheek. She was still shaking from her words with Sophie but trying to conceal the anguish she was feeling.

"Louise – thanks for looking after Finn so well – it was lovely, thanks. How's Dad?"

"He's doing well – what's the matter with Sophie?"

"I need to talk to you about that – but later." She gave a nod to indicate that the conversation was not suitable for her son's ears.

"Will I take you straight home?"

"Please – I'm exhausted – I didn't sleep a wink on the plane."

"Don't worry about Dad. He's stable and he said not to bother visiting until tomorrow."

"I bet he wants to see Sophie!"

Louise said nothing. Her father *had* been asking for Sophie but he would probably have to wait until she decided she felt like visiting him.

"I'm so glad you're home – you're the only one that can handle Mum. She's been driving her neighbours mad – you know the way she's so demanding."

"I'll get changed and do a few bits then I'll go see her – then I need to speak to *you*."

"I've got a bag of stuff in the car – it's just bread, milk, a few rashers and some fruit."

"Thanks, Louise – that was really good of you." Emma was touched.

"We are going to have our hands full for a while – Dad has to have a triple bypass."

Emma looked at her knowingly – she hoped that he would be okay but knew that she would have to be positive. It was her role as eldest sibling to support the rest of the family.

"Sugar!" Emma sighed heavily with the news. "I guess we should be glad he didn't have a heart attack. At least they've got the knack of that operation nowadays."

"It's not Dad I'm worried about."

"I know," Emma replied. Her mother would be difficult to cope with – it would be like having two invalids.

"Finn, love," said Louise, "do you want to go to the yacht club with Donal and Matt while I visit Gran with your mum?"

"Okay," Finn nodded. Now that he had his mother home he was happy to go off with his cousin again.

"Good," Louise said. She had a terrible feeling that whatever it was that Emma had to talk to her about it was serious.

Louise drove to Raheny after she had left Finn with his uncle and cousin in the Yacht Club.

"Go on, I'm all ears," she said to Emma.

"Sophie said something on the plane and I'm not sure if she's just trying to be a bitch but she couldn't make this one up."

Louise took a gulp of air and braced herself. "Go on."

Emma was close to tears. "She said that she slept with Paul – not just that – she was having an affair with him."

Louise kept her eyes on the road. She was trembling. She had hoped that Emma would never find out.

"Say something!" Emma begged.

Louise was torn. Should she tell Emma that she already knew? Probably not because then Emma would be furious that she hadn't told her.

"I don't believe it – are you sure she's not messing?"

"Why would she say such a thing?"

"To wind you up?"

"She usually tries a different tack when she's doing that."

Louise pulled the handbrake as they stopped at a set of traffic lights. She turned to Emma.

"I don't know what to say."

Emma erupted into tears. "I was just coming to terms with Paul's death – I had such a good time in Cuba. There was this really gorgeous guy – he drove a taxi and he looked a bit like Che Guevara. He was so kind to me – his name is Felipe."

"Did you have a holiday romance?" asked Louise, surprised.

"I wouldn't call one kiss in Havana a full-blown affair but I did like him."

"Where was Sophie while you were with Felipe?"

"She was with a Canadian art dealer – he was gorgeous too – I met him first but when Sophie met him she set her sights on him."

"She always wants whatever you have."

"Exactly – which makes me think that maybe she was having an affair with Paul."

Louise took off again along the road – they were nearly in Raheny.

As they came to their mother's house Louise stopped the car and turned to Emma.

"You know, we will probably never know – I mean, Paul isn't here to defend himself."

Emma sighed. "I realise that but it would explain why he was so strange before he died."

"Was he? You never said that before."

Emma hadn't wanted to admit it – to herself or to anyone else. "It just doesn't make sense why he booked this holiday and then . . ." she stopped – she couldn't go on without explaining other details. "Let's get this over with – Mum's expecting us."

Maggie Owens was sitting in an armchair with a blanket over her lap and feeling very sorry for herself.

"Mum, how are you?" Emma said, going over to give her mother a hug.

198

"Emma – thank God you're home. It's been terrible – I've had the most awful time and I'm scared in this house on my own."

"I'll make a cup of tea," Louise said to deaf ears. Her mother could have stayed on in her house if she had more tolerance of the children – it was her choice to leave.

"The shock of the burglary must be awful," said Emma. "Would you like to stay with me?"

"I think I might – this house is too big and I'm hearing noises at night."

Louise put the tea bags into the pot and searched the back of the cupboard for some coffee for herself.

She was stuck between a rock and a hard place – part of her felt as if she had to tell Emma that she knew about the affair – in case Sophie told her first that she already knew. Another part of her felt that it would devastate Emma too much to think that she had known and not told.

There was no way out.

Sophie turned the heating on in her apartment in Custom House Square. It wasn't particularly cold but she had become accustomed to the heat in Cuba. She was feeling very sorry for herself as she scanned the cupboards for provisions. She would have to go down to the Italian café on the corner to get something to eat.

Jet lag was setting in and she was meant to be back at work. She was sick now that she realised what she had done. Why had she told Emma about Paul? Maybe she needed recognition for her loss too. But instead all she had done was made Emma hate her – Emma had always protected and looked after her when she was small and she had betrayed her sister in one of the most horrible ways possible.

She changed into a pair of jeans and grabbed a warm jacket before setting off for a bowl of pasta.

The complex on the banks of the Liffey was much quieter than it had been when Sophie moved in first and many apartments were now lying idle. Things were changing too rapidly for her liking. The downturn in the economy echoed in her life.

Suddenly her mobile phone rang and she wasn't surprised to see Louise's number on the screen.

"Hello – I was wondering when you'd call."

"Is that all you have to say for yourself?"

"Don't you start – you really piss me off the way you go on with your double standards!" said Sophie, aware she was being defensive. "I loved Paul – I've been grieving too and it's about time Emma found out."

"And what do you think it's done to her? You've achieved nothing except shown what a little bitch you are! You had a chance to avoid all this and leave Emma with some good memories of her husband."

"He was my lover!"

"Give me a break – you were his bit on the side!"

"He was going to leave Emma – he had planned to bring me to Cuba – not Emma."

"I don't care what that bastard had in mind – but I do care about Emma. I don't know how you are going to get yourself out of this one – don't be surprised if Emma won't speak to you ever again."

"I couldn't care less!" But she did care.

"And what about Mum and Dad – what do you think it's going to do to them?"

"I'm not going to tell them and I bet Emma won't either."

Louise hated it when Sophie was right. There was no way that Emma would upset her mother and father.

"Just watch out, Sophie – you've done it this time."

Sophie hung up. She'd had it with people who were not there for her.

She thought of Greg and the way she had left him two nights

before. He was so gorgeous and she really felt that he was someone that she could possibly love.

But Greg hadn't been overtly keen to spend her last night in Havana with her. He let her go so that he could stay talking to a boring little Cuban man and didn't even come to her hotel when he was finished like she had suggested. The way he looked at her business card when she handed it to him before leaving left her feeling mad with herself. Greg and José – they were two men in Cuba who had treated her in a way that she had never been treated before – and never would be again if she had her way.

She suddenly wanted to get out of Dublin city and try something new. Maybe it was running away – but she felt she might be left with no choice once the reality of what she had said to Emma had sunk in properly.

Jack was trying hard to get a piece finished before the six o'clock deadline. Aoife was on his mind. After meeting Peter for a drink the night before he realised that he had to get Louise out of his head for good. But that was easier said than done.

Gerry his boss walked over to Jack's desk and put a memo on it. "I want you to go out to Beaumont hospital and cover the MRSA bug – can you do that in the morning?"

"Sure." Bugs were just where he felt he was at right now.

"I want you to interview William Fitzmaurice – he's meant to be in charge of hygiene."

This was going to be riveting. Jack nodded and put his head back over his laptop.

An icon flashed telling him that he had got mail – it was from Aoife.

I've been thinking about things and I don't want to see or speak to you for a week. Please don't contact me. I will ring you when the week is up.

Aoife

Jack was surprised by the coldness of her message. He had never known her to be that way with anyone. He couldn't reply – he had to follow her wishes. He didn't feel he could talk to Louise either because she seemed to have a lot on her plate last time he had called. He didn't want his family knowing that he and Aoife had problems either. He would put his head down and concentrate on his work.

Sophie breezed into work – glowing with sun-kissed skin. She was in the building only a few seconds before she realised that something was terribly wrong. Geraldine on reception wasn't sitting in her usual place and the coffee machine was plugged out at the wall. Harry was cleaning out his desk of all papers and personal belongings. Sophie walked up to him but he didn't stop cleaning diligently.

"What's going on?" she asked.

Harry lifted his head. "Sophie – did you have a good time?"

"Great – what's going on?"

"Haven't you heard – we've gone bust. Rod's done a runner with any cash he had left in the company. We won't even be paid redundancy."

"Hold on – is this some kind of joke?"

"I'm not laughing – we all got an email on Thursday to say that was it – the company was going into receivership and Rod had left the country."

Sophie went into her office and turned on her computer. This couldn't be happening. How could everything just disintegrate so quickly? She read through her emails and saw the one from Rod. She was sick to the pit of her stomach – when she thought of all the hours she had given to this company and how hard she had worked to get good contracts – contracts that wouldn't be honoured now. She checked the rest of her mail – most of it from disgruntled shops and buyers. Then she came across one that made her look twice. It was from Greg Adams.

Sorry the way things turned out – I'm at the mercy of the bureaucracy in Cuba – hope to catch up with you in 6 weeks????
Greg x

The email brought a smile to her face even though she hated herself for giving into this bad boy. But how could she go anywhere in six weeks? She had a huge credit card debt – thankfully her mortgage wasn't too bad but she was going to have trouble paying for her little Mazda sports car. She had never been without an income in her life – even when she was in school she had a job as lounge girl that paid for make-up and CDs. She had to tell someone her terrible news but she didn't think Emma or Louise would listen to her right now. She stormed out of the office.

"Bye, Sophie!" Harry called. But she ignored him.

She ran down the stairs and got into her car. She would go to Beaumont Hospital and see her father – Daddy had always been there for her before.

Louise went over to the reception desk and the prim lady with the spectacles on her nose.

"Excuse me, can you tell me – is Larry Owens still in the heart ward?"

The woman didn't look up. She tapped some digits into the computer and waited.

"He's in St Bridget's – he is in pre-op."

"Thank you," Louise said. Emma had been in earlier and assured her that their father was in much better form.

"Louise?"

She turned around with surprise on hearing her name called.

It was Jack and the sight of him brought a smile to her face.

"I was wondering if I'd bump into you," he said. "I've been sent to cover a hospital story. Do you have time for a coffee?"

"Yeah. How have you been? I've been thinking about you."

"I've been better. Do you remember Peter Kelly from school?"

Louise had to think for a second. "Name rings a bell – was he a friend of yours?"

"Yeah – well, we had a pint the other night – and he talked about you!"

Louise blushed. "Let's go to the canteen."

"How's your dad doing?"

"I'm on my way up to see him now – it turns out that the burglary might be a blessing in disguise – he needs a triple bypass and could have dropped dead at any time if he hadn't been diagnosed."

"That's mad."

They continued on down the corridor until they came to the canteen.

Louise heard her name called again and this time knew before she turned who it was.

"Sophie – are you only going in to see Dad now?"

Sophie shook her mop of curls. "I've had the most horrendous morning – I went into work to find I don't have a job any more." She threw her eyes over Jack and Louise could see her brain at work. "Sophie Owens – I'm Louise's sister," she said with a wide smile.

"I'm Jack."

Sophie tilted her head in acknowledgement. "It's a pleasure to meet you."

Louise felt uncomfortable. It was Sophie in her predatory form.

"So what happened in work?" Louise asked – although after what Sophie had done to Emma on the flight home she felt it difficult to look her in the eye.

"My boss shut up shop and sent everyone an email last week to say that he was leaving the country. It's bizarre. I don't know what I'm going to do – there are so many people out of work."

"Would you like to join us? We're going for a coffee," said Jack.

"I could do with one – thanks."

Louise was furious. How did Sophie manage to mess everything up – even an innocent coffee with Jack? She could see at once that he was attracted to her. It didn't seem to matter where she was, Sophie had a biological magnet that pulled men to her. She didn't have to do anything and she had them captivated.

They stood in a line and waited.

"Do you want something to eat?" Louise asked Jack.

"No, thanks."

"I'll have a chocolate muffin," Sophie said pointing to the plate on the top of the counter.

Louise put one on a tray and ordered three black coffees.

"Will you get us a table, Sophie?" Louise glared.

Sophie shrugged and set off to get somewhere to sit.

Louise smiled at Jack. "I'm sorry about that – I was hoping we could talk."

"You never told me you had such a hot sister!" Jack said, his eyes following Sophie down the room.

"She's a lethal weapon. Trouble with a capital T."

"Even I can see that – but she's really gorgeous."

"It's fun having her for a sister – not!" Louise joked.

But Jack was obviously taken by Sophie's bubbly personality and sexy appeal.

"Before we go back down to her, tell me about Aoife," said Louise.

"She doesn't want to see me for a week. She said she'll call me after that."

Louise worried for Jack. Part of her felt that he should go back and apologise to Aoife and make everything all right and another part wanted him to stay away from Aoife and be in love with her.

"I'll take that," Jack said, leaning across to lift the tray of coffees.

When they reached Sophie she was beaming and in full-on flirt mode.

"So Jack – where do you work?" she asked, taking a bite of her muffin.

"I'm a journalist. *The Irish Times*."

"I don't suppose they need any fashion designers, do they?"

"I don't know about the fashion pages – I could ask Brenda – she's the fashion editor."

"Would you? That would be so kind." Sophie gave that sad-eyed look that Louise had seen used so many times.

Louise lifted her mug and took a sip of her coffee. It would be just Sophie's luck to get a new job hours after she lost her old one.

"So, Jack – what story are you covering?" she asked.

"I have to see the head of hygiene about the MRSA bug that's sweeping through Irish hospitals. As if there isn't enough bad news!"

"I didn't realise how bad things were in my place," said Sophie. "I mean, we had orders coming in and lots of stock. I wonder what's going to happen to it all now."

"You better not tell Daddy when you're talking to him," said Louise. "He's going under a general anaesthetic in a few hours and I don't want him to be upset about anything. He's worried sick about Mum already."

Sophie rolled her eyes. "It will cheer him up when he sees me. Have you got a loan of twenty euros? There's nothing in my account and I want to bring him something to read."

Jack pulled a copy of *The Irish Times* from his bag. "Here, give him this."

"Thank you," she said with a huge grin.

Louise reached into her bag and produced a ten-euro note. "That's all I have – I need change for the car park. Are you going up to see him now?"

Sophie realised that her time was up and turned to Jack. "It was lovely meeting you. Thanks for the paper."

"You're welcome."

Louise watched as her sister sidled between the tables taking full advantage of the moves to wiggle her bottom in a way that would cause Jack to stare.

"She's something else!" Jack said, taking a sip from his coffee.

"You could say that again. What are you going to do about Aoife?"

"Nothing I can do until she contacts me."

"Be careful, Jack. Don't throw it all away."

"This is ironic, isn't it?"

Louise pursed her lips and took up her cup of coffee. "I just don't want to see you making a mistake with your life."

"Would it be a mistake? Maybe we're wrong together and meeting you has helped me to see that?"

Louise felt uncomfortable with Jack's analogy. It would imply that she had done the wrong thing by going through with her wedding – but her three children were enough evidence for her to feel that she had taken the right path and followed her destiny. Running into Jack again had caused her to question it and, although she was trying to convince him to do the right thing, she wasn't convinced herself.

"Just tread carefully – don't do anything that you will regret."

Jack looked down at his cup. "We can't change the past. For some reason our lives have crossed paths again."

Louise looked at Jack. "I just wish I knew why!"

Sophie dawdled along the corridor, peeking into each room as she passed. In the corner of a four-bed ward she saw Larry, lying on his side with his eyes closed. A bottle of Lucozade sat on the locker beside his bed.

She went in, grabbed a chair and pulled it over beside him.

His eyes opened on hearing the din.

"Sophie, you're back!"

"Hi, Daddy, what mischief have you been up to while I was away – beating up young lads, I hear?"

"Oh, Sophie, it's so good to see you!"

Sophie leaned down and kissed her father on his forehead. "So when are you going under the knife – I hear they are going to make you a brand new man!"

"I don't know what they are on about – this place is full of queer characters. I'd be better off in my own bed at home."

His face was a pallid grey and the fine lines under his eyes and cheeks had developed into bags in the short time since Sophie had been away. She had never realised how thin his white hair had become on the top of his head.

"You're going to be okay. Has Mum been in?"

"No. She's so upset – I'm worried about her – now she has this operation on top of everything else."

"Daddy, you are the one having the operation – don't worry about her – she'll have Emma running around as usual."

"Thank God you're both home safely!"

"You need to relax, Dad. Everything is going to be fine."

"I hope so. I've never had an anaesthetic before."

"You'll be like a new man when you get out of here. But, Dad, you'll never believe what happened to me. I arrived home to find out that my job is gone – the whole company shut down."

"Oh Sophie, that's terrible!"

"I know – I can't believe it."

"I have savings in the Credit Union if you're stuck. The book is in the bottom drawer of my locker at home – your mother doesn't know about it and, if the worst comes to the worst and I don't wake up from this operation, you'll get double what's in it."

"Don't be like that, Dad. Of course you will wake up – I told you they're going to make a new man of you."

"I really hope so, pet."

And for the first time in her life Sophie could see real fear etched across her father's eyes.

Chapter 17

Felipe met a newly wed couple from the Paris flight. He took their bags and put them in the back of his Renault. He had been working on autopilot since leaving Emma at her hotel door two nights before. He couldn't get her out of his head. It was unlike him to let someone touch him so deeply and he wished that he hadn't driven off so quickly on the last night of her stay in Havana. He could have tried to change his shift and taken her to the airport but he was afraid that maybe if she saw him again she would be different towards him after they had shared that one kiss and he didn't want to take that chance. Instead he was left wondering if he would ever see her again.

Felipe set off on the long drive to Varadero while the couple in the back fondled each other, oblivious to his presence. He was glad to be free with his thoughts and not to have to inform the new arrivals about his country.

He wondered if he should write to Emma – the regular post took so long but he didn't have access to a computer any more and he didn't have an email address. He felt the breast pocket of his shirt. He had put her card there for the last two mornings.

He could always try and get someone who worked in a hotel to send her an email . . . He thought of Dehannys.

At the hotel he lifted out the luggage and handed it over to the porter. The young couple were so entwined they didn't bother to say goodbye to him. He shut his car up and strolled through the majestic lobby of the hotel. The pool and gardens acted like a backdrop to the open staircase that led out of the back of the reception area.

The bar where Dehannys worked was at the beach and quite a stroll. He set off to find her and all the time was thinking of Emma.

Dehannys was polishing some glasses when Felipe spotted her. "*Hola!*"

"Dehannys – how are you and your family?"

"Well – and your father?"

"He is fine." He hesitated. "Dehannys, I need some help and I thought of you. Can you use the email in the hotel?"

Dehannys' face showed that it would not be a straightforward task. "I have an address but Diego won't allow staff into the computer room. He has Estella working there all of the time and she will tell."

"When is her day off?"

"Fridays, I think."

"Who is on then?"

"Pedro sometimes, Raphael sometimes."

"Okay – can we try on Friday if I call by?"

"We can try – who do you want to email?"

"The Irishwoman – Emma."

"She was a very good person."

Felipe nodded. He felt as if he was on a wild-goose chase but he couldn't help but try. After all, he had nothing to lose.

Emma opened her suitcase and started to remove her clothes from it. It was the first chance she'd had since arriving home and her first chance to deal with the implications of her row with Sophie on the airplane. She didn't know how she was going to look her in the eye ever again. Suddenly the doorbell rang. Emma sighed – she wouldn't get a chance to sort out her clothes now.

Louise stood at the door with her mother and a large overnight bag at her side.

"Hi," Emma said, giving her mother a kiss on the cheek.

Louise handed her the bag and with it the responsibility of their mother.

"Come on, Mum, and we'll get you set up in front of the TV," said Louise.

Maggie walked into the room. Emma and Louise looked at each other and didn't need to say a word. Maggie had developed a psychosomatic limp since the incident.

"I'll put the kettle on and make us a cup of tea," Emma said with a smile.

Louise followed her into the kitchen once she had her mother set up.

"How have you been doing?"

"Okay. Have you spoken to Sophie?"

"I rang her."

"What did she say?"

This was a tough one – Louise wasn't sure what the right answer was. "Well, she has no remorse – I think she's glad that she told you."

Emma took a sharp breath. "Coffee for you?"

"Yeah, thanks."

"I don't know how I'm going to cope with seeing her again."

"You need to sort this out. It's not like you can avoid each other for the rest of your lives."

"I could try."

"And then Mum and Dad will find out."

"I don't really care what they think any more – there's been too much skirting around issues in our family – we've been doing it all our lives – protecting Mum from this – covering up for Sophie with that – I'm sick of all the lies and deceit."

"Nothing is straightforward," Louise said, biting her lip – at the back of it all she had her own skeleton in the cupboard.

"Well, I'm not protecting anyone except Finn from now on – and I won't be judged for what I do or say. To hell with Paul – to hell with Sophie – I don't care about responsibility."

"Yes, you do – or you wouldn't have Mum coming to stay with you."

"If she gives me any grief she's going straight home."

Louise was aghast. This was Emma speaking with a completely new voice. "That guy you met in Cuba has had a big effect on you, Emma!"

Emma lifted her cup of tea from the counter. "I've crossed a bridge. Going away couldn't have come at a better time. I'm not afraid any more – what's the point?"

"What were you afraid of?"

"Now that I think about it – everything. I wasn't even able to write another book for Christ's sake. I've been so busy living my life in accordance with those around me that I wasn't fulfilling my own needs. And as for Paul – well, there aren't really words to describe how I feel about him at the moment."

Louise was startled by the new Emma. She was in a dangerous mood and Louise would have to be very careful how she handled her sister from now on.

Only one day had passed before Louise got a text message from Jack. It wasn't what she expected but she wasn't surprised either.

Can u business card ur sisters number? J

Louise was tempted to ignore the text but that would be juvenile. She did as she was asked and waited for a reply. But Jack didn't answer

Donal was back at work and in a couple of days the kids

would be back to school. She felt so empty already. What was she doing with her life? She retreated to the piano and started to play. It was Debussy again – she felt safe with him. As she played her father was having a major operation and she hoped that he would be all right. There was a shift going on in the family on such a huge scale that she worried about the final outcome.

Suddenly her phone rang. It was the person she wanted to speak to the least in the world. However she would have to humour Sophie until her current phase of mischief-making passed.

"Louise?"

"Yeah, Sophie."

"You'll never guess – that friend of yours Jack just called – he's such a dish – where did you meet him?"

Louise hesitated. "Oh, I think he did articles about the school or something."

"Well, he said that the fashion editor wants someone to do a few bits and pieces, styling and that, and she's going to interview me tomorrow."

"That's great news, Sophie." Louise was trying to sound enthusiastic but she didn't want Sophie anywhere near Jack Duggan – especially not in work.

Louise rang Jack immediately once Sophie had hung up.

"Hi, Jack."

"Louise – how are you?"

"I've been better to be honest. Look, Jack, I hope you don't mind me saying this but my sister is trouble – so watch out."

"She's only going to help out while someone is away."

"I know my sister – give her a wide berth."

Jack didn't like Louise dictating to him like this – Sophie seemed nice and he was only giving her a break because she was Louise's sister.

"Look, I probably won't even see her – I'm always on the road."

"She's dangerous – please don't ever tell her about us and our past."

"Why would I do that?"

"Just be careful."

"Forget it – I won't be seeing her. Anyway, how are you doing? How's your father?"

"He's in surgery as we speak. I'll be going in to see him later."

"Well, I hope he's okay."

"Thanks – any word from Aoife?"

"She said a week and I think she means it. I'm going out with Peter again tonight."

"Well, say hi to him – or maybe it's better to say nothing."

"Take care, Louise."

"Bye, Jack."

When he hung up she felt sad. She returned to her ebony and ivory keys until it was time to pick up Tom and Molly from their friend's house. She was anxious for her father and worried about Emma. Everything had changed so suddenly and she wondered what life was going to throw at her next.

Emma braced herself in front of the laptop. She hadn't written a word since she left Varadero. But now that she was home she was ready. Her mother was asleep in the spare bedroom and Finn was watching a DVD with his friend Gavin downstairs. He missed the company of his cousins since he came home so she arranged for Gavin to come for a sleepover. She didn't care if her mother didn't like the idea – this was her house and she would cater for her son's needs as much as her mother's.

With everybody provided for, she set off for the peace of her study. Now that she knew the reason why Paul had killed himself she felt so different. Of course she was only guessing that Paul killed himself because he got into a situation that he couldn't get out of but she knew him so well she felt she understood now why he had done what he did. The revelation had taken a great weight off her shoulders. The responsibility of driving someone to take their life had been too much to bear. But now she carried different emotions for Paul and her sister. They had done what they did and it was time for her to move on too.

Before she started, she pictured Felipe's tossed black hair and the deep-set eyes on the screen of her laptop. Their time together might have been different if she had known in Havana what she knew now.

Felipe was strong and protective that last day that they had spent together and the memories of that one moonlit kiss still rested on her lips. She reached for her handbag and the scrap of paper that he had scribbled his address and phone number on. She would love to hear his voice – the way he said "Emma" still rang in her ears.

She ran her eyes over the chapters that she had written already – Martin was a good man but life was made awkward for him through no fault of his own – she needed to change the character's circumstances and then perhaps he could get to be with the woman he was meant to be with. Somehow she felt that Martin was going to be the one to change the plot of the novel but how she wasn't yet sure. Something needed to happen – she needed a sign – something monumental that would help her make the right decisions for her characters.

Suddenly her phone rang – at once she searched for it in case it was word on her father.

Louise's voice came on the other end of the line.

"Emma?"

"Hi, Louise – any word?"

"It's good news. The operation has been a success but he's not out of the anaesthetic yet."

"Thank God. When are you going in to see him?"

"I'm in here now. They told me to go home and come back in the morning."

"Great."

"How's Mum?"

"In bed with a headache."

"Of course she is."

"I'm going to do a bit of writing tonight."

"Glad to hear it – I'll buzz you in the morning."

"Thanks, Louise."

Emma returned to her laptop – she wanted to escape. She wanted to be in her own imaginary world where Martin, her fictitious hero with Felipe's face, would do what she wanted him to do.

Donal sat back on the reclining chair in the lounge and closed his eyes. The house was quiet with the children finally in bed. He hoped that Louise would be home soon. He didn't like her being out in the car on her own at night. She had rung from the hospital to say that her father was stable after the operation and she wouldn't be long.

He felt a sudden urge for a drink. It was unusual for him when he had work the next day but he decided to go with the inclination. He went over to the drinks cabinet and took out an unopened bottle of Connemara Malt Whiskey that he had received from a client for Christmas. As the glass bottle clinked off the tumbler he was holding he heard his wife come through the front door.

"Hi," she said from the doorway. "I'm wrecked – would you pour me a G & T?"

"Sure," he said and screwed the cap off the gin. He took out the bottle of tonic and gave it a shake to check that there was still gas in it. "How's your dad?"

"He's doing well."

Louise went to the kitchen and got a glass of ice from the fridge, before returning to her husband in the lounge.

"It's been a mad few days – thanks for all of your help and support."

"I'm your husband, am I not?" He took the glass of ice from her and filled it with gin.

"I don't know what I'd have done without you," she said. "For the first time in my life I felt like an only child."

"Now you know what it was like for me!" He nodded knowingly.

"Sorry for chastising you all the times you used to go and check up on your mum before she died – I never felt that sense of responsibility before – I always had Emma there whenever there was a crisis – thank God she's home."

Donal topped up his glass of whiskey and sat back down on his recliner. "Emma has had it very tough."

"I know. I don't know how she's coped these last few months."

"She's had to carry a lot on her shoulders."

"At least you were there to help her with all of the paperwork and the will."

Donal inhaled deeply – this was as good a time as any to inform his wife – he needed to talk to her more – to come clean about his real feelings. They avoided certain issues too much and he wanted to talk to her from the heart. "That wasn't all that went with the role of executor of the will – we're lucky that he wrote one but there were complications that I never told you because Emma begged me not to."

Louise sat up in her chair. "What didn't she want me to know?"

"If I tell you, please promise that you will never tell her."

"Of course I promise." She felt extremely put out that her sister had confided in her husband about something she wouldn't tell her.

"Paul didn't die of natural causes."

"I know – he died of a heart attack."

"A self-induced heart attack."

"What are you saying?" Louise's mouth hung open.

"He knew that he would not wake up from sleep on his last night – he took an overdose of very strong sleeping tablets and anti-depressants that caused the heart attack."

"You're saying he killed himself!"

Donal nodded. "It's not totally conclusive – he could have mistakenly taken two whole bottles of pills but what do you think?"

Louise took a large gulp of her G & T. "I can't believe it," she said, shaking her head.

"The hard part for Emma to carry around in her head is why," said Donal. "She has these terrible feelings of guilt that he killed himself to get away from her."

Louise's mind was racing. She was putting facts together and getting answers to all kinds of questions that were unanswered after Paul's death. She had the puzzle almost figured out. That explained so much about the missing link in the chain of events that led to his death.

"Why would Emma not confide in us – her family?"

"She was afraid that the insurance wouldn't pay if they knew that he had killed himself and she was right – I told her not to breathe a word."

"I can't believe you never told me before now."

"It was too soon after the whole event. It's better that way – I didn't want to put you under pressure trying to keep a secret on top of all the rest of the stuff going on."

Louise felt suddenly very guilty. She was very good at keeping secrets from her husband. She had been doing it since before they were married.

"You've gone very quiet all of a sudden."

"I'm just trying to figure something out."

"The reason why he did it?"

Louise nodded.

"I've been trying to figure that out too. He had it all – Emma is terrific."

Louise didn't like hearing her husband talk about her sister like that. It made her feel inadequate. "Nobody's perfect – I've known her a lot longer than you, remember."

"My comments aren't reflective of you! What is it about you sisters? There's a constant fight for attention between you always. You're my wife – you're the one I married."

Louise stood up and went over to the drinks cabinet and topped up her drink.

"I'm sorry – it's just the way we've always been."

"Maybe if Maggie had been more concerned about you all while you were growing up, instead of worrying about herself, you might not always be in competition with each other."

"You don't understand – you're an only child."

"I know but I have three children and I see the way we are with them – they are treated equally – don't think I haven't noticed the way your father fusses over Sophie and your mother demands so much of Emma and her time."

Louise seldom spoke like this with Donal. It was more usual for them to skirt around family issues. She wondered why Donal was suddenly so frank. It hurt to hear the truth from her husband.

"It's different now that we are grown up – well, Emma and I have grown up at least!"

"You are never grown up with your own family – you will always fall into the same old patterns when you are together."

She knew that he was telling the truth and decided to take it on the chin.

"I just want Dad to be okay."

"I just want us to be okay."

Louise shivered when he said those words. "We *are* okay," she said.

"We haven't been okay for years – I can't think of a time when we were."

Louise was terrified by Donal's new voice. "I don't know what you mean."

"Can you honestly say that you are happy with me?"

"Of course – what do you mean?"

"I thought as we started to tell a few home truths about your sister we might as well tell some of our own. Do you never feel we're like mice on a treadmill?"

Louise took a large gulp from her glass. "I think we're fine."

"Oh, we're fine all right, but where is the life in our relationship? We used to be more alive together."

"But that was before the kids took over."

"We can't blame the kids all the time. Don't get me wrong, we have a good life and I am happy with you but there is a spark missing – and I never admitted it to myself."

Louise felt as if she was about to burst into tears – where was all of this coming from? "My father's in hospital and I've had a hard few weeks – months! This isn't the time to be talking like this."

"If not now – when?"

Louise took another stiff drink. She had no answer to that and the fact that her normally quiet husband should bring up such a serious issue out of the blue frightened her.

"I'm going to bed," she declared.

"Fine but we will still have to face up to the way we are in the morning and the next morning – unless you want to do something about it?"

Louise didn't answer. She went into the kitchen and got herself a glass of water.

She went straight upstairs, got into bed and turned out the light.

When she woke the next morning Donal's side of the bed was undisturbed. He had spent the night in the spare room.

Emma was about to delete the email written in Spanish as spam until she saw the subject attached: Para cliente de Sol Melia

Varadero. At first she thought it must be from Dehannys until she read the name at the end and felt her heart race.

Emma, I was sorry not to see you the day you went home. I hope you enjoyed your time in Cuba.

Maybe I will see you again some day. It is not easy for me to send this message. Dehannys is here and she says hello.

Your friend Felipe.

Emma read the short message over and over. She felt sorry for leaving so suddenly too.

She wanted to speak to him right now. She checked her watch – it was the middle of the night in Cuba. If only she had known the reason that Paul had taken his life while she was over in Cuba! A veil had been lifted since she had discovered what he had been up to in the years before he took his own life.

She needed to talk to someone – someone who wouldn't judge her – someone who would listen to her. She picked up the phone.

Two hours later she was sitting on a high stool in the Ely wine bar. Donal arrived through the door at exactly twelve o'clock as he had said he would. It was a good time of day to get a table before the busy lunch-hour trade started.

He strode over to where she sat.

She offered him her right cheek and he brushed his lips off it.

"How was your holiday? You've a great colour."

"Good – well, pretty good apart from a hiccup at the end regarding Sophie."

Donal gave a knowing nod. "Is that what you need to talk to me about?"

"Oh Donal, I'm so confused – I really needed to talk to you – you're the only sane person I know."

"I'm always there for you, Emma."

"And there's that too. You've been more like a brother than a brother-in-law to me."

Donal smiled. "I hope so."

"Well, are you ready for this?"

"Try me."

"Paul was having an affair with Sophie – from what I gather it was going on for some time before he died."

"Really?" It took a lot to shock Donal but this definitely did.

"I'm only guessing but I think she put him under pressure to leave me and he was too much of a coward to do it."

"Maybe he loved you too much to make the decision."

"If he really loved me he wouldn't have been sleeping with my sister."

The waiter arrived with the menu.

"Thank you," said Donal. "Give us a few minutes."

As the waiter withdrew Donal turned to Emma again.

"Emma, maybe he loved you both."

"Is that possible?" said Emma sceptically. "I don't think so."

"I think it is."

"Well, whatever Paul may have felt, I am twisted and torn inside – I've been berating myself for months over him and now I'm so angry with him for cheating on me."

"Paul is gone – he had his own cross to bear – he must have been in some state to do what he did."

Emma nodded. "But why did Sophie feel the need to tell me now?"

"To get it off her conscience?"

"Sometimes I wonder if Sophie has a conscience!"

"Well, maybe it has helped you understand what was going on inside Paul's head before he died."

"I wish I knew what was going on inside his head. Did he do it out of desperation or guilt? Maybe he didn't have the courage to leave me and Finn but loved Sophie so much he couldn't live without her?"

Donal wished he hadn't told Louise about Paul's suicide. He

hoped she would keep his confidence. This sudden twist in events was cutting a bit too close to the bone for comfort – everyone in the Owens family was so intertwined that they were in danger of imploding.

"We'll probably never know why he did it but the most important thing is that you move on with your life in a positive way."

"Going to Cuba was a positive experience despite the way it ended. As it turns out I met some lovely people while I was there. You've no idea of the poverty that people live in. There was this guy who was a taxi driver and he gave up his profession as a lawyer because he earns more driving tourists around!"

Donal realised by the way that Emma spoke she had feelings for this stranger.

"And what was his name?"

"Felipe. In fact he emailed me today."

"You really liked him?"

"Yes, I would really like to see him again."

"That's not exactly easy if the facts I've heard are right – isn't Cuba communist?"

"It's socialist but not the same as the Iron Curtain countries before 1990. People can leave but it is difficult and expensive. Beyond his means really."

"Emma – you're not thinking of paying for this guy to come over and visit you?"

Emma bit her lip. Louise had the same habit and Donal knew that he had guessed correctly.

"Emma, that's not a great idea."

"But why not? We got on very well and he brought me all around Havana – it would be lovely to reciprocate."

"I think you probably got too caught up with the whole holiday romance and drank too much rum."

Emma listened to Donal – she had learned that his advice was usually sound. "It is crazy, isn't it?" she said. "I just thought I'd run it by you first and I'm glad that I did – I needed to tell you about Sophie too."

"Emma, you are probably going to have to learn to live in silence with that information – at least while Maggie and Larry are still alive."

"I want to kill Sophie – that's what I want to do – and it's just as well that Paul is dead because I would kill him too."

Donal put his hand on hers. "I hate to say it but maybe Paul couldn't resist Sophie – she has that Owens charm."

"Thanks, Donal," she said wryly. "I don't know about charm but I do know she always gets her man when she sets her sights on someone." She sighed. "I do feel mixed up and confused – I just needed to talk to you."

"Well, I'm flattered and glad that you did. I'm always here for you, Emma."

Emma smiled. "Thanks, Donal. After lunch I have to go and see my dad. You know, he told Louise that I wasn't to rush in – but he wanted to see Sophie as soon as we got back from Cuba."

"That's families – you can't take it too personally."

"That's just it – we are family so it is personal. And I can't hold myself responsible for what I will do to Sophie the next time I see her."

Louise was in a state of high anxiety. Donal had been very harsh – cold even – the way he had spoken about their relationship the night before. It was the fact it was true that made it so hard to take. She drove quickly with her eyes fixed on the road.

Her mobile phone rang and she hit the switch on her steering wheel.

"Hello?"

"Louise – where is Emma? She said she was popping out for a few minutes but that was two hours ago."

"I don't know, Mum – I haven't spoken to her today."

"I asked her to buy me an *Independent* on her way back."

"I'm on my way in to see Dad. I'll give her a call if you like."

"You couldn't get the paper and drop it in to me on the way?"

Louise frowned. Sutton was not on her way to Beaumont Hospital. It would add half an hour to her journey and her next-door neighbour was minding her children while she went to visit her father.

"I'm under pressure for time, Mum."

Maggie didn't reply. She seemed to have completely forgotten what it was like to have children to take care of since her own grew up.

"I'll ring Emma – I really have to dash, Mum. Bye."

This was the way things were in the Owens household. But it was unlike Emma to shirk her responsibilities. She wondered where she was.

The last person Sophie met in the *Irish Times* office at the end of her first day was Jack Duggan.

"Have you been shown around?"

Sophie nodded. "Brenda is so nice – she said she has four days' work for me next week."

"Do you fancy going for a coffee – I'm taking a break?"

"Sounds good – thanks."

They walked around the corner until they were on Pearse Street.

"I usually pop in here," Jack said when they came to a small café.

The tables were packed up tightly together and they took a corner one by the window.

"What will you have?"

"Black coffee."

Jack called over to the waitress and ordered two coffees.

"It was good luck bumping into you in Beaumont," he said. "I'm always amazed by the law of coincidences."

Sophie smiled. She didn't think it strange at all – that was the way her life flowed.

"How's your dad?"

"He's doing well, I believe – I'm going in to see him after this." Sophie pushed her hair back from the nape of her neck and leaned forward across the table. "Where do you live, Jack?"

"I'm out in Howth."

"I like Howth – it's just a pity it's so far from the city."

"That's what I like about it."

"You're much too young to be stuck out in suburbia."

"How old do you think I am?"

Sophie sat back and looked him up and down. "About thirty-three?"

"Close enough – I'm thirty-two. I'm older than you – but I'm not going to ask you your age."

Sophie didn't reply – she was two years older than him and wasn't going to make him any wiser on little details like that.

"A few of us are going to Café en Seine tomorrow if you fancy joining us and meeting more of the crew?" said Jack.

"Sounds good."

"Where are you living, Sophie?"

"I've an apartment over by the IFSC."

"That's handy."

"It was very handy for work – but I'll have to see what happens now – Brenda said this work is only temporary."

"Temporary is as good as anyone has in this city at the moment."

The waitress arrived with their coffees and a bill. Jack reached into his pocket and paid her.

"Thanks," Sophie said, taking a sip from the cup.

"Why don't you ask Louise if she'd like to join us in Café en Seine?"

"I never socialise with my sister – especially on a Saturday night. She's so caught up with her family she drives me mad at the best of times." Sophie put her cup down and tilted her head. Why would Jack be interested in seeing Louise again? Surely he didn't fancy her? He was much younger and fitter than her. "How do you know Louise?"

Jack had realised what he had done as soon as the words had left his mouth. Now he tried to cover his mistake. "I met her in Westwood Gym."

"Oh really?" Sophie could never imagine her sister in a gym – Louise hated those sorts of places.

"Yeah – I don't know her that long at all."

"Right," Sophie said with a nod and took her cup up again. Louise had said they had met at work. There was a story here somewhere – she might go to Café en Seine later to find out more.

Chapter 18

Emma was never one to ignore Donal's advice but on this occasion her gut instinct was too strong. She had to see Felipe again. Maybe the upset with Sophie was to blame. Her inspiration was gone and all of the lovely memories she had of La Finca Vigía and Havana were entwined with memories of Felipe. Her only reservation was Finn – she wasn't sure how he would feel about a strange man from another country staying with them but she would have to put her own needs first – this time. She had rung the Cuban embassy and found out what was involved in sponsoring a Cuban citizen to come for a holiday to Ireland.

She clicked on the icon for Outlook Express and decided to reply to his email. She missed Cuba – it was such an oasis. Since coming home her days were filled with demands from her mother and Louise and she wanted to feel free again.

Dear Felipe

It was really nice to get your email. I know this may sound strange but I would really like you to visit me in Dublin. Before I say any more, please do not feel under pressure. While I was in Cuba you looked after me very well and I would like to return your hospitality.

I don't know what is involved at your end but I rang the Cuban embassy and they said that it was possible to organise – it will take a few weeks for the visa to come through.

It is coming into a nice time of year in Ireland and I would really like to see you again soon. I could ring you about this if you email me back to say that you would like to come.

Please say hello to Dehannys and tell her that I have made a parcel for her son – shoes, a computer game and an MP3 player. I sent them off yesterday but have no idea how long they will take to arrive.

With best wishes

Emma

She hoped that he would get it. Depending on his response she would phone him. There was no need to tell Donal or anyone what she had done. The relationship with Felipe was special.

Larry waved his right arm and grimaced with the pain.

"Louise!" he groaned.

"Are you okay, Dad?"

"Why hasn't Sophie been in to see me since the operation?"

Louise wanted to ask why hadn't her mother been in to see him? "I haven't spoken to her, Dad. Don't worry – things are just a bit mad – she is probably trying to catch up since getting back from Cuba."

"Emma was here earlier but she didn't stay long."

"Can I get you anything?"

"I'd like a car magazine – I want to get a new car when I get out of here."

"Good idea – it will give you something to look forward to."

"How is your mother?"

"She's staying with Emma."

"I know that but Emma is so distracted – she's not the girl she used to be – that holiday didn't seem to do her much good either."

"It's where Mum wants to be."

"Will you check up on her for me?"

Suddenly Louise had had enough. "Look, Dad – don't you think it's time Sophie took some responsibility. I'm not the only daughter and I have three kids – Emma only has one and Sophie is free as a bird. I don't want to upset you but I'm sick of everything being thrown on my shoulders at the moment."

Larry was aghast. He knew that Louise was volatile but hadn't seen an outburst like this from her about her sisters since she was twelve. "I just thought as you didn't work . . ."

"I do work – I'm a housewife. God, I'm so sick of my life!" Suddenly her eyes filled with tears.

Larry wasn't the sort of man to handle displays of emotion from his daughters – he had enough work coping with his wife.

"Does Donal know that you are this unhappy?"

Louise couldn't believe that she was having this conversation with her father – they had never had a heart-to-heart of any sort before. It was usually only Sophie that he confided in and was concerned about.

"Donal's unhappy too. He said it the other night and I can't get it out of my head."

"In what way?"

"We've got into a routine and I suppose we don't really talk about how we feel."

Larry seemed to understand exactly what she was saying. "That's just the way marriages become. Your mother has often lashed out at me over the years and I've found it is best to ignore it."

Louise felt sorry for her father – Maggie was seldom happy with anything. She remembered the trouble her father had to go to on family holidays to change apartments because there would always be something wrong with the one they were allocated once they arrived. When they ate out in a restaurant as a family Maggie would be uncomfortable with her first choice of seat and they would have to move around until she found the spot that she was happy with.

"How have you put with her all of these years?"

"She's my wife – that's just what you do." Larry's tone was resigned.

"I don't think couples will settle for that nowadays, Dad."

"That's why there's so much divorce. It's the same no matter who you are with – relationships fall into a certain pattern and each partner finds their role."

Louise smiled at her father. He was from a different generation. Maybe he was right.

"I don't know what to do about Donal – I always thought I knew what he was thinking."

"Does he know what you are thinking?"

Louise shook her head adamantly.

"Well, then – and that's the way most marriages are."

Louise understood exactly what her father was saying but somehow it didn't seem enough for her any more either and it obviously wasn't enough for Donal.

Dehannys was used to taking opportunities whenever they arose. She had to be resourceful to survive the system. Emma had promised to send clothes for Dehanny's son and he needed any help he could get – from anywhere.

"Hey, Pedro – where are you working today?"

"Hey, Dehannys – I am in the computer room." He shook his head – it was not a good day – Diego was working.

"Would you look up my email address and see if I have any messages?"

"Sure – I will do my best – but if I get caught I will have to say that you asked me."

"Of course."

"What's in it for me?"

"My father has some rum for you – I will bring it tomorrow."

Pedro nodded. It was worth taking the chance.

Dehannys was used to bartering – all of her colleagues did it. She was lucky to have a father who worked in the rum factory. Her uncle had a farm and was growing vegetables for the farmers' market – it was a great relief for her family and meant that her mother could continue running the *paladar*. This year was going to be more difficult than usual after the hammering the landscape had taken from the hurricanes. Already their ration of rice had been reduced to 4 kg per person per month and it could only get worse.

She waited patiently throughout the day – cleaning glasses and pouring drinks.

When Pedro arrived towards the end of her shift with a sheet of paper her heart lifted.

"Thank you – this is so good."

"One bottle of rum, remember – tomorrow!"

Dehannys nodded. Her head was stuck in the sheet of paper – she was trying to understand the email and wished that she had worked harder at her English lessons in tourism school. The message was made out to Felipe but she found the sentences that involved her.

She recognised the word "shoes" but would ask Felipe what "parcel" meant. Felipe would be so pleased to hear from Emma also. She folded the page and hid it discreetly in her handbag. She would be in a lot of trouble if she was found sending emails for her own purposes. Only certain professions were allowed to use email freely. She wondered how long the shoes would take to arrive.

Jack stood at the bar of Café en Seine and looked at his watch. It was nearly ten o'clock.

He felt his phone vibrate in his pocket and took it out to see who the message was from.

Where r u? Aoife

It was a shock to see her name. Five days had passed since he had received the email from her and he was surprised and pleased that she would contact him before the week was up.

In Café en Seine. U in town? J

She replied immediately.

In Malahide. Meet me 2morro in Gibneys @ 4?

Jack felt his heart lift.

OK

He put his phone back in his pocket and ordered another drink.

Sophie arrived at half past ten into Café en Seine.

Jack spotted her first and immediately made his way over to where she stood.

"Glad you could make it."

She surveyed the people standing in a group at the bar. "I thought it might be good to get to know everyone – thanks for inviting me." She batted her eyelashes and gave a Sophie look that had an arousing effect on men.

"What can I get you?"

"White wine – Sauvignon Blanc."

Jack beckoned to the barman and ordered. Suddenly a hand tapped him on his right shoulder. Jack turned around to see who it belonged to.

"Peter!" he exclaimed. "I didn't think you were coming."

"The gig I was going to was packed and the band weren't great – when you said you'd be here I thought we might head out – I didn't realise you had company though!" Peter nodded at Sophie.

She looked at his freckled Irish skin and scraggy reddish hair and nodded back.

"Uh, Peter, this is Sophie."

"Pleased to meet you," Peter said, holding out his right hand. Sophie shook it lightly.

"What will you have?" Jack asked.

"Pint of Bud." Peter turned towards Sophie and stared. "Do I know you from somewhere?"

Sophie shook her head. "I can't say you're familiar."

"I'm usually good on faces and I always remember a pretty one. Where do you work?"

"I'm doing some styling with *The Times* but it's temporary – I was in the rag trade."

Peter still couldn't figure out where he had seen her before.

"There you go, mate," Jack said, passing over the pint.

"I'm in a graphics agency," said Peter. "Maybe we were involved in some promotion work for your company?"

Sophie took a gulp from her wine glass. Maybe he worked with Paul. "Which one?"

"Evans Graphic House."

Sophie lifted her glass again. She wished she could hide behind it.

"We never used them," she said curtly.

Peter continued to stare, making Sophie feel very uneasy – she knew it was only a matter of time before he twigged where he had seen her before.

"Would you pass the remote?" Donal asked.

Louise handed it over.

"Would you like a drink?" she asked. "I'm having a G & T."

"No, thanks."

"I've been having a terrible day." Louise sighed.

"Really?"

"You've no idea how awful I've been feeling since ... ."

"I told a few home truths?"

Louise nodded.

"I know the timing isn't probably the best with your dad in hospital," he said, "but there never seems to be a good time."

"And that's my fault as much as yours. I don't know when we stopped talking."

"I don't know when we started."

"I'm afraid."

"What are you afraid of?"

"Of us."

"I'm not going anywhere, Louise. I just needed to say it and the other night it came out."

"Donal, what are we going to do?"

Donal raised the volume on the television and turned to look at the screen. He shook his head and shrugged his shoulders.

"I don't know."

Jack woke with Sophie's warm naked body by his side. He hated himself for what he had done – it was reverting back to old behaviour – but he couldn't help himself. She had made herself totally irresistible.

When Peter made the connection and recognised Sophie from a party she had attended with Paul who had worked in his office, she suddenly didn't want to be there any more. Jack wondered why she'd behaved so oddly.

It didn't matter now – he had gone back to her apartment knowing exactly what they were going to do and he only had himself to blame. He looked at his watch. It was five minutes to twelve and he had to be in Malahide by four o'clock.

Sophie uncoiled and gave a loud yawn. She looked up at Jack and smiled.

"Morning."

"Hi, Sophie – do you mind if I take a shower?"

"Go ahead." She sat up in the bed holding the sheet up to cover her breasts. Jack was no Greg Adams and he most certainly was no Paul – she wouldn't be tempted to sleep with him again.

Jack went into the shower and covered his hair with shampoo. He had to get the scent of Sophie off him. What was he thinking of? Louise had warned him she was dangerous. She was also totally irresistible.

He wasn't sure how he could face Aoife.

"Do you want some coffee?" Sophie called out from her tiny kitchen.

"Yes, please!" he hollered.

He dressed quickly and checked his phone to see if there were any messages before she returned to the bedroom

You dog!!! Peter

Jack deleted the message. It was just the sort of thing that he didn't want Aoife to see.

Sophie put the two mugs on the table and pulled out a chair.

"Thanks," Jack said, lifting the mug and taking a few swift gulps. "I'm going to have to shoot."

Sophie twirled one of her curls around her index finger. "I'll probably see you in work. We can pretend this never happened."

Jack sighed and then wished he hadn't done it so loudly. "Yeah, great – it was a good night."

"Had better!" Sophie said with a wink.

He could feel his cheeks flush. He deserved it. "Okay – see you Monday then."

"See you," she said. She didn't get up to show him the door – he knew where it was!

"Do you want me to take you in to see Dad?"

Maggie gave a little moan and turned over in the bed. "Is it morning?"

"Yes, Mum," Emma replied. "I want to go in and see him as early as possible – I'd like to try and write today."

"But it's Sunday."

"That makes no difference to me."

"I don't really think hospitals suit me."

"They don't suit anyone, Mother, but Dad's been in there over a week now – don't you want to see him?"

Maggie winced. "I haven't been very well since the terrible shock I got with the burglars – I thought if anyone understood you would."

"I do empathise – but you know Dad is the one that has had the heart surgery. Come in this once, please, Mum – he'll be out at the end of next week."

"And then I'll be left to look after him!"

Emma threw her eyes up into the air – her mother was never left with anything because she and Louise always carried the can. She had done with humouring her mother. For years she had indulged her idiosyncrasies but she wasn't willing to listen to them any more.

Aoife was sitting on a stool in the snug by the fire. She looked beautiful and Jack could feel his guilt like a weight.

"Hi, there."

"Hi," she smiled. "I didn't last very long before contacting you, did I?"

Jack sat down beside her. "I'm glad you didn't."

"How is work?"

"Work is fine, same old story!"

A big tear started to roll down her left cheek.

His heart pounded – he hated to see her like this.

"I missed you so much," she said. "I missed us. Oh Jack, it's been so hard!"

Jack put his arm around her in comfort. "I missed you too."

"What are we going to do?"

Jack kissed her on the cheek. He longed to hold her tightly.

"I didn't want this time apart – I know that I want to be with you."

"But you don't want to get married so soon?"

Jack shrugged. "I don't know – we can talk about it."

"I don't care about the wedding any more – I've just missed you so much."

"We could go home if you like?"

Aoife nodded. "Home, please."

Felipe called by the Port Royal bar in the hope of seeing Dehannys. He longed for the days when he had an email and computer as a lawyer but he had given them up in return for CUCs – until now he hadn't regretted the decision. But then again if he hadn't been driving a taxi he would never have met Emma. He felt foolish and childish thinking about this woman who was so far across the Atlantic and so difficult to communicate with – let alone have any type of relationship with.

He spotted Dehannys serving a couple at a table. She waved when she saw him.

He knew by the look on her face that she had something to show him but they would have to be secretive.

"Come into the back," she beckoned and led him into the staff quarters.

She reached into her handbag and took out the piece of paper that she had received from Pedro the day before.

"Can you understand it?" she asked.

Felipe read eagerly. A smile crossed his face.

"What is Emma going to do?" Dehannys asked.

"She says that she has sent a parcel for you with shoes and an MP3 player for your son – so that he can put music on it – and a computer game."

Dehannys shook with excitement. "Felipe, that is good news!"

"Yes, and she says that she would like me to come and visit Ireland."

"Oh, marvellous! Will you go?"

Felipe shrugged. "I don't know if it is possible. I hope so."

"That would be a great adventure."

"Who got this for you, Dehannys?"

"Pedro."

"Can he send one back for us?"

"I don't know when he will be on that shift again."

Felipe scratched his head. "I must get another contact."

"When you were a lawyer did you not have any friend who might still use a computer?"

Felipe couldn't believe he hadn't thought of it before. He reached out and embraced Dehannys tightly.

"Yes – my friend Miguel. Do you want me to say anything to Emma for you?"

"Tell her thank you and send her hugs and kisses from me and Fernando."

Felipe couldn't wait to pick up his guests and get them to Havana. They were a very rude French couple. Felipe didn't care. When he dropped them at the foyer of the Hotel Nacional he didn't care either – he just wanted to get to Miguel's office and as quickly as possible. Miguel owed him big time. He had slogged his way through university and would never have passed his exams without Felipe's help. The least he could do now was act as intermediary between him and Emma.

Miguel's office was on a side street off La Rampa. Felipe parked up his taxi and took the steps up to his dimly lit rooms two by two. Miguel's secretary sat at a desk littered with piles of papers.

"*Hola!* Is Señor Estafan here today?"

"*Sí*," she nodded and pointed to another door.

Miguel was rotund with a bald patch in the middle of his black hair. He jumped to his feet upon seeing his old friend.

"Felipe Blanco Garcia, it is so good to see you, my friend!" He embraced him warmly.

"And good to see you!" said Felipe.

"How are you doing now that you are earning all the CUCs that the rest of us only dream about?"

Felipe laughed. "It is not what it seems driving the tourists all day!"

"It is hot today – you will have a drink?"

"Maybe a coffee, thank you."

"So my friend, why do you call – it must be three years since you visited!"

Felipe hesitated – he knew that what he was asking was illegal – but that was the way when things needed to be done. "I have a favour to ask."

"Ah – I only see friends when they need something." Miguel laughed as he spoke.

"Do you still have internet access?" asked Felipe. "I need to send an email."

"I have the computer from hell – it breaks down two times per day – but, yes, I have email. Do you want to use it?"

"Yes, I met a European woman and she wants to contact me. Can I use your address?"

"Go ahead. You are lucky to have a lady with money!"

Felipe didn't want to give any more information away. He trusted Miguel but it was better to tell as little as possible – even to your friends. The walls had ears in Cuba.

Miguel went out to talk to his secretary – leaving Felipe in peace to write to Emma.

Felipe scanned the line of books above his head. All the drivel that he had to read when in university. A small English – Spanish dictionary at the end of the shelf caught his eye. He lifted it down in case he needed help with any words.

Dear Emma

It is good to get your email. This address belongs to my friend – it is okay to write to him if you like. I have thought of you many times since you left Cuba. I wish that we had more time. There is so much of my country I would like to show you. I hope that maybe some day I will see you again. It is not easy to leave my country. If you can tell me the cost of the visa and the flight I can see if maybe I can travel.

I hope that you will write to me again soon. It means a lot to get your correspondence.

Dehannys sends you love and blessings from her family and son.

Your friend

Felipe

Felipe walked out to where Miguel was flirting with his secretary.

"How are you on getting visas? I remember how it was discouraged when we were studying."

Miguel shrugged. "My friend, nothing has changed."

Emma was watching her email diligently and hit the icons swiftly when she saw a message from Miguel Estafan. The subject was *From Felipe* and that was all she needed to know.

As she read the email she felt butterflies in her stomach. She sensed his difficulties about leaving the country and finding money from the tone of the email but hoped that wouldn't stop him making the journey to Ireland.

Chapter 19

Jack was so happy to wake up with his arms entwined around Aoife's warm body. The last three weeks had been wonderful – it was that crazy honeymoon period all over again.

"I'm sorry for hurting you," he said.

Aoife looked up into Jack's eyes and smiled. She didn't need to say a thing. Their relationship had fallen back into the comfortable safe zone that she had loved living in.

"It's a pity I have to go to work," he said.

"I have to go too, but we can have an early night tonight," she said with a grin.

Jack went for his shower first and Aoife went into the kitchen and put on the kettle and some toast.

Jack's phone bleeped.

"You've got a message, Jack!"

Jack couldn't hear with the sound of the water running.

Aoife lifted the phone and hit the green button by accident – the message flashed up.

It was from a woman called Louise.

Can I c u 2day? Louise.

There was nothing sinister about the message. A few weeks ago Aoife would have presumed that it was from someone at work. Now she had an uncomfortable feeling that she didn't know Jack as well as she had thought. When Jack came out of the shower she put a cup of coffee and some toast on the table.

"You've got a message from Louise – she wants to see you."

Jack reacted the way she had hoped he wouldn't.

He looked shocked, then said accusingly, "Are you reading my messages?"

"I was bringing it to you in the shower – and what's the problem with reading your messages? I'm your fiancée – you aren't meant to be getting messages that I shouldn't see!"

"It's not that – I wouldn't look up your phone."

"I wasn't checking up on you – I hit it by accident. Why are you so upset? *Should* I be checking up on you?"

Jack was backed into a corner. "Of course not – it's perfectly normal – Louise is my old music teacher – the one we met on the pier – remember?"

"Why does she want to see you?"

"I helped her sister get a job – it's probably something to do with that."

"There's nothing wrong with that – why do you not want me to know about it?"

"It's just – nothing – nothing at all."

Aoife decided to leave it but the text message had changed the mood.

"I'm taking my shower," she said coolly. "I can't be late."

Jack looked at his phone. He didn't want anything more to do with Louise Owens or her sister. Now that he had Aoife back he would do everything in his power to patch things up. He would get married in July if she wanted. He wasn't going to risk losing her again. He went to his contacts on his phone and found Louise's number. Then he pressed delete.

The porters lifted Larry into the wheelchair.

"Are you okay, Dad?" said Louise.

"I don't need a wheelchair – I'm able to walk!"

Larry Owens had spent three weeks in convalescence because Maggie couldn't cope with the prospect of nursing her post-operative husband. Emma and Louise agreed that it was probably for the best even though it would mean a considerable amount of driving around on their part – but it would mean that regardless.

Emma caught the handles on the back of the chair. "We can manage," she said to the porters. "We'll bring the chair back."

Emma pushed while Louise carried her father's bags out to the car. She opened the car door and together they eased him onto the passenger seat. Emma helped him put on his safety-belt while Louise took the chair back inside.

As Louise emerged, Emma beckoned to her to help her put the bags in the boot – what she really wanted was to talk to her in private.

"So what else did Donal say?" Emma whispered.

"He's been saying very little since those conversations I told you about," Louise said quietly. "I can't believe he's throwing this stuff at me with Dad sick and Mum acting up."

"Well, you need to sort it out. Don't let it go on. I ignored the silences between Paul and me and he went off and had an affair."

Louise laughed.

"What's so funny?"

"I don't think Donal's exactly the affair type – do you?"

"He's a man, isn't he?"

"That's harsh coming from you, Emma."

"I know. I'm sorry. I'm still so mad with Paul and Sophie. Thank God she's kept out of my way. I want to kill her."

"You're going to have to face each other at some stage. Do you want me to act as go-between?"

"There's nothing I want to say to her," Emma said adamantly.

"I haven't seen that much of her," said Louise. "She's got some temporary work with *The Irish Times*."

"She won't like that. Who is she getting to pay for her social life?"

"I'm not sure – she's not telling me much – she knows that I talk to you."

"We had better get in the car – Dad is getting restless on his own!"

The drive from Clontarf to Raheny was short so the conversation remained light between the three until they reached the gates of 42 Foxfield.

Emma ground to a halt – a look of horror flashed over her face and she was unable to speak.

When Louise looked out of the window she realised why. Sophie's car was parked in the driveway. Louise jumped out of the car and opened the door on her father's side.

"Come on, Dad – I'll take you in – there's no need for Emma to hang around – I'm free for the afternoon."

Emma was shaking and swallowing hard.

"I'm not an invalid!" Larry protested. "I don't know why they insisted on that bloody wheelchair as I was leaving – I can walk."

Louise took her father's arm.

"I can manage better on my own," he scowled. But the scowl didn't last long as his expression changed upon seeing his daughter's car in the driveway. "Sophie must be here – did you know she was coming to welcome me home?"

Poor Dad, Louise thought. When is he going to wake up? Probably never – like most men that cross Sophie's path.

"I have to go," Emma said as she got out of the car to get her father's bag from the boot. "Have you got a hold of Dad, Louise?"

"Your mother will want to see you!" Larry exclaimed.

"She's seen plenty of me for the last three weeks, Dad – it's time you had her all to yourself."

Larry looked slightly scared by the remark. He had never known Emma to be so forthright where her mother was concerned.

"Let Emma go, Dad, she has lots to do," Louise said with a wink and nod as Emma got back in the car, indicated and slowly drove off.

Louise wondered how many other times she would have to cover up her sisters' feud from her parents.

Emma had no idea of the amount of paperwork that was required to get a visa for a Cuban national. It gave her something to focus on. She looked forward to the emails that she received every other day from Señor Miguel Estafan – each time she corresponded with Felipe she felt they were another step closer to seeing each other again. She had to get hold of his passport to get it stamped and as Dehannys hadn't received the package for her son yet Emma knew that the process would be much slower than she had originally thought.

Felipe had given his passport to a Canadian woman who promised that she would post it as soon as she reached Toronto. Emma felt that he was taking a terrible chance but when it arrived she realised that the move had saved them possibly two weeks. The cost was far more than she had expected too – so far she had clocked up over 180 euros in costs and charges and that was in Ireland. Felipe had to pay 15 CUCs at his end which was a good monthly wage for most Cubans. She hadn't been to her solicitor yet – a letter of invitation was required to show that they were genuinely friends and that the relationship was not in any way sinister and a ploy to help Felipe flee the country. She also had to vouch that she would be responsible for him financially and legally should he get into any sort of trouble while her guest.

She wished that she had Donal's help – he would be wonderful with all of this paperwork and detail but she didn't want him to know what she was doing. She swore Louise to secrecy – she didn't want anyone to know in case something went wrong. She feared that Felipe wouldn't come when they did have the visa in hand and she didn't want to appear foolish. But as the weeks passed her desire to see Felipe became greater. They had spoken four times now and she could conjure up his accent any time she wanted.

Dehannys was very excited when the big brown package arrived from Ireland. She opened the string and peeled off the tape but it had already been tampered with and put back insecurely.

A white runner boot size 34 was the first item she retrieved from the box. The other one followed and she breathed a sigh of relief. A pair of shorts with flowers like those worn by American surfers came out next – Fernando would be very happy wearing those. Then a football shirt from Barcelona was next – Fernando loved football. She searched for the computer game but there was none. Then she found a box with make-up and some costume jewellery tucked in at the back of the package. She looked for the MP3 player and found it hidden in the shoe. Some more soft fabrics and T-shirts came out that would look fine on Fernando and Dehannys thanked her lucky stars. The game would have been nice for the boy but some other child belonging to an official or a postman would get to play with it now instead.

She hoped that Felipe would call again soon. She wanted to thank Emma so much. She would buy some Cuban crafts and give them to him to take over to Ireland. He was so lucky getting this chance to see another country and how other people lived. She could only dream and wonder.

Things were becoming tense in the Scott household with each day that passed and Louise worried that they would reach bursting point. Jack hadn't replied to her texts for the last three weeks. She couldn't understand why he was ignoring her like this. She would try and phone him and then he would have to speak to her. She used her house phone as it was ex-directory and her number wouldn't show up.

He answered.

"Hi, Jack – it's Louise."

"Louise, hi," he said and she could hear the anxiety in his tone. "How are you?"

"I'm fine – I'm going to be in town today and I was wondering if you fancied meeting for a cup of coffee?"

There was a pause, then he said, "Okay – how about eleven?" he said. "Do you know the café on the corner of Pearse Street?"

"Yes. That's grand. See you then."

His tone had been abrupt but Louise figured that could just be because he was in work.

She boarded the DART and waited with thoughts flooding her head as she passed each stop.

Why was she meeting him at all? Was it purely her ego that needed massaging? Donal had become remote since telling of his feelings – it was such inconsistent behaviour.

It was five minutes to eleven when she arrived and she ordered a latte and took a seat by the window. The café was empty – a reflection of the seriously diminishing work force from the city.

Jack came through the door at exactly eleven o'clock. His hair was dishevelled and he was unshaven but looked all the better for it.

"Louise," he said formally.

"Hi, Jack," she smiled lightly.

He nodded over at the waitress to catch her attention and order an Americano.

"So, Louise, what can I do for you?"

The tone of his voice was mature and serious – so different to the way that he usually spoke to her. It threw her immediately and she wasn't sure how to respond.

"I was wondering how you were keeping and . . ." she felt foolish but had to know, "and why you were ignoring my texts."

Jack moved uncomfortably in his seat. He didn't want to have to deal with the truth – but then again maybe there was no other way to explain why he couldn't see her any more.

"Louise – it has been good seeing you again and I have to admit that at times I can't help thinking of those special times we had – especially sharing our love of music."

Louise nodded. "It's something that I have missed and that's why I was trying to get back playing for a while . . . before my father's ordeal and operation."

"And that's another reason why I haven't been in touch. You told me yourself that you had commitments and were busy."

This was true. Louise had made it clear that she was under pressure.

"I know I did – I've just been having a tough time and I needed someone to talk to."

Jack felt sorry for the woman sitting in front of him. He was a very different person to the boy he had been at the end of their affair.

"And there is another reason . . ." he started.

Louise looked into his eyes. She was hanging on his every word.

"I didn't want to tell you this but it might explain why I need to keep my distance from you . . ."

"What do you mean?"

Jack's expression was so guilty there was no way that he could backtrack now.

"Maybe being friends isn't such a good idea. I made a terrible mistake when Aoife and I were on a break. I . . ." he hesitated, "I slept with Sophie."

By the look on Louise's face she was likely to blow at any minute.

"I warned you against getting Sophie that job from the start."
Louise was shaking.

He could only try and appease her.

"Look, I made a mistake – one night with Sophie – but I was
back with Aoife the next day. It's really important that it's kept
between us." He regretted his confession already.

Louise gulped. She wasn't sure if she was going to cry or be
sick. Sophie had overstepped the mark just one time too many.
She felt like she could kill her with her bare hands if she came
into her vicinity at that moment.

Jack was relieved that the waitress arrived with his
Americano to serve as a distraction.

"Thank you," he said and took a sip.

As the waitress left, the silence between them hung heavy in
the air. Louise was so shocked she was unable to speak so Jack
said something first.

"It was just one night – it was nothing."

"Why?"

"What do you mean why? Your sister is very attractive."

Louise closed her eyes and shook her head. "I can't believe
you did this to me."

"To *you*? That's priceless. You're married and have been for
years – in fact you may as well have been when we had our
affair."

"She's my sister!"

"This may come as a shock to you but it doesn't matter
whose sister she is – Aoife is my fiancée and she is the person
that matters most to me."

Louise was trembling. She could understand the emotions
Emma had been carrying around because of their younger sister
since returning from Cuba perfectly now.

"She did this on purpose, you know."

"She doesn't know that we were ever together – I told her I
met you in the gym."

Louise shook her head. "Nice one, Jack – as if I've ever stepped foot in a gym in my life!"

"She doesn't care – about you, me or anyone but herself."

"I have to agree with you there – but, Jack, why did you?"

"It was one of those things – a disaster really."

"I hope Aoife never finds out."

"Brenda is moving to the UK and they will have a new team of people installed in two weeks – Sophie doesn't know it yet but her time is up with the paper."

It was little consolation for Louise. She wanted to hurt her sister but couldn't even tell her that she was upset.

"I'm sorry if I upset you, Louise, but you were right – I was only a silly kid back in those days and bumping into you again has made me realise that – almost losing Aoife has made me even more aware of how I really feel. I love her – I've never loved anyone more and I'm going to do everything I can to make her happy."

Louise held tight to her emotions. This wasn't what she had wanted to hear. She had hoped that she might get a boost from talking to Jack – instead her self-esteem was at an all-time low. He had reduced their affair to a ridiculous rite of passage on his part and her great love for him was now nothing more than an illusion. She wanted to cry but instead held on.

"So you see why I deleted your number and haven't been answering your texts – I think it's for the best if we don't have any contact – don't you?"

He was so cold. He had managed to hit her when she was already almost down.

"I think I'd better go." He put a five euro note down on the table. "That's for the coffee."

He stood up and held out his hand. "Thanks for taking it so well – I knew you'd understand."

He spoke like a double-glazing salesman.

Louise shook his hand limply and watched as he walked out

the door. She should never have called. She would have been happy to carry on with the rest of her life ignorant of the fact that Jack had slept with Sophie but now she would have to live with the knowledge.

Everybody seemed to be finding love and moving on with their lives – Emma was on the brink of a visit from her Cuban friend, despite the huge amount of paperwork and red tape still to be worked through. Sadly she walked to Tara Street Station, trying to contain her feelings.

Minutes later she wished that she was somewhere more private than sitting on a busy green train. She felt such a fool – she had carried loving feelings for Jack around for fourteen years and protected them carefully along with the many memories she had of the time they spent together. He was on a kind of pedestal. This was so much worse than that time in the Quay West Café when he had accused her of breaking his heart – now she had no place in it at all and she had wasted so many feelings over the years when she should have been concentrating on her marriage and her relationship with Donal. In the process she had let that slip to the point where they were in danger of breaking up and she was left with no one loving her.

As the train pulled up at Killester station she walked onto the platform. She realised that she didn't want to be home – she needed to speak with Emma.

Emma was frustrated. The system required for getting a visa was more like some sort of evil plot. But with each achievement came an even greater task to be completed. She knew how Arthur felt on his quest for the Holy Grail.

The sudden ringing on the door made her jump. She opened it quickly when her sister's outline became apparent. The red rings around her eyes were the first thing that she spotted.

"Louise – are you okay?"

"That fucking bitch!" she sobbed.

"Come and sit down in the kitchen," Emma said, following her sister as she stomped down the hallway. She hit the switch on the kettle. "What's she done now?" It had to be Sophie who she was referring to – nobody else could make them feel this way.

"She slept with Jack."

"What!" Emma was truly shocked. "When?"

"A couple of weeks ago."

"Wow – she gets around," she said bitterly. "How did she do that?"

"He didn't go into the details – I met him for a coffee in town earlier and he told me. Now he says he doesn't want anything to do with me or Sophie – he just wants to make things work out with his fiancée."

Emma put a spoon of coffee into a mug and a teabag into another. "That's good that he wants to make it work with his fiancée, isn't it?"

"Yeah, I guess – I just didn't realise how that would make me feel – you see, a few weeks ago he wanted to have an affair with me."

Emma poured boiling water from the kettle. "That would have been stupid."

Louise suddenly felt very foolish. Of course her older sister was right and listening to it in this context she realised how ridiculously she had behaved. What must Jack think of her grappling for his attention?

"I know it would have been stupid – but it was nice to feel that someone fancies me."

"Donal loves you – he's your husband – at least he hasn't been messing around like Paul was."

Louise took the mug of coffee from Emma and sipped. "You're right, of course – I just can't stand the thought of Sophie with him – I could kill her."

Emma sat down opposite Louise. She knew exactly how she felt. "You are going to have to get over this, Louise. This Jack Duggan thing has to stop. You've been torturing yourself for nothing all of these years."

"Why does she have to be our sister?"

"I don't know – she certainly has a knack for attracting our men – even when she doesn't realise it."

"She's going to be out of work soon, Jack says, but now she has this Canadian guy coming over to see her next week."

Emma sat up. "Greg?"

"That's him – the one she met in Cuba."

Emma lifted her mug and put it up to her lips. It was infuriating to think of the ease with which things fell into Sophie's lap. Greg was gorgeous, rich and coming to Dublin – and it still wasn't certain that Felipe would be able to get out of Cuba to visit her.

Chapter 20

Nearly six weeks – are you ready for me? Gx

Sophie was more than ready to see Greg. Her love life had been lean since working at *The Irish Times*. The email from Greg couldn't have come at a better time.

Hi Greg
   Where will you be staying? Maybe you could call me during the week and we can make some sort of arrangements?
   Sophiexxx

He replied a few hours later.

I'm staying in a hotel called the Merrion – have you heard of it? It belongs to a good friend of mine who collects art and he told me to look him up if I was in town. I'm looking forward to seeing Dublin again – my friend tells me that it has changed. I will be coming in at 8am on Thursday. Why don't I call you when I reach the hotel?
   Gx

Sophie was excited. She longed to see him again and feel loved. She missed Paul more than ever since returning from Cuba – she hadn't realised how empty her life would be without Emma too. So many things had changed in Dublin and she didn't know if she could stand it. Greg was coming just in time to be a perfect distraction and maybe they could become something more permanent. She was ready for commitment – it was what she and Paul were going to do.

Felipe was losing patience with the system. The government wanted proof of his relationship with Emma. All they had was one photograph taken on a phone at the harbour in Cojimar. How could he tell the authorities that they had only shared one kiss? It was the hope of seeing the beautiful dark-haired woman with the pale skin that kept him hanging on. He wondered about the rest of the world – where free people moved from country to country, not fearing their neighbours telling tales about them.

The porter greeted Sophie at the stone steps of the discreet hotel hidden behind the exceptional Georgian façades.

"Good morning, Madam."

"Morning."

Sophie ran her eyes over the stunning Jack B Yeats paintings as she passed through reception and into the drawing room. The Merrion Hotel reminded her of a stately private home rather than a place of public patronage. The fire was welcoming but too warm for early summer.

She spotted him sitting on one of the couches reading the *Herald Tribune*. He looked even better than she remembered.

Greg lifted his head momentarily – as if he detected her presence. On seeing her mass of curls which had grown since they had met in Havana – he got out of his chair and rushed over to her.

"Sophie from Ireland! How are you doing?"

He pronounced each word with such clarity Sophie couldn't detect the Canadian twang that she had recalled.

"Good to see you, Greg," she smiled as he leaned forward and placed his large soft lips on hers. "How was your journey?"

"Very good – you look beautiful."

Sophie smiled. She had spent an hour choosing what to wear and finally decided on a turquoise blue sundress and killer heels.

"My friend has spoilt me – he has given me the penthouse – from what I hear this is where Bruce Springsteen usually stays so I'm in good company, eh!"

"He does stay here – as well as other celebrities."

"My friend was very coy – said he had a little hotel in Ireland – I'm very impressed."

"What's the penthouse like?"

Sophie wasn't really interested in interiors but she desperately wanted to get Greg on his own now that she set eyes on him again.

"Let's take a look," Greg said, taking his room key from his pocket and tossing it into the air. "It's this way to the lift."

They walked down a glass corridor that led to the extended wing of the building through the perfectly manicured gardens.

When the lift doors shut Greg put his key into the lock above the button for the top floor and turned it.

"Impressive," Sophie said with a smile.

"I like the penthouse floor – it's well hidden away."

The doors of the lift opened, letting in brilliant light and views of the nearby rooftops.

"It's right here," Greg said, putting another key into the door beside them.

He held the door open for her and she entered the reception area – dressed with fine examples of classical furniture and prints of racehorses. "Would you like a tour?"

"I'd rather a drink!"

Greg grinned. "This way," he said, leading her to the lounge with its luxurious couch and vast entertainment system. "I'll get you something in the kitchen – the receptionist said it has the most underused appliances in the city!"

Sophie followed him into the kitchen which had spectacular views of Dublin rooftops.

"Tea, coffee – or something a little stronger, eh?"

"Water – sparkling – will do fine."

"We have that – and they very kindly left some pastries and scones," Greg said, lifting a large plate filled with colourful and appetising treats.

"Just the water will do, thanks."

"So how have you been – Sophie from Ireland?"

Sophie hated the way he called her that but she grinned. "Things have been better – you know that I lost my job when I got home – well, it looks like the newspaper that I had been doing some work for doesn't need me any more so I am unemployed again."

Greg poured from the bottle of Ballygowan. "I thought you were going to start up your own fashion company – what about your recycled knitwear idea?"

Sophie nodded her head. That was something that she should look into but with her father being ill and the hostility between herself and Emma she hadn't been her usual efficient self. "I need to look into it. I don't know if there's anyone left in Ireland with the money to buy exclusive knitwear."

"There are always people with money though they might hide it during a recession! Anyway, forget the Irish market – there's a big world out there!"

"And a bigger recession."

"You can't think like that – artists still painted in the thirties during the last great world recession – some of the greatest modern works were created then. Even in fashion – what about Chanel?"

Of course he was right. But things had been so difficult for her recently.

"I will do something about it on Monday," she promised. "How long are you staying?"

"I'm going back Tuesday morning. I have to meet an art dealer on Monday but I am free to enjoy the sights of Dublin until then – if you want to show me?"

Sophie did. She felt such a sense of relief in the Merrion Hotel. It reminded her of the days when she was with Paul – everything had changed and she yearned for the decadent pleasures that she once had enjoyed so much with him.

Jack wanted to look his best. He was meeting Aoife's relations in The Cellar restaurant in half an hour. He went into the bathroom of his office block with his bag containing a clean shirt and deodorant. He hated these Cullen family get-togethers. He knew that Eileen and Harry Cullen considered their daughter too good for him and it was an opportunity to give little digs. Especially since they had been apart for that short time – Aoife had completely forgiven him and was back to her wonderful self but her parents were even more cautious than they had been.

Jack ran his fingers through his hair and noticed some grey ones in the artificial light. He had to grow up and his close shave with Louise and her sister had been enough warning to help him realise what he had almost lost.

He said goodbye to his colleagues and walked out onto Pearse Street. It was a short walk up to Merrion Square and the Merrion Hotel.

Sophie held out her champagne glass as Greg refilled it. The sun was still quite high in the sky but evening was drawing in.

"Don't you love this hot tub!" Sophie exclaimed taking a sip from her glass. Lying on the rooftop deck surrounded by bubbling hot water was exactly where Sophie wanted to be – especially with a delicious dark handsome man feeding her champagne.

"Dublin is cool!"

"And you haven't even left the hotel!" Sophie said with a giggle. The champagne was going straight to her head.

"Are you hungry?"

"Starving – let's get room service?"

"Why don't we try the restaurant downstairs?"

Sophie looked at him sheepishly. "I don't want to get out of the hot tub." She didn't want to show how tipsy she had become since starting on the champagne.

"We can come back to it after dinner if you like. But you don't want to shrivel up like a raisin, eh?"

Sophie had to agree – they were in it for over an hour but with copious glasses of champagne it had felt like a few minutes.

"Okay – let me get dressed," she said, taking a bathrobe from Greg and stumbling as she stepped out of the hot tub. She wrapped the robe around her wet body. "I'll be two minutes." When she made it to the bedroom where she had left her clothes the walls started to spin. She picked up her bra and couldn't close the catch. She was much more drunk than she had realised in the tub.

Greg walked over to the rails and looked down at the perfectly manicured garden. The dome of government buildings rose above the rooftops to his right. It was a nice start to the weekend.

Emma put Finn's dinner down on the kitchen table.

"Thanks, Mum."

She had become accustomed to the two of them eating together and it was nice now that her mother had moved back home. She figured that maybe it was time to tell Finn about the possibility of a visitor from Cuba.

Now that she had sent off Felipe's passport along with the proof of their acquaintance and an international bank draft to the Irish embassy in Mexico it wouldn't be too much longer before they could settle dates for his visit. Emma wanted to pay for his flight but didn't know how to say it to Felipe without making him feel uncomfortable. So far they were coming in at four hundred euros and that would be many month's wages for him. What he had spent on her in Havana was proportionately much more than the cost of a flight. As each day passed she knew that she wanted to see him more and more. She missed companionship and intimacy – it had been a long time since she had made love – even with Paul the gaps between those times had been too long and she wanted to feel young and alive again like she had when first in love.

It was high time she told Finn. She looked at him tucking heartily into the mound of mashed potatoes and fried chicken and smiled. Her son had grown so much since his father had died. He had taken on the mantle of the man of the house. He even put the bin out and collected it without having to be asked.

"You know, Finn," she said, "when I was in Cuba I made a friend who might be coming to visit us for a while – would that be okay?"

Finn shrugged. "Sure – she can't be any worse than Granny."

"Eh, it's not a lady – it's a man."

Finn shrugged again. "If he's just on holiday that's okay – how long is he staying?"

"Nothing is set in stone yet – I don't even know for sure if he will be coming – he has to get a visa."

"What's that?"

"It's permission to leave the country and to enter Ireland. Remember when I asked for your old Barcelona football shirt for the little boy that lives in Cuba – well, people are very poor there and it is hard for them to do certain things that we take for granted."

"Sounds weird." He tucked his head into his dinner. "I'm calling for Gavin after – that okay?"

"You can stay out until nine and then straight to bed – you have school in the morning."

Finn nodded and took a gulp from his glass of milk.

"Thanks, Mum," he said, lifting his plate and putting it in the sink.

As he ran out the back door Emma realised that he would be gone soon – a teenager before she knew it and then so consumed with his own social life that he would have little room for her. She was doing the right thing allowing Felipe to visit. If it was only a holiday fling, so what! It might just be the first phase in building a life for herself. She needed to because some day she would be on her own if she didn't do something about it now.

Jack was early. He descended the stairs on Merrion Square and entered The Cellar restaurant. It was discreet and tasteful in the way that the starched white linen tablecloths echoed the stone vaulted ceilings and walls. Cream upholstered period chairs rested elegantly everywhere and a single red rose decorated the middle of every table.

In the corner he spied the table that Harry and Eileen Cullen usually booked. The maître d' came over and offered to take Jack's bag and bring him to his seat. He wanted a beer but Aoife's parents wouldn't like it. It was a small price to pay – he was so glad to have Aoife back and he would do anything to keep her happy. This dinner was another charade – a prelude to sending out the official wedding invitations and the way that Aoife's parents wanted the procedure to be done.

He looked at his watch. Aoife'd had a job in Dun Laoghaire earlier but that would be well finished by now. Suddenly he spotted her wearing a bright orange shift dress – standing out like a beacon amongst all the white in the restaurant. He rushed over to her and gave her a kiss on the lips.

"Thanks for being early!" she whispered.

"Are your folks with you?"

"Dad is parking the car," she smiled and took his hand as they made their way to the corner table.

"Have a look at the menu – I didn't want to order the wine until your parents got here."

"Good idea – you know what Dad's like about his grapes!"

They smiled at each other and leaned in over the table. Jack only had eyes for his fiancée.

"Jack – what are you doing here?"

Jack looked up – unsure who the voice belonged to.

Standing there, shaking her mop of curls, was Sophie.

Jack looked at the tall dark man at her side. He appeared to be a good deal older than his date.

"Eh, Sophie, hi." Jack stumbled over his words with the surprise of seeing her. He remembered his manners just in time before Aoife became aware of the awkwardness he felt. "This is Aoife."

Aoife held out her hand and smiled widely. "I'm Jack's fiancée."

Sophie ignored her hand, threw her head back and gave a little laugh. "That was quick, Jack – you got engaged in the few weeks since we were together!" If she hadn't had a bottle of champagne on an empty stomach she mightn't have found it so funny – or she might have had the sense to say nothing.

"Come on, Sophie, our table is over here," Greg said, taking Sophie by the elbow and guiding her over to another table.

"Bye, Jack – I hope you'll be very happy!" Sophie called with another little laugh.

Aoife was trembling and wide-eyed. "What does she mean by *since we were together*? Please tell me that you were not with that woman." Her eyes were filling up and she was trying to contain her emotions.

"Aoife, I can explain."

"Tell me that you didn't have sex with that woman!" Her voice was more animated and even though he was three tables away Greg could hear her voice clearly.

Jack swallowed hard. He couldn't lie to Aoife – he had to tell her the truth – after all, it meant absolutely nothing.

"It was a terrible mistake – it was when you said that you wanted a break for a week."

"It wasn't that sort of break – it was time out from each other – not an opportunity to go around sleeping with anyone we fancied. Anyway, it wasn't even a week!"

Jack could feel the roof of his mouth go dry. "I'm sorry, Aoife – I was hurt and confused – it's been so brilliant now that we are back."

"But we never broke up – I didn't go around sleeping with other guys!"

Her voice was louder now and even the maître d' was shuffling around his station anxiously. This sort of behaviour was not condoned.

"I'm sorry – there was no need for you to find out."

"Oh, so now it's my fault for finding out? Maybe it's just as well that we ran into your little friend. It's better that I find out now than after we are married – Irish divorces are messy."

"Please, Aoife – there's no need for that – I can explain, honestly – let's go home and talk about this."

Aoife's voice was almost at shouting pitch. "There's nothing to explain!"

Suddenly the presence of Harry Cullen and his wife overshadowed the argument.

"What's going on?" Eileen Cullen demanded.

"Take me home," Aoife said, standing up and taking her bag off the table. "We don't need to talk about invitations because there isn't going to be a wedding!"

Aoife brushed by her father and ran out of The Cellar.

Harry lifted his arm to stop Jack from running after her while his wife followed to comfort her daughter.

"Why is my daughter so upset?"

"It's a misunderstanding – that's all!"

Harry wrapped his long strong fingers around the collar of Jack's shirt. "If you have done anything to hurt my daughter I recommend that you keep as far away from me as possible – I know a lot of people in this town – don't forget how you got that job in *The Times*!" He released his grip and pushed Jack down onto his seat, then turned on his heels and left.

Jack stood up. He looked over at Sophie and Greg. She was laughing and drinking from a freshly poured glass of champagne. He walked over to them with fire in his belly. He stood at their table and glared at Sophie.

"I helped you to get some work when you lost your job – and this is how you repay me! Your sister is right – you're dangerous, Sophie Owens!"

"Take it easy, Jack," Greg said coolly. "Join us for a drink, eh?"

"No, thanks. Goodbye, Sophie – if I never see you again it will be too soon."

As he left Greg surveyed Sophie. She was sipping her glass of champagne and seemed unphased by the whole caper.

"You like causing upheaval in other people's lives?" Greg asked with a smile.

"It's other people overreacting!" she sighed.

"Maybe – or maybe you're a wicked girl!"

Sophie shrugged – she was so numb from the champagne she had little control of the words coming out her mouth. "I have to think of myself. Don't forget I was meant to be happily settled now with Paul."

"But he was your sister's husband, eh?"

"He was her husband – but he was my soul-mate."

Greg wondered if she was deluding herself. Emma was a stunning woman too and, although he would never know Paul, he guessed that he was in love with both of them. It was best to change the subject.

"Let's plan what we will do tomorrow. I'd like to see Emma again!"

Sophie rolled her eyes. "The last person I want to see at the moment is Emma – anyway I haven't seen her since we came back from Cuba."

"Why not?"

"I – I – I – eh!" she didn't want to come across as a complete bitch – after ruining one relationship so far tonight she didn't want to tell Greg that she had told Emma that she had slept with her husband. "It's a long story – do you want to go to O'Donoghue's after dinner? It's a typical Irish pub and only around the corner on Baggot Street."

Greg took a sip from his glass. Sophie was hiding something. It didn't matter to him. He was in Dublin on business and he was only filling in his time with her.

Louise pushed the washing into the machine and turned the dial. She hated it when she left her chores until the evening. Her life seemed so empty since her little fantasy had been shattered. Jack Duggan could no longer be a part of her memories – she had to get on with her future with a husband who seemed no longer very interested in her.

She would have to call and see that her parents were okay before she set off to do the shopping. Life had become so mundane again.

She grabbed her car keys and set off for Foxfield. Since Emma became so preoccupied about getting her Cuban to Ireland she was quite happy to leave the responsibility of their parents to Louise. Needless to say, Sophie couldn't be counted on for any help whatsoever.

Louise parked up at Foxfield and rooted around in her bag for her set of house keys. Since the burglary neither parent was anxious to answer the front door and insisted that all of their daughters let themselves in.

The sound of daytime TV came from the lounge and she went in there first.

Larry was sitting with a newspaper resting on his lap and a pair of spectacles on the end of his nose.

"Hi, Dad."

"Louise – I didn't hear you coming in!"

"Is Mum around?"

"No, she's gone to the shops. I'm glad you called – I wanted to talk to you about her birthday."

Louise stopped to think. "How old is she?"

"She's going to be seventy – I think we should do something nice for her – especially after all that she's been through."

"I didn't realise that she was seventy already! Well, we have about four weeks – it's the twentieth of June."

"Would she like to go out to a restaurant for a meal, do you think?" Larry asked.

Louise raised her eyebrows. "Why don't we do something here in the house?"

"You know your mother – she won't want a mess. Would you have it in your house?"

Louise thought for a moment. "Emma has a bigger house than we have and she only has Finn."

"Will you ask Emma what she thinks?"

Suddenly the realisation that Emma and Sophie would have to be together in the same room for this occasion hit Louise and she panicked.

"Leave it with me, Dad – I'll think of something and get back to you."

"We had better do it soon – we could always take a room at Clontarf Castle and have a big party and invite your cousins and all the neighbours."

If the function was big enough she would have a better chance of keeping Sophie and Emma apart. She hadn't seen Sophie since speaking to Jack and wondered how she would stomach looking at her younger sister herself.

"I'll ring up Clontarf Castle and see what they can offer – or we could always use the Yacht Club if you like."

"I hadn't thought of that – look into it."

"I'm going to Tesco – do you want me to get anything?"

"No, thanks – I'll ring you tomorrow to see what you've found out."

Louise let herself out through the front door, her mind buzzing with concern.

Greg walked down Grafton Street with such an air of confidence and ease that several heads turned as he passed.

Sophie was pleased with the reaction that the handsome Canadian was getting and proud to be walking at his side.

"Did you enjoy O'Donoghue's last night?" she asked.

"The music was great – and so was the Guinness."

"Would you like to try another pub for lunch?"

Greg shrugged. "Does Emma live near the city?"

"She's out in Sutton – it's miles away – you really are better off staying around the centre where everything is happening."

"Whatever you say!"

Sophie guided him through the Hibernian Way and out onto Dawson Street.

"I know a good place – I think you'll like it."

They took a table in the corner of Marco Pierre White Steakhouse and Sophie observed the heads turning at her handsome date.

Suddenly her phone rang. When she saw Louise's name flash up she turned it off. She didn't want to be disturbed for the rest of the weekend.

Louise drove to Emma's house. She wasn't surprised that Sophie had cut her off. She knew that she would be hiding her Canadian visitor away for the weekend.

Emma answered the door with a beaming smile across her face.

"Someone's happy!" Louise was glad to see her sister this way.

"It looks like the Irish Embassy has accepted Felipe's application for a visa."

"I'm really glad for you – when did you hear?"

"Felipe rang last night – he got a letter in the post. It's not all plain sailing though – he still has to get some stamps of approval at his end."

Louise followed her sister in to the kitchen. It would make it easier to tell her the bad news if she was already in good form.

"I'm glad you're getting somewhere. Have you any idea when he'll be coming over?"

"I've been surfing the net for flights and there's really good value from Virgin Atlantic through Heathrow – I picked up a special for the sixteenth of June so fingers crossed all of the paperwork will be through."

"That's great. I've just come from Dad's and he reminded me that it's Mum's birthday soon."

"Not until next month."

"Yes, but it's her seventieth!"

"Oh my God – I completely forgot it was a big one!"

"Exactly. And he wants us to organise a party for her!"

"You're joking!"

Emma took a seat at the kitchen table and put her head in her hands. "I don't think I can stomach seeing our little sister – and we'd all have to organise this party together."

"It's smack bang in the middle of your friend's visit too."

"Damn. I don't think I can change the flight – it's a special offer."

"Maybe it would be nice for him to see an Irish party."

"Where does Dad want to have it?"

"He wanted me to have it in our house first and then suggested Clontarf Castle but I think the Yacht Club might work out as better value."

"God, I don't think I can go through with it."

"Emma, I hate the thought of it myself! But with a bit of luck there'll be a huge crowd and we won't have to speak to Sophie for the night."

"I just don't need the pressure of Felipe in the middle of it."

"But he'll be a good distraction for you."

Emma nodded. "Maybe you're right. Will you talk to Sophie then?"

"I will try and not puke all over her when doing so! She's with her Canadian this weekend so I will call her Monday. Donal and I are going to dinner in the Yacht Club tomorrow night with the Harleys so I can ask about catering and that for the twentieth."

"Thanks, Louise. You're a star."

Louise smiled. She was taking the mantle of the family organiser from Emma for this family get-together and it felt good. She needed to feel good about herself because since talking to Jack she had felt very low.

Chapter 21

Greg was bored. He wanted to see more of Dublin than the inside of the penthouse but Sophie was determined to keep him in bed for as long as possible each day.

"Why don't we take a trip out to the sea?"

Sophie felt the need to perform for Greg. Her usual tricks weren't working. She would just have to do whatever he suggested.

"Okay – we'll get a taxi – I'll take you out to Howth."

They took a shower and dressed hurriedly. The breakfast things were splayed out on the large table of the penthouse living room. Sophie grabbed her bag and coat from where she had flung them the night before and led the way out to the lift.

"How long will it take us to get there?" he asked.

"About half an hour if the traffic is light – we could get the train instead – it would probably be quicker."

Greg smiled. "Let's do it."

They boarded a green train with Howth written above the driver's window and took a booth in the corner of the carriage.

Sophie nestled in under his arm. She wanted so badly to make this man fall in love with her and even though they had such a good time she didn't feel like she was getting to him and it didn't feel good to be the one trying to impress.

The train pulled up at Sutton station and the islands of Lambay and Ireland's Eye came into view.

"It's very pretty."

"I suppose it is," Sophie replied.

"Isn't Sutton where Emma lives?"

"Yes. We are almost at Howth."

Greg wasn't going to ask about Emma any more. Secretly he had hoped that he would see her again. It seemed such a shame to come all this way and not get to see her.

Emma looked at her watch. She had been so busy reading over Felipe's emails that she almost forgot to collect Finn. He was playing a hurling match in Howth and she would have stayed to watch but she had to do as much work as possible before Felipe came over to stay. Instead she had managed about forty words and a lot of daydreams.

She grabbed her bag and car keys and jumped into her little green Mini. It was a sunny day and warm enough to take the roof down. She felt elated as she drove up the hill past the graveyard and up towards the summit where the views of Dublin Bay were second to none.

She was so lucky to live in such a beautiful place. She turned into the GAA club where people were standing on the sidelines and cheering. She felt horribly guilty as the crowd applauded the home team for such a spectacular win over their rivals.

Finn spotted her in the distinctive small convertible and ran over with victory glowing all over his face.

"Hi, Mum – we won and I scored three points!"

"Well done, love! That's great."

"Can we get an ice-cream in Anne's on the way home?"

"Of course," she smiled. Finn loved nothing better than a 99 cone and it was a glorious day to go down to the seafront and get one.

They drove through the village and Emma parked up in front of the Pier House pub. She let Finn run into Anne's for the ice-cream while she watched the locals and visitors stroll down the east pier toward the lighthouse. It truly was a beautiful place to live. She often walked the east pier and enjoyed observing the patterns made by the masts of the yachts in the marina and the colourful fishing boats lining the wall of the west pier.

She felt very much at peace with her life. She still thought about Paul but had managed to contain her emotions and put a perspective on the whole unfortunate episode that led up to his even more unfortunate death. She had Finn and she had her health and unlike so many people burdened with huge mortgages and debts she was comfortably able to support herself and her son.

Finn emerged from the shop with two huge cones – licking one of them hungrily.

"Thanks, Finn," Emma said, taking the other and the change from him as he sat into the passenger seat.

"I love it when you take the roof off, Mum."

"I agree, love – it's a pity we don't have weather like this every day."

She pulled out onto the road and drove slowly along the seafront.

"Look – there's Sophie!" Finn called.

Emma looked to where her son was pointing and swerved with the shock of seeing Sophie with Greg at her side.

A Land Rover Jeep was coming along the road towards them and swerved suddenly to avoid the small Mini. It ploughed into a Fiesta that was parked on the side of the road.

Emma screamed with the shock of nearly being hit by such a huge vehicle.

"Mum – he nearly killed us!"

Emma parked at the footpath to avoid the debris and pulled herself together.

"We have to ring the Gardaí – that was all my fault."

The traffic piled up along the promenade and Greg and Sophie continued walking – oblivious to the collision their presence had caused.

Jack tried to call Aoife but her phone turned straight to voicemail yet again. It had been two days and two very long nights since his disastrous meeting with Sophie in The Cellar restaurant and he couldn't believe how it had all fallen apart so easily.

Suddenly his phone rang and he rushed to answer it in the hope that it was Aoife.

"Jack – it's Eileen – Aoife's mother."

"Oh hello, Eileen."

"I'm downstairs – could you let me in? Aoife asked me to get her clothes and things."

"Just press the door," Jack said. He felt an uncomfortable lump form in his throat. Apart from her husband, Eileen was the last person he wanted to speak to.

She arrived at the door with a deep frown across her forehead and an empty suitcase at her side.

Jack took the bag and followed Eileen as she stormed into the small apartment.

"Is this the bedroom?" she asked with disgust, opening the door on her left.

The bed was tossed with clothes strewn all over it. Traces of Aoife covered the small dressing table and tumbled from the half-open cupboards.

"Do you want me to help you?"

"I don't think Aoife would like you handling her garments or personal items and I certainly wouldn't as her mother!"

Jack backed in to the kitchenette and skulked behind the counter as the woman who would have been his mother-in-law cleared any trace of the woman he loved from their bedroom.

She emerged like a gladiator, triumphant and laden with spoils.

"Aoife asked me to find out a day next week that you will not be here so she can take pictures and other ornaments."

"I won't be here on Monday."

"Fine. I can't say I am happy about this, Jack, but I am pleased that my daughter had the good luck not to have married you."

Jack stared blankly at Eileen. There was so much that he wanted to say but the words failed him. He hadn't a leg to stand on.

"Tell Aoife that I love her."

Eileen smirked and shook her head. "You must be joking – you don't know the meaning of the word!" She stomped out to the lift, pulling the suitcase alongside her.

Jack threw himself onto the couch and shivered. For the first time since he was a little boy he wanted to cry. He wanted his mother to comfort him and say that it would all be all right. But he knew that what he had done could not be made all right.

Finn rang his aunt. "Louise, Mum and me have been in a car crash. Well, we didn't hit anything but a jeep swerved to avoid us and hit a parked car."

"Are you okay?" Louise's voice was high with anxiety.

"Yeah, we're okay."

"Where are you?"

"We're in Howth. We saw Sophie and then Mum swerved. She's shaking and doesn't want to drive."

"Look, where exactly are you?"

"Outside Casa Pasta."

"Donal's in the Yacht Club working on the boat – stay where you are and I'll get him to come over and help."

"Thanks, Louise."

Finn hadn't seen his mother like this since the morning they had found his father lying still on the bed. The driver of the Land Rover was busy talking to the owner of the Fiesta who had just arrived. He seemed irate and was pointing over at the little Mini.

Emma stared at the steering wheel in a trance now that the event was sinking in – she had almost killed herself and her son. Her head jerked up and she looked over at Finn who was visibly shaken.

"Are you all right?"

"I'm fine – we didn't touch anybody. Are you okay?"

Suddenly a shadow fell on the car from the towering figure of a man who looked like he was about to explode.

"You should look where you're going – I could have killed you – and you're damn lucky there was nobody in that car I hit!"

Emma looked up at the man who was in his fifties with a figure laden with experiencing too much of the good life.

"I – I – I'm sorry – I didn't see you coming."

"Well, you need to keep your eyes on the bloody road!"

Finn felt uncomfortable – he wanted to stand up for his mother but the man was so big and strong he felt frightened.

"What's going on?" a voice asked and Donal's tall figure appeared.

The driver turned and looked Donal up and down.

"Do you know this woman?"

"She's my sister-in-law."

"Well, she should be taken off the road. She nearly drove straight into me – I had to swerve and hit that car over there. Who's going to pay for the damage?"

"I will," Emma said meekly.

Finn was glad to hear his mother speak.

"Hold on, Emma – we have to find out exactly what happened." Donal was protective and although he understood the driver's viewpoint he was more concerned about his sister-in-law.

"It's okay – I wasn't looking where I was going."

"You see!" the Land Rover driver said adamantly.

"Give me your name and address and I'll see that this is handled properly," Donal said, taking a pen and his wallet out of his pocket.

"I'd like that lady's number and address – and insurance details."

The Gardaí arrived and started to divert the traffic that was building up. One of them came over to the driver of the jeep and asked him to remove it – nobody was hurt in the collision and the main priority was to clear the way so that people could carry on.

Donal handed Finn a five euro note. "Why don't you run into Beshoff's and get yourself a bag of chips?"

Finn took the money and got out of the car.

Donal sat down on the passenger seat beside Emma and put his arm around her shoulder.

"Are you okay?"

Emma nodded. "Thank God you came when you did – I really don't think I could have handled that man on my own."

"You're all right and that's the main thing. What happened?"

"I was driving along finishing off my ice-cream when Finn shouted that he could see Sophie – I took my eyes off the road and must have driven into the middle and the driver of the jeep crashed into the parked car."

"Did Sophie see you?"

Emma shook her head.

"She can cause trouble even when she isn't trying, that girl!" said Donal.

"This was totally my fault."

Donal kissed Emma on her forehead. "You're okay now. Come and get into this seat – when Finn comes back with his chips I'll drive you both home."

"Thanks, Donal. You are so good to me."

Donal smiled. Emma always made him feel so appreciated. It was a pity his wife didn't make him feel the same way.

"Would you like to have a coffee?" asked Sophie. "There's a cute little place called Il Panorama along the seafront – they do the best cappuccino in Dublin."

"Sounds good – we might get something to eat."

"What do you think of Howth?"

"Very pretty – but the Irish drivers are crazy – did you hear that crash back there?"

Sophie shrugged. "I wasn't looking."

"Do you sail?"

"My sister Louise and her husband have a boat in the marina but I don't go out. I like to stay in the city – there's more happening. Let's cross here – the traffic's at a standstill."

They opened the door into the small but welcoming café. High stools filed with patrons lined the bar and window front. Sophie spied two free stools against the wall and rushed over to take them.

"What-ah you like?" said the friendly Italian behind the counter.

"I'll have a Melbourne panini and a cappuccino, please."

Greg ordered the same for himself. He perched on the high stool beside Sophie and smiled.

"So, Sophie, what are you going to do when your contract ends with this newspaper?"

"I'll probably try and get a job back in design."

"What about starting your own label, eh?"

"This recession is more serious than I thought – I don't really think it's a good time."

Suddenly Greg's phone bleeped. He took it out and read the message.

"Everything okay?" Sophie asked.

"That was the art dealer – he wants to meet me tomorrow instead – says he has some business in London on Monday – it might be worth my while going with him."

Sophie looked up at him, wide-eyed with disappointment. "That would mean you'll be going home a day early?"

Greg shook his head. "No – two days!"

Sophie had to hold her breath to contain her upset.

"We've had a good time – haven't we, Sophie from Ireland – eh?"

Sophie nodded as the friendly Italian guy brought over two cappuccinos. She had to pull herself together – she was losing her touch and this gorgeous man was obviously not half as interested in her as she was in him.

Louise had her brown hair blow-dried straight – it was always so much shinier when the hairdresser did it. She wanted to look her very best. The Yacht Club was a beautiful venue and it should have been a treat that she looked forward to but she often felt uncomfortable when the conversation turned to racing tactics and sailing jargon.

"Are you ready?" Donal asked.

Louise turned around. She hoped that actions spoke louder than words.

"You look lovely."

"Thanks," she said. It was the most positive response she'd had from her husband in two weeks.

As they drove in his comfortable and sensible Volvo along the coast road they exchanged trivia and matters involving the children and the day-to-day running of the house.

"Dad wants a party for mum's seventieth birthday in June."

Donal nodded. "Very good. Where?"

"I suggested the Yacht Club."

"They'll be glad of the business and it's a nice venue."

"That's what I was thinking. Emma will be bringing her Cuban boyfriend so that will certainly spice the night up!"

Donal pulled up at a traffic light and slammed harder on the brakes than he normally would. "She's not bringing that fellow over here? He'll be looking for a way to get out of Cuba – she'll be setting herself up for all sorts of problems. I really thought she had more sense."

"Take it easy, Donal – what can we do about it? She's an adult and her private life is her own business."

"She's a vulnerable woman who lost her husband less than a year ago – if we don't look after her who will? Look at the mess she got in today with the driver of that jeep!"

Louise was perturbed by her husband's response. "It's not up to us anyway – you did everything you could today!"

"She only has us – Sophie has been the cause of so much pain for her – first the affair and then throwing it in her face after she was taken on the trip to Cuba."

Louise gaped at her husband. "You know about the affair with Sophie and Paul?"

"Emma told me."

"When?"

"It doesn't matter – you obviously knew but didn't think highly enough of your sister or me to confide in us!"

Louise took a deep breath – she was better off saying nothing. Emma must have met her husband and confided in him since she returned from Cuba. She was so mad.

They travelled in silence the rest of the way until Donal parked up in a spot outside the club. He locked up the car and they walked solemnly up to the door.

Louise couldn't understand what was happening to her husband and her once secure marriage. As they climbed the steps up to the bar she had to hold back the tears. She took a right at the top and let her husband go on without her. She needed to find a mirror in the bathroom to touch up her make-up and hide the distress that was bubbling underneath. She took a few deep breaths and turned to go out the door.

Judy Harley entered the ladies' room as she was leaving.

"Louise – hi. How is your dad doing? Kevin told me what had happened."

"He's doing fine, thanks."

Judy was larger than life and her flaming red shirt sang of designer brands. "That's good – I was so worried when you cancelled our last little soirée – your poor parents. It all sounded so horrific!"

They walked into the bar where Donal and Kevin were standing with two pints of Guinness in hand. Louise wondered how her once adoring husband could have become more concerned about her sister than her.

Sophie got up to answer the phone. She had never before hated Mondays. Greg had left for the airport the night before with a kiss on the cheek and a wink but with no mention of ever contacting let alone seeing her again. Whoever was at the other end of the line had better have good news or she would hang up.

"Sophie – it's me!"

"What do you want, Louise?"

"It's nice to talk to you too!"

"I've had a bad weekend and Brenda from *The Irish Times* texted to say she didn't need me any more."

"I thought you had your gorgeous Canadian visiting?"

"He went back early – and he isn't gorgeous or my Canadian!"

"Fine – we need to talk about Mum's birthday – she's seventy this year. We are having a party for her in the Yacht Club."

"When were you thinking of having it?"

"The twentieth of June – her actual birthday."

"Is Emma going to be there?"

"Of course she is! And don't think she is any happier at the prospect of having to spend an evening with you than you are with her!"

Sophie winced. "I'm not going."

"Yes, you are! And more than that, you're going to help me organise it – you don't even have work as an excuse any more."

"Why are we having this charade?"

"Daddy wants to do it for her – it's the least we can do."

"I'll talk him out of it."

"You'll do nothing of the sort. I've drawn up a list and you can do calligraphy on the invitations – that's something you're good at!"

Sophie huffed and puffed.

"You can call out this afternoon and help me with it," Louise went on.

Sophie knew there was no point in arguing. "What time?"

"After two thirty – I've got to collect the kids from school."

"Okay!" Sophie slammed down the phone.

She picked up her pillow and held it over her face with frustration. She hated her sisters and she hadn't much time for her mother. She hated her boss for running off and causing her to lose her job and she hated Greg. At the moment she hated the world. She decided to pay a visit to her family doctor on the way – she needed some help to get through the next few days and especially the run-up to her mother's party.

She called into the surgery but Doctor Lowe was out on call – in his place was a locum who was new to the area. Sophie knew what she wanted – something to relax her – help her cope. She sat down opposite the good-looking Indian man who was immediately taken by Sophie's good looks.

She laid her heart on the line telling of how terribly she was let down by her boss after her return from Cuba and how her new job was nothing more than a stopgap and she needed something to give her back her confidence. The doctor didn't want to prescribe Xanax but Sophie knew what she wanted – she had taken them before and liked the way they made her feel. Before he knew it the doctor was filling out the details on a fresh prescription. Dr Lowe was a pushover but this guy was even easier. At least she hadn't lost her touch completely with men.

The keys on the laptop clicked as Emma hit the full stop with pride. If she continued working at such a pace she could be finished with her novel before Felipe arrived. Suddenly her phone rang and she knew instinctively it was him.

"Hello?"

"Hello, Emma – how are you?"

The line was crackly.

"Felipe – have you good news about your visa?"

"I must . . . the office . . ."

He was cut off. It often happened when he rang. Cubans were given little credit for the CUCs they spent on their phones.

She dialled his number and he answered quickly. The line was a little better but still crackly.

"Are they looking for more money from you?"

"It's okay because I now have the flight ticket so they understand."

"You printed it out – that's good."

Felipe wanted to pay for the ticket himself and only agreed to let Emma book it if he repaid her once he got to Ireland.

"My friend Miguel has got his printer to work so I must get everything that I need now."

"Exactly – before it breaks down again!"

They laughed together.

"How is Dehannys?"

"She is well. She wishes she was coming to Ireland also."

Emma felt butterflies in her stomach – talking to him meant that the dream was now turning into a reality.

"I would love to see her too but I'm glad that I will have you all to myself!"

"Maybe we can have another kiss like the one in Havana?"

Her heart beat faster. "I've been reliving it over and over since I left."

"Me also."

Suddenly the line went dead. They had become accustomed to disruptions whenever they tried to communicate but somehow they didn't matter – a couple of words from Felipe were better than a lengthy conversation with anyone else at the moment. The distance didn't seem to matter either. Emma was falling in love.

Louise opened the door.

"It's half past three – what have you been doing all day?"

"That's none of your business," Sophie said, brushing by her sister and going into the kitchen where she sat at the table. "Right, show me what you want done – I haven't got all day!"

Louise got down to business. She handed a sheet of paper and a gold calligraphy pen to Sophie. Then she plonked a pile of invitations down in front of her.

"Why did you buy these? There's loads to fill in – you should have got them printed with all of the detail on them and then I would only have to write on the envelopes!"

"We haven't got a lot of time – it's less than four weeks and some of these have to go to England and the States."

"You don't imagine her brother Chris will come over from Chicago?"

"He has to be asked. And Dad said we should ask Alice. Don't make such a big deal of it. I've put the kettle on – do you want a coffee?"

"What do you think Mum will do if her sister appears in the Yacht Club after all of these years?"

Louise shrugged. She was as scared at the prospect of her mother and aunt meeting as much as the inevitable meeting of Sophie and Emma.

"Let's just do as we are asked."

"This is going to be a fiasco, you know!"

Louise didn't want to agree but she had an uneasy feeling in the pit of her stomach. There could be two different generations of feuding sisters blowing up in Howth Yacht Club and there was nothing she could do but organise the occasion.

Sophie grunted, took the first card out of the pack and reluctantly started to write.

Chapter 22

Jack walked into Harry Byrne's to see Peter – it was as close to a counselling session as he could handle. He ordered a pint and took it over to the corner that Peter had made his own.

"All right, Jack?"

"Need a refill, Peter?"

"Can't. I have the car – won't be able to stay long this evening – I've a date."

"Who is the lucky lady?"

"A girl in work – she's hot – can't believe she said yes when I asked her out."

"You've got a job – you're becoming an oddity on the streets of Dublin!"

Peter nodded. "We've been really busy – with a new client base too – lots of businesses looking for creative advertising – you wouldn't believe the amount of fast-food joints coming to us."

"You're lucky. I'm scared Aoife's dad is going to say something to my boss and put me up next for the boot."

"He wouldn't, would he?"

Jack shook his head. "I haven't heard from Aoife for two and a half weeks. This is the pits, man."

"Well, keep trying – I'm sure she'll come round."

"I wish I had your confidence."

"What are you going to do, man?"

"I don't know. I can't imagine being with anyone else. I really thought she was the one."

Peter took a drink from his half-empty glass. "You have to go after her – do you know where she is?"

Jack shrugged. "I presume she's staying at her mum's."

"Well then, get out there and go after her."

Jack took a drink from his beer – it left a tiny layer of froth along the top of his lip.

"Her father said he'd kill me."

"Of course he did – what did you expect him to say?"

Jack nodded. "I suppose I could call out on the DART."

"Go for it, man – there's no time like the present."

Jack knew that he was right.

"I'll drop you off at Clontarf Road DART station after this," said Peter.

"Thanks, mate."

Jack wasn't sure if he was doing the right thing but he had to do something.

The DART rolled into Malahide Station and Jack wondered if he could go through with it. He had only a short stroll up through Malahide Village. Aoife's parents lived in one of the nicest houses on Grove Road. He kept asking himself what was the worst thing that could happen? Harry Cullen could beat him to pulp and in a way he felt that he deserved it – it might not make Aoife forgive him but it would leave him feeling vindicated.

It was a bright evening and the sun was still in the sky. The beach looked perfect for a leisurely stroll. He tried to think positively and imagine Aoife agreeing to walk down the sandy stretch as the sun went down. That would be definitely the most positive outcome. He would have to try – sulking in his apartment in Howth wasn't going to help him win her back.

The tree-lined road was perfectly manicured with huge gates and pillars at the entrance to the sculpted gardens behind the freshly painted walls. It was a privileged address in Dublin and Aoife was a special girl who had been treated like a princess from the time she'd been born – he didn't blame Harry and Eileen for hating him the way that they did.

When he was halfway up the road he paused as the electronic gates of Aoife's parents' house started to open slowly. He wanted to hide behind a tree but didn't want to look like a burglar. The crunch of footsteps on the gravel driveway were followed by laughter and Aoife's unmistakable voice. Jack felt his heart leap and he started to walk quicker – this was perfect timing – he would get to see her without having to confront her parents.

Aoife was wearing a shocking pink dress with a white cardigan over her arm. Her blonde hair was shiny and silky and she wore a pretty pair of strappy sandals. But it wasn't her striking appearance that left Jack dumbstruck but the tall dark-haired man who was resting his arm around her waist. He looked like he had stepped out of the pages of an Armani catalogue and Jack wished that he himself had shaved at least.

Aoife stumbled as she realised who was on the footpath in front of her.

"Jack, what are you doing here?"

"I – I – I came to see you."

The Armani model quickly figured out the identity of the scruffy character who was a good six inches shorter than he was.

"I'm Karl," he said, holding out his hand.

Jack looked at it and then at Aoife. He started to take backward steps.

Aoife stood firmly on the pavement. She started to shake and let Karl put his arm protectively around her shoulder.

Jack turned and ran – like a kid who had been caught robbing from a neighbour's apple tree. He didn't look back all the way to the railway station and when the first green train came to the platform he jumped on, sat in a corner of the carriage and hid his face in the palms of his hands. He had never felt so awful in his life.

Sophie opened the wardrobe to decide what she would wear for the day. It was difficult when she had no particular place to go. So many of her clothes were boring and she would never wear them again.

Greg had left for London two weeks ago and not sent as much as a text to say if he had or hadn't enjoyed their time together. She felt utterly sick inside.

She didn't even have any money to buy a special dress for her mother's stupid birthday party. She started to take pieces of clothing that she would never wear again and fling them onto the floor. As the wardrobe became emptier and the pile on the floor larger she started to rip the clothes until some were in strips.

She threw herself onto the bed and started to sob loudly. She had never felt so sorry for herself. How did her life come to this? A year ago she was the very epitome of success.

She had a full bank account, a fabulous lifestyle, a wonderful lover and a career that most people would only dream about. Now she was left with an apartment that she couldn't afford to live in, a sports car that she didn't have the petrol to drive and no man to love her. She wondered where it had all gone so wrong.

She sat up and took a smart pair of grey work trousers and started to tear them apart. They were so well cut and stitched that Sophie found it difficult with her bare hands.

She started to use her teeth to pull the threads apart and her feet to hold the fabric steady. As the garment ripped to pieces she began to feel a sense of relief. The trousers were a symbol of the old life she had to leave behind. Things were happening outside her door on such a cataclysmic scale that her little story was no different to the many thousands who were now joining the ranks of the unemployed.

She would never be destitute – or on the streets – she could always move back to Foxfield if she had to. But the thought of sharing personal space with her mother didn't appeal.

Sophie was scared. She missed Emma and the security she had as a child when Emma was always there to stand up for her – in the playground or on the streets of Foxfield. She had burnt her bridges there. And in a week she would have to face her and the rest of her family at her mother's party.

She picked up a pink cashmere cardigan that she used to wear with Paul and held the soft fabric up to her cheek. He loved it when she wore it. He would stroke her arm gently and rub his cheek off her shoulder. There were so many good times they had shared together. She hadn't wanted to hurt Emma when she told her about Paul – all she had wanted was recognition that she had loved him too. She held the cardigan away from her and looked at it objectively. Then she angrily ripped the sleeves off and unravelled the strands of wool. She was so confused and hurting inside. If she pulled all of these clothes apart she would be kept busy for the rest of the day.

Chapter 23

Emma checked the calendar that hung beside the fridge. It was definitely June sixteenth. She switched on the kettle and put some bread in the toaster. It was eight fifteen and Finn needed to be up soon or he would be late for golf camp.

She hollered up the stairs and he grunted a reply that she couldn't hear clearly. In two short hours she would be at Dublin airport and with Felipe at last. She wondered if she would recognise him instantly. It was difficult to remember his face clearly with only one photograph as reference.

As the weeks had passed in the lead-up to his visit she had come to know him better through his emails and short telephone conversations. Her phone bill was horrendous but it had been worth it. She had learned so much about his family and life. Obtaining the visa was an experience in itself and, as in most societies no matter how idealistic they appear on the outside, the Cuban government showed itself to be fuelled by hard currency.

Finn slouched and dragged his feet as he entered the kitchen.

"Will you have some toast, love?"

"No, thanks – I'll have cereal."

He reached, with little effort, up to the top cupboard where Emma used to hide treats when he was little.

"Remember I told you about our visitor from Cuba – he's coming today."

"Yeah – you told me about ten times this week."

Emma took the milk from the fridge and put it in the middle of the table.

"He's just a guest – a friend."

"Look, Mum – it's fine. I'm busy – Gavin's asked me to play tennis with him tonight so I'll be out of your way."

"There's no need for that – I want you to meet him."

"He's your friend – and Louise said I can stay with her if I want."

"It would be nice if you had dinner with us tonight."

"I'm eating in Gavin's and he said I can have a sleepover if it's okay with you."

Now her son and his friends were organising sleepovers between themselves. Where was her little boy? Since hitting two digits the week before he was on his way to being a teenager.

"But I'd like you to meet Felipe."

"I can see him tomorrow."

Finn stood up and put his cereal bowl into the dishwasher. He went over to his mother and gave her a kiss on the cheek.

"Relax."

Emma was speechless. She took her car keys and bag and followed Finn and his golf bag out to the car.

The wheels of the plane made a loud thud as they touched down on the runway at Dublin Airport. *"Fáilte romhaibh, a chairde, go Baile Átha Cliath,"* said the air steward.

It was Felipe's first time to hear the Irish language spoken. The fields below had been green as the aircraft made its approach and all of the houses and buildings had seemed so neatly arranged and clean compared to the landscape he had left at Havana.

The passengers were in a rush to get off the plane and the click from their seatbelts sounded like dominoes dropping.

Felipe let the woman who had sat silently beside him on the hour-long flight from Heathrow airport pass him by and then the people in the rows around filed through.

He reached up into the overhead bin and pulled down the worn black bag which held his valuables.

The first thing he noticed as he descended the steps of the aircraft was the cold. It amazed him that most people around didn't seem to feel it – it must have been no more than eighteen degrees. Emma had assured him that the weather was good and they were in for a dry spell. He pulled his jumper from his bag and pulled it over his head. With his passport and boarding pass in hand he made his way to the terminal. He almost hadn't made it out of Havana. The Irish visa was a simple stamp on the back page of his passport. It bore no photographic identification and Felipe nearly had to pay the grumpy man at the emigration desk in Havana a hefty backhander to get out of the country. Thankfully another man had taken over and let him pass through to departures only minutes before the plane was due to leave.

Felipe was used to such inconveniences and he could tell by looking around at the well-dressed people who had travelled with him from London that his way of living was as alien as if he were from another planet. Felipe didn't care – once he was in baggage reclaim it was only a matter of minutes before he would see Emma again.

Emma stood at the red rope barrier which separated those waiting from those arriving. She could feel the dryness in the roof of her mouth with her tongue and her heart-rate increased. The plane had landed twenty minutes ago – she could be there for another twenty if his luggage was delayed. Her palms were sweaty and she was breathless with excitement.

Suddenly she saw him. He had a duffle bag over his left shoulder and a shabby tote bag in his right hand. His hair was now cut considerably shorter and he resembled a poet more than a rebel. His dark eyes peered nervously around the arrivals hall from under his dark brows.

She wanted to run over and grab him but the strangers around blocked their path to each other.

He spotted her through the crowd and smiled. She was wearing a pink striped dress that showed her neck and shoulders off. Her black hair was tied back loosely in a ponytail and she wore her sunglasses on her head.

She waved and started to walk quickly until they were upon each other. Then she wrapped her arms around his neck and hugged him tightly.

He let the bag in his right hand fall and returned the embrace.

"You made it!" Emma said. Her eyes widened with joy and she looked lovingly at him as he gazed back.

"Yes – thank you, Emma!"

The gaze went on and on, they were so overcome with the pleasure of seeing each other that just looking was enough for them both.

"Come on," Emma said linking her arm in his. "It's a lovely day – tell me all about your journey – did everything go okay?"

They walked out into the sunshine like two excited teenagers launching into a great adventure and talked all the way along the M1 and M50 as Emma drove in her little green Mini.

"The road is very good."

"It would make life easier for you in Cuba if you had motorways like us!"

"And this country is so clean!"

Emma shrugged. "I suppose it is now but it wasn't always like this."

"It's amazing!"

"You must be very tired?"

"No, I had a lot of sleep on the plane."

Emma proudly drove up the driveway of her modest dormer bungalow and watched as Felipe's eyes widened.

"You have a big house, Emma – for you and your son only?"

Emma had taken her lot for granted before travelling to Cuba but now she appreciated all of the luxuries that she was used to.

"Yes, Felipe – just the two of us."

She parked up and watched as he surveyed all around with amazement.

He followed her into the kitchen and she put the kettle on.

"Would you like a coffee?"

"Thank you."

Emma was prepared. She remembered how many coffees he had taken during the short time they were together.

"Where is your boy?"

"Oh, he is at golf school."

"I hope he will not feel that I am intruding."

"Of course not, Felipe – he's looking forward to meeting you," she said as convincingly as she could. "You'll see him tonight. But this afternoon – would you like me to show you around the area? There's a really nice pub called the Summit Inn and this is a perfect day to sit outside and watch the world go by!"

Felipe shrugged. "That would be good – I am happy to go out but do you mind if I take a shower first?"

"Of course – how rude of me. Let me show you the bathroom while the kettle boils."

She led him upstairs. "That's my room," she said as they passed the first room on the left. They stalled for a moment on the landing. Sleeping arrangements had not been discussed but somehow both knew that her room was where they would be sleeping later.

Emma reached into the hot-press and took out a towel and handed it to Felipe.

"There you go. The bathroom is just over there – I'll be downstairs."

"Thank you," he replied and again they stared for a brief moment.

The thrill of seeing each other was proving too much for Felipe. He longed to grab her and hold her the way he had dreamt of when he was in Cuba but for now he felt that when it did happen it had to be right. She was a widow and had to be treated with respect.

Emma smiled at him and went downstairs. Felipe joined her a short time later, looking delicious in a black T-shirt and jeans.

As soon as they had drunk their coffee, they jumped back into the car and Emma gave him a geography lesson of the area as she swept along Carrickbrack Road. She pointed out the Dublin Mountains and told him about the landmarks of Dublin Bay.

Felipe listened and watched. Their lives were even further removed from each other than he could ever have imagined.

Emma parked at the side of the road in front of the Summit Inn and got out.

"What will you have to drink – would you like to try a Guinness?"

Felipe nodded. "Yes – that would be good."

The wooden seats and tables in front of the pub were half full and a dog lay prostrate in front of them.

Inside, the pub was rather bare but a turf fire was lit in the corner of the bar and a pool table and jukebox stood in the corner at the opposite end.

"A glass of Bulmers and a pint of Guinness, please," Emma said and watched as the Russian barmaid pulled at the taps. "Would you like something to eat, Felipe? They do a good steak sandwich."

Felipe could feel the juices in his mouth at the very mention of steak. It was a rarity in Cuba to come across any food product from a cow and it was a criminal offence to kill such an animal – it could result in a sentence longer than one for murdering a man.

He nodded.

"Can I have two steak sandwiches also, please," Emma continued and then took her glass and beckoned for Felipe to follow.

They rested at the nearest outside table where the view over the treetops of north County Dublin was spectacular.

"Cheers," Emma said and clinked her glass off his. "I hope you have a nice time in Dublin."

Felipe lifted his pint, took a sip and looked over the creamy white head with intense eyes.

"I think I like Ireland very much."

She hoped he would be saying the same thing in a few days' time when she brought him to Howth Yacht Club and her mother's birthday party.

Donal stormed through the front door from work and threw his bag on the hall floor.

Louise knew from the thud that something was wrong.

He went into the kitchen where Louise was chopping some carrots.

"What's the matter?"

Donal walked over and hit the switch on the kettle. "I've been in bad form all day since getting that text from you."

"I know it's awkward but I didn't think you'd mind putting Aunt Alice and Dick up for the night – you never minded before."

"Your mother hasn't spoken to her sister for years – don't you think the feud between Sophie and Emma is going to be enough to deal with at your mum's party? Maybe I'm sick of carrying the can for your sisters. Why can't she stay with Emma? She has four bedrooms and only uses two."

"You know why! Because Emma has her friend from Cuba staying."

"It's always left to us – and we aren't exactly in great shape lately!"

The tone of Donal's voice scared her. "Look, I'll ask Sophie if she can put them up," she said.

"Your aunt won't want to stay in town."

"Well, I'll see – I'm sorry this party is causing so much hassle – I'm not exactly looking forward to it myself!"

Donal closed his eyes. "I'm going up to change – I won't be having tea."

"Where are you going?"

"Kevin wants to take the boat out – it's a nice evening."

Louise threw the knife down on the chopping board. Donal wasn't the same any more. A gnawing feeling in the pit of her stomach told her that it wasn't her aunt that was causing Donal's bad humour but the state of their marriage. He had identified their problems but they hadn't done anything about their situation. She shouldn't have let it get to this stage. Emma was the one she had always talked to when she needed help and advice but she was in her own world since returning from Cuba. She had to put her marriage right – she just didn't know how to start.

Emma led the way off Strand Road and past the Martello tower that had been built like so many others around the Irish Coastline during the Napoleonic era. The path they trekked was made by walkers and children who knew that the surrounding fields were a great place to play.

Felipe was adjusting to the comfortable temperature and at ease with the cool sea breeze that blew onshore from across Dublin Bay. They sat like two nervous teenagers and watched the Stena Seacat race along the mouth of the bay and make her way up to the River Liffey. It was good to be together – two people who were not quite lovers – yet!

Felipe had spent many nights with sweat teeming down his brow as he thought of Emma and tried to imagine what it would feel like to make love to her. Now that she was so close that he could smell her perfume he was filled with a sense of fear that to touch the beautiful woman that he had dreamed of would be too much and would shatter his illusions of her.

But so far they were happy to just be and that was enough for now.

When they got back to her house he sipped on a rioja as she peeled and chopped vegetables. He offered to help but she wouldn't hear of it – instead she insisted he sample the nachos and guacamole that she had prepared before he arrived.

He enjoyed watching her movements and made sure to control his drinking even though the rioja was one of the best wines he had ever tasted.

At last the meal was ready.

"Let me help you with that," Felipe said, taking the two plates of freshly cooked vegetables and chicken from Emma.

"Thank you," she said with a smile that melted his heart.

They took their seats at the kitchen table and clinked their glasses together. Felipe was smoulderingly handsome in the last light of day which was slipping through the window. Emma watched every move he made with his knife and fork – enjoying the familiarity of companionship. It felt so different to the last few years with Paul – Paul who had cheated on her and left her feeling so guilty. She wondered would she be able to trust this new man in her life fully.

"That was very good, Emma – you are a very good cook." He cupped his hand around hers.

"Would you like to go into the living room?" she asked.

He answered her with a longing in his eyes that said more than words.

They had been together for almost twelve hours.

"Will we open another?" she asked.

Felipe shrugged, smiling. "You are the boss!"

It was something that Paul would never have said in a million years and it sounded liberating.

Emma took the corkscrew and a fresh bottle of wine into the living room. They sat closely on the cream leather sofa, sipping on red wine and listening to strains of Cuban guitar on a CD that Felipe had given her. Unprompted, he put his arm around her shoulder and she shivered with excitement. All the work and effort they had put into organising the trip had been worth it. This was what she had missed – this was what she needed in her life.

"Thank you, Felipe," she said.

"What did I do?"

"You've no idea how much you have helped me. In Cuba you let me see that there was a future out there for me. I didn't have the guts to follow your lead then but I feel ready now."

"What changed for you?"

"On the flight home Sophie told me something – something I found very difficult to hear."

Felipe stayed silent. It was up to Emma to tell him when she wanted.

"It's changed how I see life – I realise that my marriage to Paul was a lie. I thought we were happy – we were good together but then he must have needed something else – or rather someone else."

Felipe still didn't push her – he was there to listen to what she had to say.

"It seems he was having an affair with Sophie for three years before he killed himself."

Felipe was visibly shocked.

"What are you thinking?" she asked.

"It is not nice to hear. I don't know what I can say, Emma. It is between you and your sister."

"I feel so torn inside. It had been eating me up for so long trying to understand why he killed himself and this new information is so hurtful. I don't want to be the reason that he killed himself. Was he so keen to hide his infidelity that he would do such a thing?"

"Your husband had a problem. He killed himself because he was not happy with himself."

"I should have listened to you – now I know what was going on in his life it is clearer somehow. I see why he was so confused. But Sophie I can't ever forgive – to do that to your own sister!"

Felipe reached over and caressed her cheek gently. "Don't be like that – that is not the real Emma."

"I can't help the anger I feel inside towards her."

"Don't hold it – it will make you unhappy. But now you are free – no?"

Emma nodded. She loved the feel of his strong fingers against her cheek.

"I suppose I am free now."

"Good," Felipe said and leaned forward to place his lips on hers.

They felt as wonderful as they had under the moonlight on the beach at Miramar.

Emma woke with the realisation that she was not alone in the bed for the first time since she had lost Paul. She looked over at Felipe's ruggedly handsome profile as he slept. It was the most safe and happy she had felt in a very long time.

Suddenly the telephone rang out on her bedside locker.

"Hello!"

"Emma, it's me!"

"Hi, Louise," Emma sighed. Louise knew that it was Felipe's first night and Emma couldn't believe that she would ring so early.

"Listen – Aunt Alice is coming home for Mum's party."

"You're joking – did you invite her?"

"I had to – I didn't think she'd come."

"And Dick?"

"Yes, he's coming too."

"Does Dad know?"

"I showed him the list but you know him – I doubt he even looked at it. I didn't want Aunt Alice to get wind of the party and feel left out – she's still talking to Chris in Chicago."

"Is he coming?"

"No – said he didn't get enough notice."

"When is she arriving?"

"On Friday – she asked if I would put them up. I told her that I'd make up a bed in the children's playroom!"

"I'd say she was put out at that suggestion!"

"She sure was – but I don't care – I've enough to sort out – and Donal is freaking out that they're staying. Typically our little sister seems to have gone missing!"

Felipe started to stir. His eyes opened and he looked up at Emma.

"Listen, Louise, I have to go here," said Emma hastily. "I'll call you later."

Emma put the phone on the locker and slid further down in the bed.

Felipe didn't speak. He put the palm of his hand up to her cheek and caressed it gently. Then he leaned forward and kissed her on the lips.

Their mouths melted together and they took up from where they had left off the night before.

Sophie answered the phone.

"Where have you been?" said Louise. "I've been trying to get you for days!"

"Hi – I've been working."

"You got a job?"

"No, I've been designing my own stuff."

"You've been at home all the time?"

"What's the hassle?"

"You do realise the party is on tomorrow night?"

Sophie huffed. "Of course I do – but that's tomorrow – not tonight."

"What about the preparations?"

"You said the Yacht Club will be doing the catering."

"They are but there are the decorations and menus and that!"

"Just relax – you love making work for yourself and the rest of us."

"It's not just that – Alice and Dick are coming over and they want to stay with us."

"So?"

"Well, I had hoped she could stay with you."

"My apartment is too small!"

"But there's only one of you – there are five of us and Finn wants to stay here now that Felipe has arrived."

"So our sister finally got her man over!" Sophie couldn't hide the sarcasm in her tone. She had been jealous that Emma could grieve in a way that she couldn't and now she resented the way her sister could move on with ease.

"Yes – and, as you are the only other person who knows him, the least you can be is polite to him tomorrow night."

"I've no problem with him – just don't expect me to talk to Emma."

"You better be on your best behaviour – I don't want a scene – this is Dad's gig and he wants everything to be nice for Mum."

"What time do you want me there?" Sophie asked with a sigh.

Emma and Felipe went into Dublin – it was the day before the party and Felipe had it in mind to get some new clothes.

His eyes showed amazement and wonder as he looked in shop after shop along Grafton Street. Unaccustomed to that kind of shopping, he was anxious to leave the hustle and bustle of the shops and go for lunch as soon as he had purchased a shirt and pair of chinos, so Emma led the way to Bewleys.

The waitress hurried over and put the menu into Emma's hand.

Emma glanced over it. "An Americano and a tea, please – what would you like to eat, Felipe?"

"I am not hungry, thank you."

"That's fine," Emma said, handing the menu back.

Emma guessed that Felipe could tolerate eating the food in her house but would find it difficult to cope with her paying for things when they went out.

"I have a gift for your mother – a dolphin carved out of wood."

"There was no need to buy her a gift – she wouldn't expect anything."

"I also have one for you." Felipe reached into his pocket and took out a small velvet-covered box. He opened it to reveal a fine gold chain with an encrusted pearl dangling from it. "I wanted to give it to you yesterday but now seemed like a better time."

Emma held it up against the back of her hand. "It's lovely!"

"It is – how do you say – *antica*?"

"It's an antique. It's very beautiful." She wondered what story the necklace could tell – where it had been and who had given it to some other woman before. She put it on and pressed it to her breast. "Thank you – I love it."

"You know, Emma, I did not know when I left Cuba how difficult it would be to see so many things that you can buy. People in this country have so much."

Emma wasn't sure what to say – they had so much but many of them didn't appreciate it. And what the Celtic Tiger era had shown was that material wealth hadn't made the country or its people any happier – if anything it had made them more miserable – especially since the economy had changed.

"It may look that way to you," she said then, "but we are going through a recession now and lots of people will not have it so easy."

"You know a little of life in Cuba, Emma – if my countrymen could have a small part of the things you have in Ireland they would be so happy."

Emma smiled. "But material wealth is only skin deep – it doesn't make you happy and it hasn't made Irish people happy. The people in your country have music and they dance better than anywhere I have ever been."

Felipe took her hand and cupped it in his as he had done the night before. "Music is important, nice things are important but love is the most important – do you agree?"

Emma blushed. Of course it was – it was the only thing that mattered and after sharing the last twenty-four hours with Felipe she was beginning to remember what that felt like.

Chapter 24

"How do I look?"

Louise turned around to show the swing of her black chiffon dress with its heart-shaped neckline.

"Very nice!" Donal nodded and fixed his yacht-club tie tightly under the collar of his shirt.

"Louise – do you have an iron?" a shrill voice called from the hall.

Donal turned and looked at his wife without saying anything. Her aunt had only been in the house for three hours and already she had managed to upset the children's routine and the general order of the house.

"She's just like your mother – and that's saying something!" he muttered under his breath.

"Sssh! She'll hear you."

"I don't care!"

Louise ran out to the landing. "I'll do it for you – what do you need?"

"Dick's shirt has creased in the case!" Alice handed it to her with a smile. "Thank you, lovey. You are so obliging. I hope your mother realises how lucky she is having you on her doorstep."

Louise didn't wonder why Alice's two daughters had emigrated to Australia before they had their twentieth birthdays.

Felipe came out of the shower and hurried into the spare room.

Emma caught a glimpse of him and blew him a kiss as he passed by. Finn was back home and they would have to sleep in separate rooms tonight.

"Are you ready?" she called to Finn.

The young boy emerged from his room looking uncomfortable in the stiff-collared shirt and cream chinos.

"Do I have to wear this?"

"Your cousins will be dressed up too. It will be great when we get there." She tried to sound convincing but secretly was scared of what the night was going to hold. She hadn't spoken to Sophie for so long and she wondered how she was going to feel when she saw her. Felipe couldn't have come at a better time. He was more than a distraction – he was now a support and she would take all the help she could to get through the evening.

Sophie took out the short red Jackie-O shift dress that had been saved from the slaughter she had carried out on her wardrobe a few days before. It would have to do. She had let her hair dry naturally and the curls were springing up nicely.

She didn't want to be the first there but she knew that if she wasn't there by a quarter to eight her father would never forgive her.

Larry opened the driver's door for his wife.

Maggie brushed passed him looking like an elegant older version of Sophie – she continued to carry hues of strawberry blonde in her hair and for a woman of seventy she carried it off stylishly. She was wearing a silver dress and strap sandals that a woman half her age would have difficulty walking in.

"Where are we going again?" she asked as she got in.

"Aqua – it's the restaurant on the end of the pier."

"Oh well, at least that's a nice place. I was very hurt that none of the girls called into the house today to say Happy Birthday."

"They have a lot going on in their lives, dear," said Larry as he got in on the passenger's side. "Anyway, we will see them as soon as we get to Howth."

"Emma never even phoned me."

"She has that Cuban fellow staying."

"I don't know what's got into her – she is meant to be in mourning – Paul's not even a year dead."

"Things are different nowadays." Larry said, securing his belt while his wife started the engine.

"They certainly are," said Maggie. "You get no gratitude at this stage in our lives, Larry."

"I know, dear!"

Larry put on some music to distract his wife on the route out to Howth.

"Donal said that he would meet us at the Yacht Club first for a drink," he said.

"Why do we have to go there – why couldn't we have a drink in the restaurant?"

"It's where they want to meet."

"I thought it was supposed to be *my* birthday."

Maggie drove down the west pier and took a right turn at the car park. As she pulled up, the loud hum of a sports car's engine sounded as Sophie's car came up beside them.

Sophie stepped out and zapped the alarm on.

"Hi, Mum – Happy Birthday!"

"Thank you, dear," Maggie said. "This is a terrible inconvenience dragging us to this place first."

Ignoring this, Sophie hugged her mother. Then she walked into the Yacht Club and her parents followed.

"They're coming!" Louise said urgently to Emma and she rushed over to tell the DJ to stop playing the music. The lights were dimmed and the guests, who numbered more than fifty, stood silently around the room.

Sophie appeared first and as she entered received daggered looks from Louise.

"You're late!" Louise mouthed.

Then Maggie and Larry appeared.

"*Surprise!*" the crowd chorused around the room.

The DJ started to play "Happy Birthday" and everyone sang as Maggie Owens stood there with a wide grin across her face.

Emma had to admire her father's foresight. This was exactly what Maggie wanted. She loved to be the centre of attention. Emma stood close to Felipe and watched to see if Sophie had spotted her yet. Their eyes met and the betrayal and hurt that Emma felt poured out.

Sophie turned her head and took a glass of champagne from the tray on the bar.

Her flirty glances around the room agitated Emma all the more.

"Can I get you some champagne?"

Emma turned her gaze to the handsome man at her side. "Thanks, Felipe, that would be nice – I'd better go over to Mum."

Emma walked over to her mother who was surrounded by her friends from the bridge club.

"Happy Birthday, Mum!"

Maggie hugged her daughter. "Thank you, darling – I suppose I have you to thank for all this!"

"Actually, Mum, it was Dad's idea – Louise did most of the work with the venue and invitations – I can't take credit for any of it!"

"Oh!" Maggie said as one of her neighbours rushed up to be the next to give her a congratulatory kiss.

Emma dodged Sophie on her way back to Felipe and bumped into her Aunt Alice.

"Emma – introduce me to your handsome young man – you didn't waste any time getting yourself a nice dish!" Alice said in her cultivated English accent that hid every trace of her roots on the Navan Road.

"Come over and meet him."

"Where is he from?"

"He's Cuban."

"My goodness, people are coming to Ireland from everywhere these days!"

"He doesn't live here, Alice – he's on holiday."

Felipe stood with two glasses of champagne in his hands. He handed one to Emma and offered the other to the lady accompanying her.

"Felipe, this is my Aunt Alice. She lives in England."

"Pleased to meet you," he said, holding out his hand.

"And where did you meet Emma?" she quizzed, taking his hand.

"In Cuba."

"When were you there?" Alice asked Emma.

"I went at Easter."

"How lovely! I've always wanted to go there."

"Have you spoken to Mum yet, Alice?"

Alice took a sip from the champagne glass. "I'm saving that – laying low while the mob adores her!"

There was an edge to her tone that scared Emma. Why had she decided after all these years of silence to break the deadlock and come and meet her mother face to face? Maggie had never told her daughters why they had fallen out.

"I see the way you're looking at Emma and I don't like it – just

310

remember this is Mum's party and I don't want you causing a scene," Louise said nervously.

"You don't need to worry about me – I don't plan on staying long."

"You will stay here until the end and help me to tidy up too!"

Sophie sighed and took a sip of her champagne. "The average age here is eighty – even the kids don't drag it up."

"They are all Mum's friends. Just put up with it for tonight – okay?"

Sophie's eyes were wandering around the room. She spotted the handsome man in the corner and looked twice before she recognised him to be Felipe – he looked hunky with his new short haircut and smart clothes. From what she remembered he could dance too.

She walked away from Louise, went over to the DJ and picked up a couple of his CDs.

"Have you got anything from the twenty-first century?"

"Hey, this is the music I was asked to play – the 50s and 60s."

"Well, that Frank Sinatra track is definitely the 40s! Can you liven it up a bit?"

"I'm only playing what I was told to."

"Well, don't mind my sister – she has no taste. What about something Latin – a salsa or something?"

The DJ shrugged and changed the track. The tempo was faster and the music louder. Sophie fixed her gaze on Felipe and started to walk over in his direction. She was halfway across the room when Louise apprehended her.

"Don't you dare go near Emma's boyfriend!"

"I'm only going to say hello."

"You've done enough damage!"

"Well, I'm sure Emma would love to hear that you knew about my affair with Paul and never told her!"

Louise looked at her. "How spiteful and low can you go,

Sophie? I'm beginning to think that you haven't a good bone in your body."

"It's you guys that have the problems. It's always all right for you two to mope around and wear your feelings on your sleeves. What about everything I've been through? I miss Paul too, you know – and more than Emma by the look of it!"

To Louise's relief Larry stepped over and took his youngest daughter's hand.

"Dance with your old dad?"

Sophie couldn't refuse. She would be looking for a large bail-out in the coming days. Her bank account was now empty and her credit cards maxed out. She hadn't the courage to tell him that she hadn't paid her mortgage this month either.

Felipe grabbed Emma's hand before she went to speak to anyone else.

"Please, can we go outside?"

"Of course – sorry I've been neglecting you."

She let him lead her out through the glass doors to the balcony where the views of the harbour and Ireland's Eye were stunning. The sun was setting to the west and casting pink hues on the white yachts in the marina.

"You live in such a beautiful place."

"I suppose I do. I often take a walk down the pier in the mornings to clear my head."

"Havana is so hot now. The air in Ireland is so clear and cold."

"This is summer so it actually gets a lot colder than this!"

Felipe seemed horrified.

"You need to come here in the depths of winter – we had snow in Howth this February for the first time in seven years!"

"I would like to see snow."

Emma looked out to the west and the sun which was now

turning into a big red ball as it slipped behind the restaurants and fish shops along the west pier.

"The sun is reflecting in your eyes," Felipe said with a smile. He reached his hand forward and brushed it off her right cheek. "Emma . . ."

"Felipe, how nice to see you again!"

Felipe put his hand down quickly and took a step backwards.

Sophie stood between them waving her glass of champagne in the air.

"I thought you'd have the sense to stay away from me tonight!" Emma glared at Sophie.

"I wasn't talking to you!" said Sophie.

"Well, I'm talking to you – why don't you go and amuse Alice?"

"Some people make such a fuss – don't you agree, Felipe – they have trouble letting bygones be bygones!"

Felipe hid behind his glass and took a sip.

"Excuse us, Felipe," Emma said, taking her younger sister roughly by the elbow and leading her over to the far side of the club where they would be out of sight from the other partygoers. "I've been avoiding you in case you haven't noticed because I can't stand the sight of you but, you know, I realise now that you did me a favour. My husband, your darling lover, was a man in a mess!"

"He was a wonderful man and everything would have been much better if he had left you like he was going to and made a new life with me!"

Emma had had enough – she needed to tell Sophie the truth.

"You naïve stupid little bitch!"

Sophie gasped, lifted her hand and struck her right palm off Emma's cheek.

"Feel better now, do you?" said Emma.

Sophie glared. "If anyone's a bitch around here, it's you – and none of them realise it. I know you go around like the perfect femme fatal but you bored your husband!"

"At least I'm not responsible for his death – that's something you can give yourself full credit for!"

Sophie frowned. "What are you talking about?"

"Paul didn't die of natural causes – Paul killed himself!"

Sophie's mouth dropped. Her eyes widened in disbelief. "Paul had a heart attack."

"Yes – from taking too many pills. Paul killed himself because you pressurised him into leaving me – he obviously didn't want to hurt me so he killed himself – it was the only way he saw out of the situation *you* had put him in!"

"You're lying!"

"Does the truth hurt, Sophie? You've been a spoilt brat all of your life – now it's time to grow up and live with the consequences of your actions. You've been in a dream world since you were first wrapped up in cotton wool – but guess what, little sis – it's time to wake up!"

The sound of footsteps didn't shift the girls' gaze.

"What are you two doing out here? Dad's been looking for you both to bring out the cake." Louise wished she could slip away when she saw the look on her sisters' faces.

"Sophie has been having a little lesson in life – haven't you, Sophie?"

"Come on," Louise urged. "Can't you two leave it until after the party?"

Sophie's eyes started to fill. "Like you're fucking perfect – you knew about Paul and me and never told Emma! There, Emma! How do you like that – think you can trust Louise now? She's trying so hard to be just like you – maybe she'll bore her husband to death too!" She turned and fled down the stairs and to the back gate.

"Where's she going?"

Emma shook her head. "I don't know."

"What did you say to her?"

"I told her the truth about Paul."

Louise gasped.

Emma stared accusingly at her. "Did you know about her affair with Paul all along?"

Louise shook her head. "Emma, I'm so sorry for not telling – I didn't want the family to fall apart . . ."

"Like it is now?"

"I didn't think it would do any good."

"Even after he died?"

"Especially after he died – I didn't think it would help your pain. Believe me, Emma, if I thought for a second that it would have helped I would have told you."

Emma sighed loudly. "I thought I could trust you – of all people."

"Please forgive me – I really was thinking of you."

Emma was exhausted after the outburst with Sophie and in the scheme of events Louise's secret wasn't important any more.

"Let's just get tonight over with, shall we?"

"What will I do about the cake?"

"Tell Dad to wait a while – I need a drink and time out. A great weight has been lifted off my chest at last."

"Maybe Paul can rest in peace now."

"Maybe we all can – I need to move on with my life, Louise."

"I think we all do."

Louise and Emma walked around to where the partygoers were dancing to Michael Jackson's *Can You Feel It?*

"Is that Mum and Alice dancing and laughing together?" Louise asked with disbelief.

"I think it is," Emma said, shaking her head with amazement.

Felipe came over and put his arms around Emma comfortingly. He kissed her cheek where minutes before Sophie had slapped it.

"Are you okay?" he asked.

"I am now."

Sophie ran out of the Yacht Club and up the pathway to the children's playground. She could barely see through the well of tears that filled her eyes. Her sobs were so loud a couple walking their dog along the promenade stopped to check that she was all right. She brushed them away and took a rest on one of the swings. The sky was turning to a deep blue and in the east some stars were out for the night.

She held onto the chain of one of the swings and started to push herself with her feet. As the momentum brought her back and forth she tried to forget how terrible she felt about herself. How could Paul have killed himself when she loved him so much? She thought that her love would be enough for anyone. She thought that she could have anyone that she wanted. But the way Greg had left Dublin without contacting her showed that maybe life wasn't always going to be played by her rules. It was bad enough being unemployed and having no money. She shivered as she thought about her life. She needed a cup of coffee and looked over at Beshoff's chip shop across the road. She had to pull herself together. She held onto her bare goose-pimple-covered arms.

The queue was short and Sophie joined behind a young couple who weren't long in their teens. Their innocence and apparent love for each other made Sophie tremble. The customer at the top of the line took his brown bag of food and turned around. He had taken only two steps before glancing at the girl in the red dress.

"Sophie?"

"Jack! What are you doing here?"

"I live in the apartments a few doors up. What are you doing out this way?"

"I'm at my mum's party over in the Yacht Club."

The cashier called down to Sophie. "What you like?"

"Just a coffee, please."

"So what are you doing over here ordering a coffee?"

"I had a bit of a row . . ."

Jack lifted his eyebrow. He was still angry with her after what

316

she had said to Aoife but she looked pitiful. He could easily just turn around and ignore her but curiosity made him stay.

"Who did you fight with now?"

"Emma – it's all my fault really."

The cashier put the foam cup on the counter. "That will be two euros, please."

Sophie slipped her small bag from her shoulder and snapped it open.

"Here, I'll get it for you," Jack said, reaching deep into his jeans.

"Thanks," Sophie said, taking the cup from the counter gratefully. "I was over in the playground." Jack was obviously a genuine type of guy and she had treated him terribly.

"Do you want to go back there?" he asked.

Sophie nodded and started to walk. Jack followed her – not quite sure why he was. His nights were boring since Aoife had left. He was down on his luck and secretly pleased with the company.

"Fancy eating your chips at the playground?"

"Sure – why not?"

"I'm really sorry, Jack – I was such a bitch that night in the Merrion Hotel."

"What I did wasn't right either – I shouldn't have slept with you when I was still with Aoife. I've been trying to work it through in my head for the last few weeks and I've come to the conclusion that I have to take the rap for my own actions."

Sophie took a deep breath. That was something she'd never had to do before – things used to fall into place so easily. "I didn't mean to hurt you and Aoife – I wasn't thinking – I had a lot to drink that afternoon. Is everything okay now?"

Jack shook his head. "She's met someone else."

"Didn't take her long!"

Jack nodded. "That's what I thought. Maybe I'm not marriage material."

"I know what you mean – I don't think I am either. What are your plans?"

"I've lost my job in *The Times* and I'm going back to New York!"

"I wish I was going to New York," Sophie said – and she meant it.

"It's different to here. I need to get distance between myself and Aoife. I can't stand the thought of her with someone else."

"Was she The One?"

"I thought so – then I met your sister Louise again and I was thrown."

Sophie tilted her head. "What do you mean?"

"I was her pre-wedding fling."

"You and Louise were lovers?"

Jack nodded. "Before she was married."

Sophie was shocked – and it took a lot to shock her.

"I can't believe it – you must have been very young?"

"Louise was my teacher – but we waited until I left school."

"Isn't it ironic that I should be your pre-wedding fling?"

Jack gave a little laugh. "I never thought about it that way – but it is. Only we both have different outcomes. I didn't go through with mine. Do you think Louise did the right thing with Donal?"

Sophie threw her head back and laughed. "Oh God, absolutely! They are perfect for each other – I don't know if they realise it yet though – probably won't until one of them dies."

"That sounds very morbid."

"That's the way some couples are – then when they lose each other they appreciate what they had but it's too late."

Jack put a chip in his mouth – he felt like a ten-year-old kid sitting on a swing in the deserted playground.

"I'm glad I bumped into you," Sophie said, staring vacantly in front of her. "You know, I think you are meant to go after Aoife – don't give up."

"Is this to make you feel better?"

Maybe it was. Sophie had left a trail of destruction around her and was on her own with no job or anything good to look forward to in the near future.

"Yes! Absolutely. You have to win your fiancée back for me!" Then she laughed. "I don't really care about Aoife but you're not so bad. Listen, I'd better go back to this party. Thanks for the coffee."

"You're welcome! Thanks for the advice. Say hi to Louise for me!"

Sophie walked back towards the Yacht Club, looking over her shoulder every now and again at the man on the swing. She couldn't make up to Paul or Emma but hopefully Jack would get sorted out. As she came to the door of the club she realised that she couldn't go in. She looked over at her car – she was sober enough to drive – this was her chance to make a quick getaway. Suddenly she remembered that she had her bag but her car keys were still in her coat. She skulked up the stairs and a couple of ladies from her mother's bridge club walked out of the cloakroom and held the door open for her.

"That music is very loud – you'll be deaf by the time you are thirty, dear!"

Sophie didn't answer them. She grabbed her coat – if she was quick she could escape from the club before anyone else came out from the party.

"Where's Sophie?" Larry asked emphatically.

"I don't know, Dad." Louise was getting worried too.

"It's about time we lit the candles – it's half past eleven! Lots of people will want to go home soon."

"I'll get Emma."

"And Sophie . . ."

Louise spotted Emma out on the balcony with Felipe and walked out to them.

"Dad wants to get moving – any sign of Sophie?"

Emma sighed. "I'm not about to go looking for her – let's just go ahead with the cake."

Louise gave the sign to dim the lights and moved into the centre of the room with the trolley and candlelit cake. The strains of "Happy Birthday" rang out and everyone sang along.

Maggie blushed under her make-up and batted her eyelids. She blew out the candles with great delicacy.

Larry took the microphone and coughed into it as the music came to an abrupt stop.

"Thank you everyone for coming here tonight to help share this special occasion with my beautiful wife and daughters."

Everyone in the room let out a cheer. So far no one seemed to notice that Sophie was missing.

"I am a very lucky man to be here – it took something as life-threatening as a heart operation to make me realise that. While I was spending all those hours in Beaumont Hospital, thinking that I would never come out of it, one thing kept me going – and that was Maggie waiting at home for me. She has been a marvellous wife and mother to the girls – and this is a great opportunity to tell her how much we all love her."

The room lifted with cheers as Louise pulled Emma aside.

"What will we do?"

"Just say nothing and hopefully no one will notice – damn, it may be too late for that – Alice is on the rampage with a camera."

"Emma – where's Sophie? I want to get a photo of you three girls together with your mother!"

"I think she's outside getting some air," Louise said politely taking the camera from her aunt's hand. "Why don't you go over to Mum and let me take a photo of the pair of you?"

Alice did as Louise suggested and tucked her right hand into the crook of Maggie's left arm.

"Say cheese!" Louise said as the camera flashed.

Maggie was lapping up the attention as her friends surrounded her. She hadn't noticed Sophie's absence at all and Louise wondered why she had worried – she should know her mother well enough by now.

Sophie drove like her car was on fire. She desperately wanted to go to bed in peace and quiet as far away from her family as possible. She couldn't understand why Paul had taken an overdose – maybe he had made a mistake and not meant to kill himself. There was so much that they had to live for – so much to look forward to.

She turned the bend at Clontarf Garda Station with her eyes filled with so many tears she nearly took the corner off her car with the footpath.

The East Wall was not a salubrious area to be driving through at this time of night. Sophie took the corner at the Seabank House where a crowd of youths was gathering. Her car started to make chugging noises but she didn't notice. She drove up the humpback bridge and as she started to coast down the other side she noticed her engine wasn't running. The little MX5 made it onto New Wapping Street before it stopped. Sophie looked at the dials – the petrol gauge showed that it was empty. She wasn't near a petrol station. She didn't relish leaving her little car on the road all night but she didn't have a choice. Her life was falling to pieces. She locked it and walked nervously up towards Sherrif Street. She felt in her handbag to see what money she had – twenty euros – it was something and hopefully a taxi would pass by soon. If it didn't at least she would only have a few minutes to walk before she got home. It was deathly quiet and she had walked home often before but it was usually from the south side of the Liffey and always under bright street-lights. This was not an area that a young woman should be walking in on her own and Sophie knew it.

The sound of footsteps came up behind her. She turned to see a young man wearing a hoody jacket, sneakers and baggy jeans.

"Hey – ya wan some gee-ar?" he shouted.

There was no need to shout – he was right beside her. But he had seen her open her handbag and clearly needed to get his hands on some cash quickly.

Sophie looked around. There was nobody else on the road.

"I sed do ya wan some *gee–ar*!"

Sophie was afraid to talk to the rough-looking youth and afraid to ignore him.

"I haven't got much money."

"This is good gear – buh I like the look a ya – I'll give ya dem for twenty!"

Sophie looked at him nervously. "What is it?"

"They'll help ya sleep, ya know – re-lax!"

Sophie opened her bag and handed him the twenty euros. Maybe he would go now.

The youth smiled and threw a small bottle of pills at her.

"Ple-sure doing business with ya!" He then headed off down a side street much to Sophie's relief.

She quickened her pace and soon was in Lower Mayor Street – she would be in Custom House Square and her cosy flat in a few minutes. She had her key ready and ran the last few steps as her apartment came into view. Never before had she been so glad to be home. It was one of the worst nights in her life – right up there with the night she spent after learning that Paul had died.

Maggie Owens gave Larry a wave and he knew that it was time to wrap things up. She was tired and so were most of the partygoers. She spotted Louise in the corner and called her over.

"Where's Sophie?"

"I think she's gone home, Mum."

"I want to say thank you to you all – I've had a marvellous night."

"That's good. Did we ask everyone you wanted?"

"Yes, and even someone that I didn't but I'm glad you did."

"Oh, you mean Alice?"

"I'm glad she's here. I suppose that was Emma's idea."

"No, Mum," Louise sighed. "Actually that was Dad's."

Maggie pulled her coat on and hung her handbag over her arm. She was all matter-of-fact again and it was as if the party had never happened.

"I'm glad I got a chance to sort things out. Now where is your father? I want to go home."

Chapter 25

Jack couldn't sleep. Sophie's words were ringing through his head. He didn't want to go without saying goodbye to Aoife. He went over to his laptop and started to compose an email. He had to give it his best shot.

Dear Aoife

I won't blame you for deleting this but if you do actually read this I would really appreciate it. I have decided to leave Dublin. I don't see a future for me here – it's too difficult knowing that you are so close and yet not with me. I was really wrong and you deserve so much better. I won't pretend it wasn't hard to see you with that other guy but if he makes you happy and is good to you then I wish you all the best with him.

My flight is booked for Wednesday week and if you feel that you could meet me before I go that would be more than I could hope for. Thanks for reading this – if you have got to this part of the email I hope you have the wonderful life that you deserve.

With love

Jack

He wanted to put kisses beside his name but felt now that might be too much of a liberty.

Sophie poured a generous measure of vodka into a glass and put some ice in it. She topped it up with some orange juice and went into the bedroom and put her iPod into the speakers. She lay down on the bed and closed her eyes and let the hurt and annoyance she had carried out of the party slide over her. She really wanted to feel better but the quicker she drank the vodka the sicker it made her feel.

She went into her tiny kitchenette and searched for something – a few soft crackers were all that were left in her cupboard – she had eaten the last tin of beans yesterday. She miserably remembered the times she and Paul would ring down to *Il Fornaio* for a delicious pasta dish or pizza. He used to bring her to such beautiful places. What was to become of her now? She put one cracker in her mouth and quickly spat it out again into the sink. She went into the bathroom and started to remove her make-up. Black mascara tracks ran down her cheeks. Her eye make-up remover was at the back of the cabinet – right beside her bottle of Xanax that she had given up taking. She took down the bottle and gave it a shake. There were ten pills left. Beside it was a full box of Panadol. They would mix to make a lethal cocktail with whatever she had bought from the guy on the street earlier. The vodka was making her heady and the anger from talking to Emma earlier in the evening was brewing. She took both of the boxes and brought them with her. There was no need to take her make-up off – she didn't need to look good for where she was going.

Back in her bedroom she took out the album she had made of Paul and her together. Those were the happiest moments in her life. Now she could be happy again. She could be with Paul forever. She topped up her glass with juice – she would need plenty of it.

Felipe kissed Emma awake.

"Good morning," she said with a satisfied grin on her face. "Thanks for last night."

"It was nice to meet your family."

Emma sighed. "They are awful, aren't they?"

Felipe put his hand up to her face. "It was a good party."

"Let's have a day just to ourselves. I'm glad Finn went to stay with Louise and Donal after the party."

"I hope it is not because of me."

"Of course not. He's at an awkward age."

"It is difficult for him."

Emma looked deeply into Felipe's eyes. What a wonderful sensitive forgiving man she had found!

"This is Finn's home," she said, "but we only have a couple of weeks together. I'm sure he will understand when he is older."

"But it is now that he needs you."

Emma hated it when he made so much sense. Of course he was right. How thoughtful he was. "But Felipe – I need *you*!"

That sounded good to him. He leaned forward and kissed her again.

Donal was up and dressed before Louise stirred. Her head throbbed and she wished she hadn't drunk so much.

"Where are you going?"

"Sailing!"

"I thought you were sailing on Sundays now?"

"There's a new Saturday series just started."

"We are spending less and less time together – anyone would think we were avoiding each other!"

Donal looked over at his wife. "I was with you all last night."

"When you weren't eyeballing Emma and Felipe!"

"Get real, Louise! I'm concerned for Emma – you make it sound like I've got some sort of kiddie crush on her."

"Well, do you?"

Donal reached into his cupboard and took out a fleece. "I won't dignify that with an answer."

Louise couldn't help feeling insecure. She hit her fist against the pillow. Donal was a good brother-in-law to Emma but no more than that – why did she say such stupid things when she was upset? She waited until the front door banged shut and then she ventured down the stairs.

Alice was sitting in the kitchen wearing one of Louise's dressing-gowns. She had made herself a cup of tea and was buttering some toast.

"I didn't know you were up," Louise said. "I'd have made you something."

"That's fine, dear. I hope you don't mind that I went ahead."

Louise walked over to the kettle and hit the button. Her aunt was beaming and looked different – happier.

"Did you enjoy last night?" Louise asked.

"It was a marvellous party – do you think your father enjoyed it?"

"I'd say so – he saw how happy Mum was and that's all that he wanted."

"Maggie was always the lucky one – she got the best man!"

"Don't let Dick hear you say that!"

"He knows – I'm always telling him! You're lucky like her."

Louise jolted in surprise at the comment. "I don't think so – Sophie is much luckier."

"But Sophie hasn't got a good man at her side. Larry always loved Maggie – so much."

"I guess we took it for granted growing up and thought that

all parents were like ours." She glanced at her aunt. "I'm glad you were getting on so well with Mum."

"I was anxious coming over – I have to admit. But I am very glad that I did. We aren't getting any younger and it may have been our last chance to make peace."

"What did you fall out over? Sorry, do you mind my asking?"

Alice shook her head. "It was so silly now in hindsight but I guess that's the way with family feuds – they usually start out with something very small. It was when we were all in Cornwall one summer – do you remember that holiday?"

"Yes, the weather was so hot we spent every day on the beach."

"You kids had a wonderful time. The two families had such fun – until the second last night. Well, the adults had too much to drink and your father and I were the last people up. It was all very innocent really – he gave me a hug and told me what a marvellous sister-in-law I was – we were messing. But when your mother came down to the little kitchen and saw us with our arms around each other she got the wrong idea."

"So that's why we had to leave a day early!"

"I'm afraid so. When I told Dick the next morning he laughed. Your mother was very put out and wouldn't even send a Christmas card that year."

Louise chuckled – she had no idea before this. "Such a waste of time."

"I agree – but that's families for you. It's been good that at least I've had contact with you girls – Emma was terrific for trying to build the bridges but your mum wouldn't hear anything of it."

"That's Emma – but she has changed recently."

"And can anyone blame her? It must be traumatic – losing your husband at such a young age. I think it has had a profound effect on your mother – she realises her own longevity now and everyone else's."

"Have you any plans for today?"

"I'm going into town shopping with your mother – we are going to make up for lost time!"

"Sounds good." Louise wished that she could do something for her sisters. But the feud between Emma and Sophie was much more serious than the one between her mother and aunt and that had lasted for the best part of thirty years.

Aoife's eyes filled up as she read the email. So he was going to run away. She found it difficult since moving back with her parents. They were treating her like a little girl again. Lately she had been recalling all the wonderful mornings she had spent with Jack in Greenwich Village. They had the ideal life – why had they ruined it by coming back to Dublin and trying to live like her parents?

Karl was so vain and consumed by his own career that he saw her as a trophy. She hated the way that he licked up to her father as well. If only she had stayed in New York. Things were changing by the day in her mind. She was shaken to the core after briefly seeing him on Grove Road when she was with Karl. She desperately wanted to run after him that evening. But to go back to Jack would mean turning her back on her parents and she couldn't do that. Maybe she could see him though? If she didn't tell her parents that she was in touch with him, that would be okay – wouldn't it?

Aoife had to get out of Malahide – that was something she was certain of. But could she trust Jack again? She couldn't say but she also couldn't stand the thought of living without him either. She pressed compose on her email and started to write her reply to him.

Emma and Felipe took the coast road around Clontarf. It was a brilliant sunny day and Emma was looking forward to showing Felipe around the city and enjoying its café life.

She took a left at the Garda Station, going into town via the East Wall.

As they drove along New Wapping Street they spotted a vandalised car but it took a few seconds for Emma to realise who owned it.

"I think that's Sophie's car!"

"Is anybody in it?"

"It doesn't look like it. I'm surprised it hasn't been towed away – it's causing an obstruction. I hope nothing has happened to her!"

"You must ring her."

Emma was worried. She hadn't seen Sophie since she ran out of the party after their argument. "I'll ring Louise."

Louise answered the phone. She didn't want to stop her conversation with Alice – it was enthralling to learn so much about her mother.

"Louise – it's Emma – what's Sophie's car reg?"

"It's 04D 2 something . . ."

"I think it's been stolen."

Louise felt a strange lump in her throat. "What do you mean? What's happened? Where are you?"

"I'm on one of these small streets at the East Wall – you know they all look the same. Sophie's car is parked here. I've just pulled up behind it and it's definitely empty."

Felipe got out of the car and walked around it. It was kicked in on the passenger's side but there appeared to be no other damage. He tried to open the door but it was locked.

"I haven't seen her since she ran out on the party last night," Louise told Emma.

"I don't really want to speak to her but if her car is stolen she should know where it is."

"Text her."

"I'll get Dad to."

"He's going to be exhausted. Leave it – I'll call her."

Felipe opened the passenger door and sat in beside Emma.

"It is locked but somebody maybe tried to damage it," he said.

Emma nodded. "Listen, Louise, Felipe says someone tried to vandalise it but it's locked so it couldn't be stolen."

"Where are you going?"

"I'm on my way into town with Felipe."

"I'll phone her," Louise said with a sigh, "and ring you back to tell you what she said."

When she hung up she felt guilty. Louise had been left with all of the dirty jobs lately. She on the other hand was having a lovely time with her Cuban boyfriend.

"Why don't you call Sophie?" Felipe asked.

"Felipe! You were there last night – you know some of the things Sophie has done."

"Yes, but she is your sister."

"That doesn't excuse her behaviour."

Felipe looked out the window of the car – careful to keep his opinion to himself.

Emma continued driving in silence along the quay with the River Liffey to her left. She felt bad for showing her lack of concern – Felipe had such compassion and she was consumed only by her own feelings of pride and hurt. Suddenly her phone rang out.

"There's no reply from her mobile or her landline. Where are you now?"

"Coming up to the IFSC."

"You're right beside her – why don't you check in on her?"

"I don't think I can face seeing her."

"Well, I'm in Clontarf and I have visitors – please, Emma!"

Emma looked over at Felipe. His expression was blank but she could read what he was thinking underneath.

"Okay – I'll call you when I've seen her."

Emma took a sharp right off the quays and drove into the

IFSC car park. In all probability Sophie would be nursing a sore head or sulking after running out on the party. She parked up and led Felipe onto Lower Mayor Street.

"This is very nice." Felipe's eyes were wide as he looked at the chic little cafés and symbols of hip urban lifestyle. "Sophie lives in a nice place."

As Emma remembered the tenements and smells of Havana she felt awful. What must Felipe think of the carry-on of her family? Dehannys and her family were so close and warm and welcoming and yet they had so little. In Ireland where so many lived comfortable and clean lives with every material possession catered for they bickered and fought needlessly.

Emma and Felipe came to the door of Sophie's block of apartments and fortunately a young man was walking out at the same time and held the door open for them.

"She's on the second floor," Emma said to Felipe, taking his hand.

Emma rang the doorbell and heard it ring out inside. After a few seconds she rang it again. But still no response.

"She's probably gone out," she said.

Felipe looked at Emma. He had a feeling that something was terribly wrong and so did Emma. "Try again."

Emma rang the bell and knocked loudly this time. The door of the apartment next to Sophie's opened.

"Hey – can you keep it down – it's Saturday?" The neighbour, a girl in her early twenties who looked like she had been partying hard the night before, clung to her dressing-gown and held her head as if she was in some sort of pain.

"I'm sorry – but do you know if Sophie is in there?"

The girl shrugged. "I have a key if you want to take a look – we hold them for each other – I'm always locking myself out."

"Thanks," Emma said. She followed the girl into a filthy hallway with beer cans and glasses littered along it. The apartment was decorated to the highest standard but had been abused.

"There you go," the girl said, handing the single key to Emma.

Emma turned the key in the lock. The lights were on in every room. She knew that something was terribly wrong before she went into the bedroom. With a glass of orange beside her bed and still wearing her red dress from the night before – Sophie was splayed out on top of the bed covers.

Felipe rushed over to rouse her but she was motionless. He checked for a pulse but couldn't find one.

"Call the hospital."

Emma was frozen to the spot. It was last August all over again. She couldn't bear to touch her and see if she was cold. She could vividly recall the clammy feel to Paul's skin.

"Quickly, Emma!" Felipe urged.

Emma took out her phone and dialled 999.

"Emergency services – which do you require?"

"An ambulance please – Custom House Square."

Felipe was no expert in what to do but he tried to rouse Sophie more forcefully. She wasn't responding but the fact that her forehead was lukewarm gave him some hope that she would come round.

"Hold her hand and speak to her – she needs to hear voices!" he urged.

Emma sat on the bed beside Sophie. How could she do this now? She felt Sophie's cold hand and squeezed it tightly.

"Sophie – stay with us – don't go! Is she breathing?"

"Yes."

Emma felt sick inside – the seconds passed like minutes and she was certain that Sophie was going to slip away. "Please, Sophie – stay with us!"

"What drugs – beside the bed?"

Emma looked over at two bottles and a packet of Panadol.

Suddenly the doorbell rang.

"In the kitchen," she said. "There's a switch by the door – buzz them in."

Felipe did as he was asked and Emma held tightly to her sister's hand.

The ambulance personnel rushed in and set to work resuscitating her immediately.

"What did she take?" one of them asked.

Emma handed over the two bottles and empty Panadol box.

"We'll need an escort," the medic who was working on her said urgently to the other personnel.

He placed Sophie on a stretcher and put an ambu-bag over her mouth to feed oxygen.

"Is she going to be okay?" Emma asked.

"We'll do everything that we can. Will you come in the ambulance?"

"Of course."

Felipe went over and held Emma's hand tightly. At least she wouldn't be on her own going to the hospital this time.

"I'll be there in a few minutes," Louise said, putting down the phone.

"Is everything okay?" Alice asked.

"Sophie – she's after taking an overdose – Emma has gone with her to the Mater."

"Oh my word – that's terrible!"

"Would you mind looking after the children, Alice?"

"Yes, yes – will I call Maggie?"

"No – don't do anything."

"I think I should," Alice said sternly. "You girls can't go on protecting your mother all your lives – she is seventy – not a child."

Louise sighed. "Okay then, you can call her and tell her but I am going straight in to the hospital."

Louise ran out with her bag and keys in hand. Her heart was pounding. The thought of Sophie lying prostrate and unconscious was so vivid in her mind's eye that she had to gulp back the tears.

She regretted being so hard on her. Maybe she was genuinely in a heap after Paul's death. She was in a mess herself and needed to put her family right. Everyone around her was hurting and this time it could be too late to put it right.

Jack hadn't much to pack. There were a few photographs and keepsakes that Aoife had bought that he would take with him. He couldn't believe that he would be back in New York so soon. He threw most of the junk on the table where he kept his laptop into the bin. The laptop was on and showing two messages in his mailbox. He looked twice when he saw Aoife's name attached to one of them.

Dear Jack

I'm sorry the way things ended between us. I think you are making the right move. New York suited you better than Dublin. It's good of you to let me know that you are leaving. If you like I can meet you in Howth on Tuesday afternoon. I'd like to say good-bye.

Aoife

Jack felt a lump in his throat as he swallowed. He desperately wanted to see her again – even if it was only to say goodbye.

He answered her immediately. He would be counting the hours until Tuesday.

Louise ran past reception and took a left like Emma had told her to. The stink of bleach and disinfectant didn't help her hangover. She wished that Donal was with her. He was good at times like these.

She saw Emma at the end of the corridor. At her side was Felipe, quiet and consoling.

"What's happening?" she asked when she reached them.

"They're pumping her out."

"Oh, thank God she's still alive!"

"She is but only just," said Emma quietly.

"I will get you tea, Emma," said Felipe. "Would you like some, Louise?"

"No, thanks, Felipe."

Louise sank down onto the chair outside the room. "I can't believe she did this."

Emma sat and stared in front of her. She couldn't believe she was back in casualty but this time with her sister. She was numb inside with the pain.

"Maybe she wanted to commit suicide in some grand Romeo and Juliet-like gesture," she said.

"Do you think?"

"We didn't believe her when she said that she loved Paul – maybe she did love him and wanted to show us."

"God, what if you hadn't found her?"

"I don't think she was in her right state of mind when she did this, do you?"

Louise shook her head. "What did she take?"

"There were two empty bottles of pills and a packet of Panadol beside her bed."

A female doctor came out through the theatre doors and removed her mask.

"Are you Sophie Owens' sisters?"

"Yes," they said in unison.

"We managed to clear most of the contents of her stomach – Xanax and a powerful tranquiliser – but the real damage has been done by the Paracetamol. She's lucky that you got to her when you did but her liver is in pretty bad shape."

"What does that mean?" Emma was feeling terrible for what she had been saying earlier.

"It means that she may need a liver transplant to survive. It's a precarious procedure and difficult to get donors."

Louise let out a yelp and started to cry.

Emma put her arm around her sister, still in disbelief at what was happening to her family.

"Can we see her?" Louise sobbed.

"For a little while. It's good for her to hear familiar voices – she's still unconscious but we hope she will come through soon."

Chapter 26

Larry paced up and down the kitchen. The doorbell rang and he rushed to get it.

He opened the door to Alice.

"I got here as quickly as I could – one of the neighbours is minding the children."

"She's inside." He pointed into the living room.

"Are you okay?"

"I'm fine – I want to get to the hospital to the girls."

"Should you be driving?"

Larry hadn't had the all-clear from his surgeon after his bypass but he didn't care. He knew where he had to be. He grabbed his car keys and gave Maggie a kiss before walking out the door.

Maggie burst into tears on seeing Alice.

Alice sat down beside her on the settee and put her arm around her.

"There, there – she's going to be okay, you know."

"What in God's name did she think she was doing? She's too spoilt – it's Larry's fault – he always gave her too much. It's because she's the baby."

"It's nobody's fault. Let's just pray she'll be okay."

"Why are all of these awful things happening to us? First Emma's husband and then the burglary and now this – we are good people – what have we done to deserve it all?"

Alice stood up. She didn't have any answers but somehow wondered if there was a pattern unfolding.

"Let me make you a nice cup of tea and everything will seem much better."

Maggie didn't answer. She sobbed into her wet Kleenex. The night before had been so perfect – now it was all ruined and she couldn't understand why.

Larry was trembling as he tried to reverse into a tight space on Eccles Street. His rib cage was still sore after the operation. He had to see Sophie.

His phone rang. It was Louise. He navigated his way to where she directed him.

"Dad, are you here?"

"I'm up the corridor."

"Good – I'll keep an eye out for you."

Larry was exhausted traipsing up and down the corridors. He was relieved when he spotted Louise in the distance.

She ran up to help him along and into the room where Sophie was rigged up to several complex apparatuses. However hard it was for her, it had to be so much harder for her father to see Sophie this way.

"Where's Emma?" Larry asked.

"She left a few minutes ago."

"Of course – she has her fellow staying with her."

"It's not that – just there isn't really anything we can do until she comes around."

Larry shook his head. "What could be so bad that she should do this to herself?"

Louise hadn't the heart to tell him. It wasn't her place. It was between Emma and Sophie and Paul. Her parents knowing the details wouldn't help either. Larry would be disgusted with Sophie and that would shatter their relationship. Louise felt glad to be the one in the middle. She didn't have anything to hide – any more.

Felipe and Emma sat silently in the back of a taxi. It left them off at the IFSC car park.

"Would you like to eat lunch?" Felipe asked.

Emma shook her head. "I'm not hungry."

She looked at her watch. It was two o'clock and she figured that Felipe must be starving.

"Well, maybe we should eat something. We can go to a place up the way here – they do a nice lunch."

The Harbourmaster was usually full on weekdays but it was late for lunch and a Saturday so they had their choice of tables and took one that overlooked the canal.

"What must you think of Irish people, Felipe?"

Felipe smiled. "People are the same in all the world. It is the same things that matter to everyone. Family, children, health and happiness."

"But there aren't many like my family!"

"You are not so different. We have many similar cases in Cuba – we may not have the freedom or the money but we have the same problems."

"I'm sorry that you had to be here when my family were having so many."

Felipe reached out and put his hand on hers. "I am happy that I came to Ireland now. I wanted to see your family – I want to know them."

"Well, you are certainly seeing them – warts and all!"

Felipe looked quizzically at her.

"I mean, with all their faults," she explained. "I'm glad you are here now too – it's been so good to have your help and support and I would never have passed by Sophie's if we were not going into town so she has you to thank for finding her."

"I hope she will thank me!"

Emma smiled. "I hope she comes around and is able to thank you too."

"But I want you to promise me that you will forgive your sister. Today you told her to stay alive – now you must be a sister to her."

"Felipe, you may be asking too much."

"Please – for me. We have each other – we are very lucky."

Emma had to agree. She felt very lucky indeed.

Donal was standing on the marina when he heard his phone bleep. He reached into his kit bag and took it out.

Sophie in Mater – overdose. Can u come home and mind kids Louise

Donal had to read over the message again. It was hard to digest the few words that said so much.

"Coming for a pint, Donal?" Kevin asked with a wide grin. They had come first today – it was a great start to the series.

"I can't – trouble at home."

"God, I don't know anyone that looks after their kids at weekends as much as you after doing a week's work!"

"It's a family emergency – I'll see you on Tuesday."

"Fair enough – I hope everything's okay." Kevin didn't want to know.

Donal rang Louise's number – the time of the text was three hours before.

"Hello, Louise?"

"Donal – thank God you're there!"

"What happened?"

"Sophie is unconscious and hooked up to a ventilator in the

Mater after taking an overdose when she got home from the party last night."

Donal didn't reply.

"What are you thinking?" asked Louise.

"I was wondering when something like this was going to happen – I've had a bad feeling all week."

"Why didn't you tell me?"

"You get hyper over the littlest things – there was bound to be some sort of blow-up. I didn't think we'd get through the party without some fallout."

"Will you go home and mind the kids?"

"I'm on my way there now."

"Alice was minding them but they've gone into the neighbour's while she's consoling Mum."

"I think your mother should be at the hospital with her daughter – where's your dad?"

"Here with me."

Donal sighed. "That man isn't long after major surgery – this is too much strain on him."

"I know – but you know Mum."

He knew her all right. He'd had to put up with her like he was a son.

"Look, stay there as long as you need – I'll sort things out here," he said.

He took a right at the S-bend in Raheny. He wasn't going straight home. He drove into Foxfield and up the Owens' driveway. He went up to the doorbell and rang it forcefully.

Alice answered.

"Can I see Maggie?"

"She's terribly upset."

Donal brushed by her and went into the kitchen where his mother-in-law was sitting. What he was doing was out of place and character but someone had to.

"Donal, I'm glad you are here. I need a few messages."

342

"I'm not here to do errands, Maggie – I've come to take you into the hospital. Alice, will you go back to our house and the kids?"

He spoke with such authority and composure Alice couldn't disagree.

"I'm too upset to go in there!" Maggie sobbed.

"If Sophie doesn't come out of this you will always regret it – but more important than that she may need you to come through. She needs to hear her mother's voice."

"I could phone Louise and talk to her."

Donal looked harshly at her – she had never seen him like this before.

"Let me get my coat," she said meekly.

Donal walked her out to the car and helped her close the seatbelt.

Alice sat in the back. She was dropped off unceremoniously at Clontarf and Donal and Maggie continued their journey into the Mater Hospital in silence.

Donal rang Louise when they reached reception.

Louise was so glad to see Donal – she had hated the way he left to go sailing earlier. She was more than surprised to see who he had with him.

"Mum – you came in!"

Maggie looked up at Donal and then at her daughter. "Of course I came in! Where is she?"

Louise gave Donal a questioning look but he didn't give any information away. He had taken it on himself to drag Maggie to take on her family responsibility. The strain on Larry over the years had manifested in a heart condition that he didn't even know he was carrying around. It was time that Maggie faced up to the fact that she had reared three daughters and was still an influence on how they all behaved. It took Emma to break the mould before the others started to change – if Sophie was ever going to learn to be a grown-up, her mother would have to start by setting an example and it was up to Larry to change too.

In some way Donal hoped that by changing the other members of the Owens clan he just might reach out to his wife and heal some of her insecurities.

Larry hobbled up the corridor and his face beamed as he saw Maggie in the distance.

Maggie started to walk towards him and he put his arm around her once she got near enough.

"How did you get her to come in?" Louise asked Donal in amazement.

"I told her to sit in the car and put her belt on."

Louise shook her head. "I can't believe you did it."

"She is so spoilt – I feel sorry for Larry."

"Are you afraid that will be us in thirty years?"

Donal shook his head. "It won't be."

Louise didn't like the certainty in his voice. "What do you mean?"

"We have to change, Louise. I don't know how we are going to do it – maybe we need counselling – but you haven't been happy and lately neither have I. We need to talk." He sighed. "But what is the prognosis with Sophie?"

"She's damaged her liver and she may need a transplant."

Donal pursed his lips gravely. "That girl has been heading for disaster – she's a product of all the decadence we've seen over the last few years. Sleeping with Paul was the last straw. I don't know how Emma is ever going to forgive her."

"The doctor said that she would definitely be dead by now if Emma hadn't called when she did."

"Why was she calling?" Donal asked, genuinely puzzled.

"It's a long story – Sophie had ditched her car and Emma saw it – I'll tell you on the way down – let's see how Mum and Dad are doing."

Maggie shivered and sobbed into her handkerchief. "I can't believe our little girl would do this to herself."

Larry was choked up – barely able to answer. "She reminds me so much of you."

"Of me?"

"Yes. You had the same hair when you were her age. You had the same confidence and way about you. It's no wonder I spoilt her so much."

"She was such a pretty little girl – she always shone brighter than the others – had so much talent. Why would she do this?"

"Maybe Emma would know?" Larry suggested.

"She's so engrossed in that foreign fellow – I don't know what's got into her."

"Maybe she's tired of being the good girl always."

Maggie nodded her head slowly.

"Maybe."

"But Louise has been wonderful lately."

"Yes."

"The doctor was in a few minutes ago and he said that she needs a liver transplant."

"Oh my God – what did she take?"

"Panadol. Apparently it does more damage if taken in large quantities than any of the hard drugs."

Maggie held her hand over her mouth. "Oh Larry, this is all our fault!"

Larry didn't argue – he felt responsible too.

Emma called in to Louise's house in Clontarf with Felipe.

"Alice, it's great that you were here," she said. "We had no idea we would need the extra pair of hands."

Her aunt smiled. "I'm glad that I could help. I'm having a really nice time actually – with my own grandchildren in Australia I'm lucky to see them once in a blue moon."

Emma looked at her mother's sister with new eyes now. Building bridges had been the best possible outcome of her mother's party. If only she could do the same with her own sister – but she had more to forgive.

"I'm going to take Finn home if that's okay?"

"He's out the back playing football."

"Is there anything I can do?"

"Nothing at all – I think Dick is reliving his youth outside with the boys. I'm sure there's enough food in the freezer for their tea if we are stuck."

Emma kissed her aunt on the cheek.

"Enjoy the rest of your time in Ireland," Alice said to Felipe.

Felipe gave a little smile, then went out to the car with Finn.

When he was out of earshot Alice whispered in her niece's ear. "He's a dish – I would keep him if I were you!"

Emma followed her son and Felipe out to her little Mini. Finn stood protectively at the passenger side – expecting to take the front seat.

"Will you let Felipe sit in the front for today, love? He does have longer legs."

Finn looked at Felipe and begrudgingly took a place in the back.

It didn't help instil confidence in Felipe. He was well aware of how he felt when his parents split up and his mother took a new partner. It must be very threatening for the boy to lose his father so suddenly and then see a new man with his mother.

"You like to play football?"

"I love lots of sports," Finn replied abruptly.

"Maybe we can play in your house?"

Finn shrugged. It was something he only ever did in Donal's or his friends' houses. His father hadn't liked sport.

"Okay."

A while later Emma watched with relief as Finn and Felipe kicked penalties in the back garden. She brewed a pot of tea and stood contentedly at the back door while the two played on oblivious of her presence.

That night Finn didn't want to go and stay at Gavin's or Louise's and Felipe didn't sleep in the spare room.

"I'm glad Sophie came around when both your parents were there," Donal said, handing his wife a G & T.

"You were so good to make Mum go in – it was the right thing to do."

Donal smiled. "Sometimes it's right to do what you feel in your gut even when you know it will upset those around you."

"Are you talking about us too?"

Donal shrugged. "You know, Louise, I meant what I said about the counselling."

Louise nodded. "I'll go if you want."

Donal sat down on the armchair and put his glass of Killbeggan whiskey on the small table at his side. "I just think we can do better – remember when you were playing the piano for a while recently – you seemed so happy."

Louise nodded. She was so happy when she saw Jack again – but it didn't take her long to realise that it wasn't him that she wanted but those feelings of desire and passion he had awakened in her. Playing the piano had helped and made her think about her job and how much she missed it. "Donal, I was thinking about going back to school."

"That's not a bad idea but you don't have to go back to school to teach – why don't you give music lessons in the house – God knows there are plenty of kids around here."

Louise took a sip from her drink. "That might be easier to fit in with our family arrangements."

"The kids are getting easier – you said it yourself and it would give you an interest."

Louise nodded. "I'm sorry if I've been a pain. We've been through so much these last few months."

"It's just a suggestion – I want us to get closer and I don't know how."

"You could come over and sit on the couch beside me for a start!"

Donal took the prompt and brought his glass with him.

"You know, this is great – Alice and Dick staying with your folks – your parents behaving like parents and your mother not being a spoilt child. Maybe Sophie has done everyone a favour."

Louise couldn't see it exactly the same way but she wanted peace in her family at all costs. And Sophie wasn't out of the woods yet.

"You know, when you weren't around today I felt so lost – you've always been around for any catastrophe in the family. I really need you."

"Good!" Donal said and took his wife's glass away, putting it on the ground beside his own. He put his arm around her shoulder and leaned towards her. "Now show me how much you need me!"

It was exactly the way Louise wanted to be spoken to by her husband. She smiled as his lips moved forward and touched hers. She wasn't thinking of Jack or her family or anyone else.

Chapter 27

Emma was trembling as she treaded the long corridor to St Teresa's ward. Sophie had been stable over night and her father assured her that she wanted to see her eldest sister. Felipe was at her side, an arm protectively about her.

"I don't know what I'm going to say," she said shakily.

"You will find the words when you see her."

"I'm so glad that you are here with me."

Felipe stopped and looked lovingly at her with his dreamy hazel eyes. "I am too."

He leaned forward and kissed her lips gently. It gave her the strength that she needed before facing her sister.

Felipe hesitated at the door of the ward. "Will I wait here?"

Emma nodded. "I'll have a word with her first, thanks."

Sophie was dozing, her once rosy cheeks gaunt. Emma looked at her younger sister wired up to so many contraptions – she hadn't seen her so vulnerable since she was a little girl. She walked slowly over to the side of the bed and sat down.

Sophie opened her eyes.

Emma saw pain and sorrow behind them. She felt sick inside but couldn't bring herself to embrace her.

Sophie's lips opened but she didn't smile. "Emma!"

"It's okay, Sophie, you don't need to speak."

A tear slid down the side of Sophie's nose and along her cheek. "I'm sorry."

"Now isn't the time to upset yourself," Emma said softly.

"It's been awful – I've been in such a mess." All at once the tears were streaming down Sophie's face. "Thanks for coming to see me."

"You are going to be okay," said Emma reassuringly.

"Where's Felipe?"

"Outside."

"He's a good guy, Emma. I'm glad you found him."

"Thanks. And you will find someone too."

Sophie managed a smile. She wasn't so sure. "I wish I had your optimism, Emma."

"You can't give up."

"Like Paul did?" Sophie said and then she winced. The mention of her dead lover's name sent a sharp dart down her spine.

"I don't want to talk about him." Emma's face hardened. "Just focus on yourself and getting better."

She stood up and moved away from the bed – they had spoken enough for today.

"Are you going?"

Emma nodded.

"Will you come again?" Sophie said with pleading in her eyes.

"I will."

Emma couldn't say any more than that. It had taken a huge amount of energy to go and see her little sister and a lot of painful emotions were bubbling inside.

Sophie lifted her hand and gave a small wave as Emma left the room. As her sister disappeared she was filled with a sense of regret. Not just for the damage she had done to their relationship but the trail of damage she had left around her as she had trampled her way through life to get to thirty-four years of age. With the slim prospects of a liver becoming available soon she worried that she might not get to see her thirty-fifth birthday. She sobbed uncontrollably to herself. This was the meaning of loneliness and hopelessness and it was what she felt that she deserved.

Louise was woken up by a long warm kiss from Donal.

"Good morning!" she said. A huge grin swept across her face. She was heady after the thrilling lovemaking of the night before. Donal hadn't been so passionate since their early days when he had tried to make love to her in a lift in Amsterdam. That same all-consuming desire was etched all over his face and it was like the stresses and strains of the last fifteen years had disappeared.

"I thought we'd wake the kids up last night with our enthusiasm!"

Louise's eyes watered. "I'm just so happy to be making love the way we used to – actually I don't think we used to make love like that in the past."

Donal kissed her on the nose. "Me too – but we have a lot of work to do on ourselves." He took a deep breath and sat up in the bed. "Louise, there is something I need to say to you – I didn't see the point before but as we are trying to get our marriage sorted I can't deny it any more."

Louise was numbed. She had no idea what her husband was about to say.

"It was a long time ago and you know I don't see any point in hanging onto the past – I turned a blind eye to something I saw one evening when we were still engaged. I was so afraid of losing you I didn't want to confront you with it."

"What?" Louise was terrified by what he was about to say.

"I managed to put it to the back of my mind for years but I have to say it now that we are starting afresh. One evening I called by the house in Clontarf and you were at the side gate and you were kissing a guy – he was young – looked like he could have been one of your students. I never saw him again but I was scared to say it to you. You seemed nervous about the wedding and I felt you had cold feet anyway."

The colour drained from Louise's face. She thought she was going to vomit.

"I don't know what to say," she whispered.

Donal closed his eyes. "I don't want you to say anything. I just wanted you to know that I was so afraid of losing you I didn't and haven't said anything for fifteen years but I have to say things now. I don't want you under just any conditions – if this marriage is going to work we have to always be honest with each other. I want all of you – for the rest of our lives."

"I want that too!" Louise declared. She was trembling inside.

"Good – I just needed you to know that."

"So what now?"

"Now we start again – this is our new beginning – okay?"

Louise nodded as Donal leaned forward and pressed his lips firmly on hers.

He tasted so sweet, so good. Donal was the only man for her and she regretted that it had taken her this long to discover it. She would lock all thoughts of Jack up into a box in her distant memory. She needed to live in the here and now with the man that she was going to spend the rest of her life with.

Jack could feel his heart beat in his chest. He had been here before with Aoife and let it all slip away. He knew this was his very last chance. He stood at the monument at the west pier as agreed on the phone the day before. The sound of the DART rolling along the line and into Howth station made his heart beat faster. She had said very little on the phone. He was afraid to get his hopes up too much.

In the distance Aoife's tall and elegant figure came into view and he started to tremble. She was wearing a pretty pink dress and long white cardigan and looked like an angel as she crossed the grass to where he stood. This was possibly the defining moment in his life – he didn't want to mess it up.

"Jack," Aoife said with a smile as she came close enough to see his face.

"Thanks for coming. Walk?"

Aoife nodded. They set off cautiously both feeling awkward at the absence of a kiss on meeting.

"How have you been?" he asked.

"Good," she replied. "I've got a new contract – it's very short term but the money is really good."

"You're very talented – you're never going to have a problem getting work."

"When did you decide to go back to New York?"

"When I lost my job the decision was made for me."

"Is my father to blame for that?"

Jack shook his head. "It doesn't matter who did it – they were letting people go anyway."

"Have you got something sorted for your return?"

"Nothing at the moment."

The seagulls chorused overhead as they strolled past the restaurants and Doran's fish shop. The sun was high in the sky and the sea a deep blue. It was a beautiful setting for two people who needed to be alone.

"Are you looking forward to going back?" she asked.

"I guess so – I can't stand it here . . ." he paused. He didn't want to come across as too heavy too soon. "I think it's best to be away from you – it's difficult knowing that you are so near and that I can't be with you."

Jack stopped walking and turned and looked at her.

Aoife couldn't hold back the tears – they had been building up all the way out on the DART.

Jack didn't know what to do – he wanted to touch her but was afraid. "Please don't cry."

"I'm so unhappy, Jack."

"So am I. I can't tell you how sorry I am."

"I'm mad with you, Jack – why did you have to do it?" She lifted her arms and started to beat him weakly on the chest.

"I deserve everything you throw at me, Aoife – I'm so sorry. I had to let you know that I was going and how sorry I am."

Aoife closed her eyes to keep the tears in.

Jack grabbed her clenched fists and pulled them to his chest. He leaned forward and kissed her forehead gently.

She let out a loud sob and threw her head onto his shoulder as her body flopped against his.

"Aoife, why are we apart? Do you still love me?"

She lifted her head. "Of course I do – I've never not loved you – from the moment I met you."

"Then come with me – let's go back to New York – all we need is each other."

Aoife looked down at the ground. "Coming home wasn't the great idea that I thought it would be. We had it all in New York."

"We did. And we could have that back . . . but what about your parents?"

Aoife swallowed the tears.

"I can't live my life with my parents' rules. I need to live by my own. I've been trying to do the right thing for them but it's not right for me."

Jack couldn't control his emotions. He wrapped his arms around her tightly – afraid he might crush her. He let go briefly and looked into her eyes. "What about your boyfriend?"

"I haven't got one any more. He was just someone filling in time. It's always been you, Jack – for me."

He put his arms back around her and held her tight.

"Will you come – will you follow me home to New York?"

"I will." She put her head into his shoulder and he put his arm around her waist.

They continued walking slowly past the fishing boats and the seals. Neither talked. They had said all they needed to say.

They were going home.

Louise stopped off at Emma's for a cup of tea. She knew that Emma would be alone. Felipe was spending his last Sunday in Dublin with Finn at a match in Croke Park. Louise rang the doorbell and waited. It was a different Emma who answered the door today to the one she had come to see after bumping into Jack Duggan a few months ago. So much had happened in all of their lives. Louise felt like a new person inside too.

"Hey, didn't know what time you were calling at!" Emma greeted her sister with a warm kiss. "I'm just finishing off the novel."

"I can't believe it – and with Felipe staying – well done."

"He really brings out the best in me. Have you been at the hospital?"

Louise nodded. "She's looking good, Em."

Emma followed her sister into the kitchen and they sat down at the table.

"I really hope she gets a donor." Emma said. "I can't stand the thought of her lying there."

"Will I put the kettle on?"

"Of course – sorry!" Emma jumped up. "My head's all over the place – I'm going to miss Felipe. And so will Finn – he's thrived having another man in the house – even if it's only been for a few weeks."

She hit the switch on the kettle and sat back down.

"So how do you feel your relationship with Felipe's going to go?" asked Louise.

"To be honest, it has been the most wonderful and awful

time in my life. Before going to Cuba I only had my grieving thoughts to occupy my mind. It's no wonder I couldn't write. But meeting Felipe has changed the way I view the world. He has taught me to live in the present and it's funny but, when you do that, you have a better chance of forgiving the past."

Louise nodded. "That is so true – as I found out myself – to my cost!"

"Yes, how about you? How are you doing? Any word from Jack?"

"He sent me a text to say that he's going back to New York with Aoife."

"That's good, isn't it?"

Louise nodded. "To be honest, I think Jack will be happier on the other side of the Atlantic. He was much too exotic a character to settle down to suburban Dublin life."

Emma looked keenly at her sister. "And what about *your* feelings on suburban life?"

Louise knew that Emma's question was astute and she couldn't hide the fact that there had been a dramatic shift within her own marriage. "Donal and I are starting counselling next week."

"Great! That will help."

"It's funny but now that we know we're going to deal with our relationship we've been talking every night. And not just talking!"

Emma gave her sister a wide grin. "I'm so glad – I've been hoping for the day when you would see what a great guy you have, Louise."

"You know me better than I know myself!" Louise said with a smile.

Emma stood up to make the tea. Things were taking a positive turn all around for the elder Owens sisters.

"You said Sophie looked good today?"

"She was sitting up in the bed and . . ." Louise hesitated. "She was all chat about you and her when you were kids."

Emma poured the water into the teapot and put on the lid.

"I've been thinking over the last few days and I can see why she had the affair with Paul."

Louise nodded. "We all can."

"It was attention-seeking – she needs to be in the spotlight."

"She's just a spoilt little wagon!"

"We all spoiled her. But it's more than that. Sophie has never been happy inside – always insatiable and seeking out the next thing to thrill her. This ordeal is a terrible grounding for her."

"Well, I think she's looking really good now but that's not all. Her spirits are good and she's calm in a way she's never been before."

Emma placed the teapot on the table and put two mugs down beside it. "Maybe this is the ordeal she needed to go through to see how badly she had been behaving."

"And how do you feel about her now?" Louise asked as she poured the tea.

"I feel sad that it all had to come to this – she brought this liver failure on herself. But I hope it will be her redemption and help her find a better sense of self."

"Enough of the philosophy, Emma! Would you have a few biscuits?"

Emma smiled. She was feeling philosophical – Felipe had helped her to tap into her true emotions and to find herself.

"Jaffa Cakes okay?"

Louise nodded.

"I'll get them now."

Emma handed Felipe the large brown parcel with goodies for Dehannys and Fernando.

"Thank you for such a wonderful time, Emma."

"I can't believe you're leaving – it went so quickly. I don't know how I'll manage without you."

Felipe nodded. "And I will miss you but you are strong, Emma. And I am not far away. You will see me soon."

Emma's eyes widened. "I promise. I'm looking forward to it already."

The past three weeks had shown how different their lives were – two worlds so far apart the Atlantic couldn't show how widely.

"Maybe someday soon it won't be so difficult for me to travel."

"If the regime ends lawyers will be in big demand!"

Felipe nodded. But he, like so many others, didn't think that was going to happen soon.

"I will be happy that day," he said.

"Thanks for being such a support."

"Sophie is your sister – she will need your help now."

"I know – it's not going to be easy for her."

Felipe wrapped his arms around Emma and squeezed her tightly.

"I love you."

Emma's heart filled. He had left it until the last minute to tell her – but inside she knew already.

"And I love –"

He put his fingers up to her lips. "I know."

Larry took the call.

"Mr Owens?"

"Yes."

"I have some good news."

If there was one thing that Larry Owens needed, it was good news.

"Your daughter Sophie – her liver has shown signs of recovery – we think she may not need a transplant after all."

Larry broke down in tears. The two last weeks had been horrendous – Maggie and he had visited Sophie every day and stayed until late each night.

"Are you all right, Mr Owens?"

"Yes, thank you, Doctor."

"I'm sorry that I missed you today – we've only been able to conclude prognosis in the last hour – we thought you would like to know as soon as possible."

Maggie rushed out into the hall. She wasn't wearing any make-up – her hair was flat and she had slipped into her dressing-gown on returning from the hospital.

"What is it – is Sophie okay?"

Larry hung up the phone and put his arms around his wife.

"She's turned the corner – she's not going to need a transplant."

Maggie followed her husband in tears. She put her head in her hands and sobbed.

"Thank God!"

"Everything's going to be okay from now on – I can feel it," Larry assured her and she believed him.

Emma was anxious going into the hospital but not in the same way as she had been before. The healing of Sophie's liver had coincided with the healing of the hurt that Emma had carried since finding out about her sister's betrayal.

Sophie was able to sit up in the bed and a healthy colour returned to her cheeks.

Emma entered the room and felt the emotions of relief and warmth between them.

As she took a seat by the bed, Sophie held out her hand. Emma cupped it in hers.

"Good news, Sophie."

Sophie nodded. "I'm a very lucky girl."

Emma smiled. "You've been through a lot these last few weeks."

"I've had plenty of time to think, lying here in this bed." A tear rolled down her face. "I've been so awful, Emma. How can you ever forgive me?"

"Let it go – we have to move on."

"I've missed you," Sophie admitted.

It was Emma's turn to shed a tear. She had missed her little sister – the one that she had played with so lovingly as a child. The last year had been terrible but Paul was gone and it was time to move on. She hoped for Sophie's sake that she would be able to do the same.

"We have to put the past behind us," she said softly. "It isn't going to be easy."

Sophie nodded her head very slowly. "I know. But I feel I can do it. I've changed."

"We've all changed – and Paul has to rest in peace."

Sophie felt the weight of the world lift from her shoulders. She had a wonderful sister. She had done something so awful that she had almost destroyed her whole family in the process. Lying in the bed the last few days she had been wishing she were dead but now with the prospect of a full recovery and forgiveness from her sister, she felt that she could try and be the person that she had the potential to be.

"Hi, girls!" Louise said on entering the room.

Emma turned as Louise came over and sat on the side of the bed – between her two sisters.

Louise looked down at the clasped hands of the two women and smiled. She had been through her own process of discovery over the past few months – reconciling her past and her future. The same had been happening for her sisters. The three were linked spiritually – bonded by blood from birth and a constant in each other's lives. They had crossed the Rubicon together.

Emma looked over at Louise. "What are you thinking?"

"Doing what you do, sister dear – a little bit of my own philosophising!"

Emma laughed. "Am I really a pain?"

"You're the eldest – that's your job!" Sophie butted in.

"So does that make you the brat?" Louise piped in, looking at Sophie.

The three started to laugh in unison – strong laughs that came from their bellies. They might each have their role and place in the family but they were never more united than at that moment.

"So, Emma – give us the beef on Felipe – how does he rate in bed?" Sophie asked cheekily.

Quick as a flash Emma darted a look that said a multitude until a grin started to slip from the corner of her lips.

"I can tell you one thing for sure, my sweet little sister – *you* are never going to find out!"

Epilogue

Emma slipped out through the doors of La Terraza. She wanted to be on her own for a few moments and breathe in the beautiful moonlit reflection on the calm water. It was the most perfect night of her life – a perfect ending to an even more wonderful day. Suddenly she felt a strong pair of arms grip around her waist and she didn't need to turn around to see who they belonged to.

"Are you happy, *mi esposa?*" he whispered in her ear.

She leaned back and into the torso of the wonderful man that she would be calling her husband in future.

"Very," she replied, her eyes steady on the flickering reflection of the moon on the water.

"I told you we had good luck that day when we saw the wedding, the first time you came here to Cojimar."

Emma slid around and planted a warm and gentle kiss on her new husband's lips.

"It was wonderful – we are a very lucky couple. Thank you so much for organising this – every detail was more than I could ever have wished for."

And it was – from the ceremony on the beach to the perfect reception in La Terraza. The mahogany bar was bedecked with tropical flowers and the tables covered with pretty check cloths and an abundance of delicious seafood and exotic creations that would be difficult to find in the best restaurant in Dublin.

The strains of the trumpet and saxophone lilted through the wide-open windows of the bar and onto the balcony where they stood. They both turned to look in through the windows which showed the many happy wedding guests who were dancing salsa around the bar. She smiled at her Aunt Alice and mother chatting in the corner – they were so close now – making up for lost time. At the bar Sophie sat sipping a mojito with a handsome young Cuban at her side. Emma had been very protective of Sophie after the ordeal she had been through and now she was showing a completely different side. And then there were Louise and Donal dancing in an intimate and sexy way she had never seen before. Jack Duggan had come back into their life at the most perfect time – she was pleased when Louise informed her that he was now living in New York.

She didn't always believe in happy endings – her life would not be easy, split between Havana and Dublin, but it was a choice she had to make in order to see the man that she had been waiting to meet all of her life. They were a couple now and she was as happy as she could ever be.

THE END

If you enjoyed *One Kiss in Havana*
by Michelle Jackson why not try
Three Nights in New York also published by Poolbeg?
Here's a sneak preview of Chapter One.

Three Nights in New York

Prologue

February in New York

Eve Porter wished that she had stayed in New York. Her transition to the London branch of the Just for Coffee exclusive dating agency had been good for promotion, but London didn't have the same buzz. However, just now that same "buzz" was creating a problem. Standing on a snowy Seventh Avenue, surrounded by a cacophony of blaring car horns and gridlocked traffic, she wondered how she was going to make her appointment with Lucille on time. She could always catch the subway. Most New Yorkers didn't think twice before using it – even the mayor was reported to take it to work – besides, she did get the Tube on the odd occasion now that she lived in London.

She held her breath as she descended the steps for the subway and avoided eye contact with the masses on their way to work. She pulled back the sleeve of her coat to see the face of her Rolex. John had given it to her for Christmas and even though she'd removed every trace of his existence from her flat in Chiswick she continued to wear the diamond-studded watch. One of its benefits was the dual-time system. Although it was now five years since she had left New York, she still liked to know what time it was in the Big Apple – and it was convenient when conversing with Lucille across the Atlantic.

She gave her arm a shake and the sleeve fell back over the watch as she teetered at the edge of the platform. She was anxious to be first on the carriage – near the door so she could make a rapid escape.

The tiles on the wall at the other side of the track were shiny – whiter than they should have been with the bombardment of trains passing by every few minutes. She thought she heard the train get nearer but it was only her stomach rumbling. Eating in the mornings was a chore and a cup of black coffee was usually all she could manage to keep down. She was sorry now she hadn't forced herself to eat a piece of toast at least or a few spoonfuls of muesli – anything to keep this unpleasant sinking feeling at bay. As a child she was regarded as anaemic and her doctor had warned not to fast for too long between meals. But Eve was now a professional woman and well able to make her own mind up about if and when she should eat. Another rumble from her stomach and she felt a light and airy pressure rise from the top of her spine and rush around her skull. Hypnotised by the tiles in front of her eyes and a gentle breeze brushing past her face, she began to sway.

Conor pulled the collar of his leather jacket up over his ears. The February wind was sharp and he'd known that morning they were in for a cold one as the snowflakes fell on the window of his Greenwich Village apartment. The subway was on the corner of Prince Street and as the snow fell harder he quickened his pace and plunged underground. He had to be midtown in half an hour to check on a venue for his next day's work. He had arranged to meet a friend of his who had told him about a cavernous restaurant that would be a perfect backdrop for the indie band he had to photograph – they hadn't a big budget but their manager was hot and liked to tip Conor off when he had a talented new act to market.

Conor had given up wearing a watch since a shoot with The Pixies two years before. He knew the constraints of time affected the quality of his work – and that was such a big job he really needed to get absorbed in the present and forget about how little time he had. He had taken his watch off and experienced the longest and most productive hour of his professional life.

So far doing without a timepiece had worked very well during the creative process but obviously not when it came to being punctual.

As he approached his platform he thought he heard a rumble in the distance but it was only the after-effect of a train in the next tunnel going in the opposite direction. The station was busy today – bodies everywhere. He could improve his chances of getting on by moving down the line a bit so he would be ready to jump off when he reached midtown.

Head and shoulders above most of the commuters on a busy Friday morning, he stopped short of a little old lady. She could only be from one place in the world with that lilac hair – Brooklyn. She lifted her head up and stared at the tall Irishman. It was the mixture of crystal-blue eyes and jet-black hair that made him stand out – even in New York.

He knew that she was looking at him but didn't mind. He was very lucky. Living in the most exciting city in the world with one of the best jobs, he got to go to all of the best parties and hang out with famous people. He had it all as far as his family in Ireland were concerned and this was one of those mornings where he had to agree with them.

Conor glanced over at the other side of the track. Above the heads of the other commuters he could see shiny white tiles on the wall opposite.

Then his head swung left as out of the corner of his eye he glimpsed a woman flopping off the edge of the platform. His heart gave a great leap. Was she a jumper or had she fallen?

The old lady with the lilac hair screamed, "My God, somebody help her!"

All around people were looking down onto the track – staring at the woman who was now lying face down on the steel girders.

Conor pushed through the crowd. He felt a rush of adrenaline through his body as the sound of the train in the distance started to rumble from the dark tunnel. It was too late to stop the train. Something had to be done – and fast.

At the edge of the platform two dudes laden with gold chains – boys in the hood – looked on, shaking their heads.

"She's a goner, man!" one of them said to Conor.

A force from deep inside swept over Conor like a wave. He didn't think he had the time to do what he was about to do but he didn't have a choice. He was in autopilot mode as his feet hit the steel girders. The vibrations from the approaching train rumbled down the track. Shockwaves shot through his legs as he felt it getting closer and closer. He could feel them running through the woman's body as he gathered her into his arms. She was out cold. He heaved her onto the edge of the platform, head first – it took every ounce of his energy to lift her legs. It was the elderly lady and a public transport worker who pulled her to safety.

A shrill whistle blew down the tunnel and the lights from the front of the train were approaching quickly. He tried to get a grip on the side of the platform but his palms were sweaty and he rolled off and back onto the track.

"Here, man, give me your hand!"

One of the dudes reached down and grabbed Conor's wrist. The other guy joined his friend and they heaved Conor up and onto the platform with less than a second to spare before the train swept by.

A commotion gathered around the still unconscious woman. Conor stood up and brushed his hands clean on his jeans. All he could think of was whether the woman was all right. The little lady with lilac hair held the woman's head in her lap and stroked it gently. The majority of those around boarded the train. The dudes gave him the thumbs-up from behind the doors of the carriage as it pulled away. He hadn't had a chance to thank them for saving his life.

"You're gonna be all right," Lilac Hair whispered to the woman.

Conor moved closer as the old lady brushed the strands of auburn hair from the face of the woman who was now starting to show signs of coming around. She was definitely a looker, the kind of intelligent businesswoman that he would be slow to approach in a bar – but would like to. He didn't have problems meeting women but it was usually the enigmatic and more serious type of woman that really caught his interest – so different to the models and singers that he usually dated. Her hair was pulled back in a roll and her expensive-looking full-length coat had come open to reveal a smart suit underneath. Conor wondered for an instant why she had taken the subway at all – she was more the type of woman who would be taking a courtesy car to work.

Suddenly her eyelids lifted and exposed a pair of dazed green eyes, as her head rocked from side to side. She seemed vaguely familiar but after living in the great ethnic melting pot that makes up New York for twelve years he felt most people on the planet looked familiar.

The sound of the next train rolling to a standstill disturbed his thoughts. He was going to be late.

A subway guardsman pushed his way past Conor and leaned over the woman as she pulled herself up onto her elbows.

"I have to go now," Conor said to Lilac Hair. "Will you make sure she's all right?"

"You go on. I'll see she gets home."

As the doors of the train opened, Conor reluctantly boarded it. Another subway worker was running over to the woman with the auburn hair and he knew that his part in the saga had been played. The memory of her green eyes stayed with him as the train followed the line uptown.

Eve pushed the guardsman away as he tried to help her to her feet. She grabbed her left arm as a dart of pain shot up it.

"You gotta be careful, honey," the old lady with lilac hair said kindly. "You've had a bad fall – you were nearly killed!"

Eve looked down at the old lady, clad in woolly hat and matching thick cable-knit sweater with a basket in the crook of her arm, and winced. This was definitely the last time she was ever getting the subway – what was she thinking of?

"Where's my bag!" she demanded.

The old lady looked around and picked the cream leather Gucci bag off the ground.

"Here you go, honey. I don't know what happened to your hat."

Eve grabbed the bag and with her other hand brushed back the stray auburn tresses indignantly.

"Thank you!" she said to the old lady – without meaning a word of it.

The attempts of the subway workers to calm her down were in vain. Eve wasn't sure exactly what had happened but remembered staring at the tiles on the other side of the track, feeling faint, and then one instant later falling forward. Not only her left arm but her whole body ached and felt like it was covered in bruises. Lucky it was winter and she had been protected by her voluminous coat and padded gloves. The palms of the gloves were torn – she must have broken the fall with her hands. Gridlock or no gridlock she would stick to a cab in future – and for now a quick shower in the Soho Grand was called for to wash the unfortunate episode out of her life.

"Ma'am, you need to see a doctor," the subway worker said gently. "You fell on the track – you need to get checked out."

The track! Eve put her right hand up to her head and smelt oil on her glove. She had fallen onto the track!

"You're in shock, honey!" the old lady said with a shake of her head.

"How did I get back up?" Eve asked as the realisation of what had happened to her finally took a grip.

"That handsome young man risked his own life and jumped down after you!" said the lilac-haired woman. "He was only just back on the platform when that train pulled in!"

Eve steadied herself. Did a complete stranger risk his own life to save hers? She felt uncomfortable in the presence of these people – she had to get as far away from this nightmare situation as quickly as possible. Her six-figure salary meant that she never needed to take public transport again and after this fiasco she had no intention of doing so. The entire experience was surreal.

But she was curious about this strange man who had rescued her from death. She didn't generally believe that knights in shining armour existed – especially as she was in the match-making business.

A pain shot through her left arm and she looked at the sleeve of her coat. She pulled it back to study her watch as a trickle of blood dribbled along her wrist and onto the back of her hand. It was only then that she noticed the huge rip in her coat.

One

Three months later
May

"I can't believe we're really here!" Rachel exclaimed as she slipped off her four-inch heels.

She watched her companion Nicky nervously strip as she herself had done a few seconds earlier. She was down to her shirt and jeans, and her watch was resting in the blue container.

The man in the crisp white shirt and dark tie nodded at her waistline and grunted.

"Your belt as well, madam."

Rachel leaned over and whispered in her friend's ear. "Knickers and bra also, please, madam!"

The security guard grabbed the pan filled with metal objects and shoes from Rachel and glared at them with furrowed brows. She smiled at him and gave a flick of her long blonde curls as she breezed silently through the security gate.

Nothing could dampen her mood – she hadn't been at Dublin Airport with Nicky for sixteen years. On that occasion they were students coming back from a long summer working in London to pay for their college expenses. They were both in completely different situations now and the break was well earned.

"Would your brother like us to bring anything over?" Nicky asked.

Rachel clicked the roof of her mouth with her tongue – remembering stories of fellow students begging for Tayto crisps and Lyons tea from across the Atlantic Ocean. There was little nowadays that couldn't be got in either country. Except . . .!

"Damn, I forgot to get a couple of Swiss Rolls!" she groaned. "Hang on – we'll get a few Crunchies – that will do him!" The preparations required before leaving her three children with their father for the next four days had left her little time to think about a gift for her brother Conor.

Nicky beckoned as the doors of the bar in Boarding Area B opened. "Come on – let's have a little tipple before we board!"

"But it's ten o'clock in the morning!" Rachel exclaimed.

"Exactly, and when do we ever get a chance to drink a nice crisp Sauvignon Blanc at this hour?"

Rachel nodded in agreement – there was no way that she could admit to Nicky that she often had an early morning tipple after taking the kids to school and before facing her day in suburbia. But that was part of Rachel's secret world and there was absolutely nobody that she could confide in about the insecurities attached to being a stay-at-home mum.

"What would you be doing if you weren't here?" she asked.

Nicky smiled. Normally she would be sitting at the desk of Virtue Publishing Ltd, studying the finishing touches of this week's magazine. Leaving the final editing to her PA made Nicky nervous as she knew that the young girl was chomping at the bit to slip into the assistant editorial position. But it couldn't be helped. The last time she took a break was five years ago and even now the thought of leaving her son Daniel with his friend's family was heart-wrenching. But she had dedicated many years of her life to keeping him and his needs fulfilled and the time had come to do something for herself. Besides, her fourteen-year-old son would rather spend time with his friend's family. There was a lot more on offer there – a father figure for a start. Daniel needed more men in his life and Nicky realised that painfully – even more so now that he was hitting puberty. Her own father had died when she was only fifteen so Daniel had never known him. At times Nicky was riddled with guilt and fears about the way she was bringing him up but she could only do her best as a single mum and her wages as assistant editor for a women's magazine left them both with little choice about it.

"I'm glad I'm not sitting behind my desk – that's for sure!" Nicky lifted her glass and clinked it off the side of Rachel's. "Cheers – here's to a great four days in New York!"

"Don't forget the three nights!" Rachel said buoyantly. Secretly she was worried sick. The thought of Derek at home on his own with the children sent shivers up her spine. How were they going to manage? But everyone agreed that she deserved this break badly – everyone except Derek of course. And then there was the other worry . . .

Nicky recognised the glassy expression on Rachel's face and shook her head.

"Don't go all funny on me now – you know you want to go – you jumped at the idea of visiting New York when I told you about the cheap flights!"

Rachel smiled nervously. Yes, she would miss the kids but that wasn't the real reason why she was feeling apprehensive. Her mobile phone could ring at any moment and, although she wanted it to, she didn't relish having to explain the conversation to Nicky if it did happen.

Rachel knew her friend would be furious if she knew what she had done but the feud between Nicky and Eve had gone on for long enough and a reunion was well overdue. It was great having Nicky back in her life for the last five years and this was a golden opportunity to bring the three of them together – wasn't it?

The registrar in Trinity College Dublin had been surprisingly helpful when she rang earlier in the week and the list of alumni far more comprehensive than she'd expected. The registrar said there was talk of a fifteen-year reunion of the English faculty as they had failed to organise one at ten years – this was more than likely due to the fact that they were the last of a student brain drain that had steadily dribbled out of Ireland after graduation during the later decades of the twentieth century.

The Just for Coffee company was easy to find on Google and she sent the emailed message for Eve's attention, unsure if she had changed her surname. It was as light-hearted as she could make it – surely she would answer? The rift between Eve and Nicky should be all water under the bridge by now.

As she took a sip of her ice-cold wine she felt a shot of relief. "I'm fine," she said with a smile – hoping that Eve would ring but not yet. "We deserve this!"

Nicky lifted her glass and took another sip from the frosty rim. Something inside told her she shouldn't entirely believe her friend. But, if anyone had a right to be nervous, she herself had! After all, her son was staying with a friend – not even family. She envied Rachel's stable marriage with her husband for the last thirteen years – while she herself had staggered from one disastrous relationship to the next.

Nicky sat up straight in her chair and blinked. She craved a cigarette – especially with a cold glass of wine in her hands. How was she going to get through the long flight to JFK? Then she remembered her nicotine patch – she had to put it on.

"Let's go through Immigration soon!" Rachel said.

Nicky nodded. The sooner she was on the big green airbus the better.

"I just need to go to the little girl's room for a minute," she said. How she wished that Rachel smoked too – maybe then she would understand how difficult this smoke-free flight was going to be. No cigarettes and all kinds of nightmare scenarios to conjure up about Daniel. There was only one thing to do when she boarded the big green airbus and that was drink some more.

Eve breezed through the doors of 1680 Broadway, swinging her super-light briefcase in her right hand. It felt great to be back in New York. Her last visit had been disastrous but she made sure this time that she came to the Just for Coffee offices in a cab.

"Morning, Arthur," she said to the doorman who permanently sat at the desk of the Howards Building.

Arthur nodded his head respectfully at the tall red-haired lady in the sharp grey designer suit. She didn't usually come to the offices more than twice a year but he knew who she was. Something must be up for her to visit again so soon.

"Mawnin', Miz Pawtah," he replied with his slow southern drawl. "How you been?"

"Fine, thank you."

Eve couldn't comprehend how someone could spend most of their waking hours sitting at a desk watching the world go by through glass doors. Especially a world as exciting and invigorating as New York. She imagined this poor man skulking onto the subway back to Queens in the evening, having done nothing all day but watch and wait for those who had a real life to pass him by.

Eve made her way to the lift and put her perfectly manicured fingernail on the button embossed with the number twenty-three. From that level Lucille Baron's office had a spectacular view of mid town that was a testimony to the success of the Just for Coffee franchise. In eight short years Lucille had built the business from scratch to one of the world's leading dating agencies.

It wasn't a typical dating agency where man meets woman and goes for dinner or to a show. The clients on the Just for Coffee database were all high-flying business people who were much too busy to waste a whole evening getting to know someone and far too sophisticated and intellectual to delve into the world of speed dating. Just for Coffee suited a lot of business people who could fit in an hour over lunch or in the afternoons during their heavy schedule. The hard work was put in by Lucille and her staff to ensure that the matches were made between equally successful and well-heeled individuals. They had even been involved in getting certain celebrities together but were such a professional organisation that no trace of the events would ever be leaked to the press.

Eve walked up to Lucille's secretary and the young girl sat upright in her seat. Eve had this effect on the junior members of the company – she carried an air of superiority and aloofness that made them uncomfortable.

"Hello, Ms Porter, how are you?" The secretary smiled as she searched her desk for a sheet of paper. She passed it to Eve. "This came in yesterday and I thought I should give it to you in person as you would be in the office today. I wasn't sure if it was a genuine email or spam."

Eve nodded at her and started to read the sheet of paper as she strolled over to the door of Lucille's office. The message was sent by rachelsloan@eircom.net. Subject: Reunion.

It was a shock for Eve. Rachel was a genuine type of girl – but why on earth would she contact her? She wondered where Rachel learned that she worked for Just for Coffee – she mustn't know that she had moved or she would have sent the email to the London office. She read the opening lines, which informed her that Rachel would be in New York for the weekend and included her mobile phone number in case Eve wanted to meet up. A torrent of old memories started to flood her mind and drag her into the last century. But she had an important new client to meet on this trip and really didn't have the time. She didn't know whether she would respond or not.

The door swung open when she was only a few centimetres away from it. The woman at the other side was in her early forties and perfectly groomed with poker-straight blonde hair – she beamed at her colleague with a dazzling white set of teeth.

Eve leaned forward and kissed Lucille – first on her right cheek and then on her left.

"Eve, baby, it's so good to see you!"

Lucille's blue eyes sparkled like diamonds. She had a captivating effect on everyone she spoke to but Eve wasn't taken in by all the gloss and panache of her business colleague.

"Wonderful to see you too, Lucille," she said, returning the welcome with a wide smile.

She folded the email and slipped it into her handbag as she took a seat at Lucille's desk. The stunning view of the top of the Chrysler building and the rest of Manhattan shifted her focus and steadied her nerves.

"Things must be very good if you're calling me back to New York so quickly!"

"Darling, things are fantastic. The London office is thriving in your capable hands but this particular client that I want you to meet today needs special attention and I could only trust you to look after him properly."

Lucille sat down and took out a brown file from a concealed drawer in her desk. The folder bulged with paperwork and made Eve curious about its contents.

"I've booked him into the Soho Grand so you can keep an eye on him and he does most of his business downtown so that suits. When I tell you his details you will understand why I needed you to see his file in person. I understand your reservations in dealing with Irish clients but you're the best person to handle this guy – he is real important."

Eve was intrigued but didn't want to show it by reacting too strongly.

Lucille opened the file with the reverence of a preacher about to make a sermon. She lifted the first page and cleared her throat.

"I'm really excited about this," she said. "It's rare that we get one of the most powerful men in Ireland as a client – even though he is officially retired he will never stop working."

Eve didn't often see Lucille so excited. "Is he extremely wealthy?" she asked.

"Absolutely, and he is so well connected he could open all sorts of doors for Just for Coffee! He isn't officially divorced but has been separated for years. His ex-wife has a new partner and he has two daughters – both grown up and successful in their own right."

Eve usually kept abreast of Irish news from *The Irish Times* on the internet. This man sounded familiar. "Is he looking for a permanent partner or discreet sex with someone who isn't likely to spill the beans?"

"Not sure but he's much too powerful to want his dealings with us spread all over the tabloids. He held the stopwatch for the Celtic Tiger in his hands for years."

"Go on then – tell me who he is – I know you're dying to."

Lucille grinned. She didn't often get a reaction like this from Eve. "Our new client is . . ."

A loud knock sounded on the door and Lucille's secretary appeared.

"Excuse me for interrupting, Ms Baron, but your client is here."

Eve sat up straight in her seat. Who could be coming all the way from Ireland, looking to Just for Coffee to find a partner?

"Hi, Conor, we're here!" Rachel giggled down the phone excitedly. She longed to see her brother so much. It had been three years since he had last visited Ireland and she had only ever been to New York with Derek who hated the city.

"Hey, sis! It's about time! Where are you?"

Rachel craned her neck and looked out of the window. "In the back of a yellow cab driving through Brooklyn. Will we go straight to the hotel?"

"That would be best – I'll make my way there now. How was your flight?"

"Great – no problems. Nicky drank Aer Lingus out of baby bottles of champagne and slept for the guts of three hours so it all went well!"

Nicky mock-glared over at her friend but couldn't stop a big grin from creeping out.

"You should be here in about twenty minutes," Conor calculated. "I can't wait to see ya."

"Me too – can't believe I'm here at last – see you then!" Rachel flipped the cover of her phone shut. "Look over there – that's what I told you about."

Nicky turned to where Rachel was pointing through the front windscreen and stared at the New York skyline unfolding before her eyes. Thousands of cars resembling dinkies sped back and forth over the bridge. In the distance thousands more were flying by on the overpass. The massive skyscrapers were pulsating with life and down below in the Hudson River, ferries and water taxis went about their business.

"Wow!" she exclaimed.

Rachel looked on as Nicky's eyes sparkled at the myriad architectural jewels before her.

"Nothing prepares you for your first sighting of the Brooklyn Bridge, does it?"

Nicky's mouth opened wide as the cab turned onto the massive suspension bridge.

"It's beautiful," Nicky gasped. "Look, there's the Empire State – and, oh my god, it's the Chrysler Building!"

Rachel smiled. She knew exactly how her friend was feeling. The first time Derek had brought her to New York she felt the very same. It was the eve of their first wedding anniversary and was meant to be the trip of a lifetime. The Celtic Tiger hadn't started to purr and the prospect of doing Christmas Shopping in the Big Apple was reserved for those with special concession flights or the rich and famous. The air at JFK was icy and sharp – unlike today. Christmas was everywhere in the city even though it was only the end of November. It should have been a wonderful trip but Rachel was in the first phase of pregnancy with her eldest child and suffering from morning-sickness for ten hours a day. She couldn't even go ice-skating at the Rockefeller Center – it looked so magical with the massive Christmas tree and trumpeting angels providing the perfect backdrop – such a symbol of Christmas in New York! Derek blamed her for ruining the holiday – even though it was his decision to start a family so early in their marriage.

"This is fantastic," Nicky said, looking over at her friend, unaware of the feelings of inadequacy and low self-esteem that Rachel's memories had reawoken.

The yellow cab brought them to Washington Square a few minutes later and up to the door of their hotel. Standing at the railings with his leather jacket swung casually over his left shoulder was a tall handsome man in his early thirties.

"Is that Conor?" Nicky asked, pointing out the window.

Rachel craned her neck to see. "Yeah!"

"Wow, I don't remember him looking like that – I mean, he was always kind of cute but now he's gorgeous!"

Rachel grinned and searched distractedly in her purse to pay for the cab ride.

"It's okay, I've got a fifty-dollar bill," Nicky said, reaching across and handing it to the taxi-driver.

"Thanks, Nicky, I'll get it on the way back." Rachel opened the door of the cab hurriedly. She put her four-inch-heeled boots onto the pavement and rushed up to throw her arms around her brother.

"So good to see you, sis!" he said, giving her a tight squeeze.

"It's good to be here," she replied, gently pulling away from his embrace. "You remember Nicky, don't you?"

Conor stretched out his long arm and pulled Nicky closer for a peck on the cheek.

"Of course I do – even though I was an unbearable school kid while you guys were all graduating from college."

Nicky blushed – the few years' age difference was nothing now that they were all in their thirties and she berated herself for the short-sightedness that had made her ignore her friend's younger brother.

"Let me help you with those cases," he said, leaning forward to take Nicky's.

"No, really – they're very –"

Conor lifted the first one that Nicky had left at her side and swung it up in the air. "Wow, I wasn't expecting it to be so light!"

Nicky smiled and raised her shoulders timidly. "I'm hoping to fill it for the return!"

Conor grinned. "Of course. You girls are going to hear more Irish accents than American on Fifth Avenue. This town is thronged with shoppers from across the Atlantic."

He lifted Rachel's case with his other hand and shook it – it rang hollow also.

Rachel led the way up the granite steps of the small but respectable boutique hotel. Icons from the 1930s covered the tiled walls of the foyer and there was a distinct art deco feel to the place.

"Jesus Christ!" Nicky exclaimed, causing the attractive receptionist to lift his head. "It's Denzel Washington!"

Rachel giggled. "I hope you're not going to make a show of me all over New York!"

Nicky had to stop herself from swooning on the spot – it was just as well that Rachel had made the reservation and was checking them in.

"Do you guys want to drop your suitcases upstairs and then

maybe we could go to a little café a couple of blocks away?" Conor asked. "I usually meet Alex for a coffee mid-afternoon."

"Who's Alex?" Rachel asked.

"He's a guy that I hang out with. We met at an exhibition through mutual friends and he's kinda cool – with no bullshit!"

Rachel nodded her head – she knew what he meant. He was prone to criticising the glamorous New York set in his sporadic emails.

"We'll be a couple of minutes. Do you want to come up?"

Conor looked at Nicky and then back to Rachel. "I'll let you girls do your thing and I'll wait outside. It's turned into a nice day!"

"Okay," Rachel smiled.

Conor moved out to the pavement and sat down on the steps that led up to the hotel entrance. It was a discreet boutique hotel that he had carefully chosen to cater for his sister's and her friend's needs. Rachel had warned him that Nicky hadn't much cash to throw around. That suited Conor because he liked to have his sister near him instead of in one of the many dull and generic uptown hotels where she usually stayed when she came to visit with Derek in tow. Lately, however, she hadn't been over much and he could sense that it was Derek's decision to cut back on time spent in the Big Apple. That was why he was surprised and delighted to get the email from Rachel telling of her impending trip. He would do everything he possibly could to make it a memorable experience for her.

He scanned through his phone looking for missed calls or text messages. Business had been brisk after Christmas but there was a lull now with the onslaught of summer – hopefully things would improve and he always got the odd call to photograph some of the open-air gigs. Only one missed call from Mandy and he wasn't tempted to call back and see what she wanted. A text from Alex made him smile:

Waiting for you in Tart's . . . A

"Were we quick?" a voice whispered behind his ear.

Conor turned around and smiled when he saw his sister and her friend.

"Follow me, ladies. I'm going to bring you to a real New York café!"

Nicky marvelled at the colourful shop fronts and familiar yellow traffic lights that she associated with the New York she saw on TV and in movies.

"It's so relaxed and pretty – I expected New York to be frantic!" Nicky remarked as a yellow cab stopped politely before they stepped onto a zebra crossing.

"That's because we're downtown. Live here a little while and you'll never want to go uptown."

"Oh!" Nicky replied meekly. She didn't understand what he meant but, apart from the tip of the Empire State in the distance, the buildings didn't seem that tall and life was pretty laid-back all around.

Conor beckoned the girls across a tree-lined street and over to a pretty little café with the most delicious-looking muffins and pastries filling its windows. The pale green awnings with *Once Upon A Tart* scripted across them protected those who sat out in front from the mid-afternoon sun. Sitting at a small round wooden table with a cup of coffee in front of him was Conor's friend. He was doodling on a white paper napkin and as Conor approached he looked up and smiled.

"Hey, man!" Conor said flippantly.

Alex looked at Rachel and then at Nicky – then back at Rachel again. He surveyed her blonde curls and blue eyes as a wide smile beamed across his lips.

"When Conor said he had a sister I thought 'if she's anything like him she'll have a wooden leg and a hump on her back'! But I can see that the looks in the family all went one way!"

Conor smirked at his wisecracking friend. He was used to his sense of humour and he was a good foil for his own laid-back manner.

"Rach, Nicky – it's with great misfortune I introduce Dr Alex Thoreau."

"You're a doctor?" Nicky asked in amazement. Wearing a thin leather necklace, small silver sleepers in his earlobes and a scruffy red tee-shirt, he certainly didn't look anything like her GP – not to mention his spiky white-blond hair.

"Yes, but don't let this shabby exterior fool you. Sure, if you were to have a heart attack on the spot I could do nothing to help you." He smiled as he spoke and shook his head gravely. "However, if you had a canvas and a bucket of paint I could throw something together to save your wall!"

"Doctor of Fine Art – just the guy you need in a crisis," Conor smirked. "Of course he got it in one of those American art colleges so it's pretty worthless."

Alex protested with a wave of his arms. "What about Pollock and Warhol – you guys would still be painting chocolate boxes in Europe if it wasn't for us Yanks!"

Nicky was just about to butt in and say that Picasso was European but she didn't want to seem like a total nerd already – even if she did think this artist guy was a bit of a jerk.

"Sorry, girls, he doesn't usually get like this until after his fourth whiskey of the day," Conor said with a smile. "What will it be – something savoury or sweet?"

Rachel and Nicky looked at each other and then back at Conor.

"I guess we should have a look inside," Nicky said.

"Get me a cappuccino, sis, and a cinnamon muffin!"

Rachel rolled her eyes as her brother sat down next to Alex. "Who's on holiday here?" she grinned.

The smell of cranberries and spices wafted from the kitchen to the rear of the café. Chickens and rabbits moulded from chocolate and candy mixtures decorated the shelves. At the counter an assortment of savoury delights – including frittata and pizza were on display next to the multitude of different muffins and home-baked cookies.

"I don't think I've ever smelt such gorgeous food!" Nicky exclaimed. "It's a good place to have the munchies after all that champagne I drank on the way over! Totally divine!"

"And the food isn't the only thing that's divine around here."

384

The words had rolled off Rachel's tongue before she even realised that she was saying them.

Nicky looked over at her friend with an exaggerated mixture of shock and incredulity.

"Is this my married friend eyeing up the opposite sex while her good husband is at home minding the kids? I take it you are referring to that scruffy white-haired jerk?"

Rachel felt embarrassed despite Nicky's jokey tone. And secretly she felt annoyed. Married she definitely was but Derek was no saint. He had always been difficult to live with at the best of times and recently he had become downright dismissive of her. His standards of perfection were so high that Rachel was made to feel a failure over most of the things that she did during the day.

"I didn't mean it like that," she said lightly – trying to conceal the attraction she had felt on meeting Alex. "Just he seems like a nice guy – funny!" She didn't want to dig a bigger hole for herself than she could feel herself slipping into. "I'm glad my brother's got a somewhat normal friend."

"Honey, if you think that guy Alex is normal you need to get out more. Apart from that blueberry muffin that I am going to devour in about thirty seconds, Conor's the only dish around here!" She turned to the waitress and ordered food and drinks for everyone.

Rachel paid the cashier and carried the tray out to her brother and his friend. It irritated her that Nicky had spoken so forcefully about Alex – she had hardly met him after all – and she was cross with herself for letting her.

"Sorry, girls – I should have told you," Alex said as Rachel put the tray down on the table. "I gotta shoot – not like my friend Conor here shoots – I gotta get a ten-foot by five canvas finished by six o'clock."

"Will you join us tonight?" Conor asked. "I thought I'd bring the girls to Kelly and Ping later for something to eat."

Alex lifted his sweater off the chair and casually threw it over his shoulders. "Sounds good – one of my favourite places to eat," he said with a nod of his spiky peroxide-blond hair. "That is, providing the ladies could bear spending the night with a real American."

"You're hardly a real American, Alex – your mother was from Rome," Conor quipped.

"But I grew up in Massachusetts! Later, dude! Nice meeting you ladies," Alex said with a little bow and then he was gone.

"He's a great guy," Conor said as he watched him go. Then he turned back to the girls. "What do you two want to do after this?"

"Can we do some shopping?" Nicky asked eagerly.

"Look at her!" Rachel laughed. "She's chomping at the bit. Let's take her downtown to Fifth Avenue."

Eve liked to shop around SoHo and it was one of the reasons why she chose to stay in the Soho Grand. If it was good enough for U2 then it was just about good enough for Eve Porter.

She made her way to the Armani shop first to get a few make-up essentials and she was running low on her favourite Armani Code perfume. Then she made a quick detour to get some La Perla lingerie. This trip had been organised in such a hurry she hadn't made any arrangements to meet up with her old New York friends for tonight. She looked down at her Blackberry and remembered the email that Rachel had sent. She was between two minds whether she should answer her and decided to check out her New York friends first. She typed up two emails: one to Ingrid who used to work for Just for Coffee – Eve was probably the only person in the company that she would still socialise with – and another to Tom who was a married man she liked to call for casual sex whenever she came to town. She appreciated the merits of her sex-only relationship with Tom now that she was single again. It was ironic that she worked in the matchmaking business while the need for a constant companion and partner simply didn't exist for her personally.

As she browsed through the lace-trimmed bras sized 34C she heard a bleep from her Blackberry and knew instantly who the message was from.

Hey gorgeous. Are you staying in the Soho Grand? How about 5 o c? T

She replied and then, smiling, slipped her phone back into her bag. He was so reliable. She checked her watch – two and a half hours was plenty of time to get some more shopping in – she might even have a bath before he arrived. Hell no! She'd have the bath when he got there.

As a rose-coloured two-piece set made entirely of lace was next on the rail she felt that serendipity had handed it to her. Tom loved pink! She made her way over to the cashier and joined the short queue.

Tom was always on time. He was so reliable there was no way Eve could stand him as a permanent fixture in her life. He was, like most men that she had dated and the one that she eventually married with such disastrous consequences, a solid dependable individual. She wondered if he was like that with his wife. Probably not if he could be there for her after one email. He always appeared fascinated by her and had told her he was attracted by the aloof way she carried herself. She enjoyed the way most men buzzed around her like bees when in her company – it made her feel like a honey pot.

She sprayed a little of her new perfume on her neck and loosened the belt of her luxurious black bathrobe. There was no need to beat around the bush with Tom – they would enjoy an hour of making love and perhaps order some food up to the room – then she could decide what to do for the rest of the night. She didn't relish the prospect of sharing the evening with her old college friend but part of her was curious. She still had unfinished business to thrash out with Rachel and New York was probably as good a place to do it as anywhere.

The North Loft Suite of the Soho Grand was Eve's favourite place to stay in New York now that she was a visitor. She was far enough away from all of the tourist hotels uptown and lucky that Lucille allowed her to charge the expensive room to the company. She strolled over to the large glass doors that looked out on the towering landmark of Manhattan. Later in the evening the Empire State would be illuminated like a glittering prize in the midst of the other skyscrapers and she could sit and watch it for hours. The cubist furniture and modern lines of the suite made this the perfect setting to enjoy the Manhattan skyline. She opened the door and stepped out onto the patio which was furnished with deckchair-striped couches and chairs. Maybe she should treat herself and Tom to a bottle of Bollinger – she deserved it.

Suddenly an impatient knock sounded on the door of her suite. She slowly walked over to open it – there was no need to appear overenthusiastic. She turned the handle and it was slowly but forcefully pushed from the other side. She could smell his Boss aftershave before she saw his face. Then his dark hazel eyes appeared around the door and they fixed on hers. Eve didn't want to talk – there was absolutely nothing she had to say to him. Instead she pursed her lips and drew him close enough to kiss. He smelt of work and the splattering of aftershave that he used to try and conceal the odours of the day. She didn't care – she loved his scent.

They shuffled, using tiny steps, inside the hotel suite – Eve walking backwards while Tom slammed the door with his left hand.

"Eve, baby. It was great to get your mail. I'm so glad to see you!"

Compliments didn't impress Eve. She had most of the people in her life departmentalised and her relationship with Tom was based purely on sex and she didn't want to waste the short time that they had together whispering niceties in his ear. She slipped the robe off her shoulders, revealing her nakedness. Her body was in such good shape that most women in their twenties would be envious of it.

"Wow, you are amazing . . . I've missed you!" Tom panted as he brushed his lips along her collarbone and rounded the curve of her shoulder. He was moving slowly down to her breasts when he suddenly stopped and studied her left arm. "Eve, honey, what happened to you?"

Eve glanced down at the scar along her upper arm and rolled her eyes. "I had a fall in the subway last time I was here – it's nothing – just a silly little scar." She moved her hand over to snap the buttons open on Tom's shirt.

"What happened? Why didn't you call me?"

"I didn't have enough time to see you – it was a quickie visit for our AGM."

Tom seemed hurt. "I can't believe you were in New York and didn't call me!"

Eve was getting impatient. "I said I was busy. Anyway if I wanted to be examined I'd have called a doctor."

Tom took a step backwards. "Hey, honey, I'm just concerned – I haven't seen you in months and now it's like you don't even want to talk!"

Eve snapped. "If I'd wanted to talk to you I would have phoned!"

Tom flinched at her sharp retort. It had been a crazy week in the world of fund-management and he didn't need grief from a woman that he only saw a couple of times a year – even if she did drive him crazy with desire.

Eve rolled her eyes and picked up her bathrobe – slipping it on over her shoulders as she flopped down on the square grey couch. She looked up at the dishevelled Tom as he fixed the buttons on his shirt.

"So, how's the wife?"

"Jeez, Eve, is there any need for that?"

Eve pulled punches harder than most of the guys he'd had to deal with on Broad Street in the past few days and it looked like she was in fighting form tonight.

"I'm merely asking a polite question as you came here for a chat – I thought you were here for sex!"

Tom sat down on the luxurious couch opposite Eve. His legs spread wide, he rested his palms on his thighs and shook his head. "I like you, Eve, I'm glad to see you – it's been a while."

Eve dragged her French-polished fingernails through her hair and sighed. "Yeah, well, it's been a crazy day for me – I've had emails from long-lost friends and a new client who I can already tell is going to be trouble . . ."

Tom shrugged.

"Yeah, well," she continued, "I just want to forget about it and chill out this evening . . . and I thought that you would help me."

Eve smiled for the first time since Tom entered the suite. She would give him one more chance to turn this evening around and give her what she wanted.

He cleared his throat – holding a clenched fist up to his lips.

"Eve . . ."

"Yes?"

Nothing could have prepared her for his revelation.

"Eve, Monica is pregnant."

Eve felt an inexplicable dart in her chest. She didn't give a damn about Tom's wife and she certainly didn't envy her but the fact that Tom had come to tell her the news brought a mixture of emotions up from the pit of her stomach.

"So, you're going to be a father – how lovely for you."

Tom wasn't sure if it was sarcasm or genuine regard in her tone. "I didn't want to tell you over the phone 'cause I haven't seen you for ages."

"I already told you – I didn't have the chance to call you the last time I was over," she replied sharply.

Tom rubbed his hands through his short hair. It was shades paler than it had been when Eve had first met him as more grey had crept through the black strands with time.

"I know I'm not a priority in your life, Eve, but I always regarded you as someone special in mine. But things have changed for me now . . . I can't see you when we are expecting a baby."

Eve threw her head back and laughed. "Why did you come here then?"

Tom drew a sharp breath. "I wanted to see you one last time."

"You can be so mushy. Give yourself a break, Tom. I'm really not bothered." She stood up and walked towards the door. "Actually, I'm meeting people later and I'd like to take a bath, so why don't you go home to Monica?"

Tom stood up and nodded. He knew in his heart that Eve had never really cared for him but he needed to show her the respect that he felt their relationship deserved – illicit as it was.

"Goodbye, Eve."

He leaned forward to give her a parting kiss on the cheek but she turned her head away.

"Goodbye, Tom," she replied and, as he disappeared out the door, she shut it sharply and stood for half a minute with her back leaning heavily against it.

She couldn't stay here on her own tonight. Her mind was made up – she would ring Rachel and see where she was staying. If she was in New York shopping, chances were that she would be in the Fitzpatrick like the rest of Dublin that thronged Fifth Avenue from one end of the year to the other.

She rummaged around her handbag until she found the piece of paper that Lucille's secretary had given her earlier. It was dog-eared but the mobile number was all that needed to be legible. She tapped the digits into the smooth chrome hotel phone and waited – unsure what she was going to say to her old friend. Fifteen years was a long time and all that she was certain of was that a lot had happened in both their lives.

•─◆─•

If you enjoyed this chapter from
Three Nights in New York by Michelle Jackson
why not order the full book online
@ www.poolbeg.com

•─◆─•

POOLBEG WISHES TO
THANK YOU
for buying a Poolbeg book.

If you enjoyed this why not
visit our website:

www.poolbeg.com

and get another book delivered straight to
your home or to a friend's home!

All books despatched within 24 hours.

POOLBEG

WHY NOT JOIN OUR MAILING LIST
@ www.poolbeg.com and get some
fantastic offers on Poolbeg books